Beautiful Inez

BART SCHNEIDER

Beautiful Inez

A NOVEL

Shaye Areheart Books

NEW YORK

Published by Harmony Books, New York, New York.
Member of the Crown Publishing Group, a division of Random House, Inc.
www.crownpublishing.com

HARMONY BOOKS is a registered trademark and the Harmony Books colophon
is a trademark of Random House, Inc.

Printed in the United States of America

Design by Lynne Amft

Library of Congress Cataloging-in-Publication Data
Schneider, Bart.
Beautiful Inez : a novel / Bart Schneider.— 1st ed.
p. cm.
1. San Francisco (Calif.)—Fiction.   2. Suicidal behavior—Fiction.   3. Women
violinists—Fiction.   4. Married women—Fiction.   5. Waitresses—Fiction.
6. Seduction—Fiction.   7. Lesbians—Fiction.   I. Title.

PS3569.C522374B43 2005
813'.54—dc22   2004016227

ISBN 1-4000-5442-7

10 9 8 7 6 5 4 3 2 1

First Edition

To my father, David Schneider, a generous and compassionate man, who has always played Bach with his eyes closed.

Such beauty that for a minute
death and ambition, even love,
doesn't enter into this.
   — RAYMOND CARVER

Beautiful Inez

voyant

L ANGUAGE, as Sylvia's mother was fond of saying, mimics the
human condition. What is harmless one moment can become fatal
the next. Drop a prefix, and, before you know it, what was *innocuous*
has grown *noxious*, dispensing fumes that are certain to kill you.

Take *voyeur*, which derives from the French *voir*—to see. A power-
less or passive spectator. You might define it that way, if you were willing
to strip away its unsavory meanings and free it from the clutches of
Peeping Toms.

Consider this: as a girl in Sacramento, Sylvia liked to climb trees.
She started out in the fruit and nut trees of her neighborhood and then
branched out, if you will, to the spreading oaks on the capitol grounds.
Innocuous enough, you might say. Yet the physical pleasure she took in
scrambling from limb to limb and hoisting herself into a hidden hollow
was more than matched by her exhilaration with what she saw: a long-
legged woman mowing her lawn in a pair of powder-blue shorts, a pair
of terrier mutts humping in the early morning, the opened mouth of an
ingenue as a sailor squeezed one of her smallish breasts.

Now, as a woman in San Francisco, Sylvia takes a heightened pleasure in what she sees, but she no longer worries about concealing herself.
When Sylvia moved to San Francisco last year, she found a one-
bedroom apartment, three flights up, situated along the Hyde Street
cable-car line. Home in the evenings, she watches the corner of
Washington and Hyde through her curtainless front window. Sipping a
glass of cheap burgundy and listening to a Bobby Darin record, Sylvia
watches her neighbors, briefcases and sacks of groceries in tow, climb on
and off the cable car.

She's particularly fond of the balletic passengers, who spring onto or
off of the car's running board, even when it's in motion. So far she hasn't
witnessed a single mishap among the leapers. Catlike, on their way to

their various rendezvous, they bound from curb to running board with the grace of the man leaping a puddle in the famous photograph by Cartier-Bresson. Sylvia used to imagine that she was the Parisian in the photograph, her long, open-scissored leap, reflected in the pooling water, an emblem of decisiveness.

Despite Sylvia's good high-school French—her mother used to tell her that she was born to be a linguist or an impostor, maybe both—the closest Sylvia has gotten to Paris is through a monograph of Cartier-Bresson photos, a sampling of Debussy and Ravel recordings, and the lovely baguettes at Simon Brothers, flown in every other day from Paris, that she occasionally slips under her raincoat. Sometimes she pretends that it is Paris she's watching out her window.

Watcher might be another word she could apply to herself. Socially, it would make her more acceptable, but who wants to settle for a word so bereft of nuance? Anyway, watchers have become as common as birds in 1962, now that every man, woman, and child in America has a television of their own. Those few citizens not spending their leisure time watching TV are scanning the skies for orbiting chimpanzees or astronauts. Sylvia prefers more intimate curiosities.

ONE evening, shortly after moving to San Francisco, Sylvia took a random stroll down Van Ness Avenue and saw a symphony crowd billowing out of cabs and town cars and up the grand stairway to the lobby of the War Memorial Opera House. Although she was no more dressed for a concert than a woman walking her dog, she let herself get swept along with the crowd and, with neither dog nor ticket, climbed the stairs with the concertgoers and milled about the lobby, underdressed but unrepentant.

She remembered how not long after the Second World War, as a seventh grader from Sacramento, she visited the Opera House, where delegates of fifty nations had drafted and signed the United Nations charter. She'd imagined herself as a delegate from Ceylon, one of the exotic nations from which she had postage stamps. Seventeen years later, as she milled about in the lobby without a ticket, dressed in pedal pushers and a navy blue car coat, a voice in her head announced: *The delegate from Ceylon, Sylvia Bran.*

In September, as the anniversary of her first year in San Francisco nears, Sylvia gets an opportunity to attend a symphony concert at the Opera House. Her boss at Myerson's—"The grand piano store of the West"—offers her a complimentary ticket. Although the ticket has a hole punched through it, Sylvia is ushered through a velvet curtain to a freestanding upholstered chair in a box of her own. She might as well be the queen of Ceylon.

At first, it is hard to reconcile the formality of the setting and occasion with the casual, backstage banter that follows the musicians to their seats. Some of them tune their instruments on the fly amid a cacophony of scales and eighth-note passages. Then Inez Roseman appears onstage with her violin. Of course, Sylvia doesn't yet know who the exquisite violinist is, but talk about regal. She wears her hair—a shade of blond that can't have come out of a bottle—brushed back, with a silver comb at each temple. Surely this tall and graceful figure is cut from another cloth. The knots of standing musicians seem to part for her as she makes her way, without a word, toward the front of the first violin section. Is the stunning violinist contemptuous of her joking colleagues? Do they despise her for acting as if she's too good for this world?

Sylvia pays close attention to the violinist's gestures—the lovely way she brushes a hand under her skirt before sitting; her manner of dropping a square of silk onto her left shoulder and shrugging it into place before lifting the violin and clamping it with her chin. The other violinists all seem to have more elaborate devices or padding to protect their chins and shoulders. This one, with her square of silk, is, in effect, riding bareback. The violinist closes her eyes as she begins to tune her instrument. Sylvia imagines the inner ear against which the violinist measures her A and pictures a flower within a flower. Clearly, the violinist has perfect pitch, a kind of magnetic north that draws her to its incontrovertible center. In college, Sylvia had known a French horn player with perfect pitch, and she'd always wondered what it was like for him to live among the common folk with wavering intonation.

The dashing Brazilian conductor, João Bonfa, gives his downbeat, and the opening measure of an orchestral suite by Berlioz rises to Sylvia's box. She is sitting close enough to study the supple grace of the violinist's bow arm, and, gradually, locks into the breathing pattern of the silk-shouldered beauty.

At intermission, Sylvia asks an usher the name of the first violinist sitting second stand outside.

"That's Inez Roseman; beautiful Inez." The elderly matron, whose white hair is slipping out of its chignon, turns her head dismissively. Is the gesture meant as a comment on the violinist or on the philistine posing the question? Sylvia decides the latter. Maybe the usher remembers her complimentary ticket, the one with the hole punched through it, and holds that against her.

"Has she been with the symphony for long?" Sylvia persists.

"Yes," the usher says, turning toward Sylvia. "She's been in the symphony for nearly twenty years."

"How could that be? She doesn't look like she's much past thirty."

"Well, I'm not lying to you. Some of us age better than others." The usher takes a linen hanky from her clutch and, unfolding it, reveals a small stash of lemon drops. She offers one to Sylvia.

"No, thank you."

The matron plucks a lemon drop from her linen wrap and drops it on her tongue. "Of course, Inez got into the symphony when she was very young."

"She'd have had to."

"And you know who she's married to," the usher says, in a stage whisper.

"No, I'm afraid I don't."

"Jake Roseman." The usher puckers her lips around her lemon drop. "You know, the attorney who's creating all the fuss with the colored."

Sylvia has read about him in the *Chronicle*. He seems to be something of a sensationalist. A white lawyer working on behalf of the Negroes, a favorite of the liberal columnists.

"I'll tell you one thing," the usher says, "the man has no feeling for music, even though his father played in the symphony for years."

"His father played?" Sylvia asks.

"His father was the first concertmaster under Monteux. He was Inez's teacher. But you never see the husband here. Maybe he'll come next month when Inez plays her solo. If we're so lucky."

"What will she be playing?"

The usher puts her hands on her hips. "My, you ask a lot of questions. You ought to be a reporter."

"I *am* a reporter," Sylvia says, tasting the words as she speaks them.

"What do you know?" The matron's eyes brighten—everything seems to make sense to her now.

"But you haven't answered my last question," Sylvia says.

"Your last question?"

"What will Mrs. Roseman be playing?"

"Oh, yes, the Goldmark Concerto."

"I'm afraid I'm not familiar with Goldmark."

"Karl Goldmark."

"And when did he live?"

The usher looks flustered. "When did he . . . ? He was . . ." Her hands go up to her hair and flutter in their crooked, arthritic way around the loose knot of her chignon. "He was a Romantic."

"Of course."

Now the old woman, a flirt at heart, narrows her eyes and offers a gamine smile. She holds out her hand to Sylvia. "Elizabeth Mier. That's Mier, M I E R."

Does Elizabeth Mier expect her to jot down the correct spelling of her name? Sylvia takes her hand. "Pleased to meet you," she says without offering her own name. The power of the press.

By the time the voyeur-turned-reporter is back in her box, the curious constellation of the Roseman family has woven itself around her. The French have another word, a first cousin of *voyeur* that hasn't really crossed over into English. *Voyant.* We do have *clairvoyant*, but how much more elegant to be a *voyant*, a simple seer.

Back in her seat, Sylvia Bran's career as a voyant is about to begin. As the lovely violinist walks back onstage and drops her square of silk onto her shoulder, Sylvia holds her breath.

future perfect

IT so happens that Inez Roseman is a trusting soul—a fact that might surprise her husband and even her children, who, young as they are, know plenty about trust. The common error is to confuse *trusting* with *trustworthy*, qualities that don't necessarily go hand in hand. Can "a woman of moods," as her husband puts it, be anything but unreliable? Maybe not. But there's nothing to stop her from believing that salvation, if there is to be any, might come as unexpectedly as a stranger to her front door.

Consider this: a young reporter comes to the house this morning, as completely unannounced as the Avon lady, and Inez opens the door for her. When the chimes ring, Inez is curled half-naked in a fetal position on her bed. She takes a quick inventory. The kids are off to school, and Jake made his way out the back door an hour ago, tiptoeing half-blind with an armful of shirts for the cleaners. Between his teeth he held an English muffin smeared with boysenberry jam—this to ensure that whatever garment was not stained when it walked out the door would be by the time it reached the cleaners. The reporter, it turns out, made arrangements last week, but Inez has done her best to put it out of her head.

Inez throws on a robe and opens the front door to the newspaper woman, who is hunched on the doorstep in her black trench coat. A chicky girl, as Jake would say, straight out of central casting. It is all that Inez can do to keep from laughing. Why has she agreed to such nonsense?

"I'm Sylvia Bran from the *Chronicle*."

"How do you do? Inez Roseman."

"Of course."

"You've missed him." She wants to play with the girl.

"No, no . . . I don't want *him*, Mrs. Roseman." The young woman blushes. "I called last Tuesday? . . . We spoke briefly?"

The reporter states this as a question. Inez isn't about to help her.

"I want . . . I want to talk with *you*, Mrs. Roseman."

"Well, now that we have that established, would you like to come in?"

Inez leads her guest into the living room and has her sit. Once she has a moment to study the reporter, Inez takes a liking to her. You wouldn't go out of your way to describe the girl as attractive. She has a pointy nose and wears her dirty-blond hair in bangs. She comes across as intelligent, perhaps even a little cunning. Her green eyes are quite pretty and not at all shy about taking in what she wants. Inez offers her coffee and a slice of crumb cake.

"You don't need to bother."

"Not at all. I have a pot of Folger's on and a cake left over from last night."

When Inez returns with a tray from the kitchen, the reporter gives a quick couple of claps to her hands. "I'm really excited to do this story."

"What story?"

"About your solo performance."

"It hardly seems to warrant . . ."

"I understand it's quite rare for a section player to be given a chance to play a concerto."

"Rare, but not unprecedented."

"My editor . . ."

"I'm sure your editor would prefer a story about my husband."

Sylvia Bran takes a breath and curls up her bottom lip and chin in a fetching, comic-book expression of disappointment. Then she fixes her eyes on Inez. "Would you prefer that we not do this?"

Of course, Inez would prefer not. She'd prefer to be back in bed. She'd prefer to do nothing at all. She watches the reporter push two fingers through her bangs. For some reason, Inez doesn't want to disappoint her. "No," she says. "I'm happy to talk with you."

The young woman is sitting on the yellow teak sofa, which, despite the beauty of its lines, is not particularly comfortable. Inez hands her a cup of coffee and a piece of cake. Sitting upright, Sylvia Bran seems anxious to start the interview.

"Why don't you catch your breath for a moment?" Inez says, hoping to study the young reporter a little longer.

Sylvia wants to make a good impression. She forces a smile, takes a quick bite of cake; a sprinkling of crumbs spills onto her lips. Then she pushes her plate aside and takes a walloping gulp of black coffee. A girl could burn her gullet like that.

After performing a curious exercise in concentration, shutting her eyes and breathing very deliberately, like an athlete under pressure, the reporter flips open her notebook. "Before we talk about the concert," she says, finally, pencil in hand, "I'd like to ask a few questions to put things in context. Tell me, what's it like to live with Jake Roseman?"

The reporter might have employed a little finesse. Of course, Sylvia Bran only wants to talk about Jake, Inez's famous mate.

"Subtle question," the reporter says, offering a wonderfully melodious laugh.

Inez shrugs. "Oh, it isn't that bad."

Sylvia goes at her slice of crumb cake with a sudden ferocity. Not quite finished chewing, she says, "You don't have to answer that question if you don't want."

"So what's the question?" Inez says in a nasal imitation of Groucho Marx. She wants to make the reporter laugh again.

"I asked what it was like—"

"Yes, to live with Jake. Here it is in a nutshell: everything becomes public with Jake. He's an extrovert, and I'm quite the opposite. I find the public part difficult."

Sylvia flips open her notebook and starts to dash and dot along in a remarkable shorthand. The reporter pushes a final forkful of cake into her mouth and chews for a moment. "But your husband hasn't always been in the public eye," Sylvia says, "and you're on the stage all the time."

"You're right," Inez says. "I was trained early to perform in front of an audience; groomed, you know, to have a solo career. Perhaps my temperament wasn't right for it. Jake, on the other hand, has always been a public event waiting to happen."

"So you decided against pursuing a solo career?"

"Right."

"Was that a hard decision?"

Inez stands and walks over to the side table. "Not at the time. I was young and in love and I thought I could do anything. The decisions you hardly think about are the ones your life pivots around." Inez slices a wedge of crumb cake large enough to choke the reporter. "Please, have another piece."

"I shouldn't, but it's delicious. I'm afraid I'm making a pig out of myself."

"I won't tell anybody."

Clearly, Sylvia Bran has experience interviewing the reticent. She knows when to back off and follow a lead. She eats a few more forkfuls of cake and keeps an eye on her host.

Inez draws a hand through her hair and considers the reporter. She guesses that Sylvia is twenty-five and lives with her parents. Not in the city, but in a modern rambler in San Leandro, Fremont, San Mateo. Perhaps she has a boyfriend named Ralph or Jerry who works in an electronics firm, who takes her bowling, who gave her a transistor radio for her last birthday.

As Sylvia takes her next bite of cake, Inez bombards her with questions.

"Where do you live?"

"Russian Hill."

"In the city?"

"Yes, along the cable-car line on Hyde."

"How old did you say you were?"

"I didn't say."

"Well, how old are you?" Inez is surprised by her own rudeness.

Sylvia swallows hard. She seems to have trouble remembering her age. "I'm thirty."

"You don't look twenty-five."

"I'll take that as a compliment," Sylvia says, with a certain pluck. "I was born in 1932—March 2, the night after the Lindbergh boy was kidnapped. My mother linked my birth with the kidnapping so often that I started to feel responsible for it."

"Funny, I pictured you still living with your parents in your girlhood room."

"I've already been married and divorced." Sylvia shows her left hand—a chapped, nub-nailed paw that proves nothing at all except that a bit of moisturizer is in order. "I used to wear a ring, even after the divorce, but not anymore. Maybe I've made peace with the whole thing."

Inez looks at her own ring, with its crescent of tiny diamonds. "How long were you married?"

"A couple of years."

"Not so long."

"Long enough."

"Sounds like you made the right decision."

The reporter nods and again fixes her large eyes on Inez. The kid, who might not be a kid after all, has a penetrating gaze. When was the last time someone paid this much attention to her? "Will you excuse me for a moment?" Inez says. "I'm beginning to feel a bit like a hausfrau sitting around in my robe. Help yourself to more cake."

AFTER examining the half circles under her eyes, Inez brushes out her hair and applies a dab of red lipstick to each cheek, rubbing in a bit of color. With her visitor in the other room, Inez needs to prop herself up. She begins by slipping into the linen dress she's recently picked up at Magnin's.

"How would you describe this color?" she'd asked the saleslady, who wore a boxy suit and reminded her of the designer Edith Head.

"I'd call it aubergine," the saleslady said, making an O of her thickly caked pink lips.

Inez snuck a look at the price. "It's quite a lot of money to dress up like an eggplant."

"Well, it *is* sleeveless," the saleslady chirped, as if the minimum length of fabric justified the maximum price. More likely, it was the suggestion of Jackie Kennedy that upped its price. The saleslady smiled at Inez. "I think it will look lovely on you with your nice tan arms, your cute size. Try it on."

When she returned from the dressing room she expected adoration, and Edith Head delivered.

"Oh, yes. Simple. Understated. But ravishing."

Now she lifts her violin and bow from the open case in the bedroom and strolls, as a ravishing eggplant, into the living room. She makes a point of drawing her bow across a cake of rosin more times than she needs to. She wants the reporter's undivided attention.

"My God," the reporter says, staring even more intently than before, "what a beautiful dress."

"Do you think so? I just picked it up for the concert. I thought I'd try it out on you."

"It's absolutely beautiful. Are you going to play a little from the Goldmark?"

"No, no. Forgive me, this is awfully pushy of me. This interview business has gotten me nervous. I thought a little music might relax me. You said you were born in 1932—how about I play something I performed in a recital that year?"

"I'd be honored. How old were you, if you don't mind my asking, in 1932?"

"I was ten." Inez stands in front of the reporter. "Do you know Paganini?"

"Barely. He was a virtuoso violinist."

"Right, and only mad violinists play his caprices in public."

"But you played them at ten?"

Has the reporter caught her lie? Can she possibly know that the hands of most ten-year-old girls are too small to play the caprices?

"This is number twenty, the Allegretto in D Major."

Inez draws her bow across the D and the A strings, introducing the stately theme and the drone on the D string. There is an opening calm before the madness begins with a circular flurry on the A string. As she practiced these passages—and it could go on for hours in an empty house—she pictured the elaborate scrollwork of a medieval door. As a teen, after her breasts had begun growing out of control and forced her to alter her bowing posture, she often imagined someone touching her while she practiced, and a few times she actually climaxed, her legs twisted around each other like a modern sculpture or a wrought-iron plant stand.

A successful performer of Paganini turns herself into a machine that produces breathless linear bursts as distinctly articulated as the devil's teeth. But standing before her guest at the breakfast room table, Inez mucks through a passage with a shameful smear of legato when it calls for tidy staccato. How pitiful a creature she's become, trying to impress a chicky reporter she's just met and doing so poor a job of it. Who else devotes so much time to confirming her imperfection? A simple man blessed with minor carpentry skills could have built a viable four-bedroom house in the time she's spent trying to saddle the hysteria in this three-minute caprice.

"Beautiful," Sylvia says. "Absolutely beautiful."

Inez knows enough to keep quiet. "Thank you," she says and puts her instrument down.

"What kind of violin do you play?"

"It's a Landolfi. Pietro Antonio Landolfi," Inez says in a robust Italian accent. "I've always loved saying his name. It's quite a nice instrument. Circa 1770, Milan."

"Such a beautiful sound." Sylvia closes her eyes for emphasis.

"Thank you."

"How old were you when you started playing?"

"What are you after—ancient history?"

"Our readers are curious about these kind of things."

"I was five."

"Is that when you started studying with the concertmaster, Mr. Roseman?"

"That was a few years later."

The reporter gets busy with her shorthand again. "And he introduced you to his son?"

"No, that was Jake's doing."

"How do you mean?"

Inez sits down beside Sylvia Bran on the teak sofa as the reporter flips her pad to a blank page. "I'm curious what you have in mind with this story," says Inez.

Sylvia doesn't rush to answer. "We were thinking of a longer piece for the Sunday magazine section."

Inez shrugs. "Why?"

Sylvia lifts her coffee cup and takes a dainty sip, her long nose tipping rather beautifully into the bell of the cup. Inez watches the reporter's eyelids flutter a moment. "My editor thinks that you and Jake are among San Francisco's most fascinating couples," Sylvia says. "And with your solo concert coming . . ."

"So you'll want to talk with Jake as well."

"Yes, if he'll talk to me."

"Jake? He'll talk with anybody."

"I'm really more interested in you, Mrs. Roseman."

"Why don't I believe you?"

The reporter doesn't answer. Nor does she smile. She challenges Inez with a steady gaze.

"What kind of ground rules can we establish?" Inez asks.

"What do you have in mind?"

"You promise not to print anything that I don't approve."

The reporter is silent. It seems as if she is considering the request. "I can't do that."

"Then I can't talk to you." Inez sighs.

Sylvia smiles. A disappointed smile. She rises briskly out of the Danish modern sofa.

The smart thing would be to let the reporter go. "Sit," Inez says.

"I don't want to force you to do anything you don't want to do."

"Sure you do." Inez smiles at Sylvia, the urchin with the yellow pad. "I guess I'll have to be careful what I say."

And then Inez proceeds to be anything but careful. Growing up, she was the storyteller in her little family of three. Her meek father and older sister, Bibi, sheltered and unstable, listened to anything she cared to tell them about the wider world. Inez lifts her coffee cup and takes a short sip. She smiles at Sylvia the reporter. "Would you like to hear about how Jake and I met?"

"Absolutely."

It surprises Inez how well she remembers the day, after twenty-five years. It was a sunny afternoon in the fall, and Jake was sitting on the front steps of his house, barefoot in dungarees and a T-shirt, whistling "Lovely to Look At," a song she knew from the Hit Parade. She'd never before spoken to the boy, but she knew that he was nearly seventeen years old, almost two years older than she was.

"You're Inez," he said, standing as she approached. "I don't believe we've ever been introduced. I'm Jacob Roseman. Jake." He stuck out his hand to shake, and Inez already felt at a disadvantage, as she had the violin in one hand and her music in the other.

As Jake began running his charms and Inez managed to consolidate her things to shake hands, she looked down at Jake's bare feet—his long, beautifully shaped toes—and felt desperate to get away. The music room with Mr. Roseman wasn't necessarily a relief, but it was at least familiar. An hour with the Bruch concerto might cure the distraction. When she lifted her eyes, Jake smiled at her.

"My father talks about you all the time. *Inez . . . Inez . . .* It's like a holy word in our house and, in case you haven't noticed, it's not a very holy house. *Inez . . . Inez . . .* He's very proud of you. You're the best student he's ever had. I've heard him say that. No fooling. And, you know, he's been teaching for a hundred years. Methuselah is his first cousin on his mother's side. Another thing, if you don't mind my saying, you're very pretty. Exceptionally so.

"But my father never mentions your beauty. I noticed that myself. The truth is, I've watched you come and go for years, but I never paid a whole lot of attention. You know how it is; this place is like the ferry terminal with baby violinists coming and going all day. You see people but you don't really see them. It's like watching a plant grow. Then one day you realize that beauty has been walking into your house for years."

"Oh, c'mon," Inez said.

"Forgive me. Let me tell you a secret: I've been jealous of you since my father mentioned that you don't go to school."

"I have a tutor. It's the only way I can get my practicing in."

"A likely story," Jake said and smiled like the boy in the Colgate tooth powder advertisement of the day, his large white teeth gleaming.

Inez had seen Jake at his father's recitals. She sometimes overheard the older students talk about him. He was an only child and a willful boy who told his father that he'd have no part of the violin. But he was also very bright, a chess wiz and captain of the Lowell High debate team. He'd just graduated from high school, at sixteen, and was on his way to Cal in the fall.

Jake swayed back and forth like a boy playing tag, daring her to tag him. "I don't care if you're just playing hooky," he said. "I still think you're quite a dish."

"Can you imagine somebody saying that?" Inez asks Sylvia, who's never been a *dish*, nor ever will be. The reporter bends over her yellow pad, scrawling in shorthand.

At fifteen, Inez continues, she was beginning to realize that her looks were pleasing. Teenage boys and young men showed uncommon attention. She never quite knew what to make of this phenomenon, but she wasn't going to be bullied by a frisky-boy debate champ. She lifted her head and looked directly into Jake Roseman's green eyes.

"Please don't speak to me like that. I don't like to be embarrassed."

"Sorry," Jake said, shaken by her forthrightness. "I didn't mean to embarrass you."

Inez was also taken aback by her bluntness. It reminded her of the time, two years earlier, when she'd spoken to Mr. Roseman in anger.

"I'm sorry, Inez," Jake repeated, truly contrite.

Right then, Mr. Roseman opened the front door.

"Are you harassing my student, Jacob?" Her teacher popped open his pocket watch. "Is that why we're running off the timetable? Inez, you come in here and tell me how you got that boy to apologize to you. This is unheard of. I've never heard it myself. I bet he was expounding his political theories, my son the anarchist."

AFTER Inez's lesson, Jake was waiting in the front hall. "I wanted to apologize again," he said.

"No need."

"You don't hold grudges?"

"Not usually," she said, putting her left hand behind her back and crossing her fingers.

"That bodes well for our future."

"What future?"

"The future perfect," Jake said, flashing his white teeth. "It's a tense that I adore."

Nobody had ever flirted with her so openly. Inez told herself to stand up straight. "You're odd," she said.

"Thank you." Jake bowed broadly like a circus clown. "Hey, there's something I want to ask you." He leaned back against the wall, disturbing a framed publicity photograph of Pierre Monteux. Inez watched the image of the fabled conductor swing on its hook. Monteux, the man who'd premiered Stravinsky's *Le Sacre du Printemps* in Paris, had just completed his third season in San Francisco. The photograph must have been new to the wall or she'd have noticed it before.

Sylvia the reporter looks up from her pad and smiles. "Sounds like you were noticing a lot of things for the first time."

The photograph was inscribed to Inez's teacher.

> *To Isaac Roseman, my shining light in San Francisco.*
> PIERRE MONTEUX, 1937.

Inez let out a little gasp. Perhaps it was the picture of Monteux, or the idea that she was aligned, no matter how indirectly, with musical history. More likely, it was the handsome young man standing in front of her.

"He has a lot more trophies like that," Jake said. "You should have him show you sometime."

That was about the last thing Inez would do. She gave an impatient shake to her violin case. "Did you have something else to say to me?"

"Yes." Jake stood off-balanced on one foot. She half-expected him to hop. "You know about my dad's concert next month? The first of the Mozart cycle."

Inez nodded. Isaac in his tireless desire to stay active as a soloist was presenting a three-concert series of Mozart sonatas at the Legion of Honor's new theater. Jake squared off with both feet on the floor. "I wondered if you'd like to go with me."

"With you?" Inez said, momentarily flustered. "Why?"

"Why? Because I'd like to get to know you. And I get kind of lonely, you see, going to my dad's concerts."

Inez tried to imagine Jake Roseman being lonely. It had never occurred to her that sixteen-year-old boys got lonesome, and this one seemed so capable of keeping himself entertained. She imagined that Jake traveled with a personal entourage of good cheer even when he was by himself.

"So how about coming with me?" Jake said. He lifted his chin and looked as if he was about to start whistling again.

"All right," Inez said and steered herself and her violin toward the front door.

From her father's car, she could see that Jake was standing in the picture window watching. He neither smiled nor waved, which did not strike her as peculiar. Perhaps a bit of her stoic sensibility had rubbed off on him.

A week later Jake telephoned to say that he'd be by with his family the following Friday night to pick her up, if she was still game. Inez's sister helped to pin up her hair. She wore a dress, a silk voile that Bibi had made for a recital Inez had given the year before. She'd refused to wear it then because it seemed too fancy. Now it looked wonderful to her.

Inez catches Sylvia's eye. "I know this goes against the popular perception," Inez says, "but I think that children grew up faster in the thirties than they do now." Certainly, more was expected of them, she thinks, though maybe it was just that way for her and Bibi because they didn't have a mother. By fifteen, Inez was a young woman. Well-mannered and poised. Her future as a violinist was set before she was ten. She realized that much in her little family was being sacrificed for her benefit, to pay for her tutor and violin lessons. Her father worked twelve hours a day in his frame shop. The only time he took off was to drive to lessons or recitals and occasionally to have a Sunday walk with his daughters at Aquatic Park or the wharf. Bibi became a skilled seamstress before she was out of junior high. Most evenings their small den served as a fitting room while Inez practiced. Bibi said that the women loved the bright meanderings of the violin, that it gave them the feeling that they were having their dresses fitted in Paris or Vienna.

The night Isaac Roseman's Buick pulled up, Inez and Bibi watched from the upstairs bedroom. "Enjoy yourself, Nez," her sister said. "You look beautiful."

Inez hadn't pictured a first date like this: sitting in the backseat with Jake while her teacher, dressed in his shiny tuxedo, chattered with his wife in the front. It was quiet in the backseat. She didn't mind the quiet. She never minded quiet.

"One of these days," Jake said, breaking the silence, "I'm going to get a car of my own."

Inez nodded in agreement. "I bet you will."

"Jacob," Mr. Roseman called from the front seat, "how do you propose to pay for this automobile?"

"With cash money."

"Oh, cash money."

"And if you're lucky, I'll give you a ride."

Mr. Roseman laughed. "If I'm lucky, he'll give me a ride."

"And, in case you want to know something else," Jake said, "I'm going to marry Inez."

Mrs. Roseman gasped at the absurdity of Jake's pronouncement.

"Nonsense," Mr. Roseman said. "That is nonsense, Jacob. Don't embarrass the poor girl."

Inez accepted the news of her forthcoming marriage to Jake Roseman with remarkable equanimity. She rather liked the idea, even though she hardly knew the young man. It made an odd sense. Who else was she going to marry? Clearly, the son was nothing at all like the father. Jake smiled at her in the backseat and she found herself smiling back. The deal, strange as it seemed, had been made. They hadn't even touched each other, hadn't yet held hands, but Jake blew her a kiss and she blew one back.

Inez finishes her little tale and looks up at Sylvia the reporter and then down at the ruins of pencil marks on Sylvia's notepad. Sylvia is rubbing her eyes, poor girl. What the hell kind of reporter gets tears in her eyes?

zen studies

T H E first time Jake visited Christine Newsome in her Pacific Heights mansion, she'd greeted him at the front door. But in the half-dozen years since, he's always approached the home, at Christine's request, via the trade entrance, which, though a curious form of slumming, became part of the ritual with Christine. Jake liked walking up the brick alley behind the mansion and sometimes donned a brimmed tradesman's cap to enhance the effect. Passing the trash bins in the alley even inspired a bit of vandalism. One Tuesday during the 1960 presidential campaign, Jake snuck out to the rolling front lawns of the Newsome mansion, ripped two Nixon-Lodge signs from their stakes, and buried them in the trash bins. That act of conscience, not related to the lady of the house, made his afternoon with Christine all the more pleasurable.

Christine had been his client at one time, so Jake could rationalize the trade entrance on those grounds as well. She'd hired Jake to look over business papers her husband had prepared involving property in her name. Christine was afraid that her husband, Derek, a top executive at Holmes Newsome, the accounting firm his grandfather founded, was trying to screw her. This was just one of the complications that arose when two family fortunes lived side by side in the same house. Not exactly Jake's specialty. He would have referred Christine to someone more skilled in this area, if he hadn't found her so charming. "I admire Derek's ardor," she'd said of her husband, "but I'm afraid he reserves it all for his business deals."

Every second or third Tuesday—the servants' day off—Jake makes arrangements to visit Christine. There never seems to be a hitch. In the span of two hours away from the office, Jake assembles lunch, cabs over to Pacific Heights, engages in a satisfying conversation or two, has a tasty meal, screws his heart out with Christine, and is swept back to his office, pulsing with vigor. No other ritual in Jake's life operates with such

efficiency and offers such pure pleasure. Not long after they began seeing each other, Christine entrusted Jake with a key to the trade entrance
of the Jackson Avenue Tudor and even explained the intricacies of the
security system.

On the appointed Tuesdays, Jake often strolls up Market Street and
plucks delicacies from the food marts—poached salmon fillets and ripe,
lime-scented avocado halves stuffed with chilled cocktail shrimp. Some
days he'll go pure aphrodisiac, picking up a dozen oysters on the half
shell or a pint of Siamese seviche, with the fruit of the sea pickled in equal
parts lime juice and soy. Almost always he dips into Slavin's Tropical
Health Mart for a quart of their house salad: guava, mango, and cheri-
moya, with pomegranate seeds and slices of blood orange and fried plan-
tain. As he gathers treats on Market Street for his lover, Jake feels like a
sport of twenty, whistling Thelonious Monk riffs among the throngs of
bargain shoppers and the gaggles of greaser punks and the anxious
tourists who have lost their way. He sidesteps winos outside the twenty-
five-cent theaters and hustles past flanks of dreamboy sailors, those poor,
uniformed fools who always seem to be on the prowl, in twos or threes,
for something better than they'll ever find.

Occasionally, as today, Jake calls ahead to one of his favorite restau-
rants, Vanessi's in North Beach, and has them prepare a dish for take-
out. This slight detour in the cab, and the fragrant ride to Christine's,
only heighten the anticipation. It's just these cosmopolitan jaunts
through the city that have convinced Jake that he's better off leaving his
car at home, that taking buses and cabs at his pleasure actually affords
him greater freedom.

AFTER Jake unlocks the back door and climbs the inner steps to the
pantry, he notices Christine, dangling her bare feet from a tall, black
director's chair positioned beside the double refrigerator. This is her
usual perch on their Tuesdays. Jake guesses that it's the only time all
month she spends in the kitchen. Now Christine looks up from the book
she's reading, as if she's a bit surprised to see him, as if she's momentarily torn between the book and Jake. This is also a bit of the ritual that he
doesn't mind observing. Nothing should seem automatic. Why should

she rush to him the moment he steps into the kitchen? He sets his package down on the massive butcher block and watches Christine sniff the air as she rises to come to him. She drops her slender arms over his shoulders and kisses him on the forehead.

"Missed you," he says.

"What did you miss?"

"What, you'd like a catalog of your riches, Christine?"

"Yes, give me the Song of Songs."

"If I could whistle it, I would."

Christine nods to the fragrant package on the butcher block. "What do you have in there?"

"Salad, with a Green Goddess dressing. Do you mind anchovies?"

"You know I love them."

"And a saltimbocca à la Romana."

"You didn't pick that up on Market Street."

"No, Vanessi's."

"*Mon dieu.* You must be expecting something special this afternoon."

Jake winks at her and slowly lifts the food containers out of the sack. "So what're you reading?" Christine gathers silverware and a couple of plates. He wants to believe that she hasn't really been reading at all, that the book is simply a prop, a small part of their make-believe adventure that has them now slumming in the kitchen, two plates set at the servants' side table.

"Bellow," she says, "his latest. Or at least his latest to me. *Henderson the Rain King.* It's a wonderful romp."

"Like Augie March?"

"Altogether different. This is . . . I don't know what you'd call it . . . intellectual fantasy adventure. Henderson goes to Africa."

"Like all manly men."

"You have nothing to worry about in that area, Jake."

"Nice of you to say." Jake picks up the copy of *Henderson the Rain King* and flips through it absently. He used to read. He was a great reader through his teens and twenties. He assumed it was his natural state, but at some point adult life intervened in the form of a wife and children; work; an aging, impossible father; and the goddamn Republicans. Despite seeming to the world like a happy-go-lucky soul, he is an anxious man, overmatched by work and family. How can such a man expect to sit quietly and read? Jake does word puzzles, that's his diversion; a half an hour of word puzzles are about his speed.

As Christine fixes their plates with food, he glances at her: a small, pretty woman with dull blue eyes, the cheekbones of a model, and an enchanting beauty mark above her upper lip. In the years he's known Christine, Jake's watched a wedge of gray hair broaden across her temple. Although he's tremendously fond of her, he sometimes finds her privilege a bit galling. It must be nice, he thinks, to have your days to yourself, attend the occasional charity luncheon or ballet company board meeting, drop a couple of notes to your teenage sons at boarding school, have some working stiff bring you lunch at the mansion, fornicate for a leisurely half an hour, and then spend the rest of your day reading an intellectual fantasy adventure, whatever the hell that is.

Christine smiles at him. "I'll loan it to you when I'm finished. Henderson reminds me of you, Jake. Maybe that's why I'm enjoying it so much. Seems to me, you need to have an adventure like he has."

Jake shakes out a cigarette and lights it. "A trip to Africa or an intellectual fantasy?"

"You choose." Christine hands him an ashtray, a cute brass artifact shaped like a kitchen sink.

NO matter which room she leads him to, they make love on the floor. Always on carpets or on thick-pile rugs. Each time they enter a room, they pretend it's the first time they've been there together. Jake used to keep a running tally in his mind of all the different rooms they'd screwed in, but once they'd crossed a dozen thresholds and started to make return trips, he gave up counting.

One time, they even screwed in a long hallway under a painting—an Indian miniature that expertly depicted a royal couple making love. That was early in his affair with Christine. He remembers rolling onto his back, once he was done, and noticing the Indian couple, poised inside the netted canopy of their marriage bed. You couldn't help admiring the elegance with which their bodies bent in and out of their silken garments. He wasn't in their class. There he lay, fucked out, his boxer shorts dangling around his feet. Christine smiled at him, showing off her regal beauty mark. She smoothed the black slip over her waist. "You were wonderful . . ."

"Was I?"

"For someone so distracted. Were you thinking about Inez?"

She'd caught him, but he would neither confirm nor deny. Actually, Jake had been thinking less about his wife than about their marriage bed, how bereft it seemed compared to the Indian couple's.

"Inez doesn't take lovers, does she?"

Jake did not bother to answer. He didn't like having Christine speak of his wife by name, but Christine wasn't about to pretend she didn't know who Inez was. She and her husband, like most longtime patrons of the symphony, were well aware of the presence of Inez Roseman. Christine also spoke about her husband, from time to time, without shame. "This isn't about not loving Derek," Christine said, once. "It's about sex being better with you than it is with him. And I imagine that if I were married to you, sex would be better with him."

"I'm afraid you're too modern for me, Christine," he'd said.

"What's modern? I simply know what I like and am honest about it."

"But you're not honest with your husband."

"What would be the point of that? I don't want to hurt him. Anyway, he knows."

"He knows?"

"Derek's not a stupid man, Jake. He knows as much as he wants to know."

"What does that mean exactly?"

Christine shrugged and described how her approach to infidelity derived from her study of Zen Buddhism.

"You live a charmed life, Christine."

"And your suffering is great, Mr. Roseman?"

"Epic." He watched her grin and then push the hair out of her eyes. Despite knowing better, Jake wondered if he loved her. Christine, who had a good instinct for detecting wayward sentiment, closed her eyes for a moment and said, "I want to teach you my motto, Jake: 'No attachment to either the glory or the guilt.'"

"No attachments, huh?"

"No attachments," Christine echoed.

TODAY, after dining on the lukewarm saltimbocca à la Romana and doing the deed on the floor of the billiard room, both of them are quiet for a while. Although Jake may not have absorbed the great Zen teachings of Christine Newsome, he has taught himself to be free of thought during the act and even lets himself fall asleep in Christine's arms for a few moments after. This, he thinks, rousing himself slowly, is as close as he and Christine ever come to genuine intimacy.

Jake watches Christine open her eyes. Sleepy, sated, she blushes for a moment at being watched. Even the master Zen adulteress is capable of the occasional blush.

"Saw you on the news last night," she says, as if they'd just run into each other at the supermarket. "You looked really cute in your Bermuda shorts."

"Are you laughing at me?"

"Not at all. It's refreshing to see a political man with a sense of humor."

"I think more people laugh at me than with me, but appearing like a goofball makes for a good decoy." Jake stands and pulls on his underwear. During the last year, Jake has taken to wearing Bermuda shorts to work whenever he is so moved. They are an odd enough garment for the tropics, but truly absurd in cool San Francisco. Sure, the shorts are an affectation, but he enjoys the attention they bring and the way they get people's dander up.

Christine runs a hand through Jake's hair. "So how's the political work going?" she asks.

Jake has been leading actions during the last few months on behalf of Negro hotel workers downtown. He glances at Christine. Despite her pronouncements to the contrary, he wonders if she's a closet Republican. Isn't her true alliance through wealth and family with the GOP? Sleeping with the enemy—he rather likes the idea.

"So?" Christine says, waiting for an answer.

"It looks like we have a decent compromise in the works. The Palace has offered to hire a dozen Negroes."

"Are you going to settle for that?"

"Probably. It's better than we expected. And I like being agreeable."

"You're very agreeable, Jake."

Jake watches her drop a slip over her head, her small breasts disappearing, the little pucker at the center of her slim belly suddenly sheathed in black silk. He looks down at her small feet. He loves how tiny they are. The wonder of a diminutive woman is how small she remains even as she ages.

"I'm afraid you're going to become too famous for me, Jake," says Christine.

"I'm not in it for the fame."

"So you say."

Jake pulls up his trousers and walks over to the billiard table, takes a couple of balls out of the leather net pockets, and slowly rolls one ball, then the other, the length of the table.

"There's nothing wrong with a little fame, Jake."

"I suppose not."

Christine strolls up to Jake and slides an arm around his waist. "You're good for your people, Jake."

"I'm not Moses, for Chrissakes."

At the time of Jake's political awakening in the late fifties, he'd run a solo law office for many years and begun to feel mired in a professional rut. He'd discovered almost by accident that he had a certain talent for articulating what was at stake in a social conflict, and that this talent was best served when he brought it to the street. In order to be an effective advocate for causes he believed in, work for which he was rarely compensated, he needed to draw attention to himself. The press liked an articulate kook and portrayed with sympathy the issues he championed.

As Jake bends over the billiard table, Christine kisses his neck. "I wouldn't mind calling you Moses, though."

"Don't."

"All right, I won't. So," Christine says, "how is Inez feeling about her solo concert?"

"Pretty good, I think." Jake isn't happy to have Inez mentioned as he's about to leave, but Christine is paying him back for being bristly.

"She must be practicing all the time."

"I suppose. She doesn't play much when I'm around in the evenings."

"Derek and I plan to be there for the big concert."

It seems to Jake that his method of keeping his worlds apart—a blotting out of one while the other is in play—is a far cry from Christine's Zen detachment.

Jake turns to face Christine. She is more tempting than ever, bare-legged in a fitted jersey knit dress and a pair of ballet slippers. He wouldn't mind driving a bit of a wedge between Christine and himself. It's not all it's cracked up to be, he thinks, sleeping with the filthy rich. At what point does he simply rate as another servant? Hasn't Christine had him in his place for years? And yet, as much as he'd like to wallow in his role as a victim, it's hard to cry foul when he considers the pleasure he gains in providing service.

"I'm taking Inez on a little trip," he says. "The weekend after next."

"Where are you going?"

"Just down to Carmel. Get her mind off the music. We had our twentieth anniversary awhile back and have been meaning to do something."

"How romantic."

"I don't know."

"You still love Inez, don't you?"

He's not sure how to answer, not sure of the truth.

Christine steps closer to him, and he takes her in his arms. His hand runs across the jersey covering her smooth waist. "How about we make love again? A quickie."

"I don't think that would be a good idea."

"Au contraire." He nibbles at the corner of her wide lips, then plants a tender kiss atop her beauty mark.

"You know that you love her, and that's as it should be."

"You're a strange woman, Christine, do you know that? Thank goodness I don't love you."

"Thank goodness you don't. That would really get us in trouble. We'd be finished in a moment."

Jake steps away from Christine and takes a long look around the billiard room. He wonders when they'll be back here. There are a series of framed prints on the wall. A dozen ducks. This is Derek's room, the one room in the mansion completely given to his aesthetic, the most goyish room in America. Jake has always wanted to shoot a quick game of billiards in here and then make love to Christine atop the green felt. The sound of the billiard balls cracking against one another in their webbed, leather pockets—what lovely music to fuck by.

Now he and Christine walk hand in hand down the stairs. Although he tries not to be attached to either the guilt or the glory, he can't help but feel a little of each. After all, he is a married man with chafed knees and a pleasantly throbbing prick who's just been screwing another man's wife on the carpet. Is it all a wondrous game of Clue—with his prick, from behind, in the billiard room? Much as he'd like to shoulder a little guilt—hasn't he been soiling the sacrament of marriage for years?—he's more adept at reminding himself that he's only human. Will his guilt arrive one day via special delivery? He expects it will.

Meanwhile, his Zen mistress leads him, without a word, along the first-floor hallway and through the massive kitchen, fragrant still with the detritus of their cozy lunch. Christine gives him a damp kiss on the forehead, as his hand touches the knob to the service door.

perfect pitch

EXCEPT for half a piece of crumb cake, Inez hasn't eaten anything all day. She has no appetite. She rarely has an appetite anymore. She eats only to keep up her strength—if she goes without eating on concert nights, she begins to feel faint after the intermission. She imagines the public horror of collapsing onstage. She's lost weight, but not enough to be concerned about. Jake has another view. At dinner, he'll sometimes taunt her about it. With a forkful of meat in his mouth, he'll turn toward the kids: "Your mother is wasting away."

"Nonsense," Inez says. "You're thinking of me pregnant."

"The hell I am. That was years ago. You should see a doctor," her husband says.

"I don't need a doctor."

"Look at how thin your arms are getting. If I wanted to marry Olive Oyl, I'd have married Olive Oyl."

When his father mentions Olive Oyl, Joey pipes up: "You better start eating your spinach, Mom."

At times, Inez sees the food on her plate the way an unwilling child might: gray clumps, overcooked foothills of meat and starch and vegetables. She'll take small portions and push them around strategically, as if, pea by pea, she were thinning a forest. Now, with the reporter gone and the day yawning ahead of her, she forces herself to think of something she'd like to eat. Perhaps later in the afternoon, when Joey gets home from school and has his snack, she'll fix herself a cheese sandwich.

Inez pulls off her linen dress and camisole, then climbs back into bed. She rarely had time off like this in her twenties and early thirties. The parts of her day that weren't given to practicing and rehearsing went to private students, classes she taught at San Francisco State, and a stream of occasional jobs that had an uncanny way of finding the gaps in her datebook. It was a point of honor for a young musician to be in demand and perpetually working. Inez also liked contributing more money to the household than Jake could during the period he was getting his law practice off the ground.

After her first, Anna, was born, it took her months to bounce back and, when she finally did come around, she found herself buried at home with a baby girl and a tardy diaper service, constantly arranging for nannies and babysitters, feeling guilty every time she went to work, yet sure she'd die of boredom and despair if she abandoned her career and stayed home. After Anna's first birthday, Inez returned to work with a vengeance, and it wasn't until Joey's birth, six years later, that the wheels came off the cart.

On some days off, Inez can lie in bed, half-sleeping with scarcely a thought for the time that is passing. But today, after the reporter's visit, Inez stews in a fever of reflection, remembering the night she discovered that she was pregnant with Joey. It was nearly eight years ago, ages now. The news had pitched her into a spiral of remorse. Why would she possibly want another child? She'd been thinking of it as *the fetus* because that sounded impersonal and might as easily describe something dead as alive.

The night she told Jake the news, he pranced around and insisted that they find a babysitter for Anna and go celebrate. He dragged her out that night to a jazz club called The Black Hawk. There was a piano trio playing, but Inez hardly heard the music. She focused, alternately, on how she could get rid of the baby and on how evil she was for having such thoughts. Jake, as was his habit, got friendly with the musicians between sets and brought the bass player to the table to meet her.

The man's name was Reamy. He was a slightly built Negro in a checked sport coat. He couldn't have been much more than thirty. Inez wondered how such a small man ended up playing a string bass. Jake invited Reamy to join them at the table, then ordered a round of drinks.

"He has a terrific ear, doesn't he?" Jake said, indicating the bass player.

"Yes," she agreed, though she'd hardly heard anything the man had played.

"My wife has perfect pitch," Jake bragged.

"And she's a beauty to boot." Reamy offered Inez a smile more polite than flirtatious. "I'm sorry to say I'm not blessed with it. Best I can do is walk around in my little purgatory with halfway decent relative pitch."

"It's not all it's cracked up to be," Inez said.

The bass player leaned toward her and she noted the way his bald spot shined at the crown of his head. "I've heard that perfect pitch can be a bit of a burden," he said. "I know some musicians say the problem with p.p. is that the whole world is constantly out of tune."

"It's true," she said, offering a crooked smile. "If you choose to pay any attention to the rest of the world."

Now the bass player turned toward Jake. "I see that on top of every-thing else, your wife is clever."

"Inez is a first violinist with the San Francisco Symphony," Jake said with pride, "second stand, outside."

"Stop, Jake."

"*Now* you tell me, and with p.p. to boot!" Reamy winked at Inez and coughed a guttural laugh. "How do you expect me to play my next set with her listening in on me?"

Inez loved the way the bass player had reduced her curious attribute to p.p. It had always been spoken of as if it were a noble gift from God, as if she'd been blessed with the ears of an angel. Inez found herself watching the Negro's long, tapered fingers as he lifted his tumbler of Scotch. He glanced up at her. What a useful stranger he was, an unforeseen ally. She wished that she could spend five minutes alone with him. She'd tell him everything that was going on with her, and then never have to see him again.

"The secret to a long and happy life," he said, holding her with his glance, "is to learn how to expect less of the world than you would have expected to expect."

"That hits it on the head," Jake said.

"I know what it's like to be alone," the bass player said, hoisting his Scotch. "Alone in a restaurant, alone in your bed, alone inside your own ears." He paused to sip his drink. "I was a college boy, you know. Studied music in college. Not too many of us back then."

Inez glanced over at Jake, who was in his glory, listening to the bass player. It quickly stopped being the night that they went out to celebrate the seed of a baby she didn't want to have and became the night a Negro bass player told them a story.

"I got a job when I was just out of school, backing Dinah Washington—first time I went out on the road. Thought I was hot stuff." Reamy stopped and smiled. "We did a gig in Philly along with Dizzy Gillespie's big band. Dinah and her trio with Dizzy's band—and Dizzy's bari sax player was way out of tune. Ooh, it was ugly. So I raise my hand in the air and Dizzy says, 'What's the matter?' I point to the bari player. Dizzy stares at me. 'He's outta tune,' I say, finally. Dizzy stares at me some more and says, 'How you so sure it's him?'" The bass player let loose a deep laugh.

"The thing was, nobody would talk to me for the rest of the gig. I was off-limits, ostracized, a nonentity. If my mama was there, *she'd* have turned her back on me. So, you see, I don't need to be messing around with any p.p.; I got all the ear I can handle as it is."

Jake patted the bass player on the back. "Reamy," he said, "you have time to have a glass of champagne with us? I'm going to order a bottle of champagne. Inez and I are celebrating. We're having a baby!"

The Negro turned to face her. It was clear the man didn't care much for Jake. "Congratulations. Your first?"

She shook her head, close to tears. "Our second." Surely, the bass player could see what was going on with her, or so she imagined.

"No time for the bubbly, but here's to you." Reamy tossed back the rest of his Scotch, then made his way back to the bandstand. He nodded at Inez as the pianist played a lush introduction to "Stella by Starlight." She forced herself to listen closely to the bass player, to his good ear that had gotten him into trouble. He had a warm, muscular sound. Inez closed her eyes to listen to the dark wood of his bass, how the timbre of a single, held note could provide shelter, a room to hide in. She opened her eyes and watched Reamy's long fingers pluck the thick strings. He was the engine driving the little band. He kept the beat, yet masked it in a dully polished coil of sound. There was something surprisingly unswerving about his method. It made him indestructible. Like the baby, she thought.

BABY Joey was delivered by cesarean section, just as his sister had been. The doctor who performed the surgery visited her the next day and told her, with not a little pride, that Joey had been his 157th successful cesarean delivery. She wondered how many failures he'd had and why this couldn't have been one of them. He then proceeded to outline the tortured history of the operation back to Civil War days. The stout, mustached doctor sat on the empty bed beside her and said, "Seventy-five years ago, a woman in your situation, a woman with a spastic uterus, with muscles that operate more keenly on one side than the other, would most surely have died during delivery. Infection. They didn't understand much about infection then." Dr. Covey was the man's name. In her half-drugged state, Inez thought of fat Dr. Covey and his 157 cesarean births as a mother with a covey of partridges.

A week later, Inez returned home with baby Joey. One day, when he actually slept for a few minutes, she lay naked on her side in front of the bedroom mirror. She now had two long, vertical scars, stretching nearly from womb to ribs. Dr. Covey mentioned that there was too much scar tissue from the first birth to open the same place again. When she was on her side, the twin scars looked like parallel stave lines that a music student may have drawn in his haste. Her belly button was situated perfectly at the center of the stave, like the F above middle C. A whole note that would last forever. And when she saw herself thus—depressed, doubly scarred, spastic-wombed, baby-hating, with enormous, engorged breasts hanging above her ribs like dead weights—she hummed an F and held on to it for the longest time. The virtues of perfect pitch. It would become the pitch of her breathing. F for fucked, as in *you're fucked*, she told herself, and, for the first time in her life, she uttered the obscenity out loud.

Her regular obstetrician, Dr. Seymore, called it Baby Blues and said the mood would pass within a couple of weeks. It did not pass. She wasn't able to sleep at night. She and Jake built as cozy a spot as they could in the basement, with a sofa and a remnant of Belgian carpet and a soft lamp, and Jake slept with the baby down there so she wouldn't hear the crying. That is when she began curling into a ball and became a shelled creature, armored with a layer of invisible parchment that she still wakes with every morning.

The Baby Blues became a virus, as virulent, she believed, as polio. It would not leave her. Not in a couple of weeks, not ever. There were no outer signs. That would be too easy. If it were polio, they could put her in an iron lung, let something else breathe for her. Although not physical, her paralysis was certainly grave. She had no interest in trying to explain it. How could she explain? She had a beautiful baby she could barely stand to hold in her arms. At least her own mother had the good sense to die in childbirth.

The parchment, that extra layer of skin that covered her muscles and bones and nerve endings, became the symptom by which she gauged her condition. Each morning, whether she'd slept only a wink or truly fallen off for hours, she checked to see if the extra skin was still there. It always was. She had yet to be cured and no longer expected to be.

Three months after Joey's birth, a nanny was found and Inez went back to work, a shadow of herself, perhaps, but functional enough to hold her seat in the symphony. She was forced to cut the odd jobs and the teaching, which she really enjoyed, to a minimum. All these years later, even though Jake again slept in the bed beside her, she still woke inside a skin of parchment.

INEZ dresses herself again, just before Joey is due home from school. Joey likes his rituals. A hug at the front door. Slices of French bread, buttered or with cream cheese, once in a blue moon topped with smoked salmon left over from a Sunday brunch. Then he'll sit alone at the kitchen table for the longest time, nibbling on his favorite treat, a frozen chocolate-covered banana. Inez used to wonder what went through his mind while he sat there with his banana. Did he know that she hadn't wanted him, that she could hardly stand to be in his presence for the first couple of years of his life? Of course he knew. Sometimes she asked her son what he was thinking about.

"God," he once said, without a beat's hesitation. This in a household in which religion was rarely mentioned.

"You're thinking about God?"

"Yeah, whether he ever rode a horse. He's supposed to be the best at everything, so I guess he's a good rider. Maybe God's been in a lot of rodeos. Do you think he ever rode a bucking bronco?"

"I don't know," Inez said. "I've never thought about it. Do you think about God a lot?"

Joey shook his head and took a long lick of his banana. "Nay," he said, using the negative his sister had recently been bandying about.

Usually, Inez leaves Joey to his thoughts. She'd started bribing him with the frozen bananas when he was around five: he could have a chocolate-covered frozen banana on a stick for each day that he didn't suck his thumb. Now, more than two years later, he still holds her to it.

Jake sometimes accuses her of spoiling the boy. Of course she does. She'd wanted him dead before he was born. When she brought him home, he cried constantly. What little purchase she had on her life disappeared each morning with the baby's first, probing yelp, a single-note inquiry that quickly devolved into a storm of despair. Only Anna, just six at the time, cooed at the baby.

In the first year, when the nanny was off, Inez locked herself in the closet while the baby cried, or she stood on a spot with her violin, playing a fierce Bartók sonata at fortissimo. Little Joey Roseman may have been the most tearful baby and toddler the world had ever seen. At three, he still cried up a storm. At four, when she took him to the swings at Sutro Park, he clung to her. Whenever she tried to drop him into a basket swing, he'd wriggle and fuss for longer than she could bear. He refused to let go of her fingers. Every other child in the playground ventured as far from his mother as he could. The way Joey clung to Inez, you would have thought he was an orphan.

Today, after Joey watches *The Three Stooges*, he begins his cello practice. Inez had done everything she could to discourage Joey from playing an instrument. He started begging for a violin at four, but his mother wouldn't hear of it. She'd begun playing at five and became a practicing monster as soon as she learned how to hold the bow. The last thing she wanted was a fresh version of her child-self, the one-dimensional automaton who could stand on a practice spot, inflicting measured torture on herself for hours. But Joey's grandfather wouldn't leave the business alone and sat the boy down to the piano to determine if he had a decent ear. "It's too early to know for sure," Isaac Roseman said. "The boy may have perfect pitch, he may not. But I'm telling you, it's too good an ear to squander."

When Joey turned five, Inez relented. She brought home a quarter-sized cello on loan from her violin dealer, Jan Smetna. She laid white tape on the fingerboard to help guide her son's way and gave him a few short lessons on how to hold and draw the bow. She guessed he'd lose interest in the cumbersome instrument within a week, but before long he was playing clear, coherent scales. During his second month with the instrument, Joey made a point of ripping the white tape from the fingerboard. When she asked why he had done that, her five-year-old son said, "Tape's for babies. I know where to put my fingers."

And indeed he did. The damn kid had an ear on him. Although a little clumsy with his fingers at first, he made swift corrections when he landed a fraction north or south of the pitch he was after.

"He's just like you," Isaac Roseman said, "a quick study."

As his grandfather demonstrated the virtues of long-bowing to the boy, Inez thought of the first time she'd had a lesson with Isaac Roseman. Her father had walked with her into the Roseman house. She remembers him looking down at his feet as he took off his felt hat and bowed to the new teacher. For weeks, her father had been telling her what a great man Mr. Roseman was, and how kind he was to consider teaching her. Dressed in striped tuxedo trousers with a pair of suspenders strung over a wrinkled white shirt, Mr. Roseman looked like he'd forgotten anybody was coming for a lesson. He led Inez and her father to a music room in the back of the house. It was the largest house Inez had ever been inside of, but she trained her eyes to look straight ahead so she wouldn't get lost in anything she might see. Mr. Roseman motioned for her father to sit on the piano bench. Her father lifted a hand to protest: "I'm sorry; I don't play the piano."

"I wasn't going to ask you to play," Mr. Roseman said.

It made Inez sad to see her father sit creakily on the piano bench and balance his hat on his knee. Inez was just seven years old, but she knew how to stand still for a long time.

Mr. Roseman smiled at her. "Well, are you going to take out your fiddle or are you going to just stand there looking pretty?"

Inez had never heard a violin called a fiddle, and after Mr. Roseman had her play for a few minutes, he said, "First thing we must do is to get this child a decent fiddle."

Not long after Joey started playing the cello, Inez would hear him bowing for more than an hour on the open strings. Once she went into his bedroom and discovered that her son had perfected a method of open bowing that freed up his left hand. His bow arm operated with surprising fluidity, although the instrument was secured by nothing more than his knees; meanwhile, his left thumb was tucked snugly into his mouth, the small fingers curled around his nose.

JOEY begins, as he does each afternoon, with his scales. Then he launches into the Adagio from the Dvořák Cello Concerto. He stutters through the dark flower of the theme, as if he were circling the actual music with a thick dotted line. Of course, the Dvořák is too advanced for Joey, but his teacher, Mr. Samuels, who believes the boy's a genius, offered it as an incentive. Now that Joey no longer cries and has stopped grabbing hold of her skirt or fingers, he's attached himself to the cello. Today, feeling a bit expansive on account of the reporter's visit, Inez leaves the bedroom door ajar so that she can hear a bit of cello music.

With Joey practicing, and thirteen-year-old Anna at an after-school babysitting job, Inez is free to go back to bed. It is where she likes to be best. Tonight, she won't feel well enough to prepare dinner. She'll call Chicken Delight instead, and, sooner than she can believe, the delivery boy will arrive. A miracle of the modern age, she'll have a chicken dinner with all the trimmings unpacked and on the table before Jake arrives home.

attraction

ATTRACTION. *Infatuation. Intrigue. Fetish. Obsession. Fixation.*
As a teenager, Sylvia wrote the words in her best hand, cut them from sheets of shiny white paper, and taped them in perfect rectangles to the walls of her room. She liked to stack the words in patterns. Rising doom. Mounting desire. Deepening languor.

Her mother forced the study of vocabulary on her once she hit the fifth grade. Angela, a school nurse, who'd have preferred to have been a French fashion designer or a courtesan from an earlier century, began her romance with words as a strategy for self-improvement, but it evolved into a manic study of civilization, a "lexicon for living," as she liked to say, and a distinct mode of communication between mother and daughter.

Any given Saturday might be proclaimed "Legislative Strategy Day" or "Equestrian Day" or "Phobia Day," and the kitchen walls would be splattered with lawmaking language or horsey terms or lists of things to be afraid of. Both Sylvia and her mother took a liking to phobias. "Learn them now or suffer them later" was Angela's motto.

Bathophobia: the fear not of hygiene, but of depths. *Gymnophobia:* the fear not of gym class, but of nudity. *Hamartophobia:* the fear not of pork products, but of sin. Angela never tired of pointing out that if the list of phobias seemed long, the list of manias was longer.

Attraction. Infatuation. Intrigue. Sylvia turns over each word like a flavored lozenge in her mouth. The day after her interview with Inez Roseman, Sylvia strolls the perimeter of Union Square, looking at dresses in the shop windows, imagining how some of them would look on Inez, how the fabric would drape, whether the line would complement the violinist's natural elegance or seem inhibitive. Sylvia rarely stops to imagine herself in such dresses. Although she spent hours as a child with paper dolls, dressing and undressing the figures of Gene Tierney and Maureen O'Hara, it is odd to picture their dresses on someone else. Sadly, little that she sees strikes her as worthy of Inez. The windows at Elinor's feature a wash of pastel chiffons that don't bear enough gravity for Inez, while the mannequins at City of Paris and Ransohoff's are weighted down in winter wools that, though stately, call to mind matrons in fur stoles. And then at I. Magnin she has a vision: ah, beautiful Inez in a long, creamy rose satin cut on a bias.

Sylvia considers her own visage, reflected in a side window at I. Magnin. There she is—a bright-faced woman in a close-fitting black sweater atop a crisp gabardine skirt that once belonged to her mother. She looks like a woman brimming with intention, unlike her pose of yesterday, when she appeared more like a copy girl on the *Sacramento Bee* than a *Chronicle* reporter. It was an audacious act, her masquerade. She feared she'd lose her nerve at the doorstep and slink away. At first, she wasn't sure she'd make it through the door. She doubted she'd even get a glimpse of Inez Roseman. But once she got there she took a deep breath and pressed the bell. Rather than the usual two-note summons, a mechanical phrase from Bach announced her. Bemused, she stood on her spot, ready to accept whatever awaited her.

SYLVIA'S experience in journalism consisted more of wish than fulfillment. Although she'd spent a semester as an intern at the *Bee*, her only newspaper job—her first employment in the city—was a short-lived stint in the classifieds department of the *Chronicle*.

At present, she is employed primarily "under the table." *Under the table with the crumbs*, the voice of her mother says in her head, *how sub terra of you.*

Saturdays, she plays show tunes on a Baldwin baby grand at Myerson's, for which she receives free symphony tickets, a small hourly wage, and a not inconsequential bonus anytime a piano's sold on her shift. She also works three nights a week at a cellar smorgasbord on Bush Street called The Little Sweden, where she gets to feast on shrimp and hard cheeses, herring and black bread. Although the patrons barely tip, she's fond of the place—the owners treat her like family and look the other way whenever she fills a doggie bag during cleanup.

Sylvia had stayed too long in Sacramento. She told herself that her unstable mother needed her. She kept an apartment on Calavreas Avenue, subsisting on a small inheritance from her grandmother. Each morning she strolled past the capitol with a bag lunch, masquerading as a government worker. She spent most of her time polishing her piano skills in the practice rooms at Sac State. Nothing did more to cover Sylvia's loneliness than a stroll through the music building's corridors of practice rooms. She loved the bright din of the underground hallways, the sweet cacophony of rising scales and arpeggiated blasts, the earnestness of the enterprise behind each door. Sylvia often ate lunch with a few of the studious undergraduates—music majors, as she had been—who might as well have been missionaries, given their desire to become band or choral directors in little school districts filled with Mexican children in the Central Valley. She accompanied the students at their recitals and listened like a wise aunt as they talked about their checkered romances.

About herself, Sylvia revealed little. She told them that she'd been married—a harmless if enabling fiction—but that it hadn't worked out. She told them that she wanted a future she couldn't imagine, in a city rather than a town, a love who didn't yet know that she existed. During her mornings in the practice rooms, drudging through her Hannon before playing any real music, Sylvia meditated on her future. How could she possibly reinvent herself while living in her mother's shadow?

Angela Bran's suicide, early in 1960, didn't completely break her grip on Sylvia, but it influenced Sylvia's decision to move to San Francisco. In her first year in the city, she drifted from one lowly office job to another, got temporarily trapped in a romance she could have done without, and began to entertain the notion that she preferred women to men.

On a foggy Saturday, Sylvia walked into Myerson's, the fabled downtown music store, a branch of which was the site of Sylvia's first piano lessons, and asked if they might need a piano teacher. The bohemian-looking gent on the showroom floor, who claimed his name was Myerson, snickered when she asked her question. "Everybody who can play a three-minute Mozart minuet thinks they're a piano teacher. What we need is a genuine pianist for the showroom, somebody who can give a little flair to light classics, Broadway tunes, and new numbers on the Hit Parade."

Sylvia smiled at the man, an offbeat creature wearing a devilish goatee and a string tie with a sterling silver treble clef. She enlisted one of her mother's pet phrases: "Mr. Myerson, it sounds to me like you're calling my name."

Myerson sat her down at a gorgeous, ebonized Steinway and told her to make herself comfortable.

Sylvia began by running scales. She'd never played an instrument that responded so brightly and that had so fine a sustainer. "I'm a little rusty."

"Aren't we all," Myerson said and gave a tug to the reins of his string tie. "The thing is, what we're peddling here is illusion. Fella comes into the showroom, hears the piano, song he knows, big, rich cascading-waterfall sound. God almighty, he thinks, to play like that. Plant a little worm in his brain."

Sylvia leafed through the music spread out above her and opened the score to *My Fair Lady*. "Should I play the overture?"

"Why not? Play the overture." As Sylvia started to play, Myerson leaned against the side of the piano. "I tell you, you can spot these guys as soon as they walk in. They've got the wounded-puppy look. They're weak-minded, full of cheap sentiment. Want the quick fix. Used to be, you could set them up with a player piano, nothing was expected of them. Now we have to baby them, teach them how to play 'Chopsticks,' before we sell them an instrument."

Myerson turned and smiled at Sylvia. "What do you know, she can play. She walks right in off the street and gets the job."

Sylvia bit her lower lips as she kept her left hand going.

"Tell you what I like about you, kid, you have a strong mind. You came in here and decided you wanted a job. Took a hard look at the impressive gent, who carries on the Myerson family tradition of musical excellence and spellbinding value, without blinking an eye. That shows me something. A person like you can do anything you want in this world. You want power over people, you have it. The beauty of a young lady such as yourself is that you don't even know how powerful you are. You're like the Mississippi River. Do you think the Mississippi River knows how big it is?"

Sylvia lifted her hands off the piano and folded them in her lap.

"Look over there," Mr. Myerson said, pointing across the showroom to a man standing in a gray suit. "That's Miller Beem, the most pathetic salesman you'll ever meet. I brought him on anyway. I am not a man without a heart. Okay, you want to know the truth about Miller? I was overcome with a rash of arrogance. I thought, if I can teach this guy my method of salesmanship, I can teach anyone. I found out that I'm mortal. Miller's my daily reminder. You, on the other hand, have another kind of future ahead of you."

Uncertain whether Mr. Myerson was a lunatic or just a big talker, Sylvia flipped a few pages of music and began playing "I've Grown Accustomed to Her Face."

"Lovely. Now, I'm going to give you the advance course in sales in the time it takes to play a baby minuet. Listen closely now. Your hands are important because they play the notes. Your heart is vital because it makes music of the notes. But it's your mind that brings us the customer. Your mind becomes a lasso that is both supple and strong. Do you follow me? Now, let's take our prospective customer. He might be looking forward to getting married; let's say he wants to bring a little music into the hearth. So he's come in to pick up the sheet music for *Oklahoma.* Give himself a real challenge on his ancient upright. You lay down three bars of 'Surrey with the Fringe on Top,' and as you're playing, hands in place, heart open, your mind becomes a lasso. You play three bars of 'Surrey,' toss the lasso, and, before you know it, our guy's on his knees, ready to genuflect. That's where I come in. I go up to him and offer him a cigarette. Light the man's cigarette, nod to the music. 'It's a wonderful sound,' I say, poised and ready for the guy's automatic response. Most of the time, he'll say, 'She can really play.' 'Her? She's little more than a beginner. Come on, we're not talking about Arthur Rubinstein here. A few lessons, a little practice, and with an instrument of this quality, not the priciest piano, mind you, but still, an instrument with an extraordinarily rich sound, that could be you.'"

SYLVIA picked up a couple of thrift-shop dresses and now, on Saturday mornings, wears either a chambray-blue rayon with a square collar or a swing-era teal shirtwaist and sits barelegged in Capezios at the piano. Some mornings she actually watches for the phantom gentleman, the one she'll lasso, as the notes of "Surrey with the Fringe on Top" fall miraculously under her fingers.

According to Hy, the genuine celebrities at Myerson's aren't the notables who routinely walk through the showroom on the way to signing their new records—so far Sylvia has laid eyes on Andy Williams, the Negro diva Leontyne Price, and the darling trumpeter Ronnie Reboulet—no, the real celebs are the phantom gents, the guys who may plunk down solid cash for the privilege of taking a baby grand home with them.

A couple of weeks into her job at Myerson's, Hy offered her a ticket to the symphony and let her know that there were more where they came from—four for every Friday night concert. "The reason those tickets always go unclaimed," Hy said, pausing to cough unpleasantly into a handkerchief, "is that you work with philistines, Sylvia. I count myself among them. What can I say? I've always preferred the open-face harmonies of Broadway tunes to the classics. You, you're a girl with a little more class, Sylvia. You have an affinity for the sophisticates."

WHATEVER her affinity, Sylvia feared she had made a fool out of herself the first time she interviewed Inez, but what she saw frightened her: Inez Roseman was even more beautiful in her kitchen than onstage at the Opera House. Sylvia wanted to do nothing but stare. She stuffed her mouth with dry coffee cake, the only thing that seemed to provide cover for her watching. Sylvia would have happily spent the morning admiring the bruise under Inez's chin, the marbled patch of skin, smaller than a half dollar, against which the violin rested. Did the square of silk she laid on her shoulder prevent her from having a like bruise there?

Who'd have guessed that Inez would be so easy to talk with, so vulnerable? And what did the comely violinist think of *her*? Enough to change into a fancy dress and get her violin out, enough to play a Paganini caprice, to tell things about herself that she'd barely tell her diary.

On the morning of their second meeting, Sylvia modifies her appearance. She gives her hair a light henna rinse, puts on a bit too much eye shadow, and dresses in a charcoal sheath that shows off her clavicle. "A classy man," her mother was fond of saying, "is as moved by a woman's clavicle as by her cleavage." Sylvia also wears her favorite necklace, a strand of silver pearls spaced with small medallions of abalone shell.

Sylvia picks up a fancy dessert on the way to Inez's house. Armed with the bright pink package in her string bag, she travels under a halo of invulnerability.

Inez greets her with an amused smile at the door. "You're all dressed up, dear." Inez didn't look too shabby herself. Dressed smartly in a tweed skirt and a white blouse with pearled buttons, she leads Sylvia back to the breakfast room.

"I brought something to thank you for the crumb cake."

"Crumb cakes don't need to be reciprocated, silly."

Sylvia is surprised to find Inez so affectionate on their second visit. Would it be easier if she were hostile?

"Well, what is it?" Inez says, pointing her small nose toward the pink pastry box.

"It's a berry tart from Fantasia's."

"You didn't have to do that."

"I know," Sylvia says, feeling herself turn rosy with pleasure at her own extravagance.

Awhile later, as she finishes her slice of tart, she realizes that, before pushing her plate aside, Inez has barely dented the crust of her tart. Not to her liking? Sylvia pulls out her pad and pencil and reminds herself that her purpose is to get the violinist to talk, that as long as Inez is responding to questions the contract between them is viable.

The problem for Sylvia is that she's not particularly interested in the questions and answers. She has come to admire the violinist in silence. Sylvia turns her head sideways to signal a shift toward business. "So how's the concerto coming?"

Inez takes a moment to consider the question. "I'm a little nervous, but I think it will go well. Will you be there?"

"With bells on."

"Please, not bells."

"Of course not. But speaking of bells," Sylvia says, pleased that she's managed to steer her single-mindedness back to business, "tell me what your wedding was like."

"My wedding?"

"Yes; did you have a big wedding?"

"You mean, you're still interested in doing this story?"

"Of course. Why do you think . . . ?"

"I thought you just wanted to come over and eat cake," Inez says, with a wink.

"Tell me about your wedding."

"Look, nobody wants to hear about our wedding."

"I do."

"I don't know why anybody would—"

"Human interest."

"Are you trying to turn Jake and me into a sideshow?"

Sylvia has no strategy except to appear hurt.

"I just can't imagine that anybody'd be interested. You're a scoundrel asking all these questions about ancient history."

"In my experience," Sylvia says, stalling, "people are fascinated . . . truly fascinated by the genesis of things that turn out to be big."

"What's so big about a couple getting married?"

Sylvia faces the violinist with an even gaze. "You aren't just any couple."

Inez nods, acknowledging either the truth of Sylvia's statement or its effectiveness as a ploy. "We actually had two weddings within a few weeks of each other. We were married just after I turned twenty."

Sylvia tries to imagine Inez at twenty, how lovely she must have been.

"The first time was at City Hall. Nobody was with us but my sister, Bibi. We decided against a formal wedding—Jake being Jewish, me not. But then we had a fairly elaborate folk version, a few weeks later."

Sylvia adds some dots and dashes to her pad. "What was the City Hall wedding like?"

"What was it like? We sat on benches in a courtroom full of poor couples. The young men looked like they hadn't even shaved yet. Most of them were going off to the war. Jake had a deferment while he was in law school. My heart went out to the girls. They looked scared and tired. Some, a little hopeful. I had a large bouquet of freesias that my sister had given me. None of the other girls had flowers. It occurred to me that I should divide my bouquet so that every bride in the court-room had a flower, but I held on to it. I didn't want to seem as if I was gloating. Each couple was escorted, one by one, back to the judge's chambers. It's funny, how I can still see the judge's chambers. Small and high-ceilinged." The violinist smiles, beguiled by her memory. "The room smelled oddly of mint, and there were cobwebs collecting above the photographs of FDR and Mayor Rossi. The judge, a gaunt fellow in his black robes, seemed in greater need of a benediction than either Jake or me. But, somehow, he managed to give the moment a quiet dignity."

Inez, strangely girlish, folds her hands together, like a student, embarrassed after answering a query with more candor than was called for.

"And the second wedding?"

"It was in a redwood grove in Muir Woods. Jake found a young rabbi from Berkeley. We stood under a chuppah. Four of his Berkeley buddies held up the poles that supported the fabric. The chuppah had an inscription embroidered on the cloth, in both Hebrew and English, that I kept reading to myself. *The voice of mirth and the voice of gladness, the voice of the bridegroom and the voice of the bride.* A line from Jeremiah. I remember standing there, wondering whether our marriage would be filled with mirth and gladness. Could we be that fortunate? Jake surely seemed like a man of mirth; could I become a woman of gladness? Even back then, I had my doubts.

"After Jake stepped on the ceremonial glass, our family and friends cheered a little. Jake and his mirth were off to a flying start. I closed my eyes and tried to make a picture of gladness in my head. All I could come up with was a basket of fruit. I don't know, bunches of fat red grapes drooping over brown pears. Was that enough to build a marriage on?"

Sylvia stares for a moment into the black of her cup and then drinks down her coffee. She pushes aside the reporter's pad. "Tell me about your wedding night."

"My wedding night?!"

"It's off the record." Sylvia smiles. It is an anxious moment, teetering somewhere between titillation and fright. She lifts her right hand to her mouth and starts chewing on a nail. She thinks of Hy Myerson and what he's taught her about the supple power of the mind, the way it can insinuate itself into forbidden places and make itself at home. "Women so rarely talk about their wedding nights," she says.

"Why should they?"

"I don't know. Misery loves company."

"Was yours miserable?"

"Yes." Sylvia looks straight ahead, expecting that at any moment she'll either be asked for particulars or to leave. She tries again. "What was your wedding night like?"

"You should get a job with Dr. Kinsey."

Sylvia laughs, "I've thought of that."

"You have not."

"You're right, but now that you mention it . . ."

Amused despite herself, Inez has difficulty suppressing a chuckle.

"Pretend I am," says Sylvia.

"Pretend you are what?"

"Working for Dr. Kinsey."

"Why should I?"

Sylvia tries to establish a formal tone. "Would you please tell me about your wedding night."

"No."

Sylvia nods. She picks up her pad and makes like she's reading a prepared statement. "You understand that your name will never be attached to your responses, not even in our files. We have a code that nobody can crack. What you tell us is invaluable to our research and may provide genuine solace to others."

Inez sips at her coffee. "You have a lot of nerve."

Sylvia pushes her chair back from the table, but doesn't stand. She and Inez trade glances. There is no honor in backing off now. She enjoys her host's discomfiture.

Inez lifts her chin curiously, as if, despite having no violin, she were about to play her instrument. Sylvia studies the marbled bruise under the violinist's chin.

"We spent our wedding night at the Sir Francis Drake."

"The big hotel on Powell?"

"Yes; I remember walking across the red carpet into the hotel, my arms full of freesias. We ended up in this large, mannish room with Tudor furnishings and a four-poster bed. The wallpaper featured a hunting scene. It was a helluva spot for a girl to find herself on her wedding night."

"I bet."

"I was afraid that if I closed my eyes the hounds might gain on me."

Sylvia laughs and nods at Inez in hopes of keeping her going.

"The bellboy asked Jake if he'd like the curtains pulled back. Jake looked at me—what did I want? *Open them*, I said. My first command as a wife. I must have thought that Jake was going to ravish me as soon as the bellboy left. I filled all the containers in the room with flowers. Freesias floated in the drinking glasses, in the ice bucket."

"What surprised you most on your wedding night?"

The violinist appears angry. Beautiful and mad, she inhales deeply through her nostrils, then hangs her head. "I was surprised by our nakedness. That surprised me. That could have been enough for a while. Even though I'd been touched before, I was surprised by the sensation of the simplest touch. That would have been enough. I was surprised by how quickly the rest came. Did that surprise you, Sylvia?"

Sylvia nods. She feels a sadness swoop over the room. In the silence that follows, Sylvia forces herself to look at Inez. Her full lips are open, her nostrils slightly flared.

"I think I'd prefer not to do this. I'm afraid your story's gone kaput," Inez says. "Maybe you should interview a man; you'll have better luck. You seem like a nice young woman."

Sylvia stands. Patronized, at last. Should she be hurt? Inez offers her a wistful smile. Sylvia would like to hold the older woman in her arms. She'd like to walk over to Inez and put a hand on her cheek, caress the marbled bruise under her chin.

"I'm afraid you got more than you bargained for," Inez says.

"Not at all."

Sylvia steps toward the lady of the house and, pretending that she's initiating some vaguely European form of affection, places each of her open palms on Inez's smooth cheeks. It is not quite a brazen gesture, though the violinist is caught off guard by the touch and gives a little start. Her skin is warm to the touch. A strange look comes into her eyes, wary at first, but not frightened. Sylvia wonders how long she can leave her hands on Inez's cheeks before causing a scandal. Inez inhales, not without pleasure, and slowly backs away.

god of the sea

THE weekend after the reporter's second visit, Inez finds herself alone with Jake in Carmel. The idea is both to give her a relaxing break away from the kids in advance of her solo concert and to celebrate their twentieth anniversary, which passed without fanfare a few months ago.

Mafalda, Inez's friend and colleague, happily took the kids. A twice-divorced violist who'd never had children, Mafalda was always clamoring to have the kids for a weekend. She'd known them both since they were babies, having helped Inez in the weeks and months after the birth of each of her children. Anna and Joey loved Mafalda for what Joey called her kookiness. As soon as she got away from the symphony, Mafalda slipped on fake fingernails and long, dangly earings. She knew a hundred card games and told the kids in detail about her gambling trips to Reno. Her large apartment was filled with fashion magazines, caged canaries, and an astonishing assortment of tchotchkes: hand-carved gargoyles and fertility gods, as well as clocks that performed all sorts of tricks on the hour. Still, Inez expected Joey to be sullen about being left for a weekend. Perhaps, she thought, he'd beg her not to go. But Joey burst into Mafalda's Pacific Avenue flat and said, "You still got that cuckoo clock? You still got that windup woodpecker?" He hardly turned to wave good-bye as Inez walked down the stairs to the street.

Inez enjoys the long quiet drive down the coast and is grateful to Jake for giving up on conversation when she shows little interest in it. Once in town, he leads them on a weaving tour through the sandy lanes. As they drive past the arty homes and blooming yards, Inez tries to imagine herself transplanted to Carmel. Would she be a happier soul here?

After a picnic on the beach, they stroll through shops in the village and Jake insists on buying her gifts: long silver earrings she'll never wear; an expensive pen and pencil set; a silk scarf that features watering cans, hand trowels, and potted red geraniums. Periodically, Jake is afflicted with a fever of affection for his wife that she has trouble receiving. She likens the numb, dog days of a marriage gone sour to the aftermath of a war and views her husband's odd awakenings as a form of reparation.

The first night, Inez has difficulty sleeping. Through the open windows, the sound of the waves keeps waking her. Jake had wanted to make love but she'd put him off. Why does she have no desire, not want to be touched, never want to be touched?

She thinks about her conversation with the reporter. It was less a conversation than a confession. The girl had a curious effect on her. As Sylvia was leaving, she reached out her hands and touched Inez, as gently as a feather might fall, and Inez's cheeks had flushed with heat. Inez wanted to tell Sylvia more but backed away instead. Inez felt desperate after the reporter left.

With Jake soundly asleep, Inez climbs out of bed and curls her body like a nautilus on the Danish area rug across the room. She thinks as much about the reporter as she thinks about Jake. When she falls asleep, it's in short, satisfying bursts. The night is like a full moon, the known, lit half spent with Jake, the shadow half spent with the reporter. Inez wakes, as she does every morning, heavy and listless. By the time Jake opens his eyes, she's beside him in bed, the divided night just one more of her secrets.

On their last evening, they drive down to Big Sur and run into Richard Burton and Elizabeth Taylor, of all people, standing larger than life on the terrace at Nepenthe. Or at least cutout versions of the movie stars, mounted on cardboard—stills from a yet-to-be-released movie, which was filmed in part at Nepenthe.

Jake whispers: "I prefer your beauty to hers."

"Pardon me?"

"I find you more beautiful than Elizabeth Taylor."

"I'm supposed to believe that?"

"Absolutely."

It is a lovely September evening with stars and a tolerable breeze. They sit at a choice table on the terrace, Jake offering her the seat with the widest view of the ocean. They drink martinis and champagne and eat grilled salmon. A piano trio plays cha-cha music, as Joey describes it, and couples lead each other, in a stylized swooning, around the wide granite terrace. Tipsy, Inez turns to watch the pianist, a wiry fellow in a pin-striped suit. After he announces "Stardust," Jake gets out of his chair and comes around behind her.

"What are you doing?"

"I'd like to have this dance."

Although she isn't much of a dancer—it comes more naturally to Jake—she lets herself go while they're out on the floor, the sky bright with stars, the waves splattering a hundred yards down the cliffs.

When the music stops, Jake holds her by both hands and looks her up and down, not in a salacious way, but as a middle-aged man appraising the toll twenty years of an unhappy marriage has taken on his wife. Perhaps she is crediting Jake with more perception than he has. Standing amid such majesty, awash in alcohol, he says: "You're absolutely stunning tonight, Inez, without a doubt, the most beautiful woman on the floor. Elizabeth Taylor can't hold a candle."

Shamelessly, she stands listening to this. She's taken a gander at the other middle-aged darlings and likes to think that she's above comparing herself to them. But now, as Inez considers it, she imagines that these women are able to experience something difficult for her: simple happiness. Instead of glancing around the floor, Inez looks directly at Jake, dashing in his gray suit, his red silk tie. He shakes a cigarette out of his pack and takes his time lighting it, as if the cigarette were attached to an idea that he's not sure he cares to pursue. Once he lights the cigarette, he blows a Herculean stream of tobacco vapor toward the night sky.

Back at their table, they sit quietly, breathing in the salt air. His cigarette snuffed out, Jake takes deep breaths in the manner of fitness maven Jack La Lanne. It seems as good a time as any to let him know what she's been thinking about. That it's been going on for quite a while now. That her nights are filled with imaginings that have begun to creep into her days, and the chambers of the nautilus are more comforting than human touch. Why tell him her plans? Does she want to frighten him? To have him try to talk her out of it? Or is this simply part of the ritual—to offer the fabled cry for help? She doesn't need help. She can do it herself. Then why tell? As a courtesy, or to sharpen her nerve?

Breathing normally, his face flushed with good old tobacco and alcohol Jack La Lanne fitness, Jake smiles at her. "What you thinking about?"

"I don't know."

He pitches her a perfect question and she balks. If she can't even mention the thing, how does she expect to carry it out? She certainly spends enough time thinking about it. Driving in the car. Her foot on the gas. She pictures the way the calf of her right leg will flex when she presses the pedal to the floor. There's a large parking lot at the ocean, just above The Cliff House and Seal Rock. It's often empty at night. She could get a good head of steam going in the Studebaker and drive from the far end of the lot straight off the cliff.

The other day, after the reporter left, Inez put on a jacket and walked toward the ocean. She didn't understand it at first. All that talking about herself. The reporter more curious about her than anybody has been in years, and the way Inez had yakked and yakked. The shame washed over her—a quick, unexpected tide.

It was breezy that afternoon as she walked, and she wished she'd brought a scarf. There was a blimp in the sky above Geary Boulevard. It seemed portentous—blimps have always struck her that way. A giant balloon with an idea in it. An idea for her life. The only idea she had was to end it. Inez strolled around the parking lot above The Cliff House. The lot was filled with cars. People were sitting in their cars, the windows open, pop music spilling from the radios. A man in a T-shirt, oblivious to the chill, was waxing his sharp, red Impala. She tried to picture the lot at night. Sitting in the Studebaker, at the farthest distance from the cliff. Her foot on the pedal, the real tension in the Achilles tendon rather than the calf, as she arched her heel, slammed down the pedal, the rattling Studebaker Scotsman swaying from side to side as it squealed forward and, finally, lurched into oblivion.

In the crowded parking lot, a sharp breeze blew through her hair and the salt air made her realize that she was hungry. She walked behind a row of cars, past the man waxing his Impala. She could tell that his eyes were following her. Was this all she really wanted: a witness?

Jake leans forward on his elbows, his handsome face balanced like a trophy in his hands. The man is proud of himself for choosing the beautiful terrace restaurant, for giving her the seat with the best view. Yesterday they'd driven to Pacific Grove and walked along the tide pools. As they climbed over craggy rocks, shiny with damp anemones and sea wrack, Jake said something so absurd that she'd laughed out loud. He had a stick in his hand and poked at a fat anemone. Its mouth withered to a close around the base of the stick. "Sometimes when I'm feeling down," Jake said, "I try to remind myself that I too am part of nature." She figured that Jake had read the line in a book somewhere. Jake, who'd always seemed so much more a city creature than a nature boy. But then it occurred to Inez that Jake, sensing her abstraction, her distance, her desolation, was offering his nature line as a tonic, a motto to live by. The truth was, she'd never been particularly keen on nature. She looked across the heaving mounds and clefts of ocean rock, at the pools of snails and heaps of anemones of every imaginable size, walls of opened-mouth anemones, clinging en masse to boulders and slabs of granite, waiting, like infants, for their feed. If this was nature, she didn't want any.

NOW Jake smiles at her; she needs to tell him something. She takes a deep breath and focuses on the swell of white water over his left shoulder. "Jake, I want a divorce."

"What?" he says, and immediately goes into a convulsive coughing fit. He takes out a handkerchief and blows his nose and pats his eyes, which are damp. He looks at her as if she is a person with whom he once had business but can't now place. She has the urge to wave at him. She's surprised that anything she's said can affect him so. What if she'd revealed her actual intentions?

"What the hell are you talking about?" Jake practically spits the words at her. He looks to be hyperventilating.

"Are you okay?"

Jake nods and looks away.

She watches him rearrange himself in his chair. He slips off his sport coat and hangs it on the back of his chair. Recovered now, he lights a cigarette and narrows his eyes on her. "How long have you been think-ing about this?"

"For some time."

"You've never mentioned it."

Inez wonders whether she'd be any happier as a divorced woman. Jake no longer in the house. His soiled laundry gone, his crossword puz-zles, his box scores, his pencil stubs. Although she often finds it irritat-ing, she'd miss his whistling. The jazz, like having a foreign language in the house. She'd miss his good cheer, his sweet morsels of affection.

He cheats on her, she knows; he's cheated on her for years. Can she blame him for that? She's been less than available. Certainly, he's a good father, a man concerned about his community, a good man. She watched his curiosity grow in the last years as he invited the opinion of others and tried to understand their concerns. She saw him act—protesting the crazed tactics of the House Committee on Un-American Activities, standing outside the hearings at City Hall when the police were hosing Berkeley students down the marble stairway. How he grabbed a mega-phone and stood a moment not knowing what he'd say, and then spoke against the madness of the committee and the police. If not exactly an element of nature, he stood up in front of a troubled crowd, a citizen, growing suddenly into an angel of reason. She's seen how easily people have come to adore Jake as a genuine and caring human being, which she believes he is.

Inez wonders if she could actually live in a house without a man. What would become of her and the children? Would they each shut themselves up in their own rooms for a generation, a trio of sad sacks, subsisting on Anna's macaroni, Joey's boiled hot dogs, her own over-cooked broccoli?

Jake is staring at her, waiting for a response.

"I thought you were so busy with your public life that it would hardly matter to you if you were married or not."

"What are you talking about?" Jake asks, furious. "Did you plan to surprise me? Were you going to have some shyster lawyer serve me with divorce papers?"

Jake barks at the waiter who's come over to see if they want any-thing else to drink.

Inez turns her chair to face a broader stripe of the ocean.

"I want to know something," Jake says, bitterly.

"Yes."

"Why are you telling me this now? You are so twisted. I don't under-stand how your mind works, you and your irrational moods. Anybody else would be thrilled to have a nice weekend with her husband . . ."

"Who'll have a new girlfriend by the end of the week."

"Is that what this is about?"

"No. It's more than that." And it is. But still, she finds herself think-ing about the infidelities. They began not long after Anna was born. Inez was in the midst of a period of gloominess, not as boundless as the one that followed Joey's birth, but debilitating nonetheless. She had little interest in Jake, who became, during that period, a shadowy figure who left the house in the morning and returned rumpled and weary before bed.

Up until then, she barely had a concept of infidelity. It seemed a thing that happened to people in far-off places—unstable individuals, unnatural characters, not people like her and Jake, who came from good families.

In the early days, after discovering one of Jake's infidelities, she'd tell the nanny she was sick and stay in bed all day. She'd pull the covers over her head and want to die. Later, she'd confront Jake and he wouldn't deny a thing. Contrite and kindly, he'd say that the girl didn't mean a thing; he'd gladly give her up. He was sorry for the pain he'd caused Inez. His holy calm and essential guiltlessness drove her into a rage. She wanted to know everything. With baby Anna sleeping in her crib, or tod-dling through the living room, Inez whispered a round of mean and greedy questions. *How'd you meet her? Is she a real blonde? Are her breasts bigger than mine? Does she read more than movie magazines? Where do you take her to do whatever you do? Do you buy her pres-ents? Does she call you Jakie? Or does she have another pet name for you? What does she do for you?* Then she'd cry for days and Jake would bring her tall bouquets of gladiolas, always gladiolas, a flower she can no longer experience without the dark reference of tears.

During these periods, Jake would prepare a little supper for them—a cheese omelet, a plate of toast and herring, something like that. He'd feed Anna in her high chair, clean up after her, put her in her playpen. Then he and Inez would sit at the red Formica table in the kitchen. It was a silent business. Jake sipped from a tall glass of milk, boyish still at thirty. Sometimes he'd take her hand. And later, after Anna was tucked in for the night, Inez would let him lead her to the bed, where she'd lay stiff and wounded for a biblical age, while Jake composed little speeches about his love for her and fondled her breasts. At first, this was the only way she knew to deal with Jake's treachery.

By the time of Joey's birth and the long misery that followed, Inez no longer cared about Jake's new girlfriends. She simply noted a change in him. It was like discovering that a building of the charmless, prefabricated variety had gone up in an empty lot since the last time she'd driven through the neighborhood. It became a thing she expected rather than something that surprised her.

NOW the waiter brings two snifters of cognac and sets them down on cardboard coasters bearing the image of Neptune. She lifts her glass not to drink, but to get a better look at the mischievous god of the sea as he appears on the coaster, his trident aimed forward like a champion spearfisher. Is Neptune the devil in disguise? The theme from "The Devil's Trill" floats into her head. How programatic of her. The violinist Tartini had a dream in which the devil appeared at the foot of his bed playing a virtuoso sonata. Did Tartini trade his soul for the chance to transcribe the sonata? What would she trade hers for? Does she even have one to trade?

Inez lifts her snifter and looks again at Neptune. Often when she pictures herself dead, she's in the sea. A nautilus bobbing effortlessly in the depths. A part of nature, after all. She swishes the cognac around the glass the way Jake showed her years before.

"Would you look at me, please?" Jake snaps.

"Of course."

Jake's face is red with anger. Inez feels a curious pleasure at seeing him so put out. No matter how hot he gets, she can get cooler. That is their real song and dance.

"So you're serious about this?" Jake asks, using his handkerchief to pat his forehead.

"Yes." Inez dips her nose into the glass of cognac. She doesn't want to torture the man, but neither does she want to renege. Does he think that his anger will force her to take it all back?

Jake lights a fresh cigarette, inhales deeply, blows a long, even stream of smoke, and then faces Inez. "How do you expect to tell the children?"

"I haven't thought about that yet."

"Well, maybe you should."

In fact, she thinks about the children all the time. Inez takes a sip of her cognac and enjoys the way it burns down her throat.

"Look, can we talk about this?" Jake says.

"Seems like we are."

Jake loosens his tie and opens the top button of his shirt. "I won't see other women anymore."

Inez doesn't say anything for a moment. She looks at the stripe of ocean. How nice it would be to be out there. Finished.

Jake is waiting for her to respond.

"You can see all the goddamn women you want, Jake."

"I'm not going to see any other women."

"Whatever makes you happy."

"I'm not going to see any."

He doesn't get the point—she really doesn't care. She smiles at him and follows his eyes as they narrow again.

"Now," he says, "I want you to do something for me."

She laughs out loud. Does he actually believe that his false promise merits a favor in return?

"I want you to give this a year. You feel like divorcing me a year from now, I won't try and stop you."

That, she thinks, is a grand play. The man is a skillful negotiator. She picks up her snifter and smiles down at brother Neptune.

Jake gulps his cognac. "You know, I think about when I fell in love with you, Inez. It was the first time I ever spoke with you. God, I made a fool out of myself. That was twenty-five years ago. You were the most beautiful girl I'd ever seen and now you're the most beautiful woman."

"Come on, Jake."

"I'm not kidding. I've always loved you, Inez." Jake snuffs out his cigarette and turns both of his hands palm up on the table. "What do you say, Inez?"

"What do I say?" Inez looks into Jake's open hands—all the slanting lines are supposed to tell something about the man's life.

"Will you give it a year?"

She's surprised that he's so anxious to keep his house in order. "All right," she says, allowing him to take her right hand in his. When a man's cheated on you for years, she thinks, you're hardly obliged to honor a promise to him.

Jake leans across the table to kiss her, but Inez dips her nose toward the dark bell of the snifter. It's been a long time since she's been on equal footing with Jake. Her foot is on the pedal.

Jake nods his head meaningfully and takes a gulp of cognac. "Do you believe in God, Inez?"

She laughs out loud, then holds up her coaster. "I believe in Neptune, the god of the sea."

Jake swirls the cognac around his glass but doesn't bother to inhale it before emptying his glass. "I always imagined that musicians have made some kind of spiritual pact, that that's part of the compensation for doing your type of work. I mean, after you've played your hundredth *Messiah*, doesn't it start to sink in—all that hallelujah business?"

"You're putting me on."

"Yeah, I am."

She laughs again as Jake winks at her. Is he trying to make her love him again, now that he figures he's won her back for a year?

Jake lifts his empty snifter and swirls the air around. "Where's the damn waiter when you need him?"

She watches Jake loosen a second shirt button, then roll the cuffs of his shirt to his forearms. Her mind drifts off again to Sylvia the reporter. Does Sylvia believe in God? When the kids were young, Inez and Jake used to talk about religion quite a bit. She enjoyed playing the heathen. No God, no nature. She'd been brought up without religion and was happy to keep it that way. Jake feared that given the same lack, the children would drift aimlessly through the cosmos. "Be my guest," she'd say to Jake. "They can be Jewish. I won't stand in your way."

Now she faces Jake. "You've heard of the agnostic, whose God he doesn't believe in is Jewish. That's you."

"What are you talking about?"

"You believe that everything that happens is actually supposed to mean something. You don't have a true agnostic bone in your body, Jake."

"And nothing means anything to you?" Jake snaps.

That's one she can't answer. She hears the disappointment in Jake's voice. After all the early promise—the blooming lovesong of their courtship and marriage—he holds her responsible for what went wrong because she's not a believer. Maybe it was only the virus of youth, the rush of hormones, that gave her the hopeful blush that's been missing for so long. Jake can't understand her moods, the depth of her melancholy. Maybe he would have been better off with a bighearted, happy-go-lucky girl named Roxie who would tell him how wonderful he was and never tire of having sex with him. But hadn't Jake chosen Inez, at least in part, because she was complicated? She remembers sitting with Jake on the ocean wall, on the afternoon of her sixteenth birthday. Jake was pointing toward the Farallon Islands on the horizon. "You can't really see them most of the time," he said, "but that doesn't mean they're not there. It's like you, Inez. There's so much more to you than anybody can see. You're not simple like most of the girls I know. There's nothing simple about you, and that's why I love you."

JAKE is still trying to get the waiter's attention. She watches him wave his hand at the man, who looks too young for the walrus mustache gracing his upper lip. After ordering a tequila on the rocks with a twist of lemon, Jake says, "I need a change of pace, something to lighten up my spirit a little."

Once he's gotten his drink, Jake tries to surprise her. "I don't believe in God either. And the God I don't believe in has no particular denomination. What I believe in is you . . . you and the children." He takes a sip of tequila and smiles at her. "I want to make love to you tonight, like the old days."

Inez tries to remember the old days. Love in the old days. Perhaps it wasn't as perfunctory as it's become in recent times. She'll try to honor their pact for at least one night.

"What do you say?" Jake asks.

"It's our second honeymoon, isn't it?" Inez says, smiling.

command performance

I F she had it to do all over again, Sylvia wouldn't have stolen the bottle of Arpège. Who, in her right mind, going out on a big night, wants
to smell like her mother did? She should have chosen a fragrance of her
own. Next time, at City of Paris, she'll glide the perimeter of the fragrance counters, engaging the salesgirls on the relative qualities of this
or that perfume. Can you describe its high notes? How about the fruit in
it, its woody undertones?

To make things worse, she doused herself with the Arpège. You'd
have thought she was a toddler at her mother's perfume tray. If only
she'd mimicked her mother's method: discreetly dabbing a couple of
drops behind the ears, another on the sweet spot of each wrist.

Skunked in the odor of her late mother, Sylvia has arrived at the
Opera House at six thirty, an hour and a half before the concert. Most of
the musicians won't even show up for another hour. Sylvia waits on a
cement bench in the courtyard, spying distance from the backstage door.
She wants to say a word to the violinist before she goes in. A blessing. A
prayer. No matter that Inez has probably forgotten all about her in the
two weeks since their last meeting.

As Sylvia waits, she deconstructs the word that seems to be guiding
her actions. *Anticipation.* She isolates the Latin units, or Latin eunuchs,
as her mother liked to say—*ante* for "before" and *capere*, meaning "to
take," "*to capture.*" Was that why she was here—to capture her future?

Sylvia enjoys watching the musicians arrive with so little fanfare for
their night's work. It surprises her how ordinary many of them look as
they approach the stage door—a French horn player with a prodigious
double chin, a violinist with a frayed overcoat, another with a Band-Aid
on his chin, a flutist who looks as if he might be inebriated. Sylvia
watches the approach of an elegant figure of a man in a dark coat and
beret. Another violinist. How many women would love to unwrap the

white silk scarf from his neck? Maybe he's forty-five, the type who improves with age. He smokes with so profound a nonchalance that you'd think the world was already over. European, no doubt. Viennese, she guesses. For all his worldliness, his sangfroid, she bets he spends twice as long as she does standing in front of the mirror. Vanity, her mother used to say, isn't reserved for women. And what does this cold-blooded Detlev, or whatever he's called, think of his colleague Inez Roseman? Is he jealous of her? Does he question her superior talent? Would he like to make love to her?

Sylvia moves from her perch and plants herself against the wall beside the stage door. She wishes she smoked. She tries to imagine that the world is already over, that she exists only as an afterthought, a hollow echo, a bit of commentary. And then Inez turns the corner in a pair of white heels, holding her violin. Even from a distance, she is a picture of grace. Sylvia's surprised to see her walking alone. Where is her family? Why haven't they accompanied her on this of all nights?

Inez wears a long camel cape, buttoned to the neck, and a magnificent felt hat, a conical affair in a rich caramel hue. If Jackie Kennedy were to wear a Robin Hood hat, this would be it.

Inez doesn't look up until she's nearly to the door and the surprise she registers seems genuine. "Sylvia."

The name remembered.

"I told you I'd be here."

"I'm pleased." Inez steps away from the door so that other arriving musicians can pass through. A few whisper greetings to Inez. Sylvia is amazed that her presence has slowed Inez's progress.

"I wanted to wish you well, though I'm sure you don't need it."

"I don't know what I need."

"You're going to do wonderfully."

Inez closes her eyes and then opens them in a flash, a curiously childlike gesture that seems uncharacteristic. "Do you like the hat?"

"I love it."

"Isn't it outrageous? I wish I could wear it onstage; then it wouldn't matter how I played."

Inez, it occurs to Sylvia, is caught up in the adrenaline of the moment. She might have been as friendly to anybody who'd stopped to wish her well. Sylvia wants to remind her who it is that's standing beside her. She wants to leave an imprint on the soloist, so that when her feet are spread onstage, her body might quiver with the slightest of aftershocks. Sylvia reaches out her open hand, as she did at Inez's house, and lets it fall on the violinist's cheek. Startled, but not wanting to appear so, Inez breathes in through her nose and offers a stage smile. Sylvia, her hand turned cool from the soloist's cold cheek, returns the smile, but leaves her hand in place. Sylvia is pleased by her audacity. From the Latin *audere*—to dare. Finally, Inez, with a little twist to the corner of her mouth, pulls away. She parts her lips to say something she doesn't say. Maybe it was never intended to be said. Somebody calls Inez's name, or at least part of it. "Nez . . . Nez."

Sylvia watches a short, bright-faced woman with a viola approach Inez and kiss her on the cheek.

"This is your night, Nez," the violist says.

"Mafalda!" Inez bows her head toward the violist.

"Look at that hat," Mafalda says. "What a thing of beauty. You brought it for me, didn't you? You really have an extraordinary feeling for my taste in hats."

"Go on," says Inez, draping her arm around the violist's waist.

Sylvia feels a twinge of jealousy as she watches the two musicians together. But as the violinist turns on her white heels and steps with Mafalda through the open door, Sylvia is happy to know that there are others who adore beautiful Inez.

HOW to describe the Opera House crowd tonight? *Flamboyant. Ostentatious. Redoubtable. Stately. Beguiling. Anticipatory?* Not exactly. Sylvia doesn't see anybody pulsing, as she is, with *anticipation.*

Instead of going to her seat and reading up on the Goldmark Concerto, as she'd planned, Sylvia promenades across the grand lobby. Nobody in the lobby is as nervous about Inez's performance as she is. In fact, the crowd of concertgoers, leaning toward each other in clusters of two and three, seem inordinately pleased with themselves. Sylvia had hoped the crowd would distract her from her anxiety, but it only redirects it.

She'd be better off hidden in her seat, buttoned up in her melton coat, rather than weaving in and out of the society throngs in her preposterous ensemble. She never knows quite what to wear. Tonight, after checking her coat and catching a glimpse of herself in an ornate mirror set in gilded plaster, she feels particularly absurd. She expected her sweater (a scoop-necked cashmere in muted orange acquired at Rose's Redux on Union Street) to look smart with the pleated chartreuse skirt that she'd found on the clearance rack at City of Paris. If you squinted, the skirt looked close to lime—a citrus ensemble, she dubbed it sweet and tart. But in the Opera House mirror, even in the warm, honey light of the lobby, squinting doesn't help. She looks, she fears, like some sort of loathsome accident or tropical disaster.

Still, she mingles again with the crowd on the marble floor. Is she hoping she'll find a kindred soul? A man in a pineapple suit? A skinny woman looking like an hors d'oeuvre on melba toast? She doesn't know anyone here. The men are ordinary enough in their suits, the ladies not so lovely as they imagine. Every now and then a beatnik strolls by, one gangly fellow with a bobbing Adam's apple and a sport coat short in the sleeves. A genuine music lover, no doubt. Next time she'll wink at him.

Sylvia leans against a column and reminds herself why she's here. Soon she'll be tucked away in the Myersons' box, anticipating—yes, anticipating—the moment that Inez Roseman walks onstage to a rumble of applause.

Tonight Sylvia plans to rent opera glasses and keep them trained on her subject. She'll scan the violinist's slightly parted lips, her blue eyes, hone in on the bruise under her chin. Soon enough the rest of the orchestra will disappear. The audience will vanish, too, and Sylvia Bran will enjoy a command performance.

THE only thing worse than feeling self-conscious in your anonymity is to be singled out. And it happens.

"Sylvia! Sylvia!"

She wants to believe that another Sylvia is being hailed, but she recognizes the man's voice—it belongs to her boss.

Hyman Myerson, his treble clef string tie wittier than ever under a dark blue, pin-striped suit, with a stout middle-aged woman, presumably his wife, in tow, is coming toward her.

"Well, look who's here," Hy says. "I thought we might find you. Meet my wife, Toby."

Sylvia extends her hand. "Mrs. Myerson."

"Call me Toby. Hy's told me all about you. Best showroom pianist he's had in years."

"All right, all right. Don't swell the girl's head."

"What? The girl's head is not swollen. You're the one with the swollen head."

Hy Myerson shrugs; he rolls his eyes.

Sylvia smiles at Toby, whose round, heavily rouged cheeks have the sheen of an apple made of wax.

"Can you believe," Hy says, pointing his chin toward his wife, "Toby was a dancer when I first met her? What a beauty she was. Took one look at her and I got the mind lasso going."

"Don't start."

"Who's starting?"

"The trouble is, she's too good a cook, and, on top of that, she enjoys her own cooking."

"Stop."

Mrs. Myerson turns aside. The poor woman is dressed beautifully in a woven tapestry suit the colors of honey and moss. Sylvia watches Toby open her beaded bag and pluck out a tube of lipstick.

"Sylvia's the only one from the store to use the symphony tickets," Hy says to his wife. "What does that tell you? Bunch of heathens we work with." He smiles at his pianist. "Toby and I like to make an appearance once in a while, but you really go in for the stuff."

"I enjoy the concerts, but I'm rather ignorant about classical music."

Hy nods to her encouragingly. She can tell that he wants her to keep talking.

"I was a music major in college," says Sylvia, "but all those theory classes—in one ear and out the other. Same thing with the musical forms. I remembered the stuff long enough to pass the tests, then—gone. It's pretty embarrassing. I practiced the piano for hours, but I might as well have been sitting at the typewriter for all I learned about music.

There wasn't much music in my house growing up. My mother was more fond of language." Sylvia laughs. "If anyone asked my mother if she played an instrument, she'd nod and say, 'The lingua franca.'"

Toby Myerson presses her lips together after applying a fresh stripe of rose across them. "Your mother sounds very interesting."

"That's putting it mildly." Sylvia smiles at Hy's wife. "But me, I'm left with my ignorance."

"Talk about ignorant." Toby nods toward her husband.

"What's that supposed to mean?" Hy says.

"The man makes his living from music and he can't tell the difference between Mozart and Brahms."

"Not exactly my forte."

"What exactly *is* your forte?" says his wife, nastily.

"Toby, Toby, forgive me for being alive." Hy goes through a sequence of tics—he squishes his nostrils together, lifts one eyebrow and then the other, smacks his lips three times, then rolls his shoulders as if he expects wings to sprout. He tugs on his string tie. Finally, he pulls a pack of Salems out of his jacket pocket, offers one to Sylvia, who declines, and then to his wife, who grudgingly accepts a cigarette and allows him to light it with his Zippo.

Sylvia's seen Hy run through these tics in the showroom when he becomes frustrated with a customer. Sometimes the tics follow an aborted sale, but there have been instances when they've mesmerized the customer and had the effect of clearing the slate so that Hy can swoop down again with his inimitable charm and make the deal. But what kind of fool hopes to work a flurry of tics and a tug on a string tie to advantage with his wife?

Sylvia is not above trying to help out. "I can't stop admiring your suit, Mrs. Myerson."

"Toby."

"I bought it for her in Italy," Hy says. "Sorrento, if I remember correctly. We were on a little cruise along the Amalfi coast. Her suit cost fifty thousand lira or some damn thing. A small fortune. Crazy money they have over there. You feel like you're spending your life savings on a pair of shoes. It's very becoming on her, don't you think?"

"Beautiful," Sylvia says. Then she excuses herself to rent a pair of opera glasses.

"We'll see you up in the box," Hy calls after her.

INEZ hadn't expected to get the virtuoso's dressing room. The minor soloists and second-rank divas usually get the smaller ones, but tonight they've set up the star's dressing room for her. Of course, there's no other soloist on the program tonight, but she decides not to second-guess her temporary fortune.

Inez has been in this room before. In the midforties, as a young woman playing in both the symphony and opera orchestra, she'd tiptoed in to see the vases of orchids set out for Lily Pons, who sang the title role in *Lucia di Lammermoor*. Innumerable times after concerts, she'd crossed the threshold to greet the aging virtuosos she'd idolized as a girl: Fritz Kreisler, her father-in-law's god, who struck Inez as remarkably formal given how relaxed he seemed onstage; the mechanical Heifetz, who looked right through her as if she were a glass of water; the sweet-toned Nathan Milstein, who kissed her hand and offered her a handkerchief when he noticed tears welling in her eyes; Efrem Zimbalist, who first played with the symphony in 1911 and whose son is now, of all things, a television star on one of Jake's favorite shows—*77 Sunset Strip*. Inez even stepped into this room to meet the least distinguished violin soloist of all—Jack Benny, who pretended that they were long-lost friends and had the roomful of visitors in stitches as he made up a story about being Inez's first violin teacher. "I didn't know *whhhat* to do with that child's bow hand. It was the most awkward thing I ever saw in my life. *Really.*"

Now, for a single night, the room is hers. A magnificent bouquet of South American roses sits in the center of the dressing table. Thick, long-stemmed beauties with enormous globes. She expects they're a gift from the symphony association and is surprised to see a card signed with Jake's name. There is an open box of French chocolates from Simon Brothers and a plate of sliced melon with prosciutto draped across it. Inez thinks to take a chocolate but decides not to touch the box or the plate of melon so that when the kids come backstage after the performance they can see the perfection of the soloist-for-the-night's life. The other reason for not eating the chocolate, Inez decides, after crouching to take a whiff, is that she'd probably end up with a glob of it between her teeth. That would be rich—the soloist with the chocolate smile. Inez imagines the plates of chocolates that were likely left in Mozart's dressing rooms in Vienna and Salzburg when he was little more than a child. Did he pause for fear of leaving traces of chocolate on his mouth? Hardly. The man-child probably gobbled up the whole plate of sweets. Why was it so hard to let herself have pleasure? All those hours of practice? She thinks about Sylvia the reporter. Again, the reporter's warm hand on her cheek, leaving her with a lovely benediction. Maybe the girl is part healer; more likely Inez is mad to think it.

Inez plucks from the plate a dark round gem, crowned with a violet fleur-de-lis. What in the world is inside? She dents the hard wall with her front teeth and, though she won't swallow it, she closes her eyes around the taste of dark chocolate and hazelnut. The chocolate is a wonderfully dark avenue, and then the sweet paste. Her father's favorite. Would he have been proud of her or secretly shamed that this is all she's made of her career? So much talent and no more than a single night in front of a symphony orchestra. She has no excuse. She has a hundred excuses. But only a single truth: she doesn't want to live anymore. She could explain all night long, but never satisfy the interrogators. Why is she doing this tonight? Who does she think she's playing for? What glory here? She finds a tissue and spits out her chocolate.

IN the dim light of the loge, Sylvia flips through her program. Instead of reading up on Karl Goldmark, she searches for a photograph of Inez. As the first set of curtain bells rings, she finds the miniature photo. The violinist's likeness reduced to the size of a thumbnail. Sylvia is outraged. Tonight, Inez Roseman should be rewarded with a large, beautiful photograph.

"Here we are," Hy Myerson says as he ushers his wife to her seat in the box.

Once he sits down, Hy asks Sylvia if he can borrow her opera glasses. "I think I see Jake Roseman over there in the first box. You know, the soloist's husband. I admire the man's work."

Sylvia decides to play dumb. "What does he do?"

"You don't know Roseman? Yep, there he is. Looks like he's got his kids with him. And his father. His father used to play in the symphony. He was the concertmaster, back in the days when it was a second-rate symphony. He's just another old goat now. But Jake, he's a big attorney in town, been leading protests on behalf of the Negro for quite some time. Quite the media ham. But the man does some very impressive work."

"Impressive," Mrs. Myerson mimics.

"What's the matter with you, Toby?"

Sylvia, hoping to steer clear of the marital nastiness, peers over toward the first box. She can't wait to get her glasses on the family.

Toby, on the far side of Hy, sits up tall to get Sylvia's attention. "Have you ever noticed the way men go in for heroes? It doesn't matter what their business is. They don't discriminate. Baseball players. Gangsters. Business tycoons. Union leaders. Politicians. Movie stars. Evangelists. Boxers."

"What are you talking about, Toby?"

"Leave it to Hyman. Now he goes in for a man who champions Negroes. When have you ever cared about Negroes? When's the last time you sold a piano to a Negro? You ever seen him sell a piano to a Negro, Sylvia?"

"A man's got the money, I'll sell him anything."

"But will you give a Negro credit?"

"What credit? I can't give away the store."

"See. You'll give a white man credit."

Hy shrugs, then leans toward Sylvia. "You want to know the secret to married life?" Hy points to his right ear. "In one ear and out the other."

The musicians begin to amble onstage. Sylvia loves that some of them meander to their seats without any sense of urgency. Tonight, Inez doesn't come on with the others. A happy-go-lucky young man, cracking a joke with his stand mate, sits in Inez's chair. Clearly, they've granted the soloist leave from the opening piece, a Haydn symphony. A smatter of applause greets the concertmaster as he walks onstage. Then the suave conductor, João Bonfa, appears. The man's definitely a crowd-pleaser—during rhapsodic passages, he employs the sweeping flourishes of a matador, and the critics have begun to suggest that he's a charlatan. Sylvia, though, doesn't mind a little theater, a bit of illusion.

Now the strings respond to the downbeat with a single, lush chord, a broad shelf on which a young woman could rest her chin and look at the world. Sylvia has no intention of responding to the courtly elegance of Haydn's Symphony no. 92. She's saving herself for Inez Roseman and the Goldmark. With her opera glasses, Sylvia scans the audience in the boxes and on the main floor. It's astonishing how many of the patrons look like aged gargoyles in their seats. A thirty-year-old woman begins to feel young.

Sylvia turns her glasses on Jake Roseman. He's a better-looking man than he appears in the newspapers—downright handsome, in fact, in his dark suit and crisp white shirt. Is he as anxious as Sylvia for his wife's appearance? It hardly appears so. The children seem blissfully indifferent. The cherubic boy is playing counting games on his fingers, and the pubescent daughter, who doesn't look to have either her mother's beauty or her intensity, appears to be reading from a barely concealed book in her lap. The grandfather, decked out in a faded tuxedo, sits dour-faced with his fists clenched. Sylvia puts down her glasses and listens to the measured swell of the string section.

TONIGHT, before he went out to conduct the Haydn, Maestro Bonfa dipped his head into Inez's dressing room and gave her a beguiling smile. Had there been something to it? A ladies' man, Bonfa has always maintained a formal demeanor around her. Courtly. Inez had been momentarily giddy last fall after Bonfa agreed to let her play the Goldmark this season. It set her mind off in a strange direction—a brief fantasy where she tried to imagine what it would be like to undress for Maestro Bonfa. To fall into his arms. None of it amounted to more than a curious game a middle-aged woman plays when she tries to remind herself that she's a woman.

She guessed that Bonfa was no more accomplished as a lover than as a conductor. The man had essentially lost control of the symphony. He spent most of the rehearsal time on the common repertory, barely leaving time to run through pieces that the orchestra was less familiar with. He made small, passionate speeches in hopes of compensating for what he couldn't accomplish with his baton. The last time they rehearsed the *Eroica*, Bonfa gave a history lesson, noting that Beethoven had originally dedicated the symphony to Napoléon, the liberator of the common man. "But once Napoléon became emperor," Bonfa said, shaking his head mournfully, "Beethoven tore up his dedication and retitled it the 'Sinfonia eroica.' So this music . . . this music should be played with a sense of worldly grief, you understand? Not personal grief, but worldly grief."

"I'd be all set," her stand partner, Paul Scaffidi, whispered to Inez, "if I could only find the worldly grief button on my fiddle."

Now, standing with her violin in the wings, Inez watches João Bonfa come offstage after the Haydn. He smiles warmly to her. A few beads of sweat are shining on his forehead. He adjusts his cummerbund, pats his forehead with a handkerchief.

"Are you all right, dear?" he asks and pushes back his thick black hair.

"I'm fine."

"You'll play it wonderfully. Just like in rehearsal." Bonfa comes over to her and surprises her with a kiss, not on the cheek, but on an open length of her neck. She notices the baton in his left hand, just as his right hand sweeps briskly down her left side and rests on her waist. Her mouth opens.

Inez focuses on the task ahead of her. She's known the Goldmark since she studied it as a girl. Karl Goldmark, a Jewish violin prodigy with twenty brothers and sisters, who escaped the poverty of his Hungarian village to study at the Vienna Conservatory. She takes a deep breath and senses a live current running down the center of her. She has no choice now but to go on.

WHEN Inez Roseman appears onstage, poised as a sliver of moon, in the same aubergine linen sleeveless dress that she'd worn in her living room,

Sylvia lets out an involuntary gasp, an audible response to emotions that she doesn't understand.

Hy Myerson pats her arm. "You doing okay over there? He's a handsome devil, isn't he?"

João Bonfa is in the midst of a gallant bow to Inez. "Yes," she says. "He's really something."

"Between you and me, I don't think he's the marrying kind," Hy says. "Now, let's see what Inez Roseman can do with the Allegro Moderato."

"Hush," Toby whispers. "Quit showing off that you've read the program."

"What are you talking about? I know the entire repertoire like it's my mother."

"Show me a gonif."

"This is a romantic classic. I don't know about you, but I'm ready for a little romance." Hy winks at his wife, who, despite inhaling dismissively, cannot fully resist her husband's charm.

Sylvia tries to relax as the orchestra lays down a dour, if stately, theme. A minor march that doesn't seem the slightest bit romantic. Inez stands still as a soldier. Is she counting measures until she comes in? Does she even have to count? Of course not. But Sylvia finds herself counting. At twenty bars, Inez lifts her violin—much sooner than Sylvia expects—and, in a few measures, she enters, her tone as clear as a human voice. Clearer.

Hy inhales like a man intoxicated in a rose garden. "Glorious," he whispers. Toby takes her husband's hand.

Sylvia has trouble understanding how a sound can be simultaneously intimate and forceful, bright-edged and warm. What Sylvia also finds wondrous is matching the exquisitely fluid action of Inez's bow arm with the sound. There is no separation. The sound comes as instantaneously as you witness it being made, seeming to defy some law of nature. Inez's bow arm is a wonder in itself. Sylvia is amazed by how slowly Inez can draw the bow across her violin and still achieve force, how the shift from up bow to down is not a shift at all but as even and immaculate a gesture as a single breath. The bowing strikes her as being more vertical a motion, certainly across the high strings, than horizontal, the bow deftly traveling north and south across the strings, across the body. Sylvia wonders how it would feel to be touched by a hand that has so much effect. Later, Sylvia realizes that she's held her breath, like a girl riding through a tunnel, during much of Inez's stunning cadenza.

AFTER the first movement, Inez takes in the open space of the great hall. She is coated with the weight of her own history. A habit of abstraction. A habit of disassociation. Her girlhood was spent standing on a spot practicing, the audience only in her imagination. Tonight the audience is palpable. Twenty-five hundred souls. Her family is sitting out there. This is not her girlhood room. The audience is not a wall hung with photographs. Rather than holding on to the music, or having it circulate within the closed room of her imagining, Inez would like to offer the audience what is inside her.

BETWEEN movements, all the coughers awake from their virtual slumber.

"Give them all a box of Smith Brothers," says Hy Myerson.

Just as the orchestra slips into the languorous Andante, Sylvia feels a hand drop onto her thigh. She gives a start and resists the urge to swat Hy. Toby's gaze is fixed straight ahead on Inez. Poor Toby. Sylvia lifts her opera glasses and aims them at Inez, reminding herself to breathe.

A PERFORMANCE coated with a veneer of impenetrable poise, a performance begun stoically, assumes a lush and startling intimacy in the Andante. Inez opens herself to the music's warmth, especially as she climbs to the high register of the G string. The lyric line is meant to be tentative rather than overpowering. Tentative as Sylvia the reporter's hand on her cheek. And yet what begins tentatively can end up making a lasting impression. Inez is now asking something of the audience, and letting them see her uncertainty. Life may be worth living; it may not.

Inez opens her eyes to the audience. A thin charcoal line appears across her open eyes. A horizon along which a woman could walk.

Where might it take her? She might stay alive. She might not. The fact that beauty exists in the world doesn't necessarily mean that life is worth living. Can a woman—this woman with the violin in her arms—make a rational choice to end her life? Or must she have the dogs of madness barking at her heels? She wants her most important choice to be made with controlled reason, with an unswerving command akin to this crisply articulated passage of triplets.

She glances at Maestro Bonfa, who's flipping backward in his score. The man has lost his place. She might guess that he'd given himself over to "worldly grief" if his eyes were not so stewed in fear. Thankfully, the orchestra is following her. She nods to the poor man. She will lead him in.

AS the movement weaves to a close, Sylvia Bran, an enraptured watcher, leans toward the violinist in the aubergine dress. Beside her, Hy Myerson, whose hand she'd managed to shake off her thigh, wheezes a soft bentwood curl of a snore.

as if he means it

Rising off the floor, Christine leers at him naughtily. "You're a virtuoso in your own right, Jake."

"Thank you."

Jake had watched Christine drink a half bottle of wine with lunch, but it hadn't occurred to him until after they'd finished making love that she might be a bit pickled.

"Inez must have been pleased with her performance. I thought she was magnificent, but what do I know?"

"I think she was pleased, as pleased as she allows herself to be."

"Were you proud of her?"

"Of course."

"And the kids?"

"Sure."

"Your family is beautiful, Jake. I was watching your children through my glasses—so sweet. No wonder you never mention them. Who'd want to bring up a perfect family in a place like this. You know what Derek said about Inez? He said, 'She plays it as if she means it.' I thought of that while we were screwing."

"Funny time to think of that."

"I'll tell you why. The words came into my head—*he fucks as if he means it.*"

"I do mean it."

"Yes, I know you do," Christine purrs. "Do you think it's wrong for a lady to use a word like *fuck?*"

Jake boosts himself off the floor and pulls up his undershorts. "Do I think it's wrong for a lady . . . here's what I think, Christine. I think it's perfectly all right for a lady who's just been fucking another lady's husband to use the word *fuck.*"

Christine stretches out on a wicker daybed and Jake lies down with his head at the opposite end. Christine grabs hold of Jake's right foot and bends the baby toe back until it hurts.

"Ouch."

"That's what you deserve, *fucker.*"

As pleasant as it might have been to make love on the daybed, Christine, not about to spoil tradition, made a place for them on a pair of straw mats on the floor of the second-floor sunroom.

"This is my meditation room," she'd said when she led Jake into the room.

"Are you sure you want to defile it like this?" Jake had said.

"I thought this would be a way of blessing it."

Jake was angry when he arrived. He'd brought a paltry lunch: two liverwurst sandwiches on rye and a tub of German potato salad. He thought Christine would sneer at the lunch and refuse to eat it. But she was gracious and said, "We have a bottle of Gewürztraminer in the fridge. That will be perfect with our sandwiches."

He'd wanted to pick a fight with Christine. Although the purity of their enterprise depends, in part, on his thinking of her rarely between visits, she's been on his mind a lot recently. The fact is, he hasn't been himself since the strange business with Inez at Nepenthe. Everything seems a little off center now. He'd promised to quit seeing other women, but he has no intention of stopping his visits to Christine. Add lying and betrayal to his crimes. Clearly, he will pay in full when the party's over.

In any case, something about his arrangement with Christine is bothering him. Was she too controlling? Has it all become a frivolous game for her? Can he possibly be falling in love with her, after all these years? He wishes he could come to see her more often, not just for the recreation they enjoy, but to talk with her, to tell her what's on his mind.

Jake looks across at her now; she's wrapped in a short, peach-colored kimono, bursting with blossoms. He tucks one of her small feet in his hands and begins massaging it.

"Don't hurt me."

"I'm not going to hurt you, Christine."

"Oh," she says, after he cracks a tiny bone in her middle toe, "that feels good."

Years ago, he gave Inez full body massages. He'd have his beautiful young wife lie naked on the bed with a towel draped over her rump. Sometimes, after the massage, they made love, an activity that's now become rare.

Jake lets go of his lover's foot, and Christine, who seems to have an uncanny sense of when Jake's attention has wandered, and to what location, says, "You haven't told me about your trip to Carmel with Inez."

"Do you think you should be privy to everything that goes on with my marriage?" he asks, trying to affect a light tone.

"Not at all."

"You don't tell me anything about Derek."

"You never ask. Anyway, I was just making conversation." Christine reaches forward and takes one of Jake's calves in her hands, then begins stroking it. "I have to admit, Inez has been on my mind since the concert. Your wife is a beautiful woman, Jake, and very talented."

"It's not as if that was the first time you'd seen her."

"No, but this time she was standing out front."

"Are you jealous of Inez?"

"I've never been jealous of any man's wife."

Jake pulls his leg free and stands. "Do you mind if I have a cigarette in your meditation room?"

"Not at all. I love to watch you smoke, Jake."

Jake walks over to the small bamboo stool where most of his clothes sit and pulls a pack of Viceroys—a switch from his usual brand—out of his shirt pocket. He picks up a metal ashtray, a Chinatown statue of a Buddha with a deep cleft in the belly meant for cigarette ash. Jake lights his cigarette and settles back on the wicker daybed.

"My trip with Inez was odd, if you want to know."

"Odd?"

Jake blows a long stream of smoke out of his nostrils. Christine raises her eyebrows, eager for details.

"We were having a nice enough time. Shopping in Carmel. Walking on the beach. On the last night we drove down to Nepenthe in Big Sur."

"I adore that restaurant, Jake. You're such a romantic."

Jake turns his face aside, finding it difficult to look directly at Christine. "So we had a couple of cocktails, even danced for a while out on the terrace . . ."

"Nice . . ."

Jake looks at the long ash at the end of his cigarette. "And then she asked me for a divorce."

"Oh, Jake," Christine says. She rises onto her knees and takes Jake's hands. "Did she mean it?"

"I think she meant it." Jake flicks the hanging ash into the Buddha-belly ashtray. "It frightened me."

"Of course. You love her, Jake."

"At first I was angry. I'd probably had a little too much to drink. I wanted to know how long she'd been thinking about it. Turns out it had been on her mind a long time."

"A long time? Really?"

"I was appalled."

"Why?"

"She kept it secret for so long."

"Like you've never kept anything from her," Christine says, as her kimono falls open.

"That's not the point."

"Of course not."

Jake's eyes fix on the nipple and brownish aureole of Christine's left breast.

"So did you talk her out of it?"

"No, I didn't talk her out of it."

Christine wraps herself tighter in her kimono. "Then she's filing papers?"

"Not right now."

"So you talked her out of it."

"What's your point, Christine?" Jake glares at her, but his mistress does not reply.

"We ended up talking about God." Jake laughs.

"God and divorce. That's original, at least for those not in the Catholic set." Christine rises off the daybed and pads barefoot across the room to a rattan table where the sleek, green bottle of Gewürztraminer stands beside a bowl of dried rose petals and two wineglasses. Christine pours what's left of the wine into each of the glasses, then walks back to the daybed and hands Jake a glass. "Was the talk of religion your ploy?"

"I suppose."

"Might as well bring moral indignation to the party." Christine returns to her end of the daybed, folding her legs under her, careful not to spill any wine. "So can the marriage be saved?"

"What's it to you?" he says, with a lash of venom that even surprises him.

"Sorry, mister. The truth is it means a lot to me that you stay married."

Jake pours down his wine in a gulp and hands Christine his empty glass before pushing himself up from the daybed. He walks over to his clothes and begins dressing.

Christine, holding a wineglass in each hand, places the one she's been sipping from down on the floor and shifts the empty glass from her left hand to her right. "You're really close to being an idiot, Jake." Christine hurls the empty glass against the wall next to Jake and delights at the quick explosion of glass.

Surprised, Jake shouts, "What are you doing?"

"That was satisfying."

Jake buckles his belt in a hurry. "You're crazy, Christine."

"Yes, and you, you have a way of only seeing half of what's in front of you. I know you love your wife. You may be too much of a fool to realize it. And you have children, in case you haven't noticed, who might rather have a father around than not." Christine takes a leisurely sip of her wine. "But that's all your business, Jake. Here's my business: as a divorced man, you'd be useless to me. I'm being purely selfish, but I want no part of you in that condition. If there's ever been a man who needs a wife, it's you, Jake. I won't have you coming over here in rumpled clothes, stinking from need and the pee stains on your underwear."

"Pee stains on my underwear?" Jake shakes his head for a moment and then, not at all kindly, flips Christine the bird.

"Yes, well." Christine shrugs. "Fortunately, you look like a man who aims to stay married for a long time."

depraved

SYLVIA spent the better part of a week deciding how to approach Inez Roseman again. Finally, when she works up the nerve to call and ask the violinist to lunch, the phone conversation feels like an audition.

"Lunch?" Inez says.

"Yes, well, nothing fancy. I was thinking either at my apartment or perhaps at a little Chinese restaurant in the Avenues. How do you feel about Chinese?"

"I thought we agreed that you were no longer doing the story."

"We did agree. The fact is I really enjoy your company and hope we can meet again, without a pretense."

"Without a pretense. Don't we always need a pretense?"

Sylvia laughs at the little joke. Isn't it a joke?

Inez is silent; she sounds like she's ready to hang up.

"By the way, the Goldmark was wonderful."

"That's very kind of you. I'm glad that you could be there."

Has Inez forgotten that they'd spoken before the concert, that Sylvia had left her open hand like a glowing leaf on the violinist's cheek? "I hoped the feeling was mutual," says Sylvia.

"What feeling?"

"I thought that maybe you would appreciate a friendship."

"A friendship?"

"Yes, I know it's an absurd idea," she says, stalling. Will Inez Roseman hang up on her?

"Oh, I don't know that it's absurd. It's just that I don't . . ."

"I know," Sylvia says, cutting Inez off. She doesn't want to hear the violinist's excuses and launches recklessly into a final foray. "Friendships are so passé. Who has time for friends these day? And why would somebody as accomplished as you are want to be friends with me?"

"I didn't say—"

"Forgive me," Sylvia says, wondering if she's overplayed her hand. "I tend to spit things out, especially when I'm nervous. You see, I don't always think the most of myself, but, as my analyst says, who does?"

Sylvia, pleased by how nimbly she's spun her line and invented an analyst, is delighted by Inez Roseman's response: "How about trying a Japanese restaurant? I know a little place called Miyamo that's been around since the early fifties. It's up the street from the new Japantown complex on Geary."

SYLVIA passes through an open doorway and then through the split blue curtain of the small storefront restaurant. She assumes she'll arrive first. In fact, she has the sneaking feeling that she might be the only one who comes. An old woman bows to her and leads her in past a black lacquered counter to a small row of tables with worn pillowed seats. Inez, to her surprise, is already seated at one of the tables, sipping tea.

"Am I late?"

"No, I'm early," Inez says, gesturing for Sylvia to sit.

"I'm so glad you came," says Sylvia, sliding into her chair.

"Did you expect I wouldn't?"

"I know how busy you are."

"Not as busy as you think. You must be the busy one. I'm surprised the newspaper lets you get away for lunch. Are you working on a story?"

Sylvia forces herself to look Inez in the eye. "I have the day off."

"How nice that you chose to spend a bit of it with me."

Is Inez patronizing her? Sylvia smiles at the violinist and then takes a quick look around the restaurant. The only other diners—two Japanese men in suits—seem more interested in their tall glasses of beer than in their food. The room is bare of ornament except for a bamboo screen and a large, airbrushed photo of a plate of sukiyaki.

"I know it doesn't look like much," says Inez, "but the food is good. I haven't been here for quite a while. I used to meet my father here sometimes after morning rehearsals. He had a shop nearby. After he died, I came a couple of times by myself. I don't know why I thought of coming today. You said Chinese—power of suggestion." Inez cranes her neck around. "It's kind of dingy, isn't it?"

"No, it's cozy."

"I don't know about that."

Sylvia is at a loss for what to say. She picks up a menu but can't concentrate on it. The two Japanese men are speaking to each other in bright bursts of language. Sylvia looks across at Inez's hands—how closely clipped the violinist's nails are. She would like to reach over and take hold of one of Inez's hands.

Inez looks down at her hands. "They're terribly chapped. I can't get enough lotion on them."

"Don't be silly. Your hands are beautiful, Inez."

Inez holds up one hand and then the other. "I'm sorry, but these are not beautiful."

Sylvia wonders what it would be like to have the violinist touch her, to have those fingers slowly run down her cheeks. Clearly, Inez knows everything that Sylvia's thinking.

Inez picks up her menu. "Do you know what you're going to have?"

"I can't decide."

"Me neither."

Her only hope, Sylvia realizes, is to become the reporter again. "I'm curious—what kind of shop did your father have?"

"Oh, he had a frame shop, and, because of the neighborhood, he always had a Japanese assistant. I remember one of them very well. George Kogowa."

Sylvia pushes herself back from the table and assumes the posture of a professional listener.

"My father really liked George. They hardly ever spoke, but when their work was done, they played chess together or carved animals from blocks of alder. During the war, when they put the Japanese in the camps, my father got very angry. He said they were the most loyal people he'd ever known. He wanted to give George the chess set they'd carved together, but George and his family were gone before he had a chance. I never saw my father so angry or so sad." Inez bites her lip. "You know, I can go for weeks without thinking about him, but then suddenly—" She smiles at Sylvia. "My father came to love Japanese food, which is saying a lot for an old Swede. They tend to be set in their ways—they like their fish the way they've had it all their lives."

ONCE they've ordered, the old woman brings steaming bowls of miso. It seems a small miracle to be sitting with Inez Roseman, each of them lifting lacquered bowls of steam and cloudy broth to their faces. Sylvia puts her soup down and watches Inez, who is still tipping hers. The violin bruise under her chin is more lovely than ever.

"I want to tell you again how wonderful your performance was. You played beautifully."

"Thank you."

"I can't imagine how powerful a feeling it must be, standing up there in front of a huge audience." Sylvia shakes her head. "And playing with such mastery."

"You don't need to flatter me, Sylvia."

"That wasn't my intention."

"Then what *is* your intention?"

"I don't know that I have one."

The violinist lifts her bowl of miso again. "That can't be true. I've decided that everybody is up to something. Even my seven-year-old. Or should I say, especially my seven-year-old."

"And what's he up to?"

"Oh, I don't know. This may sound strange, but I think that practically everything he does these days is focused on making his mother happy."

"That's nice."

"He knows where his bread's buttered." Inez smiles cryptically. "But you, you're a mystery, Sylvia. I'd like to know what you're planning. You're a good reporter; you have a way of drawing people out. But I'm not going to talk anymore. I'm just going to listen to you."

When the hunch-shouldered waitress approaches with their orders, Inez asks for a carafe of sake. "We might as well celebrate your day off."

SYLVIA nearly rises with pleasure off her pillowed seat at the sight of the *Deluxe* sashimi, a bounty of raw fish: yellowtail, snapper, salmon, mackerel, even octopus, along with a swell of pickled ginger shavings.

Sashimi was her mother's favorite food, and when she felt flush they haunted Sacramento's one Japanese restaurant. But Sylvia has never had such an abundant plate in front of her. She's a bit embarrassed to realize that a luxury so modest can make her swoon. But it isn't the sashimi alone that's responsible for that.

A moment later, the old woman returns with the sake. Inez is uncommonly graceful, it seems to Sylvia, filling both their cups while holding a piece of tempura aloft. She looks deft enough to pick a fly out of the air with her chopsticks. And yet Inez hardly eats a thing. She holds the tempura between her chopsticks, gesturing with it, but barely eats.

"You're not talking, Sylvia. You're supposed to talk. By the way, you mentioned something on the phone about your . . . analyst."

Sylvia lifts a slice of yellowtail with her chopsticks. "Yes."

"I've always been curious about how that works. Do you just talk about yourself for hours?"

"Not all at once." Sylvia drops the tender slice of yellowtail onto her tongue without dipping it in the tamari sauce.

Inez sips her sake. "I don't know if I could talk and talk to a man who hadn't told me a thing about himself."

"You'd be surprised how easy it becomes," says Sylvia.

"So you like your analyst?"

Sylvia lifts a shaving of ginger to her tongue. "Yes, I like him very much."

"I hope you don't mind my being so forward, Sylvia."

"Not at all."

Inez deftly breaks a piece of tempura in half but doesn't lift it from her plate. "How long have you been seeing this man?"

"Since I moved to the city; a little more than a year now."

"Will you see him forever?"

Sylvia forces a laugh. She swills her sake and holds out her little cup for a refill. "I don't know. It's not like in the movies. I don't lie down on a couch. He told me that most people he sees come in to confirm the fact that they're perfectly normal and don't need him at all."

"Is that why you go?"

Sylvia lifts a slice of salmon and swishes it through the tamari sauce. She's surprised by this line of questioning. If it's a game they're playing, it's not to be taken lightly. That's just as well. She's delighted by how supple her imagination is. She drops the salmon on her tongue. "I'm not sure. Maybe I'm trying to confirm that I'm a better person than I previously imagined. My analyst doesn't treat me like I'm insane or anything."

"That's good. How did you find him?"

Sylvia separates a shaving of ginger with her chopsticks. "An advertisement in the newspaper."

"They advertise. I didn't know they advertised."

Sylvia lets herself enjoy the fresh bite of the ginger. "It was for a study he was doing. *Divorced women wanted at Langley Porter; small stipend offered.*"

"So he pays you."

"He did, until the study was over. To tell you the truth, I . . . I kind of liked the idea of being studied."

"It sounds awful."

"I don't know; he told me that I was different from most of the women in his study."

"How?"

"Stranger."

"He didn't say that."

"Not in so many words. *Unconventional* would be more like it. Now that the study's completed, and the fee arrangement's been reversed, I do my best to study him."

Inez smiles broadly. "You're very funny, Sylvia."

"Not so funny." Sylvia smiles at Inez. Are they flirting? She wants to put her left hand down on the table and see if Inez will take it. Instead, she reaches for a slice of snapper.

"Have you always been so amusing, Sylvia?" Inez Roseman's eyes seem to be shining.

"Have you always been so easily amused?"

Inez grins at her. "If you asked Jake, he'd tell you that I'm rarely amused."

Sylvia thinks suddenly of Colleen Hass, the first friend she made in the city. They worked together in the classifieds department at the *Chronicle.* Colleen told her that she had pretty eyes and a great sense of humor. "You could be a comedian," Colleen said, "because you're off-beat like those guys—you know who I mean—Shelley Berman and Mort Sahl. They'll say anything that comes into their head, just like you."

She and Colleen often walked home from work together. Colleen lived at a residence club, the Monte Vista on Pine Street, and a few nights a week she'd sneak Sylvia into the dining room for free suppers. At first, it seemed an ideal relationship, like having a big sister to look after her. A half-dozen years her senior, Colleen was tall and chatty and drank copious amounts of Regal vodka.

Sylvia lifts the plate of sashimi toward Inez. She would like to see Inez take a slice of salmon or mackerel and place it on her tongue, but Inez demurs. Her plate is still filled with tempura.

"What do you talk about with him?" says Inez.

"Who?"

"Your analyst."

"I talk a lot about my mother."

"Tell me about your mother."

"You don't want to hear about her."

"Sounds like you don't want to talk about her, at least not with me."

"My mother was an interesting woman."

"She's no longer with us?"

This strikes Sylvia as a very strange idiom, since it seems that her mother is always *with her.* Certainly as much now as she ever was. "No, she isn't with us any longer." It's a good thing to say out loud from time to time.

"When did she die?"

"A couple of years ago."

"I'm sorry," Inez says. "A long illness?"

"You could say that. Still, her death was sudden—an absolute shock." Sylvia pauses, wondering if she should say any more. She opens her mouth again, undecided. Then she says it. "My mother took her own life." She watches, not without pleasure, as Inez's blond eyebrows point upward, revealing that she's taken aback by the disclosure.

"Oh, I'm so sorry. That must have been hard."

Sylvia nods.

"And you think of suicide as an illness?" Inez asks, not shying from the subject.

"Maybe not every one, but I believe my mother was touched."

"Touched?"

"It's a euphemism for mentally ill."

"Yes, I know."

Sylvia is surprised how calmly she can talk about her mother. It feels good to take a clinical approach.

"Would you rather not talk about her?"

"It's all right; I've made my peace, more or less." The violinist appears to have an appetite for the morbid. How much to feed her? Should she describe the death scene, what it was like to come upon? Just how much titillation of this sort does Inez Roseman go in for?

"I'm always fascinated by people's mothers, perhaps because I never knew my own."

"That's right, you said your mother died . . ."

"Yes, at my birth." Inez deflects the focus back to Sylvia. "How exactly was your mother interesting?"

The intensity Inez has brought to bear on the conversation is breathtaking. And how strange that Sylvia's mother has become the centerpiece. "My mother spent a lot of time reading vocabulary books. I think she believed a superior vocabulary would give her an advantage over others."

"Did it work?"

"Of course not. But we had some fun."

"You too?"

"Yes, words were our sport. So you better watch out, I have a sizzling vocabulary. I try to keep it under wraps."

"Why?"

"I think it's a bit depraved. That was my mother's word for us. *Depraved.* She liked to think of us as sisters. The two depraved ones. We used to make lists of words and hang them on the walls."

"It doesn't sound depraved to me," says Inez, nibbling on a small piece of tempura. "I wouldn't call it *depraved.* It just sounds like you and your mother were close."

Sylvia lifts a cluster of octopus from her tray and, as she chews on a bland, rubbery tentacle, wonders how the violinist would define the term.

WITH Colleen, she felt as if she were depraved. After an evening meal at the residence club, sometimes they'd head down the hills through a couple of seedy blocks in the Tenderloin, past Oreste's on Jones Street—a fabled restaurant that had been there before the neighborhood soured— and get a whiff of a better meal than the one they'd just eaten. "I'm going to take you in there some time, Sylvia," Colleen would say, "and buy you an order of baked green lasagna. It's their specialty." At Geary, as the traffic and excitement picked up, they'd stroll along the theater belt to gawk at the crowds stepping out of cabs in front of the Alcazar, the Geary, the Curran. Colleen liked going into art galleries and pretending that she knew things about art, as they flipped through the bins of signed lithographs by Dalí and Chagall. Colleen was especially fond of the Keanes in one gallery, paintings of large-eyed waifs that the tourists also loved.

The first time she and Colleen got into "trouble," as she used to think of it, Colleen had been going on about one of the Keanes. The painting of a dark-haired girl, with sad, moony eyes, was featured in the gallery window. Colleen made a few comments about the artist's palette and then said, "You know who she reminds me of? You!"

"What are you talking about?" Sylvia asked. "Am I that pitiful looking?"

"No, you're that beautiful."

The comment surprised her. She'd never thought of herself that way. Beauty had passed her by, and she'd accepted it. Was it a cruel joke— Colleen calling her beautiful?

They walked up the hills back toward the residence club. On Pine, Sylvia would veer west toward her apartment. But Colleen wanted Sylvia to come up to her room in the Monte Vista; she had something to show her. Once they were in the tiny suite, Colleen poured herself a large tumbler of Regal vodka and diluted it with a few dribbles of tap water from the bathroom sink. Sylvia declined an offer of the same. It was the nastiest drink she could imagine. Colleen took a catalog of Keane paintings from the pine bookshelf and lay down with it on her bed, resting her tumbler of vodka on the bedside table. "Come here," she said. "Look at these with me."

Perhaps the novelty got the better of her, but Sylvia lay down on the twin bed beside Colleen and dutifully flipped through the paintings of gypsy waifs. A curious calm came over Sylvia as Colleen took off her glasses and smiled. There was a single lamp in the room on the bedside table. Colleen reached over and turned it off. Without light, Sylvia was suddenly conscious of the noise from the street. Sylvia heard the traffic heading out Pine Street, the cars braking as they inched down the steep hill on Taylor, the *ta-ling-a-ling* of cable-car bells on California Street, the animated conversation of a couple walking down the street. At least the world would be present during whatever was going to happen to her. This was a comfort. Even in the dark, she could see the dull rose of Colleen's puckered lips move toward her brow—a soft kiss landed there, then another on her eyelid.

In her limited experience with men, Sylvia was usually overcome with dread in the moment before sex. She wasn't so afflicted with Colleen. She seemed to know how to respond. After both lids of her eyes were kissed, she opened her mouth. As Colleen reached under her blouse, tracing with a warm hand the mild curves of her side, Sylvia considered the possibility that she might be beautiful.

NOW, in the corner restaurant, Inez Roseman is the one staring, as large-eyed as the subject of a Keane painting. Inez must think she's mad, the depraved girl with the hidden vocabulary. Sylvia finds herself admiring the small mole on Inez's right cheek; she is afraid to look into her eyes. She studies Inez's eyebrows, faint blond ribbons that point upward as she smiles.

Inez reaches for a strip of salmon from her plate. "I'd be happy to be your friend, Sylvia."

Is Inez playing with her?

"Would you care for some tempura?" Inez asks.

"Yes; it looks good." Sylvia plucks what appears to be a piece of breaded broccoli from Inez's plate. She nibbles it slowly. She is trying to see how long she can go without looking at Inez. She lifts her sake cup—a lovely puce-colored ceramic dimple with a Japanese character brushed on its side—and takes a long sip from it.

the other half

As she drives Sylvia home in the yellow Studebaker, Inez peppers her passenger with questions about her work as a reporter. "What kind of stories do you like doing best? Do you ever find out things you'd prefer not to know? How much of your time is spent at a desk as compared with out in the field?" Sylvia offers a few halfhearted responses that lead Inez to a curious thought—what if the reporter is not who she appears to be? Surprisingly, Inez finds the prospect of fraud delicious, even if she happens to be its victim.

Inez glances across at Sylvia and pitches another question to test her theory: "Have you ever had to report on a death scene?"

Sylvia nods her head slowly and then looks directly into Inez's eye. "Unfortunately, I have. A couple of times. The worst was a murder-suicide out in the Sunset District." Sylvia turns to look out the side window. "It was a neat little stucco house with wedding-cake steps. The thing that got me was that there was a roast in the oven."

Inez is taken aback. So much for her silly idea.

"The bodies were in the bedroom. The detective didn't want me to see. I didn't really want to see, but I thought I should. I was filling in for someone on the police beat, but I knew that the only way to keep my stomach was to take a clinical approach, to study it."

Inez grabs the steering wheel tightly as she maneuvers around a double-parked car on Divisidero. "You're brave, Sylvia."

"I don't know about that. The place was enough of a mess without me adding to it. The poor woman was sprawled across a yellow quilt, dressed in a pair of dungarees and a factory work shirt. She had a big, fluffy slippers on her feet and a gunshot through her neck." Sylvia folds her hands in her lap.

"You don't have to tell me anymore about it, Sylvia."

"Sorry. I didn't mean to make you squeamish. You know, they found some guy to fill in right away. I don't think they like the idea of women covering murders."

"Maybe it's something women shouldn't do," Inez says. Stopped at the top of Fillmore, where some droll soul has altered the yellow street sign that once said HILL, to CLIFF, Inez smiles at Sylvia and asks, "What's your department now?"

Sylvia inhales slowly. "The society page."

"You're kidding."

"I'm afraid not. I gather items that somebody else compiles. I pitched the Variety editor the story about you and Jake and he said, 'See what you get.' You see what I got."

"That explains why I've never seen your byline."

Inez eases the Studebaker across the intersection, considering, as she often does when heading down steep hills, what it would be like to have her brakes go out, or to give the car an extra surge of gas.

Now she'd sail through the intersections of Broadway, Vallejo, Greenwich, down to the flat streets in the hollow—Union and Chestnut—colliding with what? A delivery truck? A fire hydrant? An unfortunate knot of pedestrians? She could always steer the car wide, she reasons, if pedestrians came into her path. But not now, not with the society reporter along for the ride. Jake never likes to drive with her; he says that she's a herky-jerky driver. Once, when she was driving a long stretch on a trip to Los Angeles, Jake hollered at her—"Inez, you can't play the gas pedal like it's the pedal on a bass drum." Jake had hurt her feelings, but she knew he was right—she is a herky-jerky driver. Now she shifts down to second and taps the brakes.

As they cross Union Street, Sylvia smiles at her. "You know, I live back up the hill on Washington."

"Why didn't you tell me?"

"I'm sorry, I thought I had. Anyway, I wanted to see how you'd take the hills. Tells you a lot about a person."

Inez is shocked by Sylvia's comment. "So what did you find out about me?"

"That you can be both cautious and wild. By the way, would you like to come in and have a glass of wine?"

Inez is surprised by how appealing the idea sounds. She finds much about the reporter, whatever her beat, intriguing. Further, she's surprised by the way she's been feeling with the reporter. In a word, girlish. Something she hasn't felt in ages. It's enough to make her laugh out loud.

"So?" Sylvia asks.

"Oh, I better not."

"There's the cautious response. Come see how the other half lives."

"What other half?"

"Those of us living the unconventional single life."

"All right. Just for a few minutes."

IN the time it's taken Inez to park and get to apartment number seven, her new friend, Sylvia, has changed clothes. The reporter is barefoot now, in dungarees and a man's broadcloth shirt with long tails. Her toenails are painted red. Several sticks of incense are burning. Atop a radiator shelf a trio of African violets, with shiny leaves and small, immaculate blooms, are sprouting out of old coffee cans. Sylvia's furnishings are a blend of splintering wicker and discarded crates. A love seat, covered in a frayed paisley fabric, looks as if it might goose someone with a roving spring. Low-slung brick and plywood bookshelves snake around the bottom of the walls in the main room. Why did it take her so long to realize? How dense is she? Sylvia is a bohemian. A gypsy. A beatnik. Inez becomes suddenly mindful of what's in her purse and then chuckles to herself. Is that something she really needs to worry about? What's to lose? Twenty-odd dollars and a couple of department-store charge cards. Ashamed of her thought, Inez offers her hostess a meek smile.

"Sit wherever you like," Sylvia says.

The invitation comes across as a curious dare. Inez decides against an overstuffed armchair she might have trouble getting out of and chooses a straight-back chair. At which point, Sylvia goes wild with industry. She pulls a wicker basket chair up close to Inez and drags over a wooden crate, painted forest green, to serve as a side table. Then she bustles into the kitchen nook. Inez watches her pour burgundy from a hulking gallon bottle into a quart carafe. As Sylvia bends over to select a few records on the hi-fi, the tails of her striped shirt slide up her back. Inez finds herself staring at the reporter's round bottom.

"You have a nice place, Sylvia," she says. "It has a lot of character."

"You think it's odd, don't you?" Sylvia says, pulling an album out of its sleeve.

"No, no, not at all." Inez takes out her compact and has a quick look at herself—her skin looks flushed but there's not a lot to do about it. She puts away the compact and peeks at her watch—in little more than an hour Joey will be out of school. At seven years old, in the third grade now after skipping the second, he's her little man. Inez visualizes his walk home, crossing Anza with the school patrol, then up the steep Thirty-sixth Avenue hill to the stoplight on Geary Boulevard, where Anna, walking up from Presidio Junior High, will meet him.

Sylvia stands and straightens her shirt. "You must be wondering what you're doing here."

"You asked me to come up, so I came," says Inez, offering a wry smile.

The first record drops and the needle makes contact. Ravel. His string quartet. A lovely choice.

"You like Ravel, Sylvia?"

"Yes, but I don't know anything about him." Sylvia smiles, sheepishly.

"There's not that much to know."

Sylvia bows her head. "I'm nervous having you here, Inez. I debated with myself about what music to put on. Do I dare put on something I know little about for a master like you?"

"Please. Do you think I'm going to test you?" Inez says, her eyes brightening, amused.

Sylvia shrugs. "I'm sorry, I'm nervous. Put yourself in my position— I'm barely a reporter and you're so talented. Not to speak of the fact that you're just about the most beautiful woman in the world."

"You're quite the flatterer, Sylvia."

"That's not true. The fact is, I'm flattered to be in your company." Sylvia walks toward the kitchen nook. "Would you care for a glass of red wine? It's inexpensive, but surprisingly good."

"I'll have a little glass."

Sylvia returns from the kitchen with a couple of large glasses of wine.

"That's enough wine to fell a peasant," Inez says.

"You handled the sake well enough." Sylvia touches the violinist's shoulder as she hands her a glass of wine. "So, tell me about Ravel."

"What can I tell you?" Inez carefully swirls the cheap wine around in the big tumbler and smiles at the thought of Jake doing the same with his pricey cognac. "I adore this quartet. It's the only one Ravel wrote."

"Have you played it?" Sylvia asks, holding her wineglass aloft like a rosy torch as she lowers herself into the wicker chair.

"Yes, of course." Inez takes a sip of the wine. It's not nearly as bad as she feared. "It's as if Ravel has his own genetic timbre, a particular delicacy that really comes through in the quartet. At least I think it does."

"If you say it does, it does. As my mother used to say, don't equivocate. Especially when you're talking about *timbre*." Sylvia stretches the word out as if it's a rare fruit she's tasting. With her lips still puckered around the word, Sylvia winks at Inez.

The violinist, momentarily breathless, draws in a large draught of air. Who'd have guessed that the meek reporter who came to her door had so expansive a personality?

"It's a beautiful word, isn't it? What exactly is it that creates timbre, Inez?"

"Oh, so now you're testing *me*."

Sylvia stretches her legs out in front of her. "I'm only curious. Is it a matter of tonality?"

"Formally, I s'pose timbre depends on the layering of harmonics. But when I mentioned the word I wasn't thinking formally." Inez finds herself looking at the reporter's bare feet, which are surprisingly well cared for, the nails glazed in red.

"Were you suggesting a metaphysical timbre?" Sylvia asks.

"Now you're making fun of me."

"Not at all. I'm just trying to keep up."

Inez takes a swallow of wine.

"Inez," Sylvia says, looking squarely at the violinist, "do you think two people who happen to be fond of each other create a particular timbre?"

"I've never heard the word used in that way."

"But it's not out of the question?"

Inez nods and gulps at her wine.

"Tell me some more about Ravel," says Sylvia.

"What's to tell you?" Inez says, listening to the sweet lilt of the first violin. "The music has a certain childlike quality, don't you think? But at the same time it's fastidious. Much as the man is supposed to have been. They say he collected figurines and mechanical, clockwork toys. Stravinsky called him 'the Swiss watchmaker.' Apparently, he was queer."

Sylvia laughs.

"What?"

"Just how you said that."

What did she say? Sylvia is smiling at her. It's a curious smile. Shy. Flirtatious. It's almost as if the gypsy girl with the pedicure is trying to woo her. Embarrassed, Inez takes a couple more gulps of wine. There is no almost about it. She slurps more of her wine. Without thinking, she's finished her glass, poured it down as if she were drinking juice, and Sylvia's there with the carafe to refill it. It is really nothing more than a large jelly jar. Her strange host has got her drinking wine out of a jelly jar.

Sylvia raises her jar in a toast: "To good cheap wine, to 'the Swiss watchmaker,' and to beautiful Inez."

"Thank you," Inez says and allows Sylvia to clink her glass, which, given its thickness, makes a flat thud sound.

Sylvia eases back into the wicker chair across from her.

Inez wonders whether she's lost her will or purposely suspended it. Why isn't she standing up right now and offering a definitive good-bye? What happens if she returns Sylvia's smile?

"I hope I haven't embarrassed you," Sylvia says.

"Who said anything about being embarrassed?" Inez realizes that she has turned away from Sylvia and is looking at the bare hardwood floor. She lifts her head and forces herself to meet Sylvia's eyes.

Sylvia smiles shyly. "So the fact that I have a crush on you doesn't make you feel odd?"

"I should leave."

"Why?"

"I should."

"Who says you should?"

"I think I should." Her instinct is to look at the floor again, but not to get up and leave.

"Have you ever loved a woman, Inez?"

Inez repeats the question in her head—*Have you ever, have you ever, have you ever?*—until she makes herself dizzy. Who'd have expected so forward a seduction? Who'd have expected a seduction at all?

"Are you angry with me?" Sylvia asks, drawing her lips into a pout.

"Yes, I'm furious with you." Inez says it in jest but feels a shiver of fright.

"Thank you for not leaving."

"I have to go soon."

"I hope not."

They sit silently for a moment, listening to the third movement of the Ravel, the *Très lent*, as it weaves measures of strings and light twigs into a gentle basket. With that, the phonograph needle skitters to the inner edge of the vinyl, lifts stiffly, and returns to the perimeter, waiting while the next LP drops. The overture to Stravinsky's Petroushka. Who'd have believed that composers could be stacked on top of each other like this? Any girl with a cheap hi-fi can construct her own hierarchy of composers, one record after another. Inez thinks she should stand up, prepare to leave, but she has no will for it.

"Would you mind turning over the Ravel?" she says.

"Don't you like the Stravinsky?" Sylvia says, a little hurt.

"No, I love Petroushka."

"I was so excited when you mentioned Stravinsky before. I couldn't wait to see your surprise when the record dropped."

"I guess I'm from the old school; I like to finish one thing before I move on to the next."

"Of course. I'll turn over the Ravel."

Sylvia sits for a quiet moment before getting up to flip the record. There is something defiant in Sylvia's pose. It is as if she is intent on demonstrating her poise. Look at me, she seems to be saying; I dare you to see me as homely. And if this is her dare, she's right; you'd have to subscribe to a very narrow notion of beauty to ignore Sylvia's lovely green eyes, her shrugging cuteness, the way her short hair frames her sweet, determined face. But why should Inez care a wit about the reporter's looks? What does it mean that Sylvia has become more enchanting by the moment?

Sylvia finally bounds toward the hi-fi, which is stacked on a heavy wooden crate. Inez notices the ease with which Sylvia crouches, and, again, the shape of her bottom in the dungarees. Women's bottoms have never been of particular interest to her, but here she is, captivated. Sylvia glances at her over her shoulder and Inez feels herself blush. The Ravel reenters the room as if it were meant to orchestrate the moment.

Inez is amused by the strange seduction. The whole thing feels curiously safe, as if she were watching the proceedings through a department-store window. She's more or less relaxed now. The Ravel helps. She listens to the lyric rise of the theme and wonders what it would be like to be reborn French, swaddled in a blanket of such lush and sensuous emotion, the violins woven through the muscle of the viola, the bones of the cello. How can something so graceful, she wonders, be so penetrating?

Sylvia, her glass of wine tilted against her chin, looks wistfully at Inez. "Have you ever been tempted by a woman?"

"Are you trying to tempt me?"

Sylvia's eyes fall. "I doubt that I can tempt you," she says. "You are so beautiful."

"I really better leave."

"Please, don't."

Inez stands up. She knows that it's time to walk out the door, but the coziness of the absurd apartment has wrapped itself around her. As much as anything, she's pleased to be in somebody else's reality, to have even the briefest vacation from her self-absorption, to feel her shell dissolve, if only momentarily. Whatever happens in this apartment gets to stay here, just like the wicker furniture and the shelf of African violets.

"I'm not sure what you're after, Sylvia."

"I'm not either."

Part of the problem is that she's had too much to drink. "I've got to use your bathroom. May I?"

"By all means."

Inez steps deliberately, as if along a dotted line, to the bathroom, where she sits for a long while on the toilet seat, studying a framed photograph on the wall. It's of a red enamel door with a brass knocker. Once she's peed and considered the paleness of her thighs, she looks again at the photo. Where is the door from? Clearly, it isn't in America. She's never seen a red quite like the red of this door. A Chinese red, perhaps, with a bit more orange in it? What would it be like to walk through that door? What would she enter?

Inez considers her face in the mirror. Her cheeks are no longer flushed, but she looks strange to herself, like a painterly distortion of a woman she once knew. Inez checks her watch—it's just after three. Joey is out of school by now, and up the hill to Geary. Anna has met him and walked him by the Chinese grocery on Thirty-seventh Avenue where he's bought penny candy or, if he had a nickel to spare, a pack of baseball cards. Inez reminds herself that Joey has a house key should Anna be delayed at school. As far as Inez knows, this has never happened. Soon enough both kids will be safe at home eating graham crackers and the lime Jell-O she made this morning in Pyrex cups. A while later, Joey will start on his chocolate-covered banana.

By the time she returns to the living room, Inez has forgotten about the idea of leaving. She refills her jelly jar with the cheap burgundy and sits where Sylvia had sat earlier, in the wicker basket chair. She laughs out loud at the sight of Sylvia, half swallowed in the overstuffed chair.

"There's room here," Sylvia says. "You don't have to sit over there."

Inez shakes her head. "No, I need to keep an eye on you. I'm not sure what you're up to."

"Please, sit here."

"No, I want to look at you." Once Inez realizes that she can have a hand in the seduction, she's no longer frightened. Sylvia closes her eyes. Inez can hear her breathing, or imagines she can hear breathing, across the little room. It is as if the business had begun, as if her hands were already touching Sylvia. But she is still sitting in the basket chair, sipping wine, emptying the jelly jar again.

When Sylvia opens her eyes, she looks like the most innocent girl in the world. Inez wonders if she's capable of taking this woman's heart, of offering her own? Does she have anything left to offer?

"Come over here," Sylvia says again.

"You sure seem to want me beside you."

"Yes."

Inez takes a wide, drunken turn around the coffee table and plops indelicately beside Sylvia. Inez tries to catch her breath. The two of them are silent. The whole world has stopped breathing. The moment exists in a vacuum. Inez flings her head back and feels the wine inside her, which she pictures as hot mercury, swirling to a roving pulse. Sylvia bends toward her and nuzzles the tip of her pointy nose against Inez's neck— the smallest touch, yet the sensation is so acute. Whatever armor has protected her and spared her from feeling anything for so long is gone now. Her mouth is open and hungry for everything.

Sylvia leads Inez by the hand into the bedroom, and she's surprised to see the small bed, a single bed. Inez lies down dutifully, and Sylvia lights a single candle on the dresser and then squeezes close beside her. *Look at us,* Inez thinks, *we're two in a grave.* This is the way her mind has gone soft.

She'd forgotten about the rapture of the mouth. How, when she opens her mouth to Sylvia, her entire body, though still clothed, opens, and the shy kisses quickly give way to a fierce appetite. A forty-year-old woman is not supposed to lose her head kissing a girl. Sylvia tastes like wine and berries. Inez is out of her mind with a girl.

As she begins to slip out of her clothes, she worries about her scars, the badge of her childbearing, and what Sylvia will think. Can she leave her camisole on? For the first time since entering Sylvia's apartment, her body's anthem, a single pitch, the lonely F above middle C, rises with her breathing. Her first instinct is to curl into a ball on the bed, to present herself in her usual condition, as a woman in a shell.

What surprises her next is Sylvia's bashfulness. She'd seemed so bold at first, unbuttoning her red-striped shirt and flinging it across the room. Now in a pretty brassiere dotted with pink flowerets, she turns her back to Inez, seeming less coy than shy. Perhaps the two of them should curl up on the tiny bed together and figure out how to make love the way snails do.

"It's strange," Sylvia says, "undressing in the light of the day. Maybe we should slip under the covers first."

Inez sits up for a moment, then stands. She bounces forward a moment on the balls of her feet. "I want to see you, Sylvia."

"Really?" Sylvia gives Inez a sideways glance.

"Yes. I don't just want you seeing me."

"But you're so beautiful," Sylvia says.

Inez takes off her skirt and slip and sits down on the edge of the bed to roll down her nylons. She drags a couple of fingers along her thigh and is struck by the smoothness of her skin and the thrill she feels. The long, sustained F, her breath, that familiar vibration of the tight second finger on the D string, has miraculously changed timbres. Ah, the beautiful word. Could she possibly explain to Sylvia how a pitch, heard only in her mind, has changed qualities, how the immutable F has modulated to the supple frequency of bamboo, a timbre, if you will, consonant with a body that is about to offer itself?

Now she watches Sylvia quickly unclasp her pretty bra. She turns shyly toward Inez, her small, buttercup breasts giving a half bounce.

"You're lovely."

Sylvia shrugs.

Inez drapes her nylons over a bedside chair. "You should know, I have a couple of scars."

"I won't mind."

"From having babies with some difficulty."

"Would you rather I look away?"

"Only if you think it will upset you."

"Don't be silly."

"Jake pretends they're not there."

"That's his problem."

Inez smiles at Sylvia, who is naked and lies back against a pillow, her knees drawn up high, her breasts flattened into small plates.

"You're very beautiful, Sylvia. Nubile."

"Nobody's ever called me that before."

"Just don't ask me to define the word. I'm not sure I know what it means."

"No wonder."

"I read it in an advertisement. Sounds like a lovely thing, though, doesn't it?"

"It's all in the eye of the beholder."

Inez unbuttons her blouse and takes it off. "Now, I want you to see me, Sylvia. It's funny," Inez says, laying her blouse across the chair. She lifts her camisole over her head. "I hardly ever wear a black bra."

"It's very sexy."

"I had to dig to the bottom of my underwear drawer to find this."

"You must have known."

"How would I know? You are a surprise, Sylvia." Inez leaves her bra on for now and looks down at herself. Her belly button, the holy F note, winks up at her from its position between the two incision scars. "This was the first one," Inez says, touching the left scar. "Anna. They made a little mess sewing me up, that's why there's more scar tissue. The only thing I really mind about it is the way the skin is discolored."

"Does it hurt?"

"Not at all."

Sylvia's hands move instinctively toward Inez. "May I touch it? I won't, if you'd rather not."

"Jake never has."

"Never. That man must have a problem."

Inez laughs at that. Is she really happy to be here, nearly naked on a young woman's bed? Sylvia drags her soft thumb lightly along the length of Inez's Anna-scar. Inez closes her eyes. Sylvia traces the Joey-scar with the tip of her tongue, and Inez arches her back in response. She caresses Sylvia's soft cheek and Sylvia turns, taking the fingers of Inez's hand, one by one, into her mouth. She loves Inez's hands. How can she help herself? It would be enough to make love to her hands. The fingers, so long and tapered, even with their nails trimmed to the nub. Each finger with its history of virtuosity.

"Hmmm," Sylvia says. "You have such beautiful calluses on the tips of your fingers."

"You're a strange girl, Sylvia."

"I'm not a girl anymore." Sylvia has slipped her hand under Inez's panties. "Like it or not, I'm a woman."

"I think I like it." Her thighs open.

Inez has nothing more to say. Sylvia's fingers press firmly until—oh, this. Her pulse, her softest center, wet and wanting.

"May I?" Sylvia asks.

Inez nods and her breath quickens as her panties are tugged down over her hips and the clasp of her black bra is undone.

Sylvia has given up language, too. Swapped it for sensation. She would like to draw Inez down to the depths. To take her, blood and bone and heart. The both of them helpless, falling. What if they descend *fathoms*? What if they can no longer *fathom* how deep they've gone? What if they never return?

The smooth butter-skin of Inez is the beach of a small island. Her hands. Her tongue. The flesh a swell of waves. The smell of her. Like someone roused from sleep. Fear. Desire. Salt air. The sharp smell of her privacy, of married woman, mother, heartbreaking beauty.

Afterward, Sylvia studies Inez's face—the feather of moisture over each blond brow, how Inez's eyes seek Sylvia as soon as they open. Shy. Surprised by who she's become in the last hour. The violinist has sculpted circles under her eyes. There is a papery translucence to her skin. She is so fragile, she could disappear into herself. Sylvia bends toward her and gently kisses her mouth.

INEZ feels a flash of shame as she stands beside Sylvia under the saucer-sized showerhead. The shame is like a patch of warm skin with a glow at the center of it. The water washes over her twin scars. She expects her shell to return and cover her as quickly as it departed. This time it's bound to smother her. Any time now, a blistering F, a sonic boom of a vibration will issue forth. It's one thing to be a lousy wife, a bad mother, and an inferior violinist, but now she's stooped to a new level of degradation: allowing herself to get inebriated in the middle of the day and then seduced by a beatnik girl in an apartment that smells of incense. The fact that her body is still ringing with pleasure cannot erase her shame.

Sylvia smiles at Inez and hands her a tube of Breck. "Would you mind giving me a shampoo?"

The girl has a lot of nerve.

"There's nothing I love more than having my hair washed by somebody. My mother used to do it. When I was a girl. It was about the only intimacy with her I could stand."

"I'm not your mother."

"I'm well aware of that." Sylvia blinks quickly as if she might cry.

Inez hadn't intended to hurt the reporter, or had she? She closes her eyes and listens to the blast of water from the showerhead. The surge hits the top of her head and runs over her breasts, her belly, down her legs. The swirling pool near her feet drains in a swoosh. Inez opens her eyes. "I'd be happy to wash your hair, Sylvia."

"You don't have to."

"I know I don't."

"Are you sorry that you enjoyed yourself so much?"

"I don't know that I'm sorry," Inez says.

Inez squeezes a little too much shampoo into her hands and rubs it into Sylvia's scalp. She allows her sudsy hands to trail across Sylvia's small, upturned breasts and around her hips. Her right hand—her bow hand, which seems to have a mind of its own—slides slowly down between Sylvia's legs. Pleasure. Is this pleasure?

The reporter closes her eyes. Inez is fully sober now. Neither out of her mind nor subject to illusion. She is absolutely sober, standing in a shower of her free will, fully naked, without the weight of her shell or the ringing of the long sad note in her body. In front of her is a woman of whom she has become uncommonly fond, who moans softly as Inez strokes her.

STEPPING out of the shower, Inez thinks about her kids. Surely, they're safe at home. She walks barefoot into Sylvia's front room and sees, through the window on Hyde, that there is still plenty of light in the day. If for some reason Anna wasn't able to meet Joey, he could get into the house by himself. They've gone through the drill innumerable times. Joey wears a key to the back door around his neck; he also wears a dog tag with his name and address. This, she's learned, is a dangerous combination—the house key and the identification necklace. A criminal who gets ahold of these two items has access to your house. Once, she cautioned Joey against wearing the two together and he said, "Don't worry, Mom; this is a back-door key, and robbers are dummies—they'll never figure it out." What is at risk? A few possessions, her Landolfi, which is fully insured. The only thing to be concerned about is the children's safety. And isn't she the key to their safety? Barefoot, wrapped in an orange towel, Inez reaches up and touches her bare neck. Maybe she should be the one wearing the dog tag.

By the time Sylvia strolls into the living room, Inez is dressed and standing at the front window watching a few nimble passengers climb off the cable car at the corner. She listens to the rhythmic volley of bells, watches the car jerk forward before gliding through the intersection.

Sylvia comes up to the Inez and puts her arm around the violinist's waist. "Do you have to rush off?"

"It doesn't seem like I'm rushing. But I've got to get dinner started at home."

"I bet you're a good cook."

Inez laughs. "I'm not good at all. I'm not even adequate. I'm a disgrace. I can't even make a decent meal out of a book. But they're stuck with me."

"I bet you're not so bad."

"I *am* bad. Nobody ever showed me how to cook. My family treated me like a little princess, me and my violin. My other problem is I rarely have much of an appetite, which makes it hard to cook."

Sylvia takes hold of Inez's hand. "What happened to your appetite?"

Inez shrugs. "It vanished. I think my babies took it from me."

"I'm going to cook for you, Inez."

"I'm afraid it isn't worth the effort."

As Sylvia leans to kiss her, Inez turns aside.

"Do you think it's terribly unnatural?" Sylvia asks.

"What?"

"Two women."

"Yes."

"How can you say that after we've just been together?"

Inez shrugs. "I didn't say it. You said it. Or suggested it. Or wanted me to confirm it. So I was just being obedient. I'm a married woman, for God's sake."

"Happily married?"

"No, but that's beside the point."

Sylvia takes hold of Inez's arm now. "I'm not going to let you go."

"Let's not be absurd."

Inez kisses the young woman lightly on the head.

"You're going to love me," Sylvia whispers. "You are."

Inez says the words over in her head. *Love me . . . you are.* The words are searching for a pitch to attach themselves to. They follow her down the steps to the street. They may as well be grace notes, the tidy embellishments in an overture that reveal little of what will follow.

the art of the fugue

TONIGHT, despite having nearly destroyed the lamb chops in the pressure cooker, Inez has a surprising appetite. Instead of moving the food around her plate—hiding the meat as usual behind the potato—she's gotten everything she can off the bone and is tempted to excuse herself from the table. She'd love to take her plate into the kitchen so that she can gnaw on the bone in privacy, as stray thoughts of her afternoon with Sylvia float around her.

Instead, Inez grabs hold of the dining room table and smiles across at Joey, who is slathering a slice of French bread with butter.

"You want the butter, Mom?"

Inez shakes her head and looks Anna's way. Her daughter is a strange sight—plagued with a fresh rash of acne, Anna has pulled her beige turtleneck over her chin to cover up the worst of the sores.

"I only got a B on my *Merchant of Venice* paper, Dad," she says and pushes a forkful of zucchini into her mouth, the turtleneck slipping off her chin. "All my friends got As," Anna whines.

"What do you think the problem was?" Jake asks.

Anna tugs on the turtleneck so that it covers her chin again. "Miss Harrington said that though my heart might be in the right place, I was wrong about the Portia speech and that my argument was out of control."

"What did you say?"

"That the quality of mercy is more important than any man-made law, that mercy is more important than any law, and that if Shylock had gotten his way he'd be no better than the executioners who sent Caryl Chessman to the gas chamber at San Quentin."

Jake has a bite of lamb; he seems to be thinking over what his daughter has just said.

"Hey, Mom," Joey says and stuffs a slice of bread in his mouth. "Is

Chessman that guy they killed in the jail near Marin Town and Country Club?"

"Yes," Inez says, sadly.

Although Chessman's execution two years ago had been a huge story, Inez is surprised that he entered her seven-year-old's awareness, and that Joey managed to align San Quentin with the nearby pool club the family has been to a couple of times. Inez still gets upset when she thinks of Chessman. It affected her even more than the Rosenberg executions. Two of Inez's heroes—Eleanor Roosevelt and Pablo Casals—were among the luminaries who wrote pleas on Chessman's behalf. Jake had led one of the many protests outside the prison gates. Inez remembers the morning in 1960 when she drove out to San Quentin with Jake. There was a vigil of twenty-five or thirty people. Jake, dressed in a Pendleton shirt, stood in front of the small crowd. The look of sadness on Jake's face embodied the mood of the vigil. "This man took nobody's life," Jake said softly, "but the state plans to take his. The state prefers to bury its problems than having to face them or finding a way to solve them."

Inez turns toward her daughter. "Caryl Chessman sounds like a really apt example to use in your paper."

Anna shrugs. She's only interested in her father's response.

"Hey, Mom," Joey says, chewing on another hunk of bread.

"Finish chewing," she says.

Jake, restless from sitting so long at the table, stands up and digs his hands into the pockets of his army surplus shorts. "You can't confuse mercy with the law," he says to his daughter. "One has nothing to do with the other."

"What did the guy do to make them kill him?" Joey asks.

Inez butters a slice of bread. "They say he kidnapped and robbed and hurt some people."

"But he didn't kill anybody?"

"No," Inez says and takes a bite of bread. She turns to watch Jake pacing in his shorts.

"Don't you remember the last two lines in Portia's speech, Dad?" says Anna.

Jake comes back to his place at the table. "I'm afraid not."

Inez tries to recall how many stays of execution Chessman had. Eight. She remembers a comment somebody made after they killed him—Chessman's not a cat after all; he only got eight lives.

No longer worried about her acne, Anna raises her chin, poised to recite. "'And earthly power doth then show like God's / When mercy seasons justice.'"

Jake finishes chewing a slice of meat. "Poetry is like mercy, Anna; in the end it has nothing to do with justice."

"I don't believe you," Anna says, then clenches her teeth.

"What I mean," Jake says gently, "is that we can't count on mercy."

"We should be able to," says Anna, her lips curling into a frown.

Inez stands up and looks at her family. Jake, his mouth open, regards Anna, whose head is hung, with concern. Joey, ever watchful, has slipped, his thumb into his mouth for the first time in ages. Inez loves them all. Mercy is certainly easier to feel toward others than to herself. Now she wants to lift a lamb chop to her mouth and gnaw on it. "Excuse me," she says and carries her plate to the kitchen.

AWHILE later, Inez returns to the dining room with coffee and a plate of stale molasses cookies. She sits across the table from Jake and idly dips a cookie into her coffee. Jake sits across the table from her, smoking and doing a fancy crossword puzzle in the *Saturday Review*, a double-crostic, which yields a wise saying once he breaks the code. She can hear Joey, upstairs in his room, playing scales on the cello. Anna is finishing up the dinner dishes. These are the moments of family life she most enjoys— when everybody has marked a territory and is on their own.

When the phone rings, nobody in the house shows any interest in answering. Anna finally picks it up. Sudsy from the dishes, she brings the phone to her mother with an exaggerated huff.

"Hello?"

Inez hears her soft breath first, and then her voice—"It's Sylvia."

Inez says nothing. She presses the phone closer to her ear.

"I love you, Inez."

"Hmmm." Inez glances at Jake, who's hovering like a big shadow over his magazine puzzle.

"I mean it—I love you."

"Well, that's an interesting development."

She can hear Sylvia swallow hard. "That's not what I expected you to say."

"What did you expect?"

"I don't know. Are you angry at me for calling you? I bet I've made you angry."

"Not especially. I'm just sitting here dawdling over my coffee. Jake's dawdling, too, doing a crossword puzzle. His is at least thoughtful dawdling."

Jake looks up and smiles at her, not the least bit interested in who she's talking with.

"Should I hang up?" Sylvia whispers.

"You don't have to."

"Was that your daughter who answered?"

"Yes, that was Anna."

"She sounds very grown-up."

"She's certainly trying."

Jake raises his eyebrows. He has a question.

"The composer of Turandot?" he whispers.

"Puccini."

"Perfect," he says and jots the letters down with his pencil stub.

"Puccini?" Sylvia asks.

"Jake's puzzle."

"Is he right there?"

"Spitting distance."

"When can I see you?"

"Oh, I don't think it's a good idea," Inez says.

"Why?"

"It's the kind of thing where everybody's miserable in the end. Don't you think?"

"I don't care. I want to see you."

"Yes, you've made that clear."

"But not you?"

"I didn't say that."

"Are you sorry for what happened?" Sylvia asks, her voice turned wistful.

"I have no regrets."

"It's only going to get better, Inez. Isn't it?"

Jake taps her arm. "Here's another musical one. A polyphonic composition."

"Try 'fugue,'" Inez whispers.

Jake pencils the word into the puzzle. "Yep, I should have known that."

"What was that?" Sylvia asks.

"I just gave Jake another word. *Fugue.*"

"Are you forcing the man to do musical puzzles?"

"It's not quite as it seems." Inez watches Jake bear down on the puzzle with his pencil stub. He's figured out another clue.

"It's a lovely word, *fugue,*" says Sylvia. "It has the same root as *fugitive.*"

"I didn't know that."

"Did you know that a woman can go in and out of a fugue state, that it sometimes involves wandering away from home?"

"Do you propose that's what I should do?"

"I propose, so to speak. Let's set up a time to see each other, Inez."

"You're certainly persistent."

"It's one of my virtues."

Inez glances at Jake, who's nibbling on his pencil stub. "How's next Tuesday, a little after ten? We've got an afternoon rehearsal."

"I don't know if I can wait a whole week."

"Try. It will be good for you."

When she hangs up, Jake looks up from his puzzle.

"Mafalda?" he says.

"Yes," she says. "Mafalda's having man trouble."

"She'd do better to stay away from them."

"Yes, she would," Inez agrees. She pictures Sylvia, sitting at her kitchen counter, mulling over the conversation just concluded, a jelly jar of wine in her hand.

Inez eats a second molasses cookie, and, stale as they are, she can imagine eating a third. What's gotten into her? Two is more than enough.

"I think I have this solved," Jake says, pleased as always when finishing a puzzle. "It's a quote from George Szell. 'In music one must think with the heart and feel with the brain.'"

Inez pushes the plate of cookies aside. "That sounds like something a conductor would say."

"Yeah, but what does it mean?"

"As long as it's profound, it doesn't need to mean anything." Inez stands and gives Jake a kiss on his forehead.

He smiles up at her from his puzzle. "You're certainly in a chipper mood."

"Yes, that's me, chipper. Rather scary, isn't it?"

"Well, I don't imagine it can go on for too long," he says.

"You never know. I may decide to drive you crazy with good cheer."

"Go ahead, drive me crazy." Jake reaches out and tries to squeeze her rump as she heads out of the room.

INEZ climbs the stairs to Joey's room and knocks on his door. After his exercises, the poor boy's dug in to the Adagio from the Dvořák concerto again. A seven-year-old, no matter how talented, shouldn't be playing the Dvořák, but Joey's bonehead teacher, Charles Samuels, is so intent on impressing her with her son's progress under his tutelage that he assigns music that's beyond the boy.

Inez ducks her head into Joey's room. "Sounds good."

"No, it doesn't."

"Well, you're just finding your way through it," she says, going into the tiny room and rubbing the small of her son's back.

"Sometimes I feel like killing my cello," Joey says.

"Really?"

Joey nods his head a half-dozen times and then stands his cello on its side.

Inez steps around Joey and sits facing him on the edge of his bed.

"Hey, did you ever want to bomb your violin, Mom?"

"Bomb it?"

"Yeah, atom-bomb it into smithereens."

"No, I never thought of bombing my violin."

Joey stands and makes a series of bomb sounds, flailing his arms in the air.

Inez laughs at her little bomb boy. "I used to think about jumping on my violin, though. Laying it on the floor, on the spot where I practiced, then climbing up on a chair and . . . Geronimo."

Joey climbs onto his chair. "That's what you said when you jumped, Mom . . . Geronimo?"

"I didn't jump."

"But if you did? That was your blastoff word."

Inez shrugs, but Joey isn't done with the game. He makes a flying jump off the chair, shouting his mother's blastoff word, yet careful not to get too close to his cello.

Inez wants to run a hand through Joey's cowlick and holds out her arms to him, but he stands apart.

"The good thing about a violin is that you could crush it with one jump. With a cello, it would take a few good jumps. I'd put on my cowboy boots." Joey smiles at her and climbs into her lap. "What would happen to me if I did it?"

Inez nuzzles the boy's neck and then draws a hand through his hair, slowing over the stiff cowlick. "I'd probably yell at you."

Joey looks directly into her eyes. His face is an inch from hers, and he's staring, like he did as a baby, right through her. "For how long?"

"I don't know; I'd probably yell at you for a half an hour."

"That's all? I could stand that."

Inez feels Joey's warm breath on her brows. "So are you going to jump on it?"

"No," he says, impishly. "I was teasing you."

Inez looks around Joey's room. It's sometimes hard for her to believe that he's just seven. How many seven-year-olds have a picture of Pablo Casals on their walls? Whose idea was it to tack Pablo's picture to the wall? Certainly not hers. Another wall is covered with pictures of ballplayers whom she can't identify. And there are photographs of Jake and her. Inez once asked Joey why he had no picture of his sister on the wall. "You're the only girl," he'd said, "that I want on my wall." It strikes her that she doesn't deserve to have her image enshrined on Joey's wall. She would have sold the boy down the river if she'd only been a little more clever. If she hasn't yet broken the boy's heart for good, she's bound to do it.

Joey starts to climb off her lap and she's reluctant to let him go. "Hey, Mom, you ever have a dream where you're playing a piece and your fingers get stuck on the strings?"

"No, I can't remember ever having a dream like that. You?"

He bounces over to his practice chair and picks up his cello. "No, but a daydream. I have a lot of daydreams. You want to hear my favorite one?"

"Sure."

"I'm playing a recital in front of a big audience and my fingers are stuck to the strings with airplane glue! And then I have to pee, and I run off the stage with the cello stuck to my fingers and then I'm flying with angel wings to this big bathroom, and the funny thing is that because of the airplane glue, the cello just flies with me, too."

"Do you spend a lot of time thinking about things like that?"

"All the time, Mom." Joey steadies the cello between his legs and takes firm hold of the bow.

"Maybe you're practicing too much, Joey."

"I've got to practice, Mom, if I want to be really good." He turns his head toward the fingerboard as he bows slowly through a D scale.

"You're already really good."

"Come on, Mom. You know what I mean."

Inez watches Joey's chunky fingers follow the path of an A scale. "I've told you what happens if you practice too much."

"Yeah, you become a nut."

Inez nods. It seems a strange caution to be offering a seven-year-old boy, but she wishes somebody had offered it to her.

"The thing is, Mom, I've learned how to practice and daydream at the same time."

"That's great, honey."

"That's what Mr. Samuels told me to do."

As Joey talks, Inez has a picture of her son as a man. She can see him perfectly: tall and handsome like his father. A grin on his face. Pleased, perhaps, by what he can imagine.

"Do you think Mr. Samuels daydreams when he practices?"

"I wouldn't know." It is the most comforting image: Joey as a man. Living beyond her, without her. It is practically a certainty: Joey, with his wit and wise soul, making his way successfully in the world. What more could she hope for than having her youngest child survive her? Even if she lived to be eighty, Joey, at forty-seven, would bury his aged mother. The image of a middle-aged Joey, surviving her, helps her cope with the idea of her son bereft at seven.

Inez bends to kiss Joey good night. "Will you promise to let me know before you jump on it?"

"Sure," he says, winking at her like a little man.

By the time she reaches the stairs, Joey's started up with the Dvořák again.

the mythological beast

O N Tuesday morning there's a call from the hospital. Isaac Roseman—Jake's father and Inez's longtime teacher—has had a stroke. Isaac's weekly chess buddy found him lying in the hallway of his building, beside a bag of trash meant for the garbage chute.

The end doesn't appear to be close at hand. A young doctor named Colton greets them in the hallway at Kaiser. He shakes hands with Jake—he must have recognized the attorney from the news—and flashes Inez a supercilious smile.

"I see a decent recovery here," Dr. Colton says. "He has his functions. He was alert this morning. Eager, I'd say, to get up. We think he got himself a little too excited and now he's exhausted. He's resting nicely."

Once she and Jake are alone in the room with the sleeping Isaac, Jake reacts to Dr. Colton's prognosis: "Just our luck. Pretty soon he's going to be drooling from all of his orifices."

"Stop, Jake."

"I'm not going to stop." Jake makes a slurpy sound. They both laugh for a moment, even though it's not funny. Even though it's anything but funny.

In his prime, Isaac Roseman had a certain charm that Inez learned not to trust, but after his wife died and he had nobody left to dote on him, Isaac became a bitter man. A lifetime ago, when Inez was Isaac's prized student, he'd misbehaved toward her, occasionally touching her young body. For years at a time, she'd managed to put Isaac's behavior out of her mind, especially during the early years of her relationship with Jake. What little she now remembers survives as a bare abstraction.

After pacing the perimeter of his father's hospital bed, Jake remembers a string of meetings he can't miss. "What the hell am I going to do, stand around and watch the old man sleep? He looks like some sort of mythological beast. You going to just sit here?"

"For a while."

"What good is that going to do?"

"Probably none; I just want to sit here."

Jake's hands are on his hips. Petulant like a child. She'd like to stand up and slap his face. For what? Does she have to know a reason? She folds her hands in her lap and listens to Jake's disingenuous apologies for leaving.

"Sounds like you better go," she says and watches her husband as he backs out of the door.

CURIOUSLY, Inez finds solace sitting alone with Isaac Roseman. It's almost like sitting with the dead. The sleeping Isaac has a slight smile fixed on his face. Like a baby after he's passed gas. She wondered exactly when Isaac's stroke happened. Could it have been when she was lying in Sylvia's arms? Could he have been leveled in the moment of her deepest pleasure? She tends to think like this when uncommon things happen. Like pleasure. In a rapture of grandiosity, she imagines herself to be at the center of the world, the trigger of all things, good and evil.

There's a knock at the door and Inez meets Silvio Manatelli, Isaac's friend, the man who found him.

"You're his daughter?"

"His daughter-in-law."

"Oh, yes. Heard about you," Mr. Manatelli says, touching the brim of his worn baseball cap. "The violinist, the daughter-in-law, all rolled into one. I come over to play chess and whenever it's my move, he talks. Maybe he'll talk about you, maybe he'll talk about his son. He makes me dizzy. I forget what I'm doing. Not that I'm doing so much. 'What's a matter, Manatelli?' he says. 'It's your move.' He beats me. Almost every time, he beats me. He says, 'Read the books, Manatelli; that's your only hope to beat me. Read the books.' But I don't read the books. If I want to read, I read. If I want to play chess, I play. So, how is he?" Mr. Manatelli glances over her shoulder toward the man in the bed inside. "What do the doctors say? They won't let me in there. If you're not family, you can't go in. You might as well be a garbage man off the street." The stubby man tugs on his sport coat turned shiny with age.

"They gave him some medication. He's sleeping with a smile on his face."

"He's telling himself a joke," Mr. Manatelli says. "Who else is he going to tell? I never listen to his stupid jokes."

Inez thinks of Isaac's stupid jokes. Something off-color. Or racist. Isaac became a bigot in his old age.

Mr. Manatelli looks up at her—hoping for some assurance?

"The first tests look good. They say he may recover most of his functions. But maybe you'll be able to beat him in chess now."

Mr. Manatelli nods his head and smiles. He reaches into a pocket and pulls out a small spiral notebook and a pen that he clicks a dozen times. Satisfied, he rests the pad against the wall and, creaking a bit, leans toward it. He nods to her again. "I'll write him a note." Manatelli prints each letter very deliberately. He gives his pen a final click, rips the sheet out of his pad, and hands it to Inez. "Please give this to Roseman, and if he says, 'Where's the flowers from Manatelli?' tell him I took a De Soto cab over here and that cost more money than three bunches of blue carnations."

"Thanks for coming, Mr. Manatelli."

Back in Isaac's room, Inez peeks at the note.

Get better, Roseman. I got a word for you. Say it to yourself a hundred times. Better get used to the sound. CHECK-MATE.

M ANATELLI

INEZ snoozes in the bedside chair. After she shakes herself awake and sees sleeping Isaac in his hospital bed, she remembers seeing her father in the hospital following his first heart attack. All the blood had gone out of his face. She and Bibi had come to the hospital together. They were young women by then. Inez was already married and playing in the symphony. It frightened Inez to see her father so compromised. He'd been sedated, but his eyes brightened when she and Bibi walked into the room. He couldn't yet speak, but Inez thought she saw him mouth the words, "My girls."

During much of her childhood, her father drove her to Isaac Roseman's house for lessons three times a week. He'd sit in front of the house in his Hudson and work on one of his carvings. Once a month her father walked with her to the door and handed Mr. Roseman an envelope with cash for the month's lessons. Her father didn't want her to have to handle money when she was a child. When Isaac Roseman opened the door, her father bowed to him. She always wanted to tell him not to bow, because he was the better man. Sometimes when Mr. Roseman touched her, she'd think of her father sitting out in the car with his knife and his block of alder.

INEZ strolls out into the waiting room again and sorts through the magazines. She picks up a discarded *Life* from August, with Marilyn on the cover. "Remembering Marilyn." Everybody's favorite suicide. Inez has already put in her time with this issue. She doesn't need to look at the pictures of Marilyn again. It happened just six weeks ago now and the death's fixed incontrovertibly in the public imagination. The story's been told: Be careful what you wish for. The little girl made into a goddess. Fame and glory and loneliness. The queen of peroxide and barbiturates who slipped quietly out of her life. It's an escape route that's never appealed to Inez. Who wants to fade away like a lower form of life, a dog put to sleep, too mush-brained to look open-eyed at her fate?

Inez flips past Marilyn, through a series of ads. Spun-lo panties claim to be "Runproof! Zipper proof! Ring proof! Fingernail proof! Toenail proof! Even hook and eye proof!" Chung King invites her to keep a great Chinese chef in her freezer. The new GE clock radio will transport her "from Brahms to bongos and Bach again." And because "fun is more fun when the pictures you take are finished in 10 seconds," it just may be time to get a Polaroid Land Camera. Right here in page after page of advertisements—all the reasons to stay alive.

jake's ribs

"A ND now the old man's a shell of himself," Jake's thinking, as he steps into the intersection and the grille of a red Studebaker Silver Hawk bears down on him. He lurches back toward the curb, stumbles into a parked Rambler, and falls on his rear. He takes a few slow breaths and whistles a half dozen involuntary notes—no song he recognizes. The damn Studebaker might have killed him—he can still feel the breeze of it shaving past him at thirty-five or forty miles an hour. There's a chill at the back of his neck. The package of barbecued ribs he just bought is all over the street. He stretches out his legs. Whistles something a little more coherent—"The Sunny Side of the Street." *Grab your coat and get your hat.*

Somehow, as Jake boosts himself onto the curb, his oxford-cloth shirt rips right up the back. It must have gotten attached to the rusty bumper of the Rambler. His back is sore. His pants are soiled. He'd like to sit on the curb and cry. Cars drive by, a few pedestrians seem to notice him. Does he look like a bum? A couple of stray dogs are nosing up to Jake. He unbuttons his ripped shirt, which is splattered with barbecue sauce. One dog, a black Labrador mutt with white markings on its neck, is chewing on a barbecued rib. The other, some kind of spaniel, seems more interested in Jake than in the ribs. Jake stands—a little creaky in the legs—and waves his shirt at the spaniel.

THE look on Christine's face brings back the hollow fear of the event.

"Sit down," she says. "Tell me what happened."

He slowly walks over to one of the tall kitchen stools. A guy arriving at his wealthy lover's door—even if it is the tradesman's entrance—wearing a white T-shirt and a soiled pair of slacks, needs to do what he can to stall. He wants to tell her, *Alas, Christine, there are no pee stains on my underwear.* Jake lights a smoke and thanks Christine as she hands him an ashtray. He loves this one shaped like a kitchen sink with teeny, protruding faucets that a guy can rest his cigarette on. If he had money to burn, he thinks, chuckling to himself, he'd buy a dozen of them. Christine has her eyes fixed on him, but he's not ready. "Can I have a drink of water?"

"Of course. Mineral water or from the tap? I know we have mineral water, I just don't know where it's kept."

"The tap is fine; I'm not afraid of fluoride. Do you think it's all a Communist plot, Christine—the fluoride?"

Christine smiles at him. "No, I don't think it's a plot. What's happened, Jake?"

He watches her at the sink. A petite woman with high cheekbones and a swath of gray hair at her right temple, a woman so confident that she allows herself to go gray in front of your eyes, a sexy yet sensible hedonist who happens to be somebody else's wife. She's certainly delectable today in a floral dress, a shower of yellows and greens.

"You probably want ice," Christine says.

She might as well be his accomplice in the stall. "Sure, I wouldn't mind ice, and while you're at it, how about a twist of lemon?"

"Listen to you," she says with a laugh. "You walk in here looking like you've been on a five-day binge and now you're ordering me around as if I'm a barmaid."

"Hardly. I brought some barbecued ribs; that's what's in the sack. I'm not sure I'll be able to eat them." Jake can't believe he actually went back to the barbecue shop for another order.

"Tell me what happened," Christine demands.

"Can I have the water first?" Christine's dress swishes as she comes toward him. He drinks the water in a gulp, wonders if she will offer him more. They could repeat the sequence ad nauseam. But Christine is not about to budge. A deal is a deal.

"I was almost hit by a car," he says. "A red Studebaker. A Silver Hawk. I wasn't paying attention."

"Oh. Jake."

"It doesn't sound like much, but a thing like that can change the way you look at things. Do you know what I mean?"

"Of course."

As Christine comes toward him, he sees she's deciding how close to get. She is wary of him; she needs to keep a certain distance, as you would from any changed and unpredictable creature.

"I was thinking of you," he says.

"Me?"

"Of course. I'd just picked up a big platter of short ribs at Leon's Barbecue. I was walking up here with the food. And I got to thinking . . . I got to thinking about the significance of a man bringing a woman ribs. Like Adam and Eve, although I realized that it wasn't Adam's plan to give Eve his rib. Believe it or not, this is the nonsense that was going through my head when I stepped off the curb at Geary and Fillmore."

He sneaks a look at Christine, trying to determine whether she buys his story.

"You could have been killed," she says, a hint of skepticism in her expression.

"My thought exactly. You know what saved me? I think it was the ribs. I saw the flash of the radiator grille coming at me and I clutched the package of barbecue and jumped back to the curb. I was more concerned with not spoiling the ribs than I was with my own skin."

Christine brings him another glass of water now without his asking. He sips it slowly this time. "I sat on the curb for quite a while trying to remember who I was. People walked by me as if I wasn't there. Just picture this: a white man sitting on the curb of a busy intersection in the Fillmore. You'd have thought that this was the most common thing in the world—to have a shaken white man on the curb clutching a package of barbecued ribs."

The curb he sat on, after the Studebaker nearly ran him over, wasn't anywhere near Fillmore and Geary. He'd walked a half dozen blocks since picking up the ribs, and was at some quiet, no-man's-land intersection between the Fillmore District and Pacific Heights when the Studebaker appeared. There wasn't another pedestrian to be seen. It had been less than an hour since he'd left the hospital—the old man asleep with his frozen smile and Inez ready to camp out in the patient's room for the foreseeable future. Jake had wandered a little through the Negro streets, picking up the food for his lunch with Christine, determined to go on with their Tuesday rendezvous. He didn't want to think about his father and his father's fate. Not yet. He didn't want to think about Inez. Or Inez alone in the room with the old man. Or the terrible things she'd once told him about his father.

As he walked through the Fillmore, he half expected to be noticed by somebody in the community because of the work he'd done there, but nobody recognized him, even as being a human being.

Christine, judging him free of contagion, wraps an arm around his shoulder. "Are you all right?"

"Yeah, I'm just a little shaken."

"I bet you are. What happened to your shirt and coat?"

"I wasn't wearing a coat."

"And your shirt?"

There are times when Christine is like a mother, the way she expects things to be accounted for. "My shirt got torn when I fell and there was some grease on the pavement. I just took it off and left it there. Anyway, I wanted to see what would happen if I came to your door with a pile of ribs, looking like a hobo. Will she let me in or will she pretend she doesn't know me?"

"You know you're always welcome, Jake."

"On the days that the help is off."

"This is my life," she says and gazes at him steadily. "Is there anything I can get you?"

What he'd like most would be to lie down with Christine and have her hold him.

"Can I get you a cup of instant coffee?"

"That'd be lovely."

Jake had been thinking of his father when the red Studebaker nearly ran him over. But once he scrambled back to the curb, he thought of Inez—how little he knew his wife, that he didn't begin to know what made her tick. He was often struck by the precision of her mind, which was a result, no doubt, of all the hours of practice. Her mind seemed to work overtime, as if it was charged with keeping time for the entire world. Despite her physical beauty, which had deepened with age, Jake sometimes thought of Inez as a woman without a body, always thinking and remote.

It's amazing all that can pass through a mind in an instant. As Jake fumbled the package of ribs, which exploded on the pavement, he thought about how Inez drove a Studebaker. He remembered that in the way you know, upon waking, that a curious figure in a dream is really your father. For as long as Inez has had her own car, she's driven a Studebaker, although her current model, a yellow Scotsman Sedan, is a far cry from a red Silver Hawk, with its large, round hawk on the radiator grill. Jake can still see the blazing emblem from the grille.

Meanwhile, the dark, rusty barbecue sauce had seeped onto Jake's shirt and the stray dogs found the scent. After fifteen minutes on the curb, Jake walked back down to Leon's Barbecue on Geary and Fillmore and ordered another large platter of short ribs to go. Then he did what he should have done in the first place: he stepped prudently to the curb and hailed a cab.

"You want anything in your coffee?" Christine asks.

"Black. I'll take it black." As he puts out his latest cigarette, he counts a half dozen butts in the ashtray.

Christine hands him a mug of coffee. "My survivor."

That, it seems to Jake, is an interesting way to think of himself. "I don't know what I'll be good for today," he says.

Christine takes ahold of Jake's hand and gently separates one finger from another. "We'll find some use for you," she says.

some loss

IN the late afternoon, Inez calls home to make sure the kids are safe. She doesn't bother to tell Anna, who is uncharacteristically chatty on the phone, about her grandfather.

"I got Miss Harrington to change my grade," she says.

"That's terrific, honey."

"She gave me an A–. Showed me a little mercy, Mom. Don't worry about being late; I'm going to make some popcorn for Joey and me, and then he's got his chocolate banana."

Inez returns to Isaac's room. In a while another doctor, a red-haired gnome of a man named Hintz, comes in and takes a long look at Isaac's chart. Then he peels back Isaac's sheet and blanket and Inez gets her first terrifying look at Isaac's twisted right arm, his hand frozen, claw-like. Although Isaac hasn't played for years, Inez is stunned to see the condition of his beautiful bow arm.

"Will he ever get his arm back?" she asks.

"Perhaps, to a degree," Dr. Hintz says, his thin lips settling into a smirk.

Inez wonders what's so amusing. Dr. Hintz adjusts Isaac's IV and scribbles something onto his chart. Inez asks whether Isaac has suffered a massive stroke, without knowing what she hopes the answer will be. During the doctor's discursive answer, her mind wanders oddly to Sylvia. Pleasure is more appealing than this.

Dr. Hintz is in teacher mode. "Although the word's commonly used, *massive* is really a misnomer. I suppose we have to define our terms. Personally, I object to it. It's not a medical term. Rather, if you ask me, it's architectural. Not to worry," Dr. Hintz concludes, "massive or not. This is not the real issue. There has been some loss, but much can be regained."

Inez could get a more useful answer from a fortune-teller out in the Mission District.

Dr. Hintz is not deterred. "It's going to take some work on his part. Plenty of work."

Isaac snorts in his sleep. Perhaps he doesn't like being discussed in the third person.

"Is Mr. Roseman a disciplined man?"

The question offends Inez. She stands out of the bedside chair. "Mr. Roseman was a great violinist." Great? Perhaps that's a bit of an exaggeration.

The doctor nods, then smiles at her again. His eyes, Inez notices, rest on her breasts. "What we once were," he says, "and what we are now, can be as far removed as sleeping and waking."

Inez looks down at the doctor's feet, laced into a pair of tiny brown brogues. What does he wear, size five? She thinks about how small his penis must be and smiles back at him. "I'm not expecting Isaac to play Paganini again, Doctor."

"No, not Paganini," he says, bowing his copper head toward Inez before he turns and leaves the room.

SITTING with her hands folded in her lap, Inez notices that, as the afternoon light pales toward dusk, Isaac Roseman has finally lost his smile. She considers the twisted fingers of his left hand and has a shadowy memory of the man touching her. The Mendelssohn Concerto always helped her forget. It's hard to say why the Mendelssohn. She hums a run of eighth notes from the Presto. The Mendelssohn was just one of many pieces from the standard repertory that she studied with Isaac. She played the concerto with the San Francisco Honor Orchestra, a select group of high school students. It was her first major triumph.

Her edition of the Mendelssohn was annotated by a character named Heinrich Dessauer, who offered copious explanatory remarks that she committed to memory. *The first solo is to be commenced with warm, sincere tonal production, and integrated in plain, straightforward but not brilliant or virtuoso-like style.*

She was twelve years old. *In order that the necessary increase in speed at the più presto and the last presto may be produced to best advantage . . . and her teacher would place his hand on her waist . . . the tempo should begin to grow quicker very gradually from this point.*

When Inez was fourteen, she told Mr. Roseman to stop touching her. A year later, she started to see his son and put everything about the father out of her head. Mr. Roseman talked about how to approach a passage of Brahms, and Inez would think about petting with his son, and how Jake would try to slip a hand under her skirt when they went for rides in his borrowed Chevy. She'd listen to the rise and fall of Isaac Roseman's voice and yearn for his son. Now she thinks about Sylvia. How Sylvia kissed her on the little bed. The potency of each kiss. Delicious. And Inez like a bride at forty, surrendering to so unknown an experience.

Inez sits beside her father-in-law and hums the Mendelssohn. She sees herself with Sylvia—two women sitting together on the edge of a girl's bed. She wants to open her legs to Sylvia. *Legs*, she tells herself, *not heart*, as if it were an acrobatic matter, as if she could discipline herself to give one part but not the other. The acrobatics of the living. A way to stay alive. *You are no better than a man*, she thinks. Isaac Roseman's eyelids flutter. Does he have a comment? She watches him sink deeper into his sleep, the hand that touched her gnarled atop the blanket.

the whole hand

A T times her mother called her insatiable, but it was hardly true. *Give her a finger,* Angela Bran liked to say, *and she wants the whole hand.* If anything, Sylvia had trained herself to ask for as little as possible. Her mother trotted out another cute phrase from time to time: *The way you behave, Sylvia, you'd think you were an orphan.* It wasn't until her mother had actually orphaned her that Sylvia discovered the concept of *projection.* She picked up a dog-eared psychology text in Sacramento and read as much as she could absorb about her mother, in clinical terms. On a gray Saturday in the fall, as the smell of burning leaves permeated the neighborhood, Sylvia walked toward the capitol and lit the psychology book on fire in a trash can bearing the seal of the great state of California.

Now, Sylvia has begun to fear that she *is* insatiable. Since the afternoon that Inez came to her apartment Sylvia's floated in the ether of their hours together, from the first, disorienting moments in the Japanese restaurant to the weave of the Ravel quartet and the surprising passion of their kisses, how Inez fell back, her throat long and vulnerable as she moaned with pleasure, Sylvia's private concert, and their shower together after, water turning from hot to lukewarm as they negotiated the early terms of their intimacy. The next day, Sylvia found herself in the surprising position of standing on her cable-car corner, looking up at her apartment in which so much had happened. She was dazed the whole day, but actually went to her restaurant job at The Little Sweden in the evening. Whenever an image of Inez surfaced, Sylvia bit her lower lip and did her best to replenish the shrimp, or keep track of her orders at the bar, or bring used plates to the kitchen without incident. Inez drinking cheap wine, her legs curled under her in the wicker chair; Inez on her back on the bed, revealing her scars; the stunned gratitude in Inez's eyes, after making love. It wasn't until today that the genuine worry began to kick in—what will become of Inez and Sylvia? What future does she hope for? How much can she demand?

Tonight when Hyman Myerson calls to ask if she'd like to go out for a drive in his new Impala, she jumps at the chance. She enjoys Hy's company but, more than anything, welcomes the opportunity to have a couple of hours free of worry about Inez.

"HOW are you, lovely?" Hy says, after she climbs into his shiny black Impala.

"Fine."

"You look beautiful tonight."

"Come on, Hy."

"No, I mean that. Beautiful in face, beautiful in spirit."

Sylvia flicks the foam dice hanging from his rearview mirror. "I didn't know you went in for dice."

"You like 'em? I picked them up after I got the car."

"Aren't you a little old for driving around with a pair of giant dice?"

Hy shrugs. "I *am* old." He pulls gently on his string tie, so gently that it seems that he is tuning an instrument, or synchronizing, by some miracle of puppetry, his mind and his body. Then he grins at her. Sylvia told herself that when she left her apartment tonight, Inez Roseman wasn't coming with her, that once she got into Hy's car, she was giving herself to another experience.

"Everything these days is about age, Sylvia. Age and attitude. Age and attitude and analysis."

Sylvia winks at Hyman. "Have you ever been in for analysis, Hy?"

"You mean, psychiatric analysis? You think I need that?"

Sylvia shrugs. "Maybe."

Hy bursts into a raw, biting laugh. "Naw, you'll never catch me doing that kind of stuff. If anybody's going to do any analysis on this old bean, it's going to be me." Hy's laughter sets off an ugly cough that forces him to pull out a handkerchief and spit.

Sylvia hasn't been paying any particular attention to where they are driving until she realizes that they are headed out California Street toward the Richmond District, close to Inez's neighborhood.

"The Impala drives nice," she says.

"It certainly does."

Hy pulls a small hand-rolled cigarette out of his jacket pocket and lights it up. "You ever go in for marijuana?"

She shakes her head.

"It won't grow hair on your chest," he says tightly before exhaling.

"Good," Sylvia says, taking the cigarette from him.

"Go ahead, give yourself a little lift."

She takes in a long puff of smoke.

"I'll say this for you, Sylvia, you're certainly a willing wench."

Wench, she thinks, from the Middle English *wenche*, meaning *child*. "Am I too easy, Hy?"

"No, you are a joy, Sylvia. Listen, when you inhale, suck the smoke in and hold onto it."

"Where are we going?" she asks, after nearly choking on her attempt.

"Wherever you want to go."

Sylvia shrugs and passes the little cigarette to Hy. She enjoys the faint ribbon of gauze wrapped around her forehead now and the way the houses on California Street seem to be going by faster than the car is traveling, as if there is one speed inside the car and another outside.

Hy sucks on the cigarette and then composes his face in a stoic expression. "Good evening, ladies and gentlemen," he says, in a deep Alfred Hitchcock accent.

"Good evening, sir."

Hy blows out smoke, goes into a little coughing fit, and passes the marijuana to Sylvia. "Don't worry, I'm not contagious. It's smoker's hack, from two packs of Camels a day. Since February I've given up smoking anything but this."

Sylvia takes the cigarette and draws on it, holding the smoke good and deep.

"Well, look at you," Hy says, sliding into a surprisingly good Cary Grant. "You've been holding out on me."

"I have," she says, taking a quick trail of drags. "I've had a checkered past."

Hy waits for her to explain, but she says nothing. She exhales, then draws deeply on the cigarette again, thinking of the young man at Sacramento State who introduced her to marijuana. He was a trumpet player named Dominic who, like her, spent half his life in the practice rooms. Sylvia had a crush on Dominic, but he was only interested in smoking his "sticks" and getting back to his practice. Once or twice a week she'd follow him into the tunnel between the practice rooms and the performance hall and hope that he'd suddenly want to seduce her. The doors to the tunnel were locked, but somehow Dominic had the key. He'd be chatty at first, talking about his trips down to San Francisco to visit friends in North Beach, and about jazz and how he could see a Dizzy Gillespie solo like a painting when he closed his eyes. He described paintings by de Kooning and Franz Kline. He talked about the beauty of erasures and the articulation of brushstrokes. She had no idea what he was talking about. He also said that the marijuana kept his practice sessions imaginative. It had the opposite effect on her. It distracted her, turned her skittish. Or amorous. A few times after smoking with Dominic, she sat in the practice room, touching herself with her right hand and playing bass lines with her left.

Sylvia feels pleasantly illuminated, riding in Hy's fancy black Impala with its lush red-and-white upholstery. Her forehead and the bright pulp of her brain glow like a brass globe given a light buffing. They are way out in the Avenues, very close to Inez's house, but she isn't going to think about Inez. She can bet that Inez isn't thinking about her right now either. Sylvia reaches out and gives the foam dice a nudge.

"By the way," Hy says, his British accent growing richer, "those aren't dice hanging up there, those happen to be my testicles—my balls, if I might partake of the common parlance—or shall I say they are a fair representation of their size and spotted scope." They both crack up at this. "But seriously," says Hy, pulling a large gold clip from his pocket and applying it to the end of his marijuana cigarette, "don't you ever get a little tired of all the talk about phallic symbols? What this country needs now," says Hy, shifting to a pinched, academic accent, "is an honorable set of testicular symbols. These young fellas driving around with dice in their hot rods, they don't even know they've hung up their testicles. But a man of my age and relative distinction is fully conscious of the fact and thus can take inspiration from the swinging of the giant dice. What can I tell you? I drive around for five minutes and I have a hard-on."

"Hy," Sylvia says.

"Sorry, just something a little off-color. It's my favorite hue." Hy flicks the foam dice. They swing back and forth as he drives the curving road through Sea Cliff toward the Legion of Honor. "Actually, I think they're camp."

"Like your string tie."

"Yes, I suppose. I've never grown up—that's my problem."

"I'm sure you have plenty of others."

Hy lifts the gold clip to his mouth and inhales, but the cigarette has gone out. "You're right about that . . . I have a showroom full of problems—grands, baby grands, spinets—instruments of the highest quality that never want to leave me. Sure, I have problems. I have a meshuga son who dropped out of college to become a hairdresser, a trade for which he had no aptitude. Now he's working at a dog pound. My son, the bowwow man. My daughter, Nina, don't get me started. The most beautiful girl you ever want to see. Smart. Beat me at chess when she was eight years old. I kid you not. A real nose for the books. Would sit in a room all day and read. Russians, you name it. Spoke French like a native. Her teachers were always taking me aside. This one, they said, is special. Voted most likely to succeed. What can I tell you? Broke my heart. She likes black fellas who are up to no good. And my wife, Toby— you've had the pleasure—well, Toby, how shall I say, is a wee bit off her nut . . ."

"She didn't seem like that to me."

"What do you know? Her idea of a perfect day is eight hours of soap operas and a two-pound box of See's chocolates."

"Maybe you should be taking her for a ride instead of me."

"She won't go out. Might miss something on the TV."

"She seemed to enjoy herself at the symphony."

"That was an anomaly. A once-in-a-million anomaly. Do you know what that word means?"

"Yes, I do." Sylvia is tempted to reveal her talent with words. *Deviant, aberration, irregularity*; and, if that doesn't work, slay him with etymology—from the Greek *omalia*, for *even*, qualified by *an*, for *lacking*.

"Are you trying to add yourself to my list of troubles? I don't have room for you on my list, Sylvia. You, I honor." Hy coughs wetly, that nasty hack again.

If I was home I'd be sitting in my underwear pining after Inez, Sylvia reminds herself.

"Look, I'm not used to talking like this, Sylvia. I'm not a big talker."

"You talk all the time, Hy."

"I never discuss my problems. Ask anybody and they'll tell you . . . Hy Myerson does not discuss his problems. I live by a simple philosophy: I've got the world in a jug and the stopper in my hands."

Sylvia flips down the sunshade on the passenger side and catches a glimpse of herself in the small mirror. Half-startled and young—that's how she looks. A thirty-year-old *wench*, a deviant who happens to be in love with a married woman, but who is driving around with a married man whose testicles are hanging from either side of the rearview mirror. Sylvia narrows her eyes and tries to turn herself into a desperado.

"Like what you see?" Hy asks.

"Not particularly."

"Well, I do."

"You would."

"What's that supposed to mean?"

Sylvia shrugs.

"You're a beautiful girl, Sylvia; don't let anybody tell you differently."

"Don't patronize me, Hy."

"Hey, I wouldn't know how."

Hyman turns around the circle across from the Legion and parks his car. He lifts the gold clip to his mouth again, takes out his Zippo, and lights the end. Sylvia declines the offer of the gold clip and watches Hyman take a series of little sucks at it. She turns and looks out over the dark and fog-encased expanse of golf course between her and the bay, then rolls down her window and sticks her head out into the damp air, listening to the mournful blast of the foghorns. Sylvia once took a bus up here on a clear day and decided, despite not having been in any other major city, that she'd discovered the world's most beautiful urban view—the wide blue bay, the purposeful brown hills jutting up on the other side, the bridge, poised in its balletic majesty, a perfect form, both intimate and grand. Look at it long enough, it seemed to Sylvia, and you might decide to make something of your life. Strange to think that so many people have chosen it as the place to end their lives. This evening with Hy, the damp fog fully obscures the Golden Gate.

"Shall we have a look at *The Thinker?*" Hy asks.

"I suppose we should."

Rodin's enormous sculpture sits at the entrance of the museum. A holy man, of sorts, a Western Buddha.

Once they pay their respects, Hyman says, "Can you imagine the size of the wang on that guy? I mean if it were sculpted to scale."

"I suppose it would be a wee bit bigger than yours, Hy."

"Indubitably."

They sit on the shallow step at the base of *The Thinker*'s pedestal.

"I come out here to think sometimes," Hy says. "Perfect spot. This big lug is the ideal company. Thinking man. Trouble is, I never get much of my own thinking in. He does enough thinking for the both of us."

Sylvia glances over at Hy and notices that his zipper is wide open. She can see the pink head of his penis.

"Zip up your fly, Hyman."

"Ah, Sylvia, I thought you could give me a little help. I don't get much pleasure."

"Right now!" Sylvia insists.

"All right, I'm sorry," Hy says, zipping up. He has an ugly spasm of coughing and pulls out his handkerchief to spit.

Sylvia looks out toward the bay and listens to the moan of the foghorns. Everybody wants something that they can't have from some-body else. Sylvia watches Hyman straighten his string tie and shove his handkerchief back into his hip pocket. What does she long for? Inez Roseman, of course. Inez, undressed, legs open, as majestic as the hidden bridge. When Sylvia gets home, she'll be free to think about Inez to her heart's desire.

betrayal

O N the appointed morning, Sylvia puts on a Horace Silver recording
that Hy gave her. The bluesy piano with the good beat propels her to
the kitchen nook to poach herself a couple of eggs. But in her distraction,
she drops an egg on the floor and enjoys watching it splatter. What is
happening to her? In the last week, she's imagined Inez Roseman's voice,
warm-toned yet glazed with irony, and now, on her knees wiping up the
spilled egg, she hears Inez say: *I love you, Sylvia. Sylvia, I love you.*

A half hour later, Sylvia buzzes Inez in through the outer door and
steps out to the landing. She's too anxious to wait for the knock on her
apartment door. She wants to see Inez climbing the steps, rising directly
into her apartment, into her heart.

"Hello," she calls down the stairwell, catching the first sight of the
lovely blond head. "How are you?"

"Just fine."

On the landing, they greet each other with kisses like a couple of
French women. Once inside, Inez folds her scarf into a coat pocket and
peels off the coat that Sylvia quickly takes. She brushes the hair out of
her eyes. Sylvia can do nothing for a moment but admire Inez as she
stands straight and tall in a black skirt and white blouse.

Inez takes a place on the love seat. She finds pleasure in Sylvia's
awkwardness, which she hasn't witnessed in such bloom since the first
time Sylvia came to her house for that interview.

Barefoot, Sylvia stumbles over the striped throw rug on her way to
the hi-fi, and yet she's lovely, dressed in a Chinese red skirt and a knit
top. The skirt is something special, a rayon that clings to her legs nicely.
She wears lipstick today, a red to match the skirt.

Sylvia puts on Satie's Gnossiennes and fumbles with the arm of the
hi-fi. The nasty needle bounces once and again before screeching across
the record. "Sorry," she says.

"It's all right." Inez closes her eyes and imagines a dance to go with the single-note pointillism of the Satie. When she opens her eyes, Sylvia is studying her.

"Is this music too simple for you, Inez?"

"No, I love Satie."

"I thought you might find it too elementary, but those slow notes— he's just my speed. I can imagine the way they must have rolled out of his brain."

"That's more than I can say." Inez smiles at Sylvia and takes a quick look around the apartment. Everything has been tidied up. A huge bouquet of purple mums stands in a tin vase beside the window.

"Oh, those mums."

"I tried to find them in the same color as your concert dress, but this was as close as I could get."

"They're beautiful." In the last week, as she'd taken time from the symphony to sit with her father-in-law, the urge to end her life was replaced by a steady longing for Sylvia. Inez woke each morning thinking about Sylvia. With Jake still asleep in the bed beside her, Inez pictured Sylvia rubbing sleep out of her eyes, climbing naked out of her small bed, flinching at the first chill of day. She saw Sylvia, still naked, lighting a pair of candle stubs that rose from drip-covered Chianti bottles. Sylvia, throwing on a man's broadcloth shirt in a lovely French blue. She saw Sylvia, her shirt unbuttoned, peeking out her front window at the cable-car street. Who are you looking for, sweet girl? Is it me?

And then there was the queer, gnawing twist in her belly that told Inez that she was hungry. Her long-lost appetite had returned. She couldn't remember waking with this feeling since she was a teenager. Not even when she was pregnant, eating, as they say, for two. In the last week, after she'd fed Jake and the kids their cereal and sent them out into the day, she'd fried up bacon and eggs for herself, and sopped it up with buttered French bread. If that wasn't enough, she'd make a fruit salad and have it in a tall parfait glass with yogurt.

Just as this extraordinary appetite surfaced, the dreaded heaviness, present nearly every morning since Joey's birth, had disappeared. Good riddance to the cloying parchment, this insidious curse that had made palpable her inability to feel anything save her separation from the world. She'd tried once to explain the fearsome parchment to her doctor and realized that it was like trying to explain madness or the presence of a ghost in the house. That was a treacherous part of the burden: if nobody could see it, nobody would believe it. Perhaps she had finally shed the extra skin.

"You look happy, Inez."

"Happy?" It's a funny idea, and she's certainly not ready to agree to it.

"I told my psychiatrist about you," Sylvia says.

"Should I be flattered?"

"Yes, I'd like you to be flattered." Sylvia swings her head up and strikes a silly pose to deflect the tension. Her eyes pop open, her mouth, which Inez had never realized was so elastic, stretches wide like a mime's. But before Inez can laugh at her, or laugh with her, or laugh at all, Sylvia lets her face fall back into itself. She holds herself there, without attitude or defense, and becomes, it seems to Inez, the loveliest of creatures, calm and present in a way that you'd not have expected possible of the crumb-cake-eating reporter. Suddenly, there is a gravity to the moment, in which each of them is obliged to meet the other's presence, without irony. Inez has lived for so long at an unhappy slant, she wonders if she can summon the optimism to stand fearless and straight. She worries that Sylvia expects more of her than she has to offer. Even the new Inez, with appetite and longing, will likely fall short. *There's less here than meets the eye*, a phrase Jake uses to describe politicians he doesn't like. When she first heard the phrase she thought it described her as well as anything. Who was she anyway? A woman with enough looks and talent to dazzle the lay public, but someone whose evolution as an adult has been idled by fear. Beware, Sylvia the reporter, there may be less here than meets the eye.

There's nothing to do but to bow her head. Sylvia steps toward her and rubs her cheek against Inez's high cheekbone like a cat, then kisses the corners of Inez's mouth. None of it matters, whoever she is, whoever Sylvia is. Inez thinks of the reporter's small bed, and how much she wants to be taken there.

"So what about the psychiatrist? What did you tell him?" Inez asks, trying to regain a sense of balance.

"I told him everything."

Inez wonders what everything is to Sylvia.

"He asked if you made me happy."

"He asked that?"

"Yes." Sylvia traces the line of Inez's brow with her baby finger. "I told him that happy wasn't a good enough word for it. I said that we were just getting to know each other and that there probably wasn't any future in it. He wanted to know why I felt that way. 'Because she's a married woman,' I said, 'with kids and a nice house and a great career.' He wondered how that made me feel."

"How what made you feel?" Inez says and takes hold of Sylvia's hand.

"The questionable future part. I said, 'Well, nothing's certain, is it?' He liked my saying that. He wondered how I felt about . . . about loving a woman. And you know what I did? I turned the question on him." Sylvia lets go of Inez's hand and walks toward the kitchen counter. "I'm going to slice up an orange. I have a sudden craving. Would you like some?"

"No, thank you," says Inez, dazzled by Sylvia's energy. Inez stands slowly and leans against the wall. She watches Sylvia take a large navel orange from the fruit basket and cut it into sections. The fragrance is so sweet and sharp it seems as if it's always been a part of the room.

"Anyway, I said, 'Dr. Rosconini, how do you feel about me and a woman?'"

"You didn't," Inez says, a little breathless.

"Sure I did. It made him laugh." Sylvia strips the peel from a section of orange and puts the fruit in her mouth. "Then he said what you'd expect. 'It doesn't matter how *I* feel about it, Sylvia.' 'But how *do* you feel?' I said. You know how persistent I can be, Inez. 'I don't feel one way or another,' he said. 'Liar,' I said."

"You called your psychiatrist a liar?"

"Yes, I did. And he wasn't angry with me." Sylvia bites into another section of orange. "He wants me to stand up for myself, even if it's against him."

"Sounds like you're lucky to have him."

"I think so. Now that I'm paying him, he costs me fifteen dollars a week."

"That's not so terrible."

"Well, that's through my Kaiser plan. I figured it out once—it's about the same as I spend on a week's worth of groceries. I go in for a lot of luxuries, you see. European chocolates. French lamb chops. I'm hopeless. I have no savings. Sometimes while I'm sitting in Dr. Rosconini's office and I have little to say, I think, 'There goes a cantaloupe. Say good-bye to a wedge of Camembert, a little wheel of Bucheron.'"

Inez can't keep herself from grinning. She wants Sylvia to go on with her story. Any story. She puts a hand over her mouth, a gesture, hopeless perhaps, for restraining her rapture.

"But Dr. Rosconini keeps me from going crazy. You don't approve, do you?"

"It's none of my business."

"At a certain point, everything becomes your business."

"I don't know about that."

"I'm your business, right now."

"Are you?" Inez lifts two fingers to her lips.

"But I can see that you're frightened by this business."

"I don't know."

"I'm frightened I'll scare you away."

"I don't scare so easily," Inez says.

"You sure about that?"

"No, I'm not sure about anything." Inez begins to pace the room. "Tell me something . . . I'm curious how you have so much time off from your job. Don't you ever have to be at the newspaper?"

Sylvia doesn't seem to appreciate the question. "I work a lot at night, but I'm going in this afternoon."

"I've been wondering if you're an impostor," Inez says, with a sideways grin.

"Have you?"

Inez is silent.

"What if I told you I am?"

"You are what?"

"What if I told you that I don't work at the *Chronicle*?"

Inez backs toward the door. She'd like to scoop out a deep breath, but all she can manage is a trail of shallow gasps. "Is that what you're telling me?"

"Let's say I am."

"Then who are you?"

"I'm sorry."

"Sorry?!"

"I didn't mean to trick you."

"You're not a reporter?"

"I thought you knew."

Inez stares at Sylvia, the supposed reporter. An impostor. She knew it. Who ever heard of a barefoot reporter, a bohemian journalist in a clingy red skirt? Sylvia, whoever she is, has begun to cry, her eyes brimming as if she were the one who'd been betrayed. Inez looks at the tin vase of mums and wants to knock it over, to make a flood, any kind of mess. She can practically see the orphaned purple mums scattered across the floor.

Instead, she shouts, "If you're not a reporter, why did you come to my door? Why did you do that? Who the hell are you? What's your name? Tell me your name. Is Sylvia even your name?"

"Yes," Sylvia says, looking at the floor. "It's my name. I'm sorry." She rubs her eyes. "I wanted to get to know you. I didn't think I'd have a chance."

Inez stands by the door, indignant, her cheeks flushed, her hands balled into fists.

"You can leave if you want."

"I know what I can do. You don't have to tell me that. I don't know why I'm still here."

Sylvia backs away a step. Her mouth opens, but it takes a moment for her to speak. "I saw you at the symphony. The way you came onstage. I got excited just watching you walk to your seat. I fell in love with you before I even knew your name. Before I even understood how I felt." When Inez doesn't respond, Sylvia says again, "You can leave."

"Is that what you want me to do? Game's over. Leave. Just pretend it didn't happen."

Sylvia is silent.

Inez steps toward the impostor. She'd like to slap her across the face but stops an arm's length away. "Do you do this kind of thing all the time?"

"Never."

"Just me, huh? How did I get so lucky?"

More than anything, Sylvia wants to take Inez in her arms. She doesn't dare. Inez has a blank expression on her face, as if paralyzed with fury. Sylvia reaches out toward the violinist and watches her flinch. Sylvia takes Inez's hand and holds it gently, hoping to calm her. Slowly, lightly, she drags her fingers along the soft skin of Inez's steely forearm, the iridescent skin seeming to light up as Sylvia's fingers slide up along the swell of Inez's bicep, to her shoulder, where Inez closes her eyes and tilts her head as if to hear better as Sylvia traces the delicate curve of the violinist's ear. Sylvia presses her lips to Inez's sweet lobe and exhales lightly, knowing how Inez likes that. "Could you ever want me as much as I want you?" she whispers.

"I don't know who you are," says Inez, disconsolate.

"I'll tell you."

"Do you expect me to believe anything you say?"

"I can hope so. Please, Inez."

"Why should I?" The truth is she doesn't care who Sylvia is. Let her be whoever she wants.

Sylvia's notion is to keep things going. It's an idea she learned in college music classes: the music is always going forward. If you make an error during the performance, it's folly to go back and correct it. Your reception may pivot more on illusion than competence. Never pause in midperformance to question your competence. "Will you have a glass of wine? I know it's still morning, but—a cup of plum wine and I'll tell you who I am."

"All right."

"It's sweet, I just want to warn you. I know it's not very sophisticated to like sweet things, but once in a while I like them."

It seems to Inez that the girl is afraid to stop talking, as if whatever future the two of them have together depends on her crazy will, on not leaving even the smallest space for common sense to seep through.

"Sometimes I'll go into Simon Brothers and splurge on a box of white chocolate seashells from Jacali in Belgium; other times I'm happy with an Almond Joy or a Snickers. I like to let myself enjoy things that aren't sophisticated. Do you want to know my one and only goal in life?"

Inez nods, spellbound, despite herself, by the mad impostor.

"To become so sophisticated that I don't have to worry about being sophisticated."

IN the kitchen nook, Sylvia feels as if she'd like to vomit. Go out like a dog does and eat grass in the backyard. Leave a neat pile of everything that she can't digest, of who she is, of who she is not, and say to Inez, *This is me; I am what you see.* She hears Inez take a few steps in the other room. Sylvia feels the stabbing loss of Inez already. Of course she'll leave. But then she hears the staticky beginning of the needle on the record—side B of the Satie. Inez likes to hear both sides.

Sylvia feels a momentary nostalgia for the days when life happened to people out her window. But she wasn't watching anymore. Now that her impersonation as a reporter has been exposed, she has the far more difficult task of performing as herself. She may as well see it through. Plum wine, a treat from the Orient, is all that the moment calls for.

Sylvia returns to the living room with a pair of pinch cups and the bottle of plum wine. After filling Inez's cup she watches her take the first sip worriedly. "Too sweet?"

"No. I like it," Inez says, stretching out her neck as if she has a crick in it. "Listen, I don't want to know anything about you."

"Nothing?"

"No. I wouldn't believe you anyway."

Inez hums along with the Satie softly. Clearly, the violinist wants her to pay for her crime, but she hasn't quite figured out the right punishment. Sex is sitting on the shelf above them.

"I have a gift for you," Sylvia says.

Inez looks up. "Who's the gift from? You, or the person who you were?"

"I think you're beginning to enjoy this." Sylvia reaches under the love seat for the wrapped box and places it on Inez's lap. "Read the card. It's got your name on it. You're still Inez, aren't you?"

"Ha, ha."

Sylvia remembers crafting the brief note—*A string of beauties for beautiful Inez*—which the stoic violinist puts aside as soon as she reads it.

"Open it," says Sylvia. "It won't bite you."

When Inez finally unwraps the package, she is astonished by the string of bright-colored beads, ceramic hunks, some striped, some spotted, sized like the flanges of a large finger.

"They're African trade beads. Venetian." She'd found them in a shop on Union Street.

"I can't accept these."

"Why?"

"They're too much, especially from somebody that I don't know."

"Somebody you're beginning to know. Try them on. You'll have to have them restrung—they're just on a length of knotted hemp—but you can put them on for right now."

Inez looks down at the beads and slips them gingerly over her head.

"They'd look better with your blouse off."

"What are you talking about?"

"It's the best way to judge their beauty. Then you can decide whether you want them or not."

"Oh, please."

"You know it's true," says Sylvia, unbuttoning Inez's blouse.

ONCE Sylvia has helped Inez out of her clothes she can tell Inez enjoys the weight of the smooth beads against her breasts. Sylvia strokes Inez's nipples, smiling as Inez moans faintly, her nipples tightening with pleasure. Sylvia takes one of them and then the other into her mouth, tonguing them dreamily.

AFTER they make love, Sylvia spoons Inez and strokes her breasts, the beads, the breasts. "You liked that, didn't you?"

"Yes," Inez says.

"You still haven't really let yourself go. Have you had . . . an orgasm with me?"

Inez presses her buttocks against Sylvia. "I almost had an orgasm."

"Aren't you angry with me anymore? I want you to be angry with me."

Without thinking, Inez turns and takes hold of the little bells of Sylvia's breasts and gently squeezes the nipples. She slides down in the bed so that she can get one of Sylvia's broad, berry nipples into her mouth and bites down on it hard.

"Ow, you're hurting me."

"You want me to hurt you, don't you?"

"Not really."

Sylvia takes Inez's right hand and places it between her legs. Sylvia is wet. She presses Inez's fingers against her clitoris in a circular motion, rubbing against Inez until her breathing quickens. Inez slips her index finger inside Sylvia and sends it deep. Then she adds her middle finger, and Sylvia gasps. The smell of Sylvia bursts into the room and hovers over them like a pungent veil. *Screw me*, Sylvia says, and Inez is surprised to hear the phrase. *Screw me, Inez.* Inez shoves in another finger. *Screw me, screw me.* Sylvia climbs atop her. *Screw me.* She wants to shut Sylvia up and sticks a few fingers from her other hand in Sylvia's mouth. Sylvia sucks on them furiously. Then Inez finds a rhythm, her fingers deep inside Sylvia, the walls of Sylvia a spasm around Inez's hand. *Ohhhhh*, Sylvia calls, finally. Inez keeps her eyes closed. She doesn't want to see Sylvia's rapture but can feel Sylvia's orgasm shudder through her fingers. Inez's wrist flutters as if it's gone spastic. Now Inez rubs herself against Sylvia's pubic bone. It doesn't take long.

"Close your eyes," Inez says.

"Why?"

"Close your eyes."

Inez doesn't want Sylvia to see her.

"It's all right," she says.

"Close them." Inez bites down on her lower lip and breathes hard through her nostrils.

Sylvia cups her face in her hands. "Really, it's all right."

Her mouth open just wide enough for a word, Inez whispers: *Bitch*. Then, breathless, she is scaling up the hilltop. That's how she thinks of it—as a hilltop. How many times has she climbed it? Her own Everest. She's rarely made it to the summit. She opens her mouth to gasp. The air is thinner. Oh. Oh. Oh, no. Something leaps out of her throat. A winding shriek. Sylvia, or whoever the hell she is, purrs *Good, good, good*, as Inez settles back into her arms.

AFTERWARD, they prop themselves up with pillows, just like she and Jake sometimes do after sex. Jake usually falls asleep for a few minutes. When he wakes up, he asks if she'd mind the television. He likes to watch *The Tonight Show*. She's always hated having the television in their bedroom. She doesn't want to share her bedroom with Jack Parr and Zsa Zsa Gabor, the procession of personalities. She hates seeing her husband chuckle along with the Alka-Seltzer commercials.

Sylvia doesn't have a television in her bedroom, nor does she fall asleep. Inez is pleased how long they can remain together in each other's arms, without saying a word. How long can they remain suspended like this? Inez puts a finger on Sylvia's lips.

Sylvia smiles at her. "Don't worry, I can be whoever you want me to be."

new happiness

I N the end, Inez demands that Sylvia reveal everything about herself. Inez makes the terms clear—she wants a background sketch bursting with particulars or Sylvia will never see her again. She has Sylvia jot it all down—like a criminal forced to write her confession. Even Dr. Rosconini, the wonderful psychiatrist, turns out to be a fiction. Sylvia scribbles a 250-word portrait of her mother. She crafts a bibliography of vocabulary books she and her mother used, and she names all of her piano teachers in Sacramento. She coughs up phone numbers, addresses, three generations of maiden names. Although it is useless information in a practical sense—the whole thing nothing more than another charming ruse on Sylvia's part—the transaction changes the terms of their relationship.

At the ripe age of forty, Inez hadn't expected to become a parole officer. Trained as a concert violinist, noted for her beauty and fidelity, for overlooking her husband's indiscretions, for treating her children with kindness and trust rather than heavy discipline, she hadn't expected to demand such exacting behavior from another individual. Neither had she expected, at midlife, as she was finalizing a plan to take her own life, to fall head over heels for a woman, a charlatan reporter. Does she really think that she can forestall the inevitable by rooting out the so-called truth and pursuing a relationship with a woman who's already tricked her, a creature who claims to have a "crush" on her?

On Saturday, Inez strolls unannounced into the piano showroom at Myerson's. The strains of "Bye Bye Blackbird," a burst of rhapsodic, dance hall piano, hit her as soon as she steps through the Geary Street door. She is in no hurry to identify the pianist, who is obscured by a cluster of young girls in party dresses crowded around the mahogany baby grand. A tall, tweedy-suited woman, with a huge yellow vinyl purse, stands apart from the girls, keeping a watchful eye. The woman's purse is large enough to swallow Jake's Book of the Month Club edition of *The Divine Comedy*, a volume that belongs no more in the yellow vinyl purse than on Jake's bedside table, where he insists on keeping it, because one of these nights he may just read it.

Inez plants herself across the carpeted showroom to take in the scene. Of course it's Sylvia at the piano; Inez recognizes the right hand as it makes its showy leaps. The piano playing is quite competent. If one happened to have a feeling for show tunes, a customer walking in from the street might be dazzled by the exhibition. Surely, that's the point—to dazzle the unsuspecting. Now, as Sylvia chords through her final good-byes to the blackbird, a gangly man, a dressed-up beatnik in a blue double-breasted suit and a string tie, of all things, sidles up to the woman who could smuggle Dante in her yellow purse.

Inez is trying to decide if there's something illicit about the man offering the woman a cigarette. The woman lowers her eyes, and the man in the blue suit sparks a small flame with his Zippo. Meanwhile, Sylvia, who's dressed simply in a cream-colored shift with a delectable ballet neck, turns to talk to the girls. They adore her. Inez adores her, but she's decided this morning to stay in the shadows.

Sylvia hoists the smallest of the three girls onto her lap and shows her how to tinkle her baby paw up a C scale. The other girls pester the pianist for a chance at the instrument. Their mother stands with her hands on her hips and watches the scene at the piano. The way she bites on the filter of her cigarette and inhales for all she's worth reminds Inez of Susan Hayward in one of her death-row scenes in *I Want to Live.* The man in the blue suit shifts his weight from one foot to the other and offers his kindliest rogue smile. He's doing his damnedest, Inez realizes, to sell the woman a piano. Lifting the girl off her lap, Sylvia spots Inez standing by the sheet music and mouths her name, the tip of Sylvia's tongue settling between her teeth for the long "Z" of Inez. A negotiation's begun for the purchase of a piano. The woman unbuttons the jacket of her tweed suit to expose her white blouse. She wants the sales-man to know that her breasts are good-sized, as if that will factor into the final price. The man in the blue suit nods, it seems, in recognition. All in a day's work. Although the girls are clamoring for Sylvia's atten-tion, she keeps her gaze fixed on Inez, who, in the splendor of the moment, backs away, swallowing the final vowel of her lover's name after she's mouthed it.

ON Thursday, after her matinee concert, Inez decides that she'll visit Sylvia that evening in another of her worlds. Late in the afternoon, her children wander into the kitchen making noises about dinner. Inez is seated at the kitchen table, sipping a massive gimlet from a San Francisco 49er tumbler. All the other glassware is in the dishwasher. She needs to start a jelly glass collection like Sylvia's. Either that, or buy some new glasses. Anna has been breaking them. Every time Anna empties the dishwasher she seems to break another glass. Clearly, she's doing it on purpose. It seems a strange way for a thirteen-year-old girl to seek attention.

"What do you want for dinner?" Inez asks. It's been a warm October day. Earthquake weather, as people are fond of saying. "We hardly have anything in the house."

"How about a tuna casserole?" Joey says, naming his favorite food—his pathetic idea of a wholesome, home-cooked meal, but one he knows he can't ask for often as his mother doesn't care for tuna.

Inez turns toward her daughter. "What do you think about that, Anna?"

"Okay with me."

Although her appetite is the best it's been in years, Inez still cannot abide the notion of tuna. It's hard to say what she despises most: the smell of the open can or the too-rich odor of the baked-in-Pyrex casserole, featuring Uncle Ben's rice and Campbell's cream of celery soup. No one else in her family seems to mind the smell of tuna, which lingers in the drain even if she rinses away the tiny scraps of fish and runs the disposal with sucked-out lemon halves. Inez takes a final swig of her gimlet and thinks to hand the 49er glass to Anna to see what she'll do with it. Toss it across the room for all I care, girl. Instead Inez puts the glass down and decides that once she distracts the kids she'll pour in another jigger of gin and a splash of lime juice.

"Will you guys help me prepare it? I have to go out tonight."

"Where are you going?" Joey asks.

Inez doesn't bother to answer.

"Are you going with Daddy?"

"No, I have an unexpected rehearsal. Will you help me, Joe?"

"Sure. Whatcha want me to do?"

"There's a couple of fresh loaves of sourdough in the bin. Will you slice one and get the butter out?" Suddenly, she's ravenous. Her mighty appetite is coming home to roost.

Going through a loaf of sourdough with Joey is among her happiest times in the house on Thirty-ninth Avenue. There have been times when bread is the only thing she'll eat for days. Sometimes Anna will join them for the simple feast, but Anna doesn't approach a loaf with the same fervor. To ensure that both Anna and Joey will spend a little time with her in the kitchen, Inez will splurge occasionally on a little smoked salmon, which they lay with cream cheese atop slices of French bread. Joey was born with a hard heel of bread in his mouth. Inez gave him crusts of bread to teethe on. Jake was afraid baby Joey would choke on the bread. Nonsense, she said. The real issue was that Jake didn't trust her with Joey, although he'd never come out and say that. She'd been a bad mother, she wouldn't argue that point, but she'd never set out to purposely harm her son.

When he was five, Inez showed her son how to hold a serrated knife and safely slice a loaf of French bread. Once, while Joey was handling the bread knife, Jake hollered at her: "Don't let him play with that knife." "He's not playing," she answered.

Some Thursdays after matinees, she'll drive by Larabaru Bakery on Sixth and Balboa and buy a couple of afternoon loaves, still cooling on the racks outside, and when Joey gets home from school, they'll take turns hacking away at a loaf. Joey sits up on the kitchen counter and, between slices of bread, tells his mother more about his day than Anna has told cumulatively over eight years of school.

"You want to do the tuna recipe," Anna asks, "from the dummy cookbook?"

"Sure, unless you want to find another," Inez says and bites into her first thick slice of buttered sourdough.

"No, let's stick with the dummy." Anna pulls the red plaid *Better Homes and Gardens* cookbook off the shelf.

In the last year, Inez has led Anna through the "Easy Meals" section. Together they've mastered "Skillet Spaghetti," "Fillets Elegante," "Hurry Seafood Curry," and "Speedy Chop Suey," not to mention the tuna casserole. It seems a pathetic legacy to leave a child, but maybe Anna can build on it. Inez considers the sum of what she learned at home about cooking: how to boil an egg. Her sister had done all the cooking. Anytime Inez showed any interest in helping to prepare a dish, Bibi said, "Your job is to practice. I'll do the cooking."

Now, thirty years later, her daughter digs through the pantry shelves for the Star-Kist. Inez anticipates the smell of tuna before a single can is located. She takes another slice of bread and spreads it with as much sweet butter as is decent.

"Should we try something a little more complicated tonight, Anna?"

"Like what?"

At the far counter, Joey starts a chant: "Tuna, tuna, tuna."

Inez chews on her bread—she could finish the whole loaf herself—and pours another shot of gin into the 49er glass, tinting it with a splash of lime juice.

"Why don't you bring the dummy cookbook over here, Anna? And, Joey, give me another slice."

"Wow, Mom, you'd be good in a pie-eating contest." Joey slides the loaf from Larabaru completely out of its sleeve and starts to wield the bread knife as if he were Zorro.

"You be careful with that thing."

"I'm real careful," Joey says. "How many more do you want?"

"Let's stick to one at a time."

After plucking a couple of Star-Kists out of the stack of cans and setting them on the counter, Anna tilts her head sideways, assuming a classic posture of teenage indifference. She strolls toward Inez with the cookbook.

AS Anna aligns the first can of Star-Kist with the blade of the can opener, Inez stuffs another slice of buttered bread in her mouth as if a glut of sourdough, in all its dark and twisting savoriness, might overwhelm her olfactory sensitivity. It seems to work. Either that, or not even the smell of tuna bothers her anymore. With a crust of bread half in and half out of her mouth, she steers her mind from tuna to lovely Sylvia, whom she'd once thought homely. Sylvia, stuffing her mouth with crumb cake. Sylvia, the impostor.

WHEN Jake steps in the front door, neither whistling nor calling hello to the house, but hauling his heavy briefcase like a man who believes his work is never done, Inez surprises him with a whiskey sour, in a glass from the set meant for company.

"Thank you." Jake grabs the drink as soon as he's parked his briefcase by the front door. "Aren't you having one?"

"No, I've already had a gimlet."

"Have another."

"I already have."

"Good for you."

"Yes, but not exactly wise—I have an unexpected rehearsal tonight."

"What are you talking about?"

"You know, Eugene Ormandy is guest conducting this week."

Jake gives her a skeptical look. "Why didn't you let me know?"

"It just came up this morning. Maestro Ormandy isn't very pleased with 'the condition of this orchestra.'"

"You could have called," says Jake, glaring at her.

"I didn't think it would matter to you one way or the other."

Jake shrugs. She follows him into the living room and watches him collapse onto the sofa with his drink.

"You look tired, Jake."

He knocks a cigarette loose from his pack, kicks off his shoes, and puts his feet up on the coffee table. "I need to talk with you about something."

"I can't now, Jake."

Jake takes a large gulp of his drink.

"I'm going to be late if I don't run."

"You're making this up," he says, angry.

Inez grabs hold of her violin case and faces her husband with a calm, steady look. "I'm not in the habit of lying to you, Jake." She might have a future as an impostor herself.

As she shifts out of her pose, Jake says, "We've gotta do something about the old man."

Inez thinks about her father-in-law, the reports she's heard of his steady recovery in the past couple of weeks—all but his old bow arm functional. "I can't talk about that now. Are you hungry? Anna's making up a tuna casserole."

"Cat food," Jake says and blows a stream of smoke in Inez's direction.

"It's Joey's favorite."

Jake stands and begins to pace. "He has to leave the hospital next week."

"What do you mean? The man had a stroke."

"Yes, and now he's getting around in a wheelchair. He's beginning to walk with a crutch. He's cursing anybody who gets in his way. Throwing food. They won't keep him after next week."

Inez realizes that she hasn't seen Isaac since the day he was hospitalized. She's done her best to forget he exists, which has been her basic strategy toward Isaac for years.

"We have to move him somewhere," Jake says.

"Then move him."

"I can't find a place that will take him. There are waiting lists."

Inez stands, impatient. "I told you I can't talk about this now."

"Where are you going?"

"To a rehearsal. Are you deaf?"

Jake shakes his head. "You never have rehearsals in the evening."

"We never have Gene Ormandy."

Jake snuffs his cigarette and glares at Inez. "How many gimlets have you had?"

"Just two."

"Two gimlets before rehearsal. Can you drive?"

"Of course I can drive."

"Be careful."

"I'm always careful."

INEZ, fortified by three oversized gimlets, quaffed from a football glass, drives very slowly to The Little Sweden. On her way to the restaurant, the radio is playing, of all things, the overture to Stravinsky's Petroushka. Does Sylvia now have control of the airwaves? Apparently not, as a sudden news bulletin interrupts the Stravinsky. President Kennedy is speaking to the nation. She likes the sound of his voice, how, even with the absurd accent and patrician diction, he conveys a certain intimacy as he speaks to the masses. But the man seems strangely tense today. Leave one tense man at home and pick up another on the radio. She'd rather hear the rest of the Stravinsky. She switches off the radio and hums the charming, neoclassic theme from Petroushka. The only difficulty with driving after drinking three 49er gimlets is that she'd like to close her eyes as she hums the Stravinsky and imagine the original dancers from the Ballet Russes. Did Nijinsky dance with them at the premiere? She imagines the dancers prancing about the stage in feathery blue and reddish costumes, appearing as odd as creatures dropped from the moon. Why hadn't she been a dancer?

Even though she's tipsy, the fifteen steps down to The Little Sweden are familiar. Had she come here with Jake and the kids? Her father? She spots Sylvia as soon as she steps into the cellar restaurant. It's Thursday evening, and Sylvia, fetching in the black-and-white getup of a Swedish maid, is, again, right where she said she'd be. She offers her puckish shrug at the sight of Inez and twirls around in a happy circle with three dirty plates balanced in her arms. Not exactly the Ballet Russes, but surely a sight for sore eyes. Inez is soon seated in Sylvia's section. She remembers sitting at a similar table with Jake, her father, and Bibi. A dozen years ago now? Little Anna at home with a babysitter. Was that the night she realized her father was terminally sad, sitting over his plate of Swedish dumplings, the night she understood that Bibi, more than being a little odd, might be going out of her mind?

Sylvia comes over to the table and curtsies deeply. It is a lovely gesture, and Inez is tempted to ask her to do it again. Instead, Inez hums the opening notes of "Bye Bye Blackbird."

"I was impressed with your piano playing, Sylvia."

"Don't embarrass me."

"You're multitalented."

Sylvia blinks her eyes, coquettishly. "Do you think so?"

"Absolutely."

"Maybe I should become a journalist and interview you? You're a famous violinist, aren't you?"

"Fame is fleeting."

"Don't be glib."

"It is. Just like love."

"It doesn't have to be that way," Sylvia says, holding Inez's attention with a steady gaze.

"How would you know?"

"I'm not talking about fame," Sylvia says, folding her arms in front of her. "I don't know anything about that."

"But you're an expert on love?"

"I know some things."

Inez offers the Swedish maid a coy smile. "You're a big talker. It's all those vocabulary words."

"If you only knew. What if I called you my *amorósa*, Inez?"

"I might not have any recourse."

Sylvia bends down close to Inez and whispers, "Meaning both my lover and my glass of sweet oloroso sherry."

"You're making that up, Sylvia."

"Not a word of it." Sylvia stands up straight. "Shall I bring you an aperitif, or do you already have an appetite?"

"Actually, I'm half stuffed with bread. My secret addiction. But what do you recommend?"

"Is this your first time to The Little Sweden?" Sylvia asks primly, the proper waitress.

"No, I believe I've been here before."

"Fine, then you know that we're a Swedish smorgasbord. You fill your plate with whatever you like. We can also grill a nice piece of fish for you, if you'd like."

"Yes, and what do you recommend?"

The cook rings a bell. Sylvia turns an eye toward the kitchen and then back to Inez. "I like the shrimp and the hard cheeses. The dumplings are always good. You might care for some of the salads and the cardamom cake. It reminds me of a wonderful crumb cake I once had." The cook's bell rings again. "I'll be back; somebody's order of trout is up."

Despite all the bread, Inez does have an appetite. Perhaps she'll have a few dumplings. Now she remembers the night with Jake, her father, and Bibi. The old Swede at The Little Sweden. Her father's loneliness loomed large that night. He had been a widower for years. She'd never realized how lonely he was. He sat with a plate of dumplings that he barely touched. Jake kept encouraging him to get more food. "Max, get another plate, something you like better—the creamed herring, or the meatballs in lingonberry sauce. The shrimp."

Her father shook his head and looked down at his dumplings. "This," he said, "is sufficient."

"Papa knows what's good for him," her sister said.

Bibi, her father's caretaker, appeared to need somebody to look after her. In the last year Bibi had started acting strange. Always a paragon of hygiene, Bibi had stopped bathing regularly. Her hair was often dirty. Never a churchgoer, she began attending services daily. When Inez spoke with her father about these oddities, he said, "She's all right; leave her alone." Which is exactly what she did. Inez had a baby at home; she didn't need to worry about an eccentric sister.

That night long ago, Bibi, after eating a neat plate of salads and a few slices of hard cheese, took a ball of brown wool and a pair of knitting needles out of her sewing basket.

"What are you making, Bibi?" Jake asked her.

"A pair of socks."

"For your father?"

"No, he has plenty of socks. These," she said, "are for baby Jesus." Inez looked at her father's face then. His expression didn't change. Had he even heard Bibi?

A s a girl, Inez used to wade out into the ocean with her father. He loved to get out into the saltwater. That's how he referred to it. *Should we take*

a dip in the saltwater? The only times that she could picture her father
as a young man were when she saw him in the ocean. On those warm
Sundays, on fall days like this, warmer than most days during a San
Francisco summer, they'd leave the car in the shade by Sutro Park and
walk down to the beach with a sack full of sandwiches and a bag of towels. Her father seemed a different man from the one who worked all day
in his frame shop or drove her to violin lessons. *Shall we take a dip?* he'd
say. Once in a while, they'd go out farther than she could stand. One
time, wading out into the ocean, her father let go of her. He hadn't
meant to scare her, but there she was, bobbing in the saltwater beside
him. Instead of going down under the waves, she simply bobbed. It
seemed a kind of miracle. Her sister was standing on the shore. Bibi
wouldn't go into the ocean. She said it was too cold, too dirty. She said
that the jellyfish might bite you or the giant squid could turn you ink-
colored for the rest of your life. Inez and her father kept drifting farther
out into the ocean. Bibi started waving at them, becoming a little frantic,
and Inez—maybe she was ten years old—began to wonder how long
they could stay out there before they'd wrinkle up or turn blue, the
undertow pulling them under. It was as if she and her father had made a
tacit pact—a mutual understanding that they could just as easily give
themselves to the saltwater as not. She hasn't thought about that for a
long time—her father and her in the ocean.

INEZ helps herself to a frightfully large plate of food: the meatballs in
lingonberry sauce, chilled shrimp, a small hill of dumplings—the meal
her father couldn't be persuaded to partake of. She adds a healthy
wedge of Gouda, a thick slice of black bread, and a scoop of apple pudding that she has the strange desire to eat first. When Sylvia returns,
Inez asks for a glass of Wente Grey Riesling. The Riesling was her
father's wine. The man had the lovely habit of keeping a bottle on the
floor beside his right foot. A couple of times during the meal, he'd reach
down for the long-necked bottle, pull the cork, and refill his glass. A
small pleasure in a simple man's life. Did her father believe it unwhole-
some to have a bottle of wine on the table as he dined with his two
daughters? What had he wanted for his daughters? He never really said.

In a sense, Inez had been taken away from him. It's doubtful he had any desire to raise a prodigy. But here was a girl with extraordinary talent— or so he was told—and he had no choice but to let her be shaped by people who knew better. She used to wish that she'd never been given a violin. That she could have remained her father's younger daughter, a simpler creature, a happier soul.

Toward the end of his life, after he closed the shop, Inez would visit him some mornings. Her sister tended to leave the two of them alone. They'd sit quietly at the kitchen table. Once the pleasantries had been dispensed with, there was little to say to each other. Inez had come to think of her father as a man who'd lived his entire life with only a single idea passing through his head. Strangely, she never had a clue what the idea was. She reasoned that a man who'd immigrated from the Old World and fought all the little battles necessary to establish himself in this world was entitled to nurse a single, phantom idea for the rest of his life. Might Inez have been a simpler soul like this? A good mother, perhaps, a decent wife?

Her father would fold his hands in front of him when she visited and sit ruddy-faced and silent as a plum. Then he'd smile at her.

"What, Daddy?" she'd say.

"Nothing, I just like to look at you."

What did he see? What did he want to see? She found it hard to sit there and let herself be appreciated. In these moments she'd wonder about her mother. Being born motherless was her natural condition, and she accepted it as such, like somebody else might accept being born blind. But when her father smiled at her, she'd think how if she'd had a mother, then maybe she could have remained a child, at least for the duration of her childhood. What might it have been like to have had a childhood? If she wasn't so disciplined, she might be crying right now— a forty-year-old woman, tipsy on gimlets and Grey Riesling, sitting alone at her table at The Little Sweden—she'd break down and sob like a child.

But she has everything under control. She finishes her apple pudding. She's cleaned her plate. Wouldn't her father be proud of her? Her father. What would he make of his two daughters now? The older, good daughter who looked after him, the one who was lost after he died, wasting away now in a mental asylum, and the younger, talented one, the beauty, the one he sacrificed for, who hardly had time for him in the end . . . what exactly has become of her?

The other day, as she and Sylvia sat on the edge of Sylvia's small bed, feeding each other ripe figs, Sylvia licked her lips and said, "I like to think of all the terrible things they can call us. *Wanton, depraved.* I'm learning to accept my depravity, if that's what they want to call it. Who says there's only one way to be a woman, to be a human being?" Was she talking about more than just sex? Inez still isn't sure. The sex has been wonderful. Sex with a woman. If that's depravity, Inez can imagine a lifetime of it.

Now she watches her faux reporter stroll across the restaurant in her milkmaid outfit and thinks of Sylvia's girlish body with the small breasts, the nipples standing up like ripe berries. It's true, she wants Sylvia. And yet there's something else she wants—to be a good girl, to be her father's good girl, even if that was never part of his wish. Are her desires mutually exclusive? *I'm happy,* she'd tell her father, if she could. *I have a new happiness in my life.* He wouldn't ask for an explanation. He wouldn't call her depraved. She only wishes she could sit a moment longer with him at the kitchen table. She'd love nothing more than to have the light of his modest smile shine on her as she savored *her* single idea.

Sylvia is back at her table again. "Hungry, eh?"

Inez looks down at her plate, which is almost empty. "I'm being a pig."

"Hardly; you should see some of the people who come in here. Why don't you go back for another plate?"

"Are you trying to fatten me up?"

"Yes, I want you fat." Sylvia watches as Inez nibbles on a last shrimp. "I can get off early tonight since it's slow. Would you like to come up to my place?"

"Can't tonight."

"You sure?"

Inez nods, even though she'd love to be with Sylvia in her dark apartment. She imagines the candlelight. The two of them naked. The clang of the cable cars outside. And yet, Inez enjoys a certain satisfaction in controlling the pace of the affair.

Sylvia whispers, "But I want you," before carrying away Inez's dirty plate.

"I know," Inez says and is left at the table with her own ache.

the news

O N Tuesday morning Sylvia gets a call from Hy Myerson.
    When the phone rings, she's sitting by the window sipping Tang from her favorite embossed jelly jar, pleased not to have to join the morning parade of office workers.

"Hy, here. So what do you think, is the sky falling?"

"Huh?" In a flurry of syncopated clangs, a cable car brakes across the intersection. Sylvia watches a woman in a gray-and-white suit run half a block before leaping onto the car. It's a beautiful leap. What wonders take place outside her window every morning. She wishes she could share them with someone. Will she ever have the pleasure of waking up with Inez Roseman beside her?

"What, you haven't had your coffee yet?" Hyman says. "Take a look at the sky, is it falling, or do you see anything peculiar whizzing through it?"

"I don't know what you're talking about, Mr. Myerson."

"Don't mister me, this is Hyman speaking. So, what's the deal, are you jumping out of your skin with fear like everybody else?" Hy falls into a miserable cough and takes a long moment to recover.

"You're leaving me in the dark, Hy."

"What? You don't get the news in your part of the world? We're half a sneeze away from World War III. Castro and the Russians have missiles aimed at us. President Kennedy addressed the nation last night. He's playing chicken with the Russkies. It's straight out of the superhero comics. One guy shooting missiles at the other. Everybody's smoking cigars. What did I tell you? The whole world's gone phallic. If you ask me, it's nothing but smoke. But they're talking about grave danger, the gravest danger we've faced in years. What's the matter with you, Sylvia, don't you watch TV?"

"I don't have a TV."

"And this makes you a superior person?"

"That and other factors."

"Touché, darling. You know I agree with you. I'm your biggest fan, Sylvia. Always."

She thinks of Inez hearing the grave news, the way it must have registered in her lovely face, a hushed surprise, deepening the crinkles under her eyes. Did she get the news from her husband or the television? She imagines Inez sitting on the edge of her bed, unclasping her garter, the TV blaring, rolling down one of her nylons, and then, absentmindedly, remembering the other. Who did Inez think of first when she found out? Her children, of course.

"So are we in real danger, Hy?"

"My question to you. Is it a ruse, or the genuine article? I'll tell you this, if they haven't started already, people will be jumping off the bridges momentarily. You have plenty of sensationalists walking around out there—a city filled with second-rate thespians just looking for a reason to play dead forever. Myself, I don't subscribe to the party line. I take a jollier view. Come what may. Got the world in a jug . . . you know the drill. That's my position. What the hell are we going do about it anyway? So, with that noble sentiment in mind, I'm calling to ask for your company. You free for dinner tonight?"

Sylvia wonders about the chances of seeing Inez and realizes they aren't good. "Dinner?"

"Yes, dinner, supper, that meal that, at least in my country, generally comes after lunch." Hy dives into another wheezing cough. He is a geezer, but he's also her friend. She glances toward a few people on the street. Hyman's news has fractured the morning. Five minutes ago everybody on the street looked ordinary, now they've gained gravity, become stoic, the woman in the gray-and-white suit taking a leap of faith, each of them carrying on with their little bundle of fear.

"Look, I'm in the mood for something Italian," Hy says, recovering his voice. "How about you? What say we run over to North Beach, go to the Green Valley or the New Pisa? One of those joints that serve family style. We can be a family of two."

c rations

A T ten in the morning, Jake gets a call from Christine at work.
"Are you frightened?" she asks.

"Not especially. You?"

"Me neither. I think we're supposed to be. There must be something the matter with us. Ice in our veins. Stone hearts. Derek has already started to make preparations."

"What's the point?"

"The worse thing is to remain idle. Or so the dictum goes. I happen to think that idleness is the most wonderful thing ever invented, but it takes all kinds, Jake. Anyway, I'm calling to say you needn't bring food."

"Aren't we eating?"

"You sound horrified at the prospect of missing a meal."

"It's a ritual I'm attached to."

"There's food already here. If you have a Swiss Army knife handy, you might bring that."

"What's going on? Are we butchering a rabbit?"

"There will be no blood, Jake, if I can help it."

"Tell me what's going on?"

"You'll have to wait and see."

"You're a tease, Christine."

"Mmm-hmm."

"So, there's nothing I can bring?"

"Oh, what the hell, you might pick up a loaf of bread."

"All I have is a little penknife, Christine."

"We'll make do."

JAKE hands over his sack as soon as he's in the kitchen. "Here's the bread, and I also picked up a hunk of gooey cheese."

"You shouldn't have."

"I couldn't resist."

One of the virtues of their affair, Jake realizes as Christine leads him down through the massive basement, past the laundry room and the booming furnace, is how it seems to start fresh each time they see each other. There is a history, of course, but they rarely refer to it. The odd times, like the last visit, with Jake in shock after his run-in with the Studebaker Silver Hawk, recede, and all that remains of their history is a memory of pleasure.

"Where are you taking me?" Jake asks.

"You'll see."

Their affair always exists in the present tense. There's a lot to be said for that. It's like traveling, with little baggage, to one of those Scandinavian countries in the middle of the summer. With the sun shining twenty-odd hours a day you can live by your wits and not have to worry about tomorrow.

"Hope you like mazes," Christine says. "They're one of Derek's pet projects."

Jake looks up to see a course of fake juniper hedges that must stand seven feet tall. While Jake muses about what the rich will think of next, he loses sight of Christine, who's passed through the first series of archways. Soon, he's breathless and needs to tell himself not to panic, that he won't be lost forever in the artificial hedges of a Republican basement in Pacific Heights. What if the maze isn't actually Derek's creation, Jake wonders, but Christine's? Clearly, the woman has a richer imagination than Jake does. Her ability to keep him off balance is part of her fascination, part of what makes her such a good lay.

Finally, he emerges into a clearing. Christine gives him a quick smooch, and he's flabbergasted to find himself standing on the edge of a miniature golf course, painstakingly contoured as a model of the Bay Area, with hills, bays, and bridges, as well as a number of city landmarks.

Jake admires the model. The damn thing has a surface of felt that he's tempted to touch. His eyes scan east from The Cliff House, past the Palace of Fine Arts and Coit Tower to the Ferry Building. "Does Derek come down here to putt?"

"No, he's really not much of a golfer. He had it built for the boys when they were young. God, how they loved it. They'd be down here for hours. Sometimes I could hear them through one of the vents, pretending to broadcast their tournaments. They'd take turns being Ben Hogan and Arnold Palmer."

Jake notes a crackle of emotion in Christine's voice. She mentions her sons so rarely he's decided they must be stepchildren. Why else would you farm them out to eastern prep schools during the year and to camps for most of the summer? But they *are* her children. Was it Derek's choice to send them away? The poor woman must have a hole in her heart. He thinks of his own children—weeks go by and he hardly sees them, what with his long days in the office and the demands of community work.

Christine takes his hand again. "You ready to go down?"

"I thought we were down."

"You ain't seen nothing yet, kiddo."

She leads him along a corridor to a steel door. After she opens it, they descend a dozen steps to a matching door that opens onto a wide passageway of poured concrete, painted the color of beach sand. Along the walls are shelves with linens and blankets and batteries, racks of wine, and an astonishing array of canned goods. As he walks through the corridor, Jake reads the stenciled labeling on some of the cans: PEAR QUARTERS, BEANS AND WIENERS, CHEESE SPREAD, SPICED BEEF, TURKEY LOAF, APPLESAUCE.

Jake gasps when they reach a large, open room.

"Welcome to Derek's foxhole," Christine says, fanning out an open arm graciously.

Jake tiptoes around the room in awe. "When did he have this built?"

"A few years back."

Jake takes a gas mask from a hanging hook and swings it from its black strap.

"That's only here for decoration," Christine says. "In the event of an atomic bomb, this shelter's supposed to reduce gamma ray exposure by a factor of one thousand. I don't exactly know what that means, but it seems to make Derek very happy. Apparently, there's a very sophisticated ventilation system. State of the art for bomb shelters."

"That must be a comfort," Jake says, still swinging the mask.

"Oh, absolutely. We'd be perfectly safe, you understand. Only hitch, we might have to stay down here for weeks, maybe months."

"But think of all the pear quarters and spiced beef you could enjoy."

"Exactly."

Jake cranes his neck around the vast shelter. "And where does Derek keep his collection of shrunken heads? Doesn't he have the heads of a few Communist schoolteachers?"

"Oh, no," Christine says, "Derek collects the heads of liberal attorneys. By the way, you're next."

"Cute."

Christine unfolds a pair of canvas camp chairs and pulls them up to an oak dining table that's already covered with a checkered yellow cloth and set with plastic picnic plates and cups. Christine places the bread and cheese down on one plate and then lights a squat candle inside a hurricane lamp. "Derek tells me that when we finally come out from the shelter, we might be the only people alive."

"Well, that would simplify things," says Jake, loosening the strap of the gas mask and pulling the massive snout over his own.

"You look fetching, Jake."

"Like a cockroach," Jake says, his voice muffled.

"A charming one."

Jake comes up behind Christine and pokes at her neck with the snout of his gas mask.

"Ooooh, that's weird," Christine says and pushes Jake away.

After some effort, Jake takes off the mask and kisses Christine sweetly on the ear. "I thought we could eat down here today," she says, "and make love like it's the last day of our lives."

"I didn't think you believed in this stuff, Christine."

"I don't, but I'm never one to miss an opportunity." She takes his hand and leads him to the table.

"And what exactly are we going to eat?"

They sit down across from each other. "Along with the French bread and gooey cheese? We have C rations."

"You think I'm going to eat canned ham and lima beans?"

"You can't be a snob, Jake. This is survival."

In a moment they are sipping Côte du Rhone from plastic tumblers and poking holes in ration cans with folding can openers. Jake would like to dig into the bread and cheese but realizes a sporting effort is required of him.

Christine has a certain fire in her eye as she jabs at her can of spiced beef. "According to Derek, these can openers are called P-38s, because it takes approximately thirty-eight pokes to get a ration can open."

Jake is the first to break through and gallantly offers Christine a taste of C-ration turkey loaf.

THEY make love slowly on a double cot. This is first time Christine has let them make love off the floor. It seems fitting that they needed to descend to the deepest underground for the pleasure.

"Tell me," she says, opening her eyes, "what if it were us two?"

Jake lifts a few strands of hair from her eyes. "Us two?"

"Who survived down here. The only two people left alive."

Jake props himself up on an elbow. "We could have some rough-and-tumble food fights. How would you like to get hit with a faceful of spiced beef?"

"Seriously, Jake."

"How can you be serious about this?"

"Would you miss your family terribly?"

"I suppose."

Christine grabs ahold of Jake's face and stares right into his eyes. "You suppose. Is that all?"

"Come on, Christine. Don't you think it's a little hard to imagine how you'd feel about anything if you were living inside a science-fiction movie?"

"Don't you miss your family right now?" says Christine.

"Right now?" Jake is not quite sure that he knows what she means. He looks away from Christine. He has a strange taste in his mouth that comes from something other than the C-ration meal.

"I miss my family now," Christine says and covers her mouth with a hand.

"But your boys are always gone, Christine."

"I miss them more than ever now."

Jake takes hold of his lover's hand and whispers, "What's happened to all the Zen detachment?"

"We're talking about the end of the world, Jake."

"We're playing a game, Christine."

"Yes, and you're not playing very well."

Jake gets up to find a cigarette. "How would you like me to play?"

"What would you say at the end of the world?"

"I love you."

Christine sits up on the cot and folds her hands around her knees. "You don't love me, Jake, and I don't want you to. You love your wife, you fool. You should figure that out, you know, before the end of the world. That woman *should* divorce you. I would if I were her."

Jake finds his pack of Pall Malls and lights a cigarette. He flicks an ash into the empty turkey tin.

"This is not a game, Jake. Tell me what you're worried about at the end of the world."

Jake sits beside her on the cot. He feels his breath shorten and a bit of panic set in. He concentrates on his cigarette for a moment, inhales sharply, and blows out a long stream of smoke. "There's something strange going on with Inez that I can't figure out. She seems more content than I've seen her in a long time, but I don't trust it. She seems happier, but I know that I don't have anything to do with that happiness. It's as if she's discovered some purpose. She has a glow about her."

Christine reaches out a hand for Jake's cigarette. Takes a couple of puffs. Hands it back to Jake. "Do you think she's pregnant?"

"Oh, God, I hope not. Anyway, that's the last thing in the world that she'd want."

"Maybe she's seeing someone."

Jake laughs a moment at the idea. "I can't imagine that. Inez? Who would she be seeing?"

"Hard to say. Who are you seeing?" Christine takes his cigarette again.

"Nobody besides you."

"And who am I to Inez? Does she even have a clue about me?"

Christine hands back the lit butt of Jake's cigarette and he shakes another from his pack, lights it off the stub, and hands it to Christine. "It doesn't sound viable to me," he says. "I don't think it's so much the morality of the thing, I just don't think Inez would want to bother with the trouble."

Christine faces him. "Is this a lot of trouble for you?"

"No."

"There can be compelling reasons, you know." Christine runs her tongue slowly over her lips, then draws on the cigarette.

"She isn't one for anything messy, anything unpredictable."

"And that's what I am, Jake—messy and unpredictable?"

Jake doesn't answer but stares straight ahead.

"Look, now I've gone and put a fright into you."

"Fright? What fright?" Jake says, snapping to. "Here's an idea—how's about we stay down here until the world's over?"

"I like it," Christine says and leaves a trail of kisses across Jake's brows.

Jake closes his eyes. It would be nice, it seems to him, to keep them closed for a long while.

the blindfold

A FTER pasta and a couple of glasses of hearty house red, Hy sug-
gests that they mosey over to a coffee shop on upper Grant.

"You ever go over to The Blindfold on a Tuesday night?"

"I've never been there."

"The place is filled with poets and artists, motorcycle guys and
queers, every kind of degenerate you can imagine, and on Tuesday
nights the audience is required to wear blindfolds while the poets read
their poems. It's quite a spectacle, especially if you don't keep your
blindfold on."

"I don't believe you about the blindfolds."

"It's true. They say it allows one to better hear the true essence of the
words."

Sylvia snorts. "Why do you go?"

"For the poetry, of course. I've become a connoisseur of bad poetry.
And for the girls."

"You're shameless, Hy."

"I tell you, there's nothing like a roomful of blindfolded girls. They
listen with their mouths, I swear to God. Sensual deprivation can have a
profound effect. Take away their eyes and they open their mouths. The
blindfold is meant to enhance the aural experience. That's aural with an
a," Hy says, with a wink.

"Yes, I got that." She thinks *aura, breath, breeze.* From the Greek.

As they walk up Grant, past the shuttered Shaman Shop, Hy tells
Sylvia about the unfortunate proprietor, a man named Bockley who lost
his shirt betting on long shots at Bay Meadows. Sylvia wraps her scarf
tightly around her neck—there's a chill in the air—and thinks of Inez,
wishing that they were out in the night together. But she's with her boss,
Hy, who walks slightly ahead of her, his hands dug deep in his trouser

pockets. He likes the idea of being her guide. Sylvia wonders what she's doing with a man twice her age. It's a little late in the day for digging up a father figure, especially in the form of a would-be hipster, a character more pathetic than she is, who still holds out a ridiculous hope of seducing her.

Hy stops outside of another storefront. "The Infidelity Tea Shop," he announces. Sylvia turns to face the lit window that, under the hand-lettered sign, INFIDELITY, features a number of teapots, suspended miraculously in the pouring position, their spouts tilted expertly toward the empty belly of the teacup in their neighbor's pattern.

"See," Hyman Myerson says. "Infidelity is in the air."

"It may be in your imagination," Sylvia says, leaning against the teapot window. "But that's where it's going to stay."

Hy takes his hands out of his pockets and looks at them in the light of the window. He seems surprised that they are his hands. Sylvia notices his hard, thick nails before he turns his hands palm up.

"I've become an old man overnight," says Hy.

"You're not an old man," Sylvia says and thinks of her mother. Angela Bran didn't give herself a chance to grow old, and did her best to smother Sylvia's life. Her mother, the superstitious school nurse, who routinely recited a vocabulary of phobias as if it were her catechism, had grown afraid of everything and did her best to spread that fear. She warned Sylvia incessantly against moving to San Francisco. "It's the loneliest place in the world," she said. "You'll end up with one friend, if you're lucky, and he'll be sitting next to you on a bar stool."

Sylvia turns away from the shop window to face her friend. Hy seems like he's been as busy with his thoughts as she's been with hers. He extracts a wrapped toothpick from his coat pocket, pushes it through its paper wrapping, and pokes mercilessly at his gums. Sylvia looks at Hy's yellowing teeth, dotted with gold fillings, and is reminded of a photograph she once saw from World War II. A man dead on the street in London after a bombing. The photograph focused on the man's shoes, which had been patched multiple times. Despite the dead man's sincere and humble efforts to persevere, to keep his life patched together as well as he could, it was erased in a random moment. That's what she'd thought when she'd seen the photo. Now, seeing that he's raised blood from his gums, it strikes her that Hyman Myerson is dying.

Sylvia turns back to the window and studies the hearty spout of an orange Fiestaware pot pouring its ether into a delicate floweret-bordered porcelain cup. *Infidelity.* She isn't interested in giving the word a gloss. Her mother would be disappointed. Angela Bran would have had her believe that words were what mattered in the end, that commentary was more important than action. Commentary takes precedence, Sylvia supposes, if the only action that inspires your imagination is to take your own life. To hell with her mother. To hell with her mother's words. To hell with her mother's suicide threats. Her grisly attempts. Her final achievement. Sylvia glances at Hyman, her dying friend. She decides to confide in him.

"What?" he says. "You're looking at me funny."

"There's something I want to tell you."

"So tell me."

"There's this person."

"What person?"

"This certain person."

"So what about him?"

"I think I'm in love with this person."

Hy puts his hands back in his pockets. "I take it you're not speaking about me."

Sylvia shakes her head.

"So tell me about this guy."

"Well, this certain person . . ."

"He doesn't have a name?" says Hy. "What's his name?"

Sylvia looks into Hy's face, his blotchy skin, the great leathery pouches hanging under his eyes. In all the time she's spent with him—on the showroom floor at Myerson's, sharing a pasta dinner, sitting beside him at the symphony—she's never allowed herself to guess how old the man is. The sadness in Hy's face sits naturally in his sunken eyes and among the folds. Why hasn't he shown her this face before? The beautiful gloom of Hyman Myerson.

"Can I confide in you, Hy?"

"That's up to you," he says, raising his chin to signal his willingness to listen.

"I'll be interested to see how you respond."

"A little test of character, huh?"

"I wouldn't go that far."

"That's a relief." Hy runs his tongue across his gums and seems to savor the taste of his own blood.

"Anyway, this person . . . this person happens to be a woman."

"A woman. Goddamn." Hy, waving his hand toward Sylvia, dives into another spasm of coughing. "It's not what you said," he gasps. He reaches into his pocket for a handkerchief, excuses himself, turns his back, and spits into the handkerchief. Once he's collected himself, he turns back around and to Sylvia. "I didn't know you had it in you, dear." His eyebrows go up. "So what's her name?" he says, turning away to cough again.

"Hy?"

"I'm fine. What's her name?"

"Are you okay with this, Hy?"

"If you think it bothers me that you go that way, you've got that wrong. Live and let live is what I think. So am I going to meet this person?"

"I don't know."

"Keeping her for yourself?"

"For the time being."

Hy nods his head a moment and then gets caught up in the rhythm of his nodding. "Look, Sylvia, I got a confession to make to you."

"What?"

Hy tugs on the strings of his tie as if that might dislodge his words.

Sylvia looks past Hy—a yellow Studebaker, a later model than Inez's, races past them up Grant Avenue. Sylvia feels light-headed and leans against the shop window.

"I've wanted to tell you . . . wanted to give you a heads-up . . ."

Sylvia forces herself to look directly at Hy. "That you're dying?"

"How did you know? Toby tell you?"

"Nobody told me."

Hy sighs.

"What is it?"

"Cancer. Emphysema. The lungs are shot. The breathing mechanism is about to go kaput."

Sylvia lays her head on Hy's shoulder.

"Let's not get maudlin here."

Sylvia whispers: "How long have you known?"

"A year. You?"

"A few minutes."

"For a psychic, you're a little slow on the draw."

"Are you scared?"

"No more than everybody else these days." Hy turns and begins walking up the street.

Sylvia falls in step behind him.

"I've been dreaming a lot lately . . ." Hy turns aside to cough and spit into his handkerchief. "Dreaming these phone conversations with friends I haven't seen for years. They're not conversations. More like I dial them up and they don't answer but I can hear them on the other end and I can tell what they're doing. Sitting on the beach, playing pinochle, ordering a beer at a bar. Whenever I want to say something to one of my old pals, a voice says: *Leave him alone, just listen.*"

Hy stops at the corner and leans against the street sign—Grant and Vallejo. "And something else that's really strange," he says, his eyes brightening." All I want to do—I mean besides having sex—all I want to do anymore is sell pianos. Give a guy a death sentence and all he wants to do is more of what he's done his whole life. Who knew? Maybe it's a homing instinct. I think of my father all the time now, and my grandfather, who was one of the great Jewish pioneers of California. One of the big three, in my estimation. Levi Strauss sold denim for work clothes. Zellerbach sold toilet paper. And Moses Myerson sold the first pianos to the brothels of California. Heh. Hence our motto: *A Myerson for every house.* As luck would have it, the family business ends with me. Nobody to pass it onto."

"What about your children?" Sylvia asks.

"Don't make me cry—neither of them is suited. It's just as well. The industry has gone to hell. Used to be, folks either had a piano or a player piano. Now they have a hi-fi. I call it death by high fidelity. If I had my way, I'd die on my feet selling every last instrument in the store."

Sylvia turns aside as her eyes brim with tears.

"Chin up, girl. For all we know, World War Three is bearing down on us a lot faster than my little cancer."

"Oh, Hy," she says, "you have a real knack for solace."

SYLVIA had imagined neat rows of audience members wearing uniform eye covers like the 3D shades she once wore on a date with Colleen at the Coronet Theater on Geary. But in The Blindfold Café people's eyes are covered with scarves, and scraps of fabric and leather of every imaginable hue. Some are sunken into overstuffed monstrosities, others sit on the edge of creaking straight-back chairs, turned toward the stage. A long-haired blond woman in sandals and a sundress is chanting a barely audible poem about the uses of nectar. To make up for their visual deprivation, people seem to be going out of their way to make gleeful sounds of assent, as they smoke and gulp coffee or grope for paper sacks with bottles of wine being passed to them by a friend. The floor is sticky with spilled coffee and who knows what else.

Sylvia and Hy find a pair of vacant stools toward the back of the room under a painting of a brooding Negro bassist. On a wall to their side is a series of crude but glowing landscapes painted on cracked canvas window shades still attached to their rollers. Sylvia unknots her scarf and lets it fall open. With its pattern of prehistoric fish on an aqua ground, the scarf reminds her of a Paul Klee painting. She stole it from Magnin's a couple of weeks after first visiting Inez. She'd wanted to see if the violinist's sleeveless aubergine dress was still available so that she could hold it up on its hanger and muse about Inez. But she never got back to the dresses. After stealing the scarf, she sensed that a store detective was following her. Sylvia draws the scarf over her eyes and knots it. As her last bit of thievery before a self-imposed rehabilitation, the scarf is doubly precious.

The smell of smoke seems stronger with her blindfold on. Hy erupts into a spasm of coughing.

"Too smoky for you, Hy?"

"Nah," he says, hacking. "You look grand in a blindfold, Sylvia."

"Shh. Just let me know if you want to go."

"No, no, I'm all right. Just getting used to the atmosphere. Pardon me." Sylvia hears him spit into his handkerchief. "You fit right in," he whispers, momentarily recovered. "You're born to be a beatnik. Me, I'm too old. If they ask me why I'm not playing along, I'll tell 'em I'm the fuzz."

Sylvia puts two fingers over her lips and tries to hear the words the poet is chanting, but in their back corner spot it is difficult to make out any more than a smear of amplified language.

Hy taps her on the wrist and whispers. She can hear him pushing off his stool. "Listen, I'm going to go to the bar and pick up a drink. Can I get you something?"

"Yes," Sylvia says, delighted at the thought of adding alcohol to the sensory adventure of this night. "Bring me a Bloody Mary."

"You've got it."

"Goody. I may have to peek at it when it gets here."

AFTER Hy leaves, Sylvia slips her scarf beneath her eyes and gazes around the room. What an ideal spot for a voyant—a world in which everyone else is wrapped in blindfolds. Sylvia sees an open table far closer to the stage and moves toward it. Surely Hy will find her. Sylvia settles into a bentwood chair and pulls her scarf over her eyes. Now, for better or worse, she can hear the poet.

> *"Why not gather up our sweet holdings?*
> *Why not climb onto each other's shoulders?*
> *Why not penetrate the city's bloodless marrow with a*
> *needle of nectar."*

A silence follows and Sylvia isn't sure whether the poem is finished. Then comes a smatter of applause. Sylvia sneaks a look at the blond poet as she climbs off the platform and embraces a Negro in overalls and an Abe Lincoln top hat. The Negro steps onto the platform chanting. *"Red is under your work boots, under your trowel, under your bed."* Sylvia blinds herself again with the scarf, enjoying the poet's sweet and witty drawl, the words a glowing vapor in her mind.

"Red is under you, underwood, and undercover.
Red your memory and red your heart.
Red your mama's throat calling your name.
Red the petaled lips of your lover whispering.
Red her tongue in the jelly and yours in the jam.
Red the color of your firstborn's head, bursting from his
    mama's womb.
Red is who you are, who you aren't, who they want you
    to be.
Your personal trail of blood, the crooked lines of your
    humiliations.
Red is your eyes grown weary in winter.
Red is your unctuous undertaker, licking his rosy lips as
    he lays you out."

A loud cheer goes up as the red poem draws to a close. Sylvia sneaks a look at the top-hat poet as he nods happily and waves his hat in front of him. "I call that poem 'Red Scare,'" he says. "I happen to favor the color red and think it's about time we take it back from the politicians."

Sylvia remembers her Bloody Mary and wonders what's keeping Hy.

"It's one thing to be color-blind," the poet says, "but another to sit blindfolded in a country without justice. Now they're trying to make Cuba into the villain. They have already done that with the Russians. But I look at Cuba and all I see is a bunch of poor colored people trying to live their lives. I wrote this next poem this morning out of my worry."

Sylvia, her scarf now tied around her neck, looks around for Hy.

"A fanciful collaboration, if you will," says the poet, "with Ezra Pound. I call it 'One Missile, Two.'"

A hoot goes up from the blindfolded crowd. Sylvia stands, beginning to grow worried about Hy. The poet, in a deeper voice now, blasts his words through the microphone.

"And then went down to the ship
to drink rum and smoke Cubans.
Set keel to breakers: the brown mama rolled
tobacco leaf on her thigh as I ate her pie."

The crowd cheers after each of the poet's lines. Where the hell is Hyman Myerson? Sylvia sees guys in leather, guys with beards and torn jeans, barefoot girls in leotards and wool skirts, most of them in home-made blindfolds of one sort or another. She begins to weave toward the bar through the motley throng of beatniks. The top-hat poet is whipping the crowd into a frenzy. Sylvia hears bursts of amplified language as she pushes her way toward the bar.

"Man of no fortune . . . fortune hunter . . ."

The bartender wears a black leather patch over one eye, leaving himself enough vision to get his job done. She needs to holler to get the bartender's attention.

"Hold your horses, chicky."

"Unsheathes his narrow sword . . ."

She tries to stay calm, boosts herself onto a stool.

"His nuclear missile . . ."

"Have you seen a man, an older man?" she asks the bartender.

"Unguarded, unprotected, unrepentant."

"Old guy, string tie?"
"Yes."

"He goes up the long ladder."

"In the head. Passed out for a moment."

"Peers down on the cadaverous dead."

"Oh, no. He wasn't drinking."

"The missiles . . ."

"He didn't look so good. We called an ambulance, just in case."
Sylvia pushes her way toward the men's room.

"The missiles . . ."

She is almost to the bathroom door when she hears the wail of a
siren. She stops still a moment. Tells herself to breathe.

"The missiles . . ."

The siren is growing closer. Her mother would have her deconstruct
the word. *Siren.* Picture a winged creature, half-woman half-bird, steering sailors toward the rocks. Even at a time like this.

"Count them, for they are our currency."

But she thinks of a wounded animal instead.

"One missile, two."

The siren, an electronic aria in the night, is making the crowd edgy.
The siren and the poet, a combined frenzy.

"Knock down their shanties,
knock down their towns.
One missile, two, one missile, two."

A roar goes up from the crowd. Sylvia yanks open the bathroom
door and spots Hy lying on his back by the sink. Somebody, perhaps the
bartender, has propped up Hy's head under a couple of bar towels; the
string tie is ripped off, his shirt open to the ropy folds of his white neck.
As the ambulance pulls up, the siren curling back into itself, Sylvia can
hear a slight wheeze coming from Hy as his chest rises and falls. She
crouches beside him.
"Hello, beautiful."
"Are you okay? You in pain?"

"The slight . . . the slightest twinge," he says, his breathing labored.

A pair of medics in starched white shirts and trousers burst into the bathroom.

"The ambulance is here, Hy."

"Good. Let them . . . know . . . I'm here."

"They know, Hy."

"Thing that dis . . . disappoints me . . ."

"Hmmm?"

"I wanted . . . wanted . . . see you drink a Bloody Mary . . . in a blindfold."

circumstances

It's been three days since President Kennedy's dire speech to the nation, and the entire world is gripped by the high-stakes standoff: Soviet missiles aimed at the United States as the navy enforces a strict blockade of Cuba. The frenzy of fear seems to have bypassed Sylvia. Or so it seems to Inez, perched in the window seat of Sylvia's apartment, a hearty bowl of niçoise salad in her lap. As for Inez, she's fascinated by the prospect of the world ending. And yet, she's surprised that she'd rather not have it happen anytime soon.

Inez dips a fork into her salad. "So you're not afraid of this missile thing?"

Sylvia, who's sitting cross-legged on the floor in a cute pair of pink pedal pushers, shakes her head. "Hy thinks it's a big bluff."

"Yes, but what do you think, Sylvia?"

"I tend to agree with Hy. I think it's a grand game of chicken and, fortunately, everybody's chicken."

Inez is tired of hearing about the oddball character from the piano shop. He's all that Sylvia's talked about since Inez got here. Now, given his terminal illness, Hy's ascended to mythical status. Inez thinks about her father-in-law. Jake keeps threatening to bring the old man home to live with them, but she's hoping Jake will find someplace else for him. The prospect of Isaac Roseman in their house is more frightening than any missiles.

"The thing about Hy," Sylvia says, holding a forkful of tuna in the air, "the thing that really makes his illness sad, is that he's so young at heart."

Young at heart; Inez finds the phrase galling. Perhaps because she's always felt *old at heart.* The consequence of being a prodigy rather than a child. *She has an old soul,* Isaac Roseman once told her father, *and it's our job to cultivate it.* Inez blames the process of cultivation, at least in part, for turning her into so separate a creature. After the first charmed years with Jake, Inez became who she's been for years, a distant woman, a step outside of her own time. The relationship with Sylvia has changed that, but how can she trust that Sylvia is who she says she is, or feels what she claims to feel.

Inez pushes her salad around with a fork.

"I can't believe Hy's dying," Sylvia says.

Inez takes a bite of salad. It's dry and fishy tasting. What does she expect; it's tuna.

Sylvia tells Inez about The Blindfold Café, how her boss collapsed there while she was with him. Talking about it brings her close to tears. Inez wonders whether the sentiment is legitimate. Inez climbs off her perch by the window, puts down her salad, and sits cross-legged beside Sylvia on the floor. "I'm not as agile as you are," Inez says, taking hold of Sylvia's left hand. What begins as a gesture of comfort quickly turns. Once Sylvia is within her grasp, Inez wants to squeeze her hand. She wants to hurt her, to make a modest impression. Inez is surprised by the force of her grip. She keeps squeezing the hand. Sylvia stares back at her. "You're hurting me," she says calmly.

"Sorry." Inez lets go. "I didn't mean to hurt you."

"Apparently you did."

Inez glances at Sylvia, who's sitting perfectly relaxed, flexing and unflexing her sore hand.

"You've fallen in love with me, Inez. And now you're confused. That's enough to make any reasonable person angry."

"You don't know what you're talking about."

"I think I do."

Inez stands and returns to her spot by the window. The street is perfectly quiet now. No cable cars. No pedestrians. Nothing but parked cars. She should force herself to leave, but Sylvia has cast her usual spell. Sylvia pushes her salad aside and massages her palm with the opposite hand. "I'm sorry I've talked so much about Hy," Sylvia says, working her thumb in slow strokes. "I'm upset about his condition."

"I didn't realize you were so close to him."

Sylvia sighs. "I've learned a lot from Hy."

"Like what?"

"You're not really interested."

"I just asked you . . ."

"You're jealous."

"I'm not jealous." Inez stands.

"What are you going to do, leave? You crush my hand and then you walk out."

"Is your hand crushed?"

"No."

"You have a flair for the dramatic," Inez says, with satisfaction. Standing, she has more control of the situation. She can walk out of this apartment right now, if she chooses, and leave Sylvia with her "crushed" hand, musing about her dying mentor.

"I don't want you to leave."

"Why not?"

"I want to go to bed with you."

Inez smiles. "You're a sex fiend."

"Now who's being dramatic?"

"Is that the only reason you want me to stay?"

"No. Sit down."

Inez sits across from Sylvia in the wicker chair. "So tell me what you learned from Hyman."

"He taught me a way of using my mind to get what I want."

"Has it worked?"

"Yes, it has," Sylvia says, her eyes fixed on Inez.

ONCE they go to bed they stay there a long time. Sylvia is even more daring today than usual. Perhaps "the crisis" has filled her with false courage. What, Inez wonders, if the prospect of death, instead of provoking fear, turned everyone into fearless sensualists? What if America turned degenerate, a little like Germany between the wars? "Fatality," as her stand partner Paul Scaffidi is fond of saying, "can be so ennobling."

Inez inhales deeply. Despite the scented candles, the room is still gamy with the smell of their lovemaking. How can a woman who's spent so much time imagining her own death feel such satisfaction? What if pleasure were as habit forming as misery?

Sylvia smiles mischievously and climbs out of bed. "I have a treat for you."

"What kind of a treat?"

"You stay there."

Inez watches Sylvia slink off toward the closet. She pitches her voice down an octave. "And now what you've all come for. Please welcome, the one, the only—Sylvia Bran!"

"What's this?"

"I'm going to strip for you," says Sylvia, behind the closet door.

"But you're already naked."

"I was," says Sylvia. She extends a bare leg into the room.

Inez hardly considers herself a connoisseur of the female body. She's known her own, she's getting to know Sylvia's. As a girl, she'd seen her sister's body, but Bibi, like her daughter, Anna, was modest.

When Jake began to cheat on her, Inez thought a lot about the female body. What drove men so crazy about this particular formation of flesh? She remembers once wandering through the Rexall on the corner of Sutter and Powell and noticing a couple of men at the magazine rack flipping through girlie magazines. She could see bursts of pink flesh fly by. They flipped through page after page of rosy-nippled breasts and perfectly rounded rumps as if they were skimming through a sample book of floor coverings. These men were all business. Inez kept expecting a lusty grin, a bit of snigger caught in the throat. Occasionally, a guy shifted his weight from one foot to the other, but that seemed to be the sole reflex to the miles of female flesh.

After she'd found all her necessary purchases, Inez circled back to the magazine rack. She picked up a magazine called *Nugget*. The girls wore tiny bits of fur and satin. They leered at the photographer—an attempt to look sexy. Inez flipped through a few other magazines as methodically as the men. The large breasts—Inez thought of them as *boobs* as she was standing there—didn't do a whole lot for her. She was rather taken, though, by the curves that ran, page after page, from waists to full hips. She might have convinced herself that her only interest was aesthetic, that this was little different from flipping through a book of Matisse still lifes, if it wasn't so clear that the sheer naughtiness of the activity was appealing.

INEZ can see little more than the arms of a red silk kimono as Sylvia begins to show herself from behind the closet door. Sylvia slowly flutters into view, the kimono barely reaching her knees. She does a low, swirling dance like a flower in the *Nutcracker*. She lets the red kimono slip off one shoulder. She grins at Inez impishly, as if to say, *Geez, I don't know what got into me.* Finally, Sylvia halts directly in front of the bed and shimmies, the red kimono sliding to the floor. Inez does her best to honor Sylvia's moment. "Beautiful," she says. Sylvia's small breasts swell above a push-up bra. Her rear end makes a cute package in black panties.

But Inez is alarmed by how girlish and white Sylvia looks. It's hard for Inez to believe that she's just performed carnal acts with this woman, who appears more innocent the naughtier she gets. As a con artist, her innocence is clearly her most valuable asset. When Sylvia unclasps her bra and her small breasts bounce freely, Inez becomes aroused. This is how Sylvia wants it.

"Come here," Inez says.

INEZ considers leaving while Sylvia showers. She could write a short, sweet note and creep away. This has to be the high point in the relationship. A rational woman would know that nothing could get better or less complicated. But Inez decides to call home instead.

The sweet boy answers: "Roseman residence, Joey speaking."

"My, you have exquisite phone manners. Who taught you those beautiful manners?"

"Hi, Mom."

"Anna meet you at the corner?"

"Yep."

"You get some candy?"

"A cherry Tootsie Roll Pop."

"That sounds good. How'd it go at school today?"

"Okay. Miss Fambrini talked about the Russians. She said that this was a good time to make sure we said our prayers at night. Bobby Kent kept raising his hand and saying, 'Why, Miss Fambrini? Why should we say our prayers?' "

"Did you say prayers in school?"

"No. We memorized a Robert Frost poem today. Miss Fambrini talked a lot about Cubanmissiles. Mom?"

"Yeah?"

"Is Cubanmissiles a country?"

"No, Cuba is a country."

"I thought maybe Cubanmissile was a country, too."

Inez's eyes tear up as she listens to Joey.

"Don't tell anybody. Okay?"

"Don't tell anybody what, honey?"

"What I said about Cubanmissiles."

"I won't tell anybody. So, what are you doing now?"

"Watching *The Three Stooges.*"

"Are they silly?"

"They're really silly, Mom." He starts laughing and talking so fast he can hardly get the words out. "You know . . . you know Larry? You know the bald one in the middle? I don't mean the fat one, Curly, he's bald all over, but Larry, who's kinda skinny, but bald in the middle of his head."

"I think I know which one is Larry."

"You know what happened to him? He fell in a big tub of fat."

Joey starts to laugh really hard now, thinking about Larry in the vat of Hollywood fat. Inez pictures Joey's baby teeth as he laughs.

"And then . . . and then you know what he does? He pulls out his hair. And he says: 'I'm just a victim . . . a victim of circumstancers.' "

"Do you know what a victim of circumstancers is?" Inez asks, the dutiful mother, taking every opportunity to offer a lesson.

"No," Joey says and starts to laugh again. "What is it, Mom?"

"It's really called circumstances. It means the things that happen to people that they don't have a lot of choice about."

"Like big tubs of fat?"

"Exactly."

"Larry has a lot of circumSTANCES. You should of seen the one . . ."

Joey begins laughing again and pretty soon Inez is laughing with him, laughing at the whole idea of them having a conversation about *The Three Stooges* and the "Cubanmissiles." It is the longest telephone conversation that she's ever had with Joey. Then Joey's laughter comes to a sudden halt. "I'm going to practice the Dvořák some more, Mom. I'm going to get back to it right away."

"You don't have to practice, honey."

"Yeah, I do."

"Watch *The Three Stooges.*"

"It's almost over, Mom; I don't need to watch the rest. I'll turn it off."

"Don't," Inez wants to shout into the receiver. She thinks of her son sitting down with his half-sized cello. A seven-year-old with a taste for cartoons and imbeciles. "I don't think you need to practice any longer."

"Don't you think I'm doing any good with the Dvořák?"

"You're doing great."

"I know I can get it better. A lot better."

"That's not the point. You're only seven!"

Joey is silent. She's frightened him.

"Listen, do what you like."

"Maybe now . . . maybe now that Grandpa's here . . ."

"Grandpa's there?" Inez says, confused by what she's hearing.

"I thought maybe he could help me with the Dvořák."

"Your grandfather is there?"

"I mean even though he played the violin, I bet he could help me."

"When did Grandpa get there?"

"This morning."

"Is your father there?"

"He's at the store. Getting Grandpa seltzer."

"Is your sister there?"

He doesn't answer but screams directly into the receiver: "ANNA, ANNA."

Inez tries to calm herself, but the idea of Isaac in the house is almost more than she can bear. It's a temporary arrangement, she tells herself, only temporary.

"Hi, Mom," Anna sounds bothered to have been called to the phone. Inez does her best to stay cool. "How are you, kiddo?"

"I'm all right."

"Any news about the Cuba deal?"

"No."

Anna has seemed more disturbed by the crisis than Joey, but she isn't about to reveal anything to her mother.

"I think we're almost in the pink," Inez says, unable to resist the urge to offer comfort.

"In the pink?" Anna objects. "I thought the whole deal is that we're fighting the pinkos." The poor girl is ensconced in what Jake's dubbed the "splitting hairs" phase of adolescence.

"I think we're going to be all right," Inez says.

"If you say so."

"Not that I have any expertise. . . ."

"I know, Mom. Joey tell you about Grandpa?"

"Yes, he did."

"Wow, you sound really excited, Mom."

"I was surprised it happened today."

"Dad set him up in the TV room. That means Joey's going to be in your room all the time now."

"Why?"

"To watch *your* TV. Unless you think he's going to watch *The Three Stooges* with Grandpa."

"How does Grandpa look?"

"He can walk and talk and everything. His arm's all twisted up."

"His bow arm."

"I guess. He started yelling at Joey."

"He what?"

"As soon as Joey got home from school, he made him get out his cello. And when he started playing, Grandpa yelled. *What's the matter, can't you hear? Don't you listen to yourself when you play? You're flat. Can't you hear?*"

"That's terrible!"

"Dad's here," Anna says, and, before she knows it, Jake is on the phone.

"Inez?"

"Did you get him the seltzer?"

"So you heard."

"Couldn't you find another place for him?"

"I couldn't secure a place in a nursing home. I told you there are waiting lists. And the hospital threatened a lawsuit if we didn't get him out of there."

"You're an attorney."

"Don't start."

"I hear he's already been hollering at Joey."

"He wasn't hollering."

"You're defending him now?"

"I'm not defending him. Where the hell are you, anyway?"

"At Mafalda's." Inez concentrates on sounding casual, odd as it is, sitting half dressed on the bed of someone whom she's just made love to.

"You're sure spending a lot of time with Mafalda."

"We're catching up with each other."

Sylvia walks into the room naked, wet from the shower, and shrugs, comically, once she notices Inez on the phone. Inez watches a trail of moisture slowly ease down her lover's neck and over her left breast, as she explores the closet again.

"When will you be home?" Jake asks.

"I don't know. I may stay for supper."

"Don't do this to me, Inez."

"I'm not doing anything to you."

Sylvia returns to the bedroom, wrapped in a short robe now, the sash tied in a bow. She winks at Inez and puts one end of her sash in Inez's hand, then backs away slowly.

"Look, I'll be home a little later," says Inez, watching as Sylvia's robe falls to the floor.

"I need you, Inez," he says.

"This will give you a chance to sort things out with your father," Inez says. She gently slips the receiver onto its cradle as Sylvia places one knee on either side of Inez's pelvis and leans down, brushing her nipples against Inez's belly, her hair showering Inez with delicious drips.

~

IN the *Chronicle* this morning Inez had read about a construction company in San Bruno that could build a fully viable air-raid shelter in your backyard in three days. Inez remembers this now, as she lounges in the dusk light listening to a Frank Sinatra record. She laughs out loud at the thought of the construction crew descending on one of her neighbors' yards and digging a big hole. Inez has no interest in having an air-raid shelter in her yard, no interest in trying to protect her family from what they can't be protected from. All she wants is the shelter of this apartment, the friendly squeal and bright bells of the cable cars outside, the smooth gangster crooning "Witchcraft" and dear Sylvia at the stove pulling together a quick supper. No husband, no children, no father-in-law, no violin, no history. A suspended moment in which nothing outside of the realm of this little apartment exists.

Inez, as slothful as she's ever been in her life, sits in Sylvia's kimono on a stool in the kitchen watching her talented friend braise lamb chops and steam a pot of Uncle Ben's rice.

"All we do is eat," Inez says.

"Eat and make love, the measures of a life well lived."

"Who said that?"

"I did."

Sylvia, in an orange apron and nothing else, is somehow fetching with a jack-o'-lantern emblazoned on her chest.

"You make a rather skinny pumpkin."

"Yeah?"

"That apron's meant for a plump girl with a fat behind."

"Do you wish I had a fat behind?"

"No, I like your behind the way it is."

Sylvia adds crushed garlic to her creation, then circles behind Inez and peels the kimono off her shoulders, threading her hands under Inez's arms to cup her breasts. Unlike Jake, who grabbed and squeezed, Sylvia holds onto them gently in a kind of communion.

"You're going to smell like garlic," says Sylvia in her ear.

"I don't care."

Sylvia kisses Inez on the corner of the mouth then slides her tongue into Inez's mouth, the lamb chops sizzling in the skillet. Sylvia groans and returns to the stove.

Inez rolls her head around naked and woozy. "I smell like garlic," she says.

"Yes, and how do you like your meat?" Sylvia says, blowing Inez a fat kiss.

"Rare."

toy soldiers

B Y the time she arrives home, the kids are in bed and the old man's asleep in his new quarters in the TV room. Jake's left a terse note on the kitchen table:

Everybody's tucked in. Had to run out to a labor meeting.
Don't wait up.

J.

Inez tries to picture the woman that Jake's laboring with. A bottled blonde or a redhead? Beside Jake's note is a fat, unopened envelope from Napa State Hospital. Her sister. She doesn't want to open the envelope. She hasn't seen Bibi for a few years. She stopped going up to Napa after her last visit. That was 1958. *So what's new?* she'd asked Bibi. *Tell me how you are. How about the food here? It's all right, you can complain. Do you want me to talk with your doctor? Don't you ever want to get out of here, Bibi?* But Bibi didn't answer. She glared at Inez for half an hour, refusing to speak.

Call it survivor's guilt, call it sheer cowardliness, this is the part of Inez's life that she's most ashamed of. And Bibi has made it worse by forgiving her. Bibi is without guile. She sends cards that she's pasted together during craft class. Lovely things, really. Collages made out of scraps of fabric. How she gets these materials is hard to say. The staff must know her history as a dressmaker and bring in the scraps for her pleasure. They're kinder to her there than Inez is.

Inez takes the cards out of the envelopes when they arrive, admires the crooked beauty of the collages and forces herself to read the notes inside. Then she takes a kitchen match to Bibi's cards and drops them in the fireplace. How can Inez respond to a woman who no longer exists, who's nothing more than an arched and crinkled filament of ash?

But this fat envelope from Napa State Hospital troubles her. Is Bibi dead at age forty-five? Businesslike, Inez slices open the envelope with a paring knife. No card. No curious quilt of fabrics. But a sheaf of small sheets covered in Bibi's tiny, precise script. Inez considers burning the missive *before* reading it. That would be the purest approach. Instead, she reads it slowly as if the message has come from some divine and lucid source.

Dear Inez,

How are you? How are the children? How is your handsome husband? I think of him a lot. Not that way. I've taught myself not to think that way. No, I think of Jake because he's funny. I remember him as being funny. Is he still funny? I wonder what it would be like to live with somebody who's funny.

Believe it or not, we've heard about the missiles in Cuba. At least some of us have. We saw President Kennedy on TV. What a good-looking man. The staff here didn't know what he was going to say, so they let us watch, at least those of us that they don't worry about much. The stable ones. Inez, can you believe anybody regards me as stable? It's all relative, they tell me. Next thing you know, they'll say we're all relatives. They don't pay so much attention to the radio here. It's on all the time in the rec room so I listen to the news bulletins. I know what's going on.

Are you scared, Inez? I'm not scared, but then I don't have much to lose. You have a lot to lose. When I hear violins on the radio I think of you. They don't play much real music on the radio here, but pop music with strings. 101 Strings. The music is meant to calm us. Sometimes when they play 101 Strings, I try to take away a hundred strings so that there's only one left, one pure violin. But mostly I hear them all.

Sometimes I sit down to the piano in the music room. The piano's no good but I can't really play anyway. I play the little bit of Bach that I know. The beginning of the Largo from the Harpsichord Concerto in F Minor. But it's not very good. Sounds stiff. Like toy soldiers, marching in line over little puddles. That's how I thought about it one day — my fingers were stiff like soldiers. Somebody showed me a game to play with my hands in case I get bored, but I never play it.

Here's what you do with your fingers in case you get bored: you start with your pointer finger on one hand and go down the row of fingers on your other hand and back again, starting with the pinkie. You can say it out loud, or you can say it in your head. Johnny, Johnny, Johnny, Johnny, whoops, Johnny, whoops Johnny, Johnny, Johnny, Johnny. That's how I sound playing Bach on the piano. Johnny, Johnny, Johnny, Johnny, whoops, Johnny, whoops Johnny, Johnny, Johnny, Johnny. Except I think of it as Johann, Johann, Johann, Johann, whoops Johann, whoops Johann, Johann, Johann, Johann.

I think about Mama. I wish you could remember her. She was beautiful. I think of her playing the piano. I remember how her beautiful hands rose away from the keys with a little flourish at the end of a piece, but I can't recall the sound of her playing.

Mama was proud of that piano — the Baldwin baby grand. Sometimes she let me help her clean the keys. We did it with milk, little cups of milk and a rag. She called it milking. *"Let's begin the milking," she'd say. "Don't use too much, just a little dip. We don't want the piano to smell bad." I'd start on the top keys and Mama would start at the bottom. "Meet you at middle C," she always said. That's one of my happiest memories. There were so many keys, I thought we had all the time in the world. That was before I knew about all the things that could go wrong in a little person's life, in a little person's head. That's what Mama called me sometimes — a little person. A little person doesn't slurp when she sips her soup. A little person eats over the table. A little person doesn't whine when she's supposed to take her nap.*

The piano here is not so nice. It's called a Kimble, which seems a funny name for a piano. Nobody's taken care of it very well. It's gone out of tune and I don't think it will ever be back in tune again. I think about that a lot — the piano being out of tune. The piano should be in tune. We need the piano to be in tune more than other people need it. This piano is not well-tempered. If anybody else around here loses their temper, they get more medication, but not the piano. The piano has been allowed to lose its temper forever.

Sometimes I want to ask them for a cup of milk and a rag so I can clean the keys. But the thing that stops me is that I'm afraid they'd think I was crazy. That's a joke we say around here — what if they think I'm crazy?

Sometimes I wonder, Inez, will I ever see you again? Will I hear you play the violin before the end of the world? I don't really think it's coming soon—the end—but I see fear, sometimes, in the eyes of the people who work here. That scares me. I used to see Mama crying all the time. There's a nurse here named Rose Carlentini. I love Rose. She's sweet to me. The fear isn't really in her eyes, but in her mouth. She's held her lips funny since President Kennedy made his speech. Her lips look like they're holding a pebble in place and that pebble is her fear. But what do I know? Maybe she's holding a cube of sugar in her mouth and it doesn't have anything to do with fear. I'm giving this letter to Rose to mail for me. She said she would, but maybe I am only writing to myself. That would be all right. Maybe Rose will read the part about her. One time Rose said: "Maybe Inez will come and visit and bring her violin. Then she could play for us." I laughed for a long time after Rose said that and then she said: "On the other hand, Bibi, maybe she won't come, or maybe she won't bring her violin."

I told Rose that you are very busy, but that you are thinking of me. I think that's true. I really think that's true, because you and I had the same mother and father, even if you didn't know our mother. We grew up in the same house and told each other secrets. But, no matter what you do, Inez, I love you and don't believe the world is coming to an end.

Your sister, Bibi

Instead of building a pyre to burn Bibi's letter, Inez curls up on her bed and reads the letter once more. If it were possible for Inez to coil herself so tightly on the bed that she suffocated, she would do it now. If only she could cry. Instead she remains in her sturdy body, which, if she didn't intervene, would likely go on until she was eighty, the troubled conscience within the body glowing like a polluted sunset.

Inez closes her eyes. Just a few hours ago she was happily in bed with her lover, but now it seems like a frivolous entertainment, a child's game played as an adult, a dream that she recalls only in its barest outline. Yet her mad sister, whom she hasn't seen in several years, is so present that she might as well be tiptoeing around Inez's dark bedroom, guided by a luminescent needle, trailing a length of thick, black thread.

Although only five years older, Bibi had been her mother. Nobody had looked after Bibi. No one could have guessed that she needed looking after, a woman-child with so rosy a disposition. Bibi shined more light on Inez than anybody had. Never married, she'd seemed content to live with their father. She cooked for him and sewed for him and searched for his car in the downtown streets when he forgot where he'd parked it. When he began to truly fail, she fell apart. A gifted dressmaker and seamstress, she could no longer be left with a needle and thread because she'd sit quietly and sew her fingers together. Inez discovered her one day, after their father had been put into a home, sitting in his bedroom rocker, blood everywhere and a bemused smile on her face.

"What happened?" Inez screamed, running in circles around her sister. Bibi held up her left hand, delighted. Inez couldn't believe what she was seeing. Thick black thread was strung through each of her fingers down to her thumb. Her hand had become a web.

"I've finished," Bibi said, "a perfect white glove, Nez."

At the hospital, after they'd given Bibi painkillers and the stitches had been taken out and she'd been bandaged, after she'd been given a shot for tetanus and wheeled to the mental ward, where Bibi and Inez sat for two hours waiting for Bibi to get admitted, Inez asked her sister why. "Why, Bibi? Why did you do it?"

"I needed to," her sister said. "And now I'll have to do it again."

"Why?"

"Look," she said and held up her undamaged right hand. She spread her fingers wide. "The minister says that if we are true believers, our bodies are nothing more than vessels for the Lord to fill. We must become gloves. Jesus fits us perfectly if we make a place for him. I was making a place for him."

When Bibi spoke, her eyes brightened. She held her head high. She was on her way somewhere. Not a churchgoer until the last few years, Bibi had started going every day. It seemed an innocuous enough activity. Inez had even begun to wonder if she'd found a boyfriend there. Inez pictured a tall, oafish, religious bachelor who'd lost his parents as well. But, no, her sister had simply gone mad.

Inez did her best not to panic in the waiting room. "If I weren't able to spread my fingers," she said, "I couldn't play the violin."

"Nez, you aren't meant to sew your fingers together," Bibi said, all-knowing. "You already have the Lord, Inez. He comes to you through your music."

Inez wanted to scream, *The Lord has nothing to do with me or you.* Inez looked at her sister in a glazed wonder.

Bibi lifted her bandaged hand and considered it for a moment. "I'll have to try again," she said.

As Bibi spoke, the fingers of Inez's left hand ached right through the calluses. *Don't leave me, Bibi.* Even though she and Bibi were the only ones sitting in the small room with baby-blue walls, they were kept waiting ages. They could hear a boy wailing beyond the doors; he sounded like a German shepherd with a human vocabulary, demanding and insistent.

Inez had put in a call to Jake at his office—he was supposed to meet them as soon as he finished with a client. Where the hell was he? Soon, Bibi would be brought in to speak with a psychiatrist. Soon she would be taken away. She was perfectly calm; Inez was the agitated one. Inez stood up and started pacing. What were they going to do with her sister? The wailing voice of the canine-boy seemed to be coming through the heating vent. Inez had words with the broad-nosed receptionist. *What the hell's taking so long?* The receptionist looked at Inez as if she were the crazy one.

Bibi came up to the desk to calm her down. "Why don't you come and sit down, Nez?"

"You certainly have a lovely voice," the receptionist said to Bibi.

"Why, thank you."

You would have thought the two of them were at a tea party.

"If you think about Jesus," Bibi said, after Inez sat back down, "you have to believe he'd have been happier to have his fingers sewn together than to have a huge spike driven through his palms."

Inez took a long look at her sister. She had a beatific smile on her face. She seemed thrilled about the idea of being crazy.

"Do you think about Jesus much?" Inez asked.

"Yes, but no more than I should."

It was at this point that Jake Roseman burst through the swinging doors and looked around wildly until he noticed the two of them, sitting right in front of him.

Bibi let out a screech of hilarity. "Jake."

Jake's big head of black hair, just beginning to show gray, was all windblown. Inez was surprised by his fake red bow tie clipped to a wrinkled oxford-cloth shirt. His black corduroy sport coat was hopelessly frayed at the elbows. Never could a man look so beautiful and rumpled at the same time as Jake Roseman.

Inez took Jake aside to explain what had gone on, then he came and sat beside Bibi. He took her right hand in his. Inez tried to give the two of them a little room but stayed close enough so that she could hear what they said. Jake bowed his head. Bibi had always felt great affection for Jake, and he was fond of her.

"How do you feel now?" he asked in a low voice.

"Just fine. They gave me some painkillers."

"If you do something to yourself that requires painkillers, then you're doing something wrong. You shouldn't be causing yourself pain."

Bibi nodded respectfully.

"Inez says you want to sew the fingers of each of your hands together."

"That's right."

"Then you'll not be able to sew anymore."

"I've done enough sewing."

"You're tired of sewing."

"Yes."

"You know there's a way you can quit doing it without sewing your fingers together."

"I know that, silly."

Jake tried another tack. "What do you plan to do with your hands once they're all sewn up?"

"Maybe I'll be a Jewish wife," Bibi said.

Was she joking for Jake's sake?

Bibi lifted her right hand from his, and, together with her bandaged paw, cupped both hands in front of her face and rocked her head back and forth.

Not long before, they had invited Bibi over for a Shabbat dinner. At times, Inez played at being a Jewish wife on Friday nights, even though she never had any intention of converting. It was something that started after Anna was born, a sacrilege probably, her doing this, but Jake got a kick out of it. After she'd done it a couple of times—blessing the candles with a made-up mumble and with her hands cupped in front of her face as she'd seen Jake's mother do—Inez found that she liked it. They had a little ritual in their lives, false as it might be. Their small daughter sat fascinated at the table. The illusion of the perfect family was in place. After a couple of months of it, complete with homemade matzo-ball soup and bad Jewish wine, they invited Bibi over to share in the ritual.

Bibi was still sitting with her hands over her eyes. Jake stood up and paced around the waiting room. He lit a cigarette and looked to Inez for help.

"Bibi's saying the blessing over the *shabbos* candles."

Bibi, her eyes still covered, murmured her assent.

"How will you light the candles?" Jake asked.

"What do you mean?" Bibi asked.

"With your hands sewn together."

That seemed to stump her. She thought about it a minute. "I guess I won't be able to be a Jewish wife."

THE need to urinate forces Inez out of her stupor and into the bathroom. She brings the Princess phone with the long cord from the bedroom, thinking to call Sylvia. She needs to secure her bond with Sylvia before everything turns dark. As the phone rings, she imagines Sylvia's apartment as she left it: dishes piled up on the kitchen counter, sheets scattered across the small bed, the floor of the bedroom strewn with half of Sylvia's wardrobe. Inez had finally left in a hurry, panicked that if she didn't leave Sylvia's apartment she might find it hard to leave at all.

Sylvia answers in a groggy voice.

"Did I wake you?"

"Yes. Is something wrong?"

"No, no, I'm sorry. I missed you."

"You missed me?"

"I shouldn't have let it ring so long."

"What if I told you that I was dreaming of you, Inez?"

"I wouldn't believe you."

"You're so skeptical."

"You've given me reason."

"Everybody asleep in your house?"

"Except Jake; he's out seeing someone tonight."

"What's good for the goose."

"He brought home his father, set him up in the spare room, then took off for his 'labor meeting.'"

Inez stares at herself in the mirror, phone at her ear. She looks sad.

"Inez? Are you there?"

"Yes, I'm here." She sits back down on the toilet cover.

"I thought I'd lost you."

"You haven't lost me, but you should know that I'm sitting on the toilet seat."

"That puts things in perspective."

"I'm not going to the bathroom. I wouldn't talk to you while I was going to the bathroom."

"So, the bathroom? Do you just happen to like the atmosphere?"

"Privacy."

"Ah. You have your father-in-law there now."

"And the children. I once slit my wrists in here."

"You . . . what?"

"I slit my wrists." Inez listens to the gasp on the other end of the line and realizes that she's said something that she shouldn't have. "It was years ago. I was going through a hard time."

"Why are you telling me this now?"

"We were talking about the bathroom. I remembered the incident, that's all. There was no point to my telling you."

"Why didn't you tell me before?"

"It never occurred to me."

"Inez, is this why you're calling so late? If you're thinking about harming yourself, I can come right over. I can catch a cab like that."

"No, no. It's nothing like that. You have the wrong idea. Anyway, when I did that I was just fooling around."

"People don't fool around with that."

"*I* was fooling around. There was hardly any blood. The cuts were superficial. I cleaned it up myself and didn't even end up with any scars." Inez remembers the running water as much as the blood. The two faucets, the hot and the cold—no updated plumbing in this house—each running its own pinkish swirl through the blood.

"When did this happen?"

"Years ago."

"When?"

"What does it matter?"

"Tell me."

She thinks of telling Sylvia a little about it. Isn't this the type of thing you share with somebody you're intimate with? Isn't this a form of intimacy? Wouldn't it be good to share, especially now that it's over? She likes to think it's over, even if it's only in remission. How to begin? She thinks of herself as a child at the doctor—open your mouth, please, and say "ahhhh."

"I had trouble after Joey was born. I didn't bounce back so well. The fact is, I couldn't stand to hear him crying. There were other things, but I couldn't stand the crying. The crying felt like little tack nails being pierced into my head. The same nails over and over again. First the mallet hammered them in and then the claw yanked them out. Over and over. The trouble is I already had Anna—she was six then. I didn't need another baby. I wanted to cry all the time, but I didn't. The baby was crying. I had no appetite. I didn't want to get out of bed. I didn't want anybody near me. No one. I didn't want to play the violin. My husband was cheating on me. The baby was crying. The baby was always crying. I lay in bed and imagined myself in a box, lined with yards and yards of cotton. Beautiful white cotton. You can't believe how much the baby cried."

And there, she's said it, or said something; she's certainly said too much. There's a silence now on the other end of the line.

"Oh, Inez, I'm so sorry."

Now to pretend that it hadn't happened in earnest. "It wasn't so bad."

"How can you say that?"

Inez doesn't answer. She's already said enough.

"How long did it last?"

"Not long," she lies, wondering if it has ever truly ended. Parts did. The need to cry.

"Inez, this sounds serious. Did you ever see a professional about this? Did you talk to anybody about this?"

Inez can feel Sylvia's intensity on the end of the line. She hadn't wanted this part of her life cracked open. You can't share what's most private. There are things you can't share with anyone.

"Is that why you called?" Sylvia says.

"No, you just got me thinking of memorable times I've spent in the bathroom." Inez forces a laugh.

"This isn't funny, Inez. When you think about suicide, what sort of ways do you imagine doing it?"

"I don't think about suicide." The impostor is trying trick questions on her. When, sir, did you start beating your wife?

"But you told me you slit your wrists, so you must have thought about it a lot of times before you tried that."

Perhaps Sylvia should have been an attorney.

"Let's say I have a tendency. But most people who have tendencies never act on them."

"Does Jake know about this?"

"What's to know?"

"Maybe you should tell him."

"I'm telling you."

"Do you want me to tell him?"

"No."

"I think he should know."

Inez shifts to a more assertive tone. "Look, this is something I've told you in confidence, Sylvia. I'm not going to tell people that you go around impersonating journalists and who knows what else."

"This is different."

"Trust me, I'm not going to do anything."

"I think Jake should know about this."

"Quit being an ass. Should I tell Jake what I do when I'm at your apartment?"

"That's up to you. I'm worried about you, Inez."

"You have no reason." Inez stands again in front of the mirror.

"Should I come over? I could grab a cab."

"You have nothing to worry about."

"Really?" Sylvia says, beginning to sob on the other end of the line.

"No, nothing to worry about." Inez could look at herself for five minutes without blinking. "Sylvia, let's forget about this conversation."

"I can't do that, Inez; I love you," Sylvia says brokenly.

"Listen, there's nothing to worry about."

"Nothing?"

"Not a thing. It's old news."

"I told you that I went through this with my mother."

"I know."

"I couldn't stand to go through it again."

"You won't have to."

Inez is beginning to feel weary. Sylvia's sobs have started to become a breathless event, a heaving oceanic business that seems like it could go on forever. Inez holds the phone away from her ears. Enough already. She puts the phone up to her mouth. "You'll just have to trust me," Inez says, holding her own eyes captive in the mirror. "Now, go to sleep, sweet one. Go to sleep, now."

Sylvia is still weeping. *For crying out loud,* Inez wants to say, *enough.*

the mind lasso

To Sylvia's surprise, Hy is back at work on Saturday morning, decked out like an aging mannequin in a fancy men's shop. She welcomes the normalcy of his being there, his unusual clothes notwithstanding, as her life grows dense with complications. She's cried for days after her conversation with Inez, flooded with images of her mother. The halfhearted suicide attempts, almost always in the summer when Angela Bran, the good school nurse, found herself adrift with too much time on her hands. The wrists slit, then bandaged, then covered in long-sleeved shirts, unnatural in the hot Sacramento summer. For a few years after Sylvia moved out, her mother stopped cutting herself. Sylvia believed the worst was behind them, but then her mother's experiments with pharmaceuticals began, and one Sunday morning in July, when they were supposed to meet for brunch, Sylvia found her mother dead. Angela Bran was in her bed, propped up against half a dozen pillows, a broad swath of ruby-red lipstick caked on her lips. Her mother, who despised makeup, had applied a thick foundation and a hideous blue-black eyeshadow. Beside the pills, her mother's note:

> Dear Sylvia, the only hope for me is to become eternally somnolent, from the Old English, the Latin and French. Ah, the somnus of sleep. Forgive me.

This morning, worn out, her eyes still red and bleary, Sylvia has finally managed to put her mother out of her head. It's not so easy with Inez. How does she stop thinking about Inez offering her beautiful white wrists to a razor? The violinist's casual confession was no accident. Suicide, it seems to Sylvia, is a form of attack, and before it's launched comes the probe. Sylvia hasn't decided on a response but thinks the first step is to back away, retreat to her comfort zone, be the voyant again.

She sits at a Baldwin piano, one of her favorites. At least Hy has no desire to die at his own hand. As disease overtakes him and he grows steadily more breathless, he'll probably wish he could live longer.

It isn't the typical Hy holding forth this morning, though. Despite the fact that he can barely breathe and that he should be in the hospital, a special edition of the man has shown up today. He's draped in tailored clothes she's never seen: a camel-hair sport coat atop a starched broadcloth shirt, the hue a fancy men's shop might dub "coral." Hy's silver cuff links feature a pair of linked eighth notes that nicely match the freshly buffed silver treble clef medallion at the throat of his string tie. He's wearing a pair of moss-green flannel slacks and well-shined loafers.

"Look at you," she says. "What a sight for sore eyes." As she says this, she laughs to herself and wishes she had a pair of sunglasses to hide her eyes. Fortunately, Hy doesn't notice her condition. It's taken all his concentration to dress like a dandy and remain standing.

"So you like the ensemble?" he asks.

"Handsome."

Hy nods his head and winks at her—the cool cat. Clearly, he doesn't want to be reminded of his physical collapse last week. Thus the fancy dress and the touching bit of bravado.

Still, Sylvia can't help asking, "What's the occasion?"

Hy inhales slowly through his nose, seeming to repeat the question to himself. "I intend to sell . . . a record number of pianos, so I thought it would behoove . . . behoove me to dress nicely for my public." He steadies himself against the piano. "You hear about the . . . about the Cuban missile business going kaput?"

"I did."

"If it was ever anything . . . in the first place. Anyway, all that bullshit, pardon . . . pardon the expression, is done. Everybody's breathing a sigh . . . of relief. People are so goddamn happy to be . . . alive, they're going to come out and buy . . . themselves a piano."

Shy Miller Beem, whom Hy has described as the worst salesman in the Western world, comes up to admire his boss. Miller, dressed in his usual gray suit, starts to say something, then just shakes his head.

"You can't believe how beaut . . . how beautiful I am, Miller?" Hy says.

"No, I can't."

"You're not supposed to be sur . . . surprised."

"Miller's always surprised," Sylvia says. She opens a book of music and chords the intro to "I Feel Pretty" from *West Side Story.*

"Listen to her. . . . We're going to sell a shit . . . a shitload of pianos today, Miller."

Miller backs away, blushing, and resumes his position across the showroom. Although not really a salesman, Miller looks good standing there in the suit, which fits him surprisingly well. One Saturday morning, before Hy came in, Sylvia heard Miller playing a Chopin sonata. She was surprised by the timorous fellow's facility. He played the Chopin with more personality than she'd have imagined Miller could project, but as soon as he looked up from the keys and saw her standing there, he quit playing and slunk off the piano bench.

Hy turns toward her now. "Why did I ever hire a shy faggot?"

"Because you're a kind man." Sylvia turns a couple of pages, then segues into "Tonight."

Hy shrugs. He's having a harder time breathing. He inhales slowly through his nose. It looks like he's trying to invent a new way of smoking without smoke. "So, how's that . . . that girl of yours, Sylvia?"

"She's fine."

"You going to keep her?"

"I'm not sure. I'm not sure I can."

"She giving you . . . trouble? She doesn't realize how . . . wonderful you are? She doesn't deserve . . . you."

Sylvia lifts her hands from the piano and folds them in her lap.

Hy puts a hand on her shoulder and for a moment she lays her cheek against it.

"I'm sorry."

"Thank you," she says and feels herself getting weepy again. "Let's not get maudlin now, Hy."

"No, ma'am."

She can sense him watching her as she closes her eyes, the tears streaming.

"Maud . . . maudlin isn't good for sales. Listen, you are my pride . . . my pride and joy, Sylvia."

She opens her eyes and faces him.

"So tell me . . . tell me what you really think . . . about my ensemble."

"It's beautiful, Hy."

"Truth is, I was looking for a shirt . . . that was a redder red. Like . . . a boiled crayfish red. But I ended up settling for . . . what would you call this red?"

Sylvia wipes her eyes. "Coral."

"Not . . . coral. That's a girl's color. Coral. Trouble with you . . . you don't know anything about men's clothes."

"You're wrong about that. I bet you bought that shirt at Toole-James."

"How did you know?"

"And the slacks, I'd say the slacks . . ." But Sylvia can see that Hy is distracted. A terrible weariness has come into his face. "Are you all right?"

"Fine," he says and digs for another breath. "Just going to sit for a minute . . . til somebody comes. You should start playing. You start playing, Sylvia, and sud . . . suddenly . . . customers. That's your power."

Sylvia watches Hy slump onto the nearby bench of an ugly blond spinet.

"What do you want to hear?" she asks.

"*My Fair Lady*? You always . . . do a fine job with that."

Sylvia quickly launches into "Wouldn't It Be Loverly."

Hy offers a wan smile from his piano bench.

"Wouldn't you feel better if you were home?" she asks.

"I'll be fine. I'm just going to . . . lie here a minute. Keep playing. Tell me one thing . . . How'd you know I got that shirt at Toole-James?"

"I used to frequent Toole-James."

"Come on."

Sylvia segues into "With a Little Bit of Luck" and tells Hy about her infatuation with downtown. "I discovered Toole-James when I first moved to the city. The place is a little intimidating. But after I'd been there a couple of times, I dared myself to steal a souvenir—something extravagant."

"Stories."

The supine Hyman is dying in front of her eyes. She has two choices: to break down crying again or entertain him. Keeping her eyes on Hy, she segues into "I've Grown Accustomed to Her Face."

"Lovely," Hy says and kindly prompts her. "So you're a thief?"

"Upon occasion."

Hy grins. "So what did you steal?"

"Well, I was thinking of a hand-painted silk tie, or a pair of opal cuff links. You know how they leave the jewelry around on the countertops, just ripe for the picking." She dives into "The Rain in Spain," adding a rapid rhumba beat. "The men in Toole-James weren't my type and I wasn't theirs. Even the salesmen seemed impervious to me."

"Must have been blind."

"No, they took one look at me and decided that I'd more likely pull out a feather duster than buy the silk shirt that I was fingering. I ended up stealing a fake red turtleneck, a silk dickey. I stuffed it into a coat pocket."

Hyman laughs until he's forced to sit up on the ugly blond piano bench and cough into his handkerchief. Getting ahold of himself, he says, "For a shiksa, you're quite . . . quite the storyteller."

Sylvia shakes her head. "Of all the things I could have stolen. When I got home I was ashamed of myself. Not for stealing the thing, but for stealing something so paltry. I stuck the dickey in the pocket of an old coat and hung it in the darkest corner of my closet."

"And that's where the story ends?" Hy asks, wiping his brow.

"Nope. I had a moment of inspiration." Sylvia modulates down to "I Could Have Danced All Night." She smiles at Hy, who is leaning on an elbow. "I don't want to shock you."

"It's too late for that."

"Well, I decided my fascination with Toole-James was a sign."

"Of what?"

"That I should dress myself as a man."

"You want to dress . . . like a man?"

"I was curious. I picked up a blue oxford-cloth shirt and fleshed out my ensemble at a thrift shop on Divisidero. I chose a pair of ash-gray gabardine trousers and a young man's herringbone sport coat that draped beautifully over my shoulders. It's true, Hy. I spent hours admiring myself in front of the mirror. I want you to know, that when I choose to, I make a beautiful man."

"That's not how I see you."

"I'm sorry, Hy."

Hy shrugs.

Sylvia looks across the showroom floor, then whispers, "We have a customer."

Hy boosts himself up off the piano bench, then slides the silver medallion down the cords of his string tie and lifts the tie over his head. "Here, Sylvia, this is for you."

"I can't take that."

"What are you talking about? Try it . . . with your sport coat when you're not . . . wearing your dickey."

"Oh, Hy."

"Come on, don't get all gushy . . . on me. We've got a customer."

SYLVIA is amazed at the way Hy snaps to. Up on his feet with a little bounce, he says to Sylvia, "I know this woman doesn't look . . . like the type, but she wants to hear *West Side Story.* Trust me."

"Mood?" Sylvia asks.

"Mild schmaltz. Just like you did before—start with . . . 'I Feel Pretty,' go on to 'Tonight,' then . . . then juice it up a little with . . . 'Somewhere.' This is going to be a quick one."

Sylvia watches as Hyman steps toward the slim, graying woman, weaving his way through a row of uprights. Despite his condition, he negotiates the narrow spaces as if he were Cary Grant, a bit debauched, maybe, a trifle rumpled. A minute later he is offering the woman, who appears to be a witty but viceless aging maiden devoted to her nieces and nephews, a mentholated Newport, a gesture that pleases her even though she declines the offer.

Sylvia attacks the piano with as light a touch as she can manage. Does the gracefully aging customer, who's always been considered attractive despite never marrying, *feel pretty* as dapper Hyman follows her through the showroom? Sylvia can see that the customer is more interested in Hy's proximity than in the roomful of pianos in front of her. At a certain point, midway through "Tonight," Hy stops on a spot and allows his charge to wander alone among the larger instruments. "The trick," Sylvia once overheard Hy telling Miller Beem, "is to get them to miss you, to miss your presence, to have them feel like they're lost without you. This is where the art comes in. This is when you choose the piano that seems appropriate for them to buy. And when you get good, really good, you toss your mind lasso around the piano you want them to buy and pull it toward them." Of course, Miller Beem has yet to master the mind lasso. In his first six months at Myerson's, he's sold nary a piano. But that isn't Miller's purpose. He'd been hired, as had his predecessors, to stand in his gray suit and greet customers. Nothing particularly effusive is expected of him, simply the unassuming smile of a human welcome mat. But as his illness has progressed, Hy has felt a necessity to pass on the tricks of his trade to all his employees.

When the slim, gray-haired maiden approaches the blond spinet, Sylvia plays the chords to "Somewhere" and notices Hyman wink at Miller Beem. The mind lasso has clearly been set. All three of them know it. Even the aging lass must know that she has little chance of leaving without the title to the ugly spinet. Why, Sylvia wonders, did Hy choose this instrument for the lassoing? Because it is homely? Or was Hyman forestalling his death by unloading the piano in whose shadow he'd just survived a near-death repose?

A little later, after Hyman closes on the mahogany baby grand, a $3,500 instrument, with a couple who's never played a lick of piano, he strolls over to Sylvia and compliments her on her playing. He'd requested something flashy for the couple, and she'd obliged with the overture to *Rhapsody in Blue*.

"Your instincts are glorious, Sylvia," he says, and signals for Miller Beem to come over. "See how it's done, Miller? The next one is yours." With this, Hyman excuses himself and goes off to rest on the long, padded bench of a Steinway grand.

WHEN Sylvia returns from the ladies' room, where she's washed her face and done her best to brighten herself, Inez Roseman, sumptuous in a rose-colored cashmere sweater and a long black skirt, is backed against the keyboard of the ebonized Baldwin. Miller Beem is standing thirty feet from Inez, performing the mind lasso. A proper voyant would hide herself behind a pillar and watch this curious game play itself out. But Sylvia is afraid that if she stands watching for too long she'll begin to cry again. She takes a deep breath and steps promptly out of the shadows.

"Sylvia, Sylvia," Inez calls sotto voce. "Thank God."

"What are you doing here, Inez?"

"I needed to talk with you. Who is that man?"

"That's Miller. He's trying to sell you a piano."

"He hasn't even spoken to me. Would you please tell him that I don't want a piano, that I already have a piano. It's like he has a grip on me."

Sylvia gazes at Inez. If the mind lasso is this effective, she wonders if it could be employed to tie a person to their life? And yet, what's the sense of holding someone against their will? She walks over and stands beside Miller for a moment. "Good work with the lasso."

"Thank you."

"I think you've got her where you want her. Only thing, she's a friend of mine. She's not interested in buying a piano. She came to see me."

Miller Beem exhales a long, ragged stream of breath, and then slowly turns his back on Inez.

Inez sighs and her body quivers for a moment. She seems hesitant, like an animal who's just discovered its liberty. Sylvia tries to watch the violinist dispassionately. It is a difficult task. Inez starts at the sight of Hy Myerson, sleeping on the Steinway bench. "Who's that?"

Rather than classical snoring, Hy emits a series of high-pitched sighs.

"That's my boss," Sylvia says.

"Mr. Myerson? Shouldn't we do something?"

"There's nothing to do. Hyman should stay home, but he insists on coming to work. He has trouble breathing, the medication wears him out, but the only thing he cares about is selling pianos. He's already sold two this morning. He thinks today's going to be a banner day."

"And Miller? Is that his son?"

"His protégé."

"Sylvia, I need to speak with you."

"Not here."

"Can we go somewhere? The ladies' room?"

"I only have a moment."

IT is a humble bathroom with a single stall and a porcelain sink, etched with cracks.

"The other night," Inez says, "was an aberration. My suicide chatter. It won't happen again. As I said, it's old news."

"Whatever you say."

"Don't be like that."

"Like what?"

"So cool."

"You shouldn't have kept it from me." Sylvia doesn't want to be pulled back in. Which of them is operating the lasso?

"Don't worry." Inez reaches up and traces the bones of Sylvia's cheek.

Sylvia closes her eyes. She can't resist the smooth tips of Inez's bow fingers as they glide over her left cheek, leaving a mark of desire, a lush vibrato, rippling in their wake. Sylvia kisses the violinist's left hand and opens her eyes. "I need to go, Inez."

"Wait." Inez reaches inside the neck of her sweater and pulls out the strand of African trade beads that were tucked under. "I've had them restrung and knotted on silk. Don't they fall nicely?"

Sylvia nods. The markings of each bead appear remarkably distinct against the rose-colored sweater. It's all Sylvia can do not to reach out to the beads or run her hands over the cashmere.

"I love them," Inez says. "They're one of the nicest gifts I've ever gotten."

Sylvia pushes open the bathroom door. "I have to go," she whispers.

"You're all right with the other night?"

"No, I'm not all right."

"What can I do?"

Sylvia shakes her head.

Inez takes Sylvia's face in her hands, kissing each eyelid sweetly. "Can we keep it between us?"

"Yes," says Sylvia, panting slightly from the violinist's kisses.

"There's something else," Inez says.

Sylvia faces Inez's serious eyes.

"I had a letter from my sister at the state hospital. The missile thing frightened her. I need to visit her."

Sylvia nods.

"Will you come with me?"

"Why would you want *me*?" Sylvia says, coolly.

"Do I have to explain why I want you? All the reasons I want you? Will you come, Sylvia? I need you."

"I'll have to think about it."

"Don't punish me, Sylvia. May I give you something?"

"What's that?"

"This."

Sylvia tastes Inez's sweet tongue.

BACK on the floor, Sylvia is surprised to see Hy smoking beside a tall, loose-limbed gentleman with a trim mustache. Hy has shed his camel coat and opened the collar of his coral shirt. How empty his neck looks without the string tie and its silver medallion, now coiled in her purse. Hyman seems to be chewing on the smoke as he sucks it down into his spoiled lungs. His last cigarette?

"Sylvia, we were won . . . wondering where you'd gone. Mr. Mathews would like to hear . . . the ebony Steinway."

"Of course." Sylvia walks to the piano, glancing over her shoulder toward the ladies' room just as Inez emerges, the African trade beads visible now, framed by the rose-hued sweater. Sylvia looks away as Inez turns and walks head down toward the street door.

Sylvia must put the violinist out of her head. She smiles up at the tall man. "Anything in particular you'd like to hear, Mr. Mathews?"

The man shakes his head. "Anything is fine. You choose." He takes a long draw off his Newport and blows the smoke out of his nose.

He must be the idealized customer Hy always talks about. Sylvia peeks at Hy, who, leaning against the far end of the Steinway, is blowing smoke rings. Sylvia can see Miller Beem creeping forward.

Sylvia sits at the stately piano. There is a determined shine to its ebony surface, which makes playing it an occasion. Sylvia spends a moment silently pumping the sustaining pedals, as if she were pumping life into the instrument. The two men stand close to the piano. What are they expecting?

As Sylvia opens into the lilting theme of "Surrey with the Fringe on Top," Hy holds his hand out toward the piano, as if to say, *Behold this, my friend; there may never be more grace exhibited on this planet.* Hy reaches up to pull the strings of his tie and realizes that it's no longer there. He trains his eyes on Sylvia and they quickly become moist. Hy offers Mr. Mathews a fresh Salem. "Isn't she won . . . wonderful?" Hy says. "A proper salesman would tell . . . you that it's all the piano. That you . . . could go home . . . in an hour and play like that. Not true. Sylvia here is some . . . something special. Now, I don't mean to imply . . . that there's any . . . anything wrong . . . with the piano. It's the finest piano we have at Myerson's, the finest available on the West Coast. Can you hear . . . the richness of its sound? How crisp its re . . . response? The way the act . . . the action, un . . . unparalleled in my judgment, con . . . contributes to the clean . . . to the clean artic . . . articulation? This is a piano to die for. I'd . . . I'd wager . . . wager my life on that."

night picnic

THE kids and the old man are asleep tonight when Inez returns from the monthly jaunt down the peninsula with the symphony. The Saturday night concert and the round-trip bus ride always leave her a little spent.

Jake is smoking in the dimly lit living room, a whiskey sour in his hands. "You must be beat. Come have a drink with me in the backyard."

"The backyard?"

"Yeah, it's nice out. There's stars."

"Nature boy," she says.

"That's me.

The day after his father came to roost with them, Jake went out and bought lawn furniture. "The old man hates the outdoors," he said, by way of explanation.

Inez excuses herself to change and, a few moments later, steps out to the backyard, in a cotton nightgown. Although it's still warm enough, the air is like a damp tongue, reaching through the cotton to her skin. She sees a wisp of smoke rising from the corner of the yard. The magnificent blue and white globes of the hydrangeas are visible. Also, the perfect pink camellias, which in their setting of firm and shiny leaves remind her of corsages. The camellia is just as lovely floating in the water of a chipped bowl. Although she can't see the roses, she can smell them. No matter that she rarely prunes them, they still grow, a bit choked, perhaps, into the light of day. Inez is grateful for the garden, something that thrives with so little attention from her. What else in her life has provided her with more than she's given it? She thinks of her father and her sister. She thinks of her children, and stands a moment, sadly contrite.

"Over here," Jake says, from a corner of the garden.

As Inez steps closer, she can make out Jake, sitting cross-legged on a blanket, clad only in his shorts. "What do you think this is," she whispers, "a nudist colony?"

"Hey, the neighbors can't see back here. Sit down. Isn't it a beautiful night? I'll never understand why it's warmer in October than it is in July."

"It's called fog, Jake."

"Gosh, you smell wonderful," he says, handing her a whiskey sour.

Inez takes a short sip. She never cared for whiskey until Jake showed her that she could drink it like this.

"Roasted almonds," he says.

"What?"

"That's how you smell."

She can make out his face, the sweet smile, in the glow of his cigarette. She sits down on the blanket beside him.

"To beauty," Jake says, clinking her glass with his.

"You can't even see me in the dark."

"I can see you."

She doesn't say anything but catches another glimpse of him in the cigarette light, his eyes steady, a man planning his next move. She tells herself to give in, if not to the man, then at least to the damp night air. Why not?

"You're so beautiful, Inez. I can't believe you ever married me."

"Maybe that was my first mistake."

"You think so?"

"I don't know."

He scoots closer to her and kisses her neck.

His damp lips surprise her and she leans away.

Jake tilts his head back, draws on his cigarette, and blows a stream of smoke toward the sky. He reaches out his hands. Inez sinks down toward him as he fondles her breasts, his thumbs going back and forth across the cotton fabric above her nipples, his cigarette still between two fingers.

"What do you think you're doing?" she says, feeling herself swoon under his touch.

"What do *you* think I'm doing?"

"Going after what you want," she says, sitting up straight.

"You don't want it?" he murmurs, kissing her ear.

"I didn't say that."

Jake faces her directly. "Don't you ever have any desire for me?"

It's a fair enough question and the answer is yes. "I do," she says. She lifts her glass of whiskey sour and sips at it. Jake lights a new cigarette off his old one. In the flare of light, she catches his wistful look. He leans on an elbow to prop up his big, open face. What's alarming is how much he is himself: a man in the middle of his life who's traded so much on his charm.

Some mornings, still in bed, she watches him dress by the bureau. He must think she's sleeping. Noting his lips as they pucker into a soundless whistle, she marvels at how he wakes with such good cheer and bears so little resemblance to the man she's made into the devil. Long-limbed and muscular, his body has kept its shape pretty well over the years—she used to love to sling an arm around his broad shoulders, to lay her head in the hollow of his belly. She sometimes wishes she could do it now. Is that desire? She's wanted him to hold her countless times, to curl up beside him in bed, to have an entire day go by like that. She's learned to keep it to herself. She can't trust the man—she's not even sure she has any respect for him—but that doesn't stop her from wanting him.

She sips her drink, holding her gaze on Jake. She can't get over how large his features are. There is something outsized about them, like the hands and feet of a Rodin sculpture. Is it simply that she's grown used to the intimacy of Sylvia's little bird face with its long, pointy nose? Her husband of twenty years, whom she's always considered as handsome a man as she's ever known, appears grotesque with his sprawling nose and his large, open lips; his brown eyes, so full of meaning; the loose skin under his eyes, a pocket for all the woes he hasn't shared with her. How maddening to have this man, whom she'd just as soon write off as a philandering clown, present himself as the aching face of humanity. She recognizes the ploy—sincerity as a marketable guise, yet another tool leaping from the counselor's briefcase. Or is she simply demonizing him? She wants to be so angry at him. She wants to blame him for everything. Didn't they once love each other? Didn't he promise her a future? Hasn't he taken it all away? Taken her for granted. Relied on his chippies. Driven her to what? A woman? A woman who reminds her of herself long ago. A daring young woman with an actual personality, whoever she is.

Jake draws on his cigarette, then touches her hand. "So how are you?" he says.

"I don't know."

Jake takes hold of her hand.

Inez thinks to pull away, but breathes a moment instead. She notices the blue hydrangeas. They have no fragrance. She closes her eyes and tries to imagine a smell for them.

"You look like you've been doing some serious thinking," Jake says.

"I'm always thinking, Jake."

"I know. You do enough thinking for the both of us." He takes a deep drag off his cigarette and slowly exhales smoke out through his nostrils. "So tell me, Inez, how's your soul?"

Inez chuckles at the glibness of his question—a Jake Roseman specialty, and yet she finds herself wondering. She faces him. "I wish I knew."

Jake snuffs out his cigarette in the grass, then kneads her shoulders—a light massage. "I've missed you," he says. "You've been gone so much, and now with the old man . . ."

"It's a difficult time," she says, hoping to cut things off. When Jake is this genuine, he's hard to resist.

Jake leans over and kisses her, not on the lips but on the bridge of her nose. It's a gentle, cautious act. A man dipping his baby finger into the water to test the temperature before fully partaking. She reaches out and takes hold of Jake's face, that large globe of expression, hoping to control in her hands whatever intimacy might pass between them.

She used to wonder if their sex life might have been salvaged had she been the one who regulated the pace of the foreplay. The concept was like a foreign language to Jake—he referred to it as *the stall*—and by the time she realized that she could have a voice in the matter, that she could demand that Jake slow down and include her spirit in the act as well as her body, it was too late for them. She used to wonder if Jake hurried through sex with his bimbos. They must be made differently than she is. Or maybe Jake's discovered a new breed of rocket-age women who roar off instantly to orgasm. She prefers to believe that each of Jake's girls aches like she does. But being inferior beings—which is the only way that she can conceive them—their cheap agony is short-lived and hollow.

Jake has a hand under her nightgown now and she clamps her thighs around it before he can get where he wants.

"Aren't you getting enough from whoever your latest is?"

"You're the one I always want."

As Inez opens her legs to Jake, she feels herself shiver. From the night air, or from the touch of him?

"Let's see how slow you can go."

"You talk too much," he says.

With that, they both laugh, because it's always the other way around. She lets Jake slide her nightgown up over her head. She's naked in the backyard. She lets him kiss her. He runs his hand down her side, along her ribs.

"My violin," he says, softly.

"I am not your violin," she says, as quietly.

Jake curls up beside her. This is a new strategy. He is going to make her want him. She does want him, but she can't let him know that. As soon as she lets him know, he'll be on top of her. She won't be ready for him. Then he'll get angry that it always turns out the same.

Her hope, her foolish hope, is that if they lie there together long enough, they'll arrive at some sort of mutual desire. But all he is really doing is counting: one thousand one, one thousand two, one thousand three, just like the boys playing football on the street. Late afternoons, before a symphony, when she forces herself to lie down and take a little rest, she sometimes hears these football boys hollering: one thousand one, one thousand two . . . Once, when she asked Jake, he told her that the boys had to count to a certain number before they rushed the quarterback. Now she feels herself go tense beside Jake as she anticipates his coming to the end of his count.

What's most frightening is how ordinary it seems. When Jake climbs atop her, she consents. She is a willing participant. Or, more accurately, a participant without will. But did she say no? Of course not. Without saying yes, without saying no, the wife of twenty years is laid in the backyard.

One time, years ago, when Jake was angry after a particularly listless session in bed, he called her a Swedish ice queen. She thought it had a rather nice ring to it.

"You mean I strike you as *frigid?*"

"I didn't say that," Jake said.

They both knew that the F word was a no-no. If you uttered it, it might prove irrevocably true. The self-fulfilling prophecy. But she was way past the point of being spooked by such things. In fact, she'd wanted to say it, not that she even knew what the word meant. She could have talked all night about her peculiar lack of responsiveness, which was maybe not so peculiar after all. She'd sure spent a long time thinking about it. Far more time than Jake had. He'd pretty much shoot his wad and roll over. A moment later he'd have ferried out to deep sleep and she'd prop up a couple of pillows and consider her condition. Jake seemed to have made peace with it, as if he'd had the misfortune of marrying a woman with multiple sclerosis.

After Jake called her a Swedish ice queen, she said, "Oh gosh, I always wanted to be royalty."

They'd been married for ten years by then, and she'd spent so many nights wondering what was wrong with her that she'd gotten a little bit bored with the question. She either needed another participant in the discussion or it was time to turn the argument on its head. What if Jake shared some of the responsibility for her frigidity? That was the kind of ridiculous thinking that reading Dr. Kinsey led to.

NOW Jake, sated, climbs off her and turns over to sleep, naked as a baby on the blanket. Nature boy. Inez is tempted to leave him outside, but she doesn't want to be party to the scandal it would cause if he was discovered by the children, or worse, by his father, sprawled without his clothes in the backyard. With a little effort she gets his shorts on and drags him to his feet.

"Want to do it again?" he mumbles, his eyes not even open, but his pink prick making its way through the slit of his shorts.

"Inside, inside," she says, urging him forward.

The house is quiet. Asleep. Fortunately, Jake is also asleep once he hits the bed. Inez is afraid of sleep just now. If she slept now, she might slip back into her role as the long-married wife and never be able to climb out. She turns the bedside lamp on and looks at Jake, peaceful in his sideways sleep, his lips bunched as if he means to kiss the air. The man is sated. At rest. Should she take some credit for this? Hardly.

Sometimes after sex with Jake, a profound aversion sets in. Tonight, she's unable to rid herself of his smell. Even after she's washed herself, showered, the air around her is filled with his particular odor. She used to love his smell—an earthy caraway, or so she imagined, rising through a light blanket of whiskey and tobacco. Now she finds the smell cloying. She thinks of Sylvia, the touch of her skin, the cool glow of it. How happy she's been, luxuriating in the province of Sylvia's smell: the knotty fragrance of sex glazed with the clean floral tinge of a surprisingly good perfume. Sometimes the smell of a floral soap rising. Of lavender. Talc. Salt. The intimate, randy taste of Sylvia's vagina. The faint but comforting smell of dry blood. A tinge of some Givenchy fragrance rising from her lover's skin.

But now Inez is oppressed by the smell of her sleeping husband. He'd hardly been on top of her a moment, a train passing through the station, and yet his imprint is insoluble. She could stand under the shower for an hour, to no avail. How to wash away twenty years that haven't gone the way she wanted? What exactly had she wanted? That's the hitch. She hadn't known what to want, had imposed little will. And Jake? Jake had simply been Jake. Find a vacuum and fill it. Who could blame him? Wasn't he probably a better man than most? She'd become the vacuum. Does she think she is unique in this? The only woman in America waiting for divine inspiration? Wishing that her husband, although no better trained in sacrificing his pleasure and convenience than she is in satisfying herself, will lead her to the promised land? Why hasn't she learned to be content with her emptiness or, like other women, to be practical: to measure what she has and doesn't have in other ways?

She could spend the rest of the night making an inventory that would look good on a balance sheet. Two beautiful children. A pleasant house. An enviable career, employing a bit of her talent. A husband who provides, in a manner of speaking. And what does she provide? Who exactly is the ingrate here?

Inez steers her mind to Sylvia's apartment. Who'd have guessed that you could make a paradise out of two rooms filled with cheap wicker chairs and jelly jars, three floors above the cable-car tracks? The photograph in Sylvia's bathroom of a red door, a glorious color that makes her shiver every time she sees it, perhaps because it reminds her that the world is more various than she ever imagined. Ravel, Satie, Sinatra on the hi-fi. Dancing in the middle of the big room. A striptease in the bedroom. Love on the small bed. A meal of lamb chops and Swiss chard. Succulent.

Inez would like to think that she has found herself in those rooms, found a true if crooked love in Sylvia. A tenderness outside of her experience. Perhaps what she loves most about Sylvia is that for all the woman's trickiness, she's as sincere as anybody she's known aside from her own children. She'd hand Sylvia her heart, if she could, and be done with it.

What would Inez have to trade to stay in those rooms above the cable-car tracks? Everything, is the humble answer. And what price to remain where she is? Live the second half of her life as the respected wife of Jake Roseman. She can see how it would unfold. Mother of two grown children, grandmother, grown weepy waiting for her children to call, her facility on the violin waning, life dissolving slowly through the shadows, the aches and pains. She hasn't a choice. A woman like her isn't brave enough to walk away from her family, her children, and go on living. She cannot make so sharp a left turn in her life, nor can she sit idle.

Inez touches herself under the covers. She thinks of Sylvia's tongue, the taste of Sylvia. The smell of Jake diminishes. Inez slowly pushes the covers off her side of the bed and begins to rub herself in earnest. For once, her body is determined to triumph, as she lies naked atop the sheets, glowing in the lamplight, slowly bringing herself to climax.

The door to their room, which may not have been properly closed, is now ajar. Inez cannot bear to think that one of her children is lurking in the doorway. She looks up, in quivering fright. Isaac, her father-in-law, her old violin teacher, is leaning crookedly in the doorway, taking it all in.

skeleton key

"You want to hear something amusing?"

"Of course."

"The other night, Inez and I made love in the backyard."

"In the backyard, huh?" Christine pushes her plate to the side, her sandwich barely touched. "You're getting awfully adventurous for an old married couple."

Jake isn't sure why he's brought this up. He'd been telling her about his father, the fact that the old man is now living in the house. He takes a bite of his pastrami sandwich. "We've run out of privacy in the house."

"And you've discovered it under the stars."

"Mmm-hmmm."

He and Christine are sitting at a sewing table in a large third-floor room. The presence of the single bed covered in a rose-patterned quilt pleases Jake. On the side of the bed is a geriatric sewing machine sunken in an oak cabinet. A slim-waisted mannequin in a snug summer dress is facing out the room's only window.

"There's something awfully sweet about this room," Jake says, quickly gazing around it.

"I used to spend hours up here," Christine says wistfully. "When the boys were little I liked to make them outfits—velvet overalls, pajamas in a wild zebra pattern."

"She reminds me of you," Jake says, pointing toward the mannequin at the window.

"I hope I'm a little more expressive than she is," Christine says.

"Indeed." Jake reaches across the table and pats Christine's cheek affectionately.

"So how was it?" Christine asks, keeping her eyes trained on Jake.

"How was what?"

"Your backyard party with Inez."

"Oh . . . it was fine."

"Fine," Christine says, with a smirk. "That's not a very descriptive answer."

"Did you expect a blow-by-blow?"

"Well, I figured you brought it up for one reason or another." Christine picks up a wedge of pickle from her plate and takes a bite. "But, really, I don't expect a damn thing, Jake. That's the secret to my happiness."

"You seem to have a lot of secrets."

"You have no idea. You've only heard the ones I'm willing to share. So tell me about Inez in a general, nondescript way. You can leave out all the body parts. Have you figured out what's going on with her? Is it still going on?"

"I don't know."

"You don't know what?"

Jake lights a cigarette. He doesn't want to be badgered by Christine. He blows a stream of smoke off to the side and hopes her eyes will follow it, but it's he who watches the smoke.

"Well?" Christine says.

"I still don't know what's going on with her."

"Have you asked?"

"What am I going to ask her?"

"Ask her who's betraying whom. Isn't that the question we're always at the point of asking our spouse? Or have we already decided? It's them."

Jake reaches to the floor and picks a large red pincushion out of an open sewing basket. He pulls out a few pins and needles and, one at a time, jabs them back into the cushion.

"I hope you're not performing voodoo on me," says Christine.

Jake shakes his head and drops the pincushion back in the basket. He picks up a thimble and fits it on his baby finger. "No, you've just got me thinking. Inez still has this glow about her. It's as if she's on her way somewhere."

"But you don't know where?"

"No, I don't."

"And you don't want her to go?"

"Not especially."

Christine reaches into the sewing basket and pulls out a spool of white thread, breaking off a length with her teeth. "Have you thought about telling her that?"

"What's to tell? That I'd rather she not go, though I'm not sure she's going at all, to a place I can't imagine."

"You could tell her that."

"Right."

Christine takes a small needle from the pincushion, wets the end of the thread, and guides it through the needle's eye. "Women happen to find men attractive when they admit that they're confused, when they admit anything, really, but especially when it shows that they've been paying attention." Christine looks up at Jake, then takes his hand.

Jake faces her. "What are you going to do with that needle and thread?"

"I have a loose button. Why the strange look?"

"I don't know. I once knew a woman who hurt herself with a needle and thread."

"Anybody I know."

"No."

"I have no intention of hurting myself, Jake."

"Good."

Christine begins to unbutton her blouse.

Jake turns and looks at the mannequin in the window. He wonders if she has a name. Inez. There's a name for you. Inez and Bibi. A pair of names. There'd been a letter from Bibi recently and Inez mentioned a desire to visit her sister. It's been awhile since Jake's thought about his sister-in-law and what she did to herself with a needle and thread. He and Inez never talk about Bibi. They rarely talk about anything from the past. It's an unwitting strategy to leave things unmentioned. The burial mounds of a long married life. And now Christine talks to him with an unnerving frankness. It feels wrong to talk with her about Inez, as if he is betraying both of them.

Jake lights a cigarette and watches Christine drawing the needle and thread through the bottom button of her blouse. He takes in the pale skin of her belly, her small breasts, cupped away in the snug black bra.

Jake wouldn't mind being in a room like this by himself. A smaller room. As a boy, he used a skeleton key to lock himself in an attic room that nobody ever went in. A maid's room in a house without a maid. There was a small bed in there with a metal frame. It creaked when he lay down on it. After he'd locked himself in the room, he'd sprawl out on the bed and weep. Nobody in here, he'd say, but us skeletons. The weeping could go on for hours. It was all he ever did in that room. He never did it anywhere else. When the time came that he no longer cried, he stopped going into the room altogether, but for years, until he went off to college, he carried the skeleton key in his pocket.

Christine smiles at him, kindly. It's as if she's caught a glimpse of him in the little room.

"You know, Jake, for such a bright, lovely man, you really are a fool."

Not exactly what he expected from Christine. He gives her a sideways glance.

"Hey, there's a lot to be said for the fool, Jake. He's the one who survives in the end. Think about his image in the tarot cards. This guy walking along merrily, not worrying about where he's going to step next, because he's pretty sure the sidewalk's going to rise to meet him."

A HALF hour later, Jake's angry. Angry at Christine. Angry with himself. He sits on the bed, one sock on, one in his hand, and watches Christine dress with no particular interest, yet he watches her closely. She stands bare breasted and pulls on her panties. Her tiny feet are splayed on the straw mat. She smiles at him as she steps into her black drawstring pants. She goes to the closet and hangs the blouse she's just sewed a button on. He hears her shuffle through the rack of clothes. The whole house, it seems to Jake, is a game for Christine and when he's here he's just another part of her game. She brings out a red silk blouse and slips it over her bare breasts. The blouse has a Mandarin collar and frogs for buttons, but Christine leaves the blouse unbuttoned, her small breasts slightly fallen, lovely banded in red silk.

"It happens to everybody," Christine says.

"It hasn't happened to me. At least not with you."

"Then you're Superman. You were thinking about your wife. You don't think about her when you should, and you do when you shouldn't."

"How do you know what I'm thinking?"

Christine fastens the top frog of her blouse. "I don't know. I guess. It's better than knowing. Knowing carries a certain arrogance about it. Guessing is a much more fluid affair."

"Thanks for the treatise."

"Anytime."

Jake pulls on his second sock and stands up in his boxer shorts. "Hey, I'd really prefer if you wouldn't talk about my wife."

"Me? It seems like you were the one who brought up your wife— screwing her in the backyard. I was just making conversation."

Jake bows his head. "I'm sorry, Christine."

"You don't have to tell me you're sorry. Tell it to your wife."

Jake pulls up his slacks, buttons his shirt. He looks toward the mannequin in the window. "By the way, does the woman over there have a name?"

"No, I've never named her."

"I think she should have a name," Jake says.

"I'll think about that. See if I can come up with something for her." Christine finishes fastening the frogs on her blouse. She comes over to Jake and drapes her arm around his waist. "I'm sure it won't happen next time, Jake."

"How can you be sure?"

"I can't. I *guess* it won't happen again. Don't be an asshole, Jake. Maybe it *will* happen next time, and the next, and the next after that. Maybe you'll retire from sexual activity altogether and decide to race cars or take up Zen Buddhism."

"Or tarot cards," Jake says.

"You could do worse."

Jake lightly runs the back of his hand over Christine's cheek, then unbuttons the top two frogs of her blouse and reaches inside, taking gentle hold of one of her breasts.

everything precious

EARLIER in the week, a couple of days after her father-in-law had spied on her, Inez told Sylvia about the horrid incident. The old man had a way of killing something in her and now, as he creeped around the house in his soiled pajamas and flannel robe, downright raffish with the spirit of recovery, Inez backed into a quiet world and began to grow her protective skin again.

At first, the prospect of seeing Sylvia frightened her. What if Sylvia struck her as an oddity, a gnomish freak of nature who had no business being in her life? Her alternate fear—that she was slipping back into a shell from which she might never emerge—was as much responsible for propelling her to Sylvia's apartment as her foot on the gas.

Sylvia, who'd been distant and suspicious the last time they were together, was kind and even forgiving when Inez called early in the morning to see if Sylvia might be free at midday. Barefoot in a black leotard and purple pedal pushers, her young lover greeted Inez warmly and embraced her. In a moment they were petting and talking baby talk. At the window, they watched cable cars trundle by in each direction. After Inez confessed her tale of woe, Sylvia told her that senile old men have no more power than what you're willing to give them. Although Inez knew the business with her father-in-law was more complicated than that, she let herself spend a couple of hours, in the middle of a Thursday, feeling beloved. They made love, as they had the first time, to Ravel, but this time to a new recording of his rhapsodic *Daphnis and Chloé*. Inez, thinking it better to tell everything that she could bear telling, even confessed to making love with Jake in the backyard.

Sylvia curled her nose.

"He is my husband, after all."

"Was it good?" Sylvia wanted to know.

"No, it wasn't good. It's never been as good as with you."

Later, Sylvia served an elaborate lunch. After eating, Inez wanted nothing more than to stay on, cuddle with Sylvia on the twin bed, listening to the hi-fi. Yet she had no choice but to return home.

THIS morning, Inez awakes with a simple thought: *everything in this life is precious and I don't want any of it.* It strikes her as the type of proverb a suicide might carry around with her. She hears it in her head as if it were a fragment of a Schubert lied. Once Jake and the kids are gone, and she is alone in the house with the old man, she wishes she could stay in her room all day and hum the lied. *Everything in this life is precious . . .*

Instead, she cooks a large breakfast for her father-in-law—her own appetite has deserted her again—and leaves it, as he sleeps, to turn cold on the breakfast room table. After she showers, she dresses for success— although she doesn't want any of it—in a tailored suit, an imitation Coco Chanel, with rose piping.

As soon as she sees Sylvia, waiting under her building's front awning, the Schubert lied comes back into her head and she tries to force it out. Dear Sylvia is clearly precious. Dressed in a pleated skirt with black tights, a rayon blouse the color of ripe cantaloupe, and a string tie like the one her boss wears—a silver ornament embossed with a treble clef—Sylvia, hidden behind a pair of dark glasses, looks like a beatnik girl on her way to the rodeo. How better to dress for a visit to a mental asylum? At her side, Sylvia holds a straw sun hat adorned with a moss green ribbon. For a moment, Inez wishes she could drive off right now and abandon Sylvia, in her cowpoke getup, under the awning. Instead, Inez pulls up to the curb.

Sylvia presses her freshly painted lips together and walks to the open window.

"Am I all right?"

"You look fetching."

"I wasn't sure how to dress."

"Yes, the nuthouse is a fashion challenge, but you'll be a genuine hit."

"Inez, you look lovely."

Inez looks down at her Chanel knockoff. "Thank you."

"I can change."

"Don't be silly. Get in."

Once Sylvia is seated in the Studebaker, Inez tries her best to give herself over to Sylvia's charms, to everything precious she has to offer. "Where'd you find the hat?"

"It's from a little shop on Maiden Lane. Hy gave it to me. He gave me the string tie, too."

"How is he?"

"He's failing. I think he'll go quickly now."

"I'm sorry."

"Thank you."

Sylvia drops the straw hat on her head and then turns the rearview mirror to have a look at herself.

"It's darling."

"Do you think so?"

"Yes, and it provides perfect cover." Inez dips her head under the brim and kisses Sylvia on the corner of her mouth. "Bet you never expected me to do that in the light of the day."

"Not exactly." Sylvia, playing the tart with a certain majesty, slips the tip of her tongue out of her mouth and lets it roam back and forth across her red lips. "I'd love to go to bed with you right now. You could park the car and we could go up to my apartment and make love like men and women do—really quickly."

"We better not. It's so hard for me to get up to see my sister. If I go upstairs, I'm going to want to stay."

"You're a tease," Sylvia says, slipping a hand on Inez's thigh.

"You should talk."

The bells of an approaching cable car begin clanging a block behind them.

"Let me steal one more," Inez says, craning her neck again under Sylvia's wide brim.

IT'S a Monday morning without much traffic, and Inez is going quite a bit faster than the speed limit. Sylvia keeps an eye on the driver, uncertain whether to ask her to slow down. She'd rather not be included in Inez's suicide plan, if such a plan is in the works. She doubts it. Not now, not this way anyway. She's grateful for her sunglasses. They remind her of the distance she needs to keep from Inez. She can do anything she wants behind her sunglasses. Cry, if she must. She may never again take off her dark glasses in Inez's presence. She imagines Inez is worried about the visit with her sister. But perhaps she's thinking about nothing more than the woman sitting beside her. The fact that she loves her. As if such a thing could be a fact or stay a fact. Her eyes begin to water, and she looks out the window to her side. The hills of Sausalito, Mediterranean dream houses, a brushstroke of woods, the deep blue of the bay. People live in boathouses down there. Where will she live in ten years, when she's Inez's age? Where will she live when she stops knowing Inez? It's a strange question to ask, her love of Inez so ripe, now as she sits beside her.

Inez slows the car down to something close to the speed limit and it feels to Sylvia as if a fever has broken.

Inez turns toward her. "Sylvia?"

"Yes."

"This isn't meant as a loaded question, but have you ever been inside a mental hospital?"

"No, but my mother used to tell me that that's where I'd end up."

"She said that?"

Sylvia nods.

"What a terrible thing to say to your daughter."

Hope you never end up in a place like this is what her mother actually said. Sylvia was fourteen, the first of several times her mother was kept on suicide watch in the psychiatric ward at Sac General. Her mother's boyfriend, Ricky Benoit, a sportswriter, whom she wished her mother would marry, brought Sylvia to visit. Poor Ricky seemed defeated by her mother. "Your mother has troubles," Ricky said on the ride over. "Real or imagined, I understand this. But I don't see what's the matter with her talking them over with me. Thing about Angela, thing about your mother, she thinks even her troubles are too good for me."

Her mother sat in a bathrobe with long sleeves so Sylvia wasn't able to see what she'd done to her wrists. At least she wasn't chained to the bed the way they show in the movies. They kept her sedated instead. They didn't want her to become manic and start chanting exotic vocabulary. Someone had talked her mother into putting on makeup. Her face had sharp edges and rouge had been worked into her cheeks.

"Why do you keep looking at me like that?" her mother said. Sylvia trained her eyes on Ricky Benoit, who wore a green plaid sport coat and had his wavy black hair slicked back with Vitalis. He usually looked like a no-nonsense guy who could sell a lot of used cars or Fuller brushes. But in the hospital room, Ricky was nervous and couldn't help jiggling something in his coat pocket.

"You got nothing to worry about here, Angela," Ricky said, "nothing to worry about."

Out of the corner of her eye, she could see her mother shrug. Her mother wasn't worried about worrying.

"Nobody needs to know about this thing," Ricky said. There was some concern that her mother would lose her job if the school found out what she'd done to herself. Nobody wants a suicidal school nurse. "And I'll be looking in on Sylvia. She's a big girl, can take care of herself, but I'll be looking in. So, you see, things are all right there."

That's when her mother said it. It was an innocuous thing to say, yet highly noxious. *Hope you never.* It planted a seed. Became a mantra— *Hope you never.* It sharpened Sylvia's instincts. As they were about to leave, Sylvia asked her mother a question, posed less out of curiosity than to keep the thin strand of communication with her mother intact for another moment. Angela Bran's eyelids were beginning to droop over her eyes—the latest round of sedative doing its work—when Sylvia asked, "What's the worst thing about this place, Mom?"

At first, her mother looked like she was going to sleep on the question, but then she turned her head sideways and made a frightfully cogent statement. "The worst thing about this place is that the people here are afraid of language. They think that language is evil, that it's going to come out and strangle them. Not only are they afraid of words, they're afraid of ideas. They're afraid of opinions, they're afraid of personality. If they could eat little capsules and shit little capsules and think little capsules, that's what they'd do, which doesn't make it that much different from the outside. But still. Hope you never end up in a place like this."

NOW, as the highway climbs away from the bay, Sylvia looks down the embankment with sadness. She turns toward Inez, whose eyes are fixed on the centerline. She seems abstracted and tightly coiled.

"Is there something I should know about the hospital, Inez?"

"The hospital?"

She watches Inez's face soften as she makes sense of the question.

"Not really. Strange things can happen in there. A few of the patients may start conversations with you as if you've been talking together for years."

"Do you think your sister will know when she sees us?"

"Know what?"

"That we're lovers."

"How would she know?"

"I don't know. She might. If she's sensitive."

"She won't know."

Sylvia is hurt by Inez's response. Perhaps she was fishing for affection, but Inez didn't have to be so cool about it. Sylvia blinks back tears. "Maybe your sister is gifted with special perception."

"Do you actually believe crazy people are clairvoyant?"

"It isn't about clairvoyance, Inez. The fact is, anybody could see that you're nuts about me."

This makes Inez chuckle in the deep-throated way that Sylvia loves.

"Would you care to make a wager?" says Sylvia.

"What's to wager?"

"I say your sister figures us out in the first fifteen minutes we're with her."

"Not unless you tell her."

"I won't say a word. Here's how it works. If I win the bet, and there's no question that I will win, we go to a motel directly after the visit and make love."

"And if I win?"

"We go to a motel directly after the visit and make love." Sylvia tugs on her string tie in the manner of Hyman Myerson, then dips the wide brim of her hat over her face. What lengths she must go to, to hide the fact that she's in tears.

IT feels strange to Inez, walking through the long, polished halls of Napa State Hospital, toting a violin. They march up the center hallway of Building Three, the walls painted a creamy lime. Her stomach is already knotted. She can sense herself trying to disassociate. Sylvia, looking like an oddball with her string tie and dark glasses, strolls along beside her. Was it a mistake to bring her? She doesn't need anybody else to worry about. "This place sure makes you want to mind your p's and q's."

"Haven't you been minding them?" Sylvia asks.

"Oh, I don't know," Inez says, a bit distracted.

Although the building isn't familiar to Inez, it is predictably sterile and forbidding. On this floor, there's little sign of life. Along either side of the hallway are rows of shut white doors. A mausoleum of madness. Inez marches forward with little thought to Sylvia.

"You seem to know where you're going." Sylvia needs to hurry along to keep up.

"I know we're in the right building; this is the one they said she was in."

They stop at a reception station and a small, hawk-nosed woman in a black-and-white uniform—name-tagged Iris—neither nurse nor social worker, consults a thick directory of names while puffing on a Lucky Strike.

"She's not in this building," the woman says.

Before thrusting a directory at Inez, the small woman puts a hand over her pack of Lucky Strikes, as if Inez's query has only been a ruse to steal her cigarettes. Inez scans the list up and down for Bibi's name and panics when she doesn't see it, as if Bibi herself has disappeared. But there she is on the next page: Building Two, Ward D.

They pass through a courtyard, a couple of benches facing a dry fountain, and make their way toward another monstrosity.

Once inside Building Two, Sylvia begins chattering. "After my mother suggested that I might end up in a nuthouse, I fantasized about the kind of place I wanted it to be. I imagined a lovely garden, with clusters of bougainvilleas drooping all year long."

"There is no such place."

"Oh, there must be some private hospital like that somewhere."

"Well, this isn't it."

Sylvia stops her by a wall of high windows. Not to look out—the windows are covered in steel mesh—but to talk without the brisk pace of their footsteps.

"I think I got the idea about the beautiful madhouse after seeing *Lust for Life*," says Sylvia. The filtered light reflects in her sunglasses. "It played in downtown Sacramento for so long I went to see it three times. There's a scene in which van Gogh—or Kirk Douglas in a terrible red beard—is committed to a charming nuthouse in Provence. He's got his easel set up in a pasture. It's very bucolic."

Inez can't believe that Sylvia is telling her a story, as if they were in a department store or museum, as if Bibi wasn't close by and the baroque afternoon wasn't about to unfold.

"I can't remember if there were any bougainvilleas, but there's this young nurse or nun there to serve just him, to bring him wine and plates of grilled trout. I wanted to be in that place. I wanted the young nurse to look after me. I wanted the grilled trout."

"Why are you telling me this now, Sylvia?"

"I wanted you to be privy to my nuthouse fantasies."

"Thank you."

"Inez, don't worry. Everything's going to be all right."

"Thank you. I'd like to believe you." Inez turns back toward the hallway, leaving Sylvia dazed in the filtered sunlight.

ONCE they find the station leading to Ward D, where Bibi lives, they are told to make themselves comfortable in the visitor's room across the hall. A thin, mustached guard in a starched white shirt and pants nods to them as they walk into the room, a large, sunny space, its windows also covered with wire. The puce-colored walls are shiny from countless coats of semigloss. The man in white stands against one of the walls.

Sylvia and Inez each take a seat along the wall. As they wait, Sylvia studies some of the others in the room. A tall, slender woman, whose hair falls into her face, stands beside the window, writing furiously with a pencil stub on a large pad of yellow paper. She scrawls an intense streak, filling a page, then flipping it over with a grandiose gesture before leaping to the next page. Sylvia can see that Inez's attention is fixed on the scribbler as well.

"Maybe she spent too long pretending that she was a reporter."

"Ha, ha," Sylvia says.

She turns to watch an older couple, dressed in clothes that look left over from the Depression. The man wears a brown suit that has gone shiny. A soiled gray homburg rests on his knee. His trousers are too short for him, exposing his hairless white legs. He sits with his head bowed. Thin strands of his white hair gleam with hair oil. His wife, a woman in thick spectacles, wears a homely, putty-colored suit that looks like she sewed it herself, sometime after her eyes began to fail. Atop her small, animated face is a queer black hat overwrapped mummy style with a length of pink lace. The hat is adorned with a bunch of wooden cherries. It looks like a proper place for birds to nest. The old couple are huddled around a small table with a middle-aged man. The prodigal son. The man, decked out in a resident's blue smock, is surprisingly handsome. He seems to be staring at the foot of air above his mother's hat. Maybe he's watching sparrows fly in and out. His mother is talking at him non-stop, as if her banter might awaken his attention.

"You know how Audie is. She can't ever make up her mind about anything. Should she go back to work? Should she go back to school? Should they trade in their car? I told her that with a husband like that somebody's got to make up their mind. Somebody needs to set a policy. You should see that house, Jack. The floors are sticky. I can't stand sticky floors. I think it's fruit cocktail or soda pop from the kids. The thing is, Audie never seems to notice."

Her husband lifts his head and, without looking toward either his wife or his son, says: "Enough about Audie."

"He never likes to talk about Audie," says the woman in the hat, indicating her husband. "I don't know what it is about him and Audie."

The son doesn't seem to know either. He appears content to stare at the sparrows Sylvia's imagined for him, flying in and out of his mother's hat.

Elsewhere in the room, another couple, perhaps in their mid-thirties—the man neat in a crisp white shirt, knit tie, and blazer, the woman in the telltale inmate's smock—sit holding hands and whispering. Sylvia notices a trim little bald-headed man sitting at a small table with a deck of cards. He has the look of a plumber, a man who, because of his size, specializes in getting into tight spaces underneath the sink. In his present residence, he's had to trade his pipe wrench for a deck of cards. He shuffles and then cuts them repeatedly, making Sylvia think of a man washing and drying his hands ad infinitum at the kitchen sink. She wonders if the lapsed plumber ever has a playing partner, if he ever deals the cards. In another world, Sylvia would sit down at the table across from him and say, *How about a hand of rummy? Are we playing five-card stud, or aren't we? I'm in the mood for a little spit-in-the-ocean.* Just as she thinks this, the man quits his shuffling and looks up at her, smiling, as if to say, *What's your fancy?*

BIBI's hair has turned gray since she last saw her. Inez wonders if that's why she has it cut so short. She is forty-five now, so you can't exactly call her prematurely gray. Bibi smiles when she first glimpses her baby sister. It's hard to say whether it's Inez or her violin case that's got Bibi smiling. A large, muscular nurse—Mrs. Carlentini—brings her into the visitor's room. Inez, conscious of Sylvia sitting beside her, stands up quickly without making a reference to her friend.

Despite the gray hair, Bibi looks girlish. It may be the way she's biting her lower lip, or perhaps it is just how slight she seems next to Mrs. Carlentini. As a young woman, Bibi hadn't been attractive. Her face was pocked during adolescence, her eyes gray and beady, and, despite having a small face, she'd inherited their father's hawk nose. But now, at middle age, after salting away the last decade in an institution, she looks cute, even buoyant.

"You brought it. I never thought you'd bring it," Bibi says, nodding toward the violin in its case.

"Sounded from your letter like you felt like hearing some music."

She smiles. "You got my letter, Nez."

"I did."

Inez hurries over to greet her sister, but Bibi makes no motion to come forward.

"How are you, Bibi?"

"Me?"

Inez can see that her sister's attention has shifted to Sylvia.

"This is my friend, Sylvia Bran."

Sylvia stands and smiles.

"At first . . . at first I thought you were one of us. But then I didn't recognize the shoes and you're not wearing . . ."

"How do you do, Bibi?"

Her sister doesn't respond at first. Mrs. Carlentini has backed away, allowing Bibi to be the guest of honor. Bibi, still five feet away, looks alert, her head held high, her hands folded proudly in front of her like an athlete poised to receive a medal. She begins to nod her head in a quick, rhythmic way, as if she were counting out a piece of music in an eccentric time signature. Once she settles into her tempo, the nodding becomes less pronounced and she entertains Sylvia's greeting. "I'm fine, thank you. I'm very excited to see Inez with her violin."

Inez puts her arms around Bibi.

"You're like mother," Bibi says, immediately freeing herself from Inez's embrace. "She was a big hugger. At least that's what Daddy always said. 'She was a traitor to her race,' he said. 'Svedes are not supposed to hug people.'"

Bibi laughs at that. A fat bouquet of a laugh that Inez fears will go out of control, but Bibi quickly cuts it off. She assumes their father's voice again. "'A Svede wants to be quiet, gloomy, and resigned to his fate, which is quiet and gloomy.'"

Inez has forgotten how good a mimic Bibi is. She can hear their father's voice in the room.

"That's why they named you Inez."

"What do you mean?"

"They wanted you to be a hugger, so they came up with an exotic name. You were supposed to be a Mediterranean hugger."

"You made that up, didn't you, Bibi?"

Bibi shakes her head. "Me?" But Bibi can't keep herself from grinning. She has a better sense of humor than Inez does. That's something else Inez has forgotten.

"Well, I don't think the name worked. I'm a real Swede."

"But you just hugged me."

"And I didn't want to let you go."

That is true. The very smell of Bibi brings back her childhood. Inez holds her again and pokes her nose against her neck. Bibi tolerates her for a moment and then stands up a little stiffer. Inez lets go reluctantly. How has she allowed Bibi to stay so many years in this place?

BIBI takes a deep breath, as if to cleanse herself of the physical contact. Then, like a proper hostess, she turns toward Sylvia, who is still standing.

"Thank you for coming to visit me at dear old Napa State."

"I'm very happy to meet you," Sylvia says.

"Napa State is what people call it here, as if the hospital were their alma mater, but most of us will never leave."

Sylvia walks over and shakes Bibi's hand.

"Thank you." Bibi takes a hard look at Inez, shifts her eyes to Sylvia, and then back to Inez. "Do you still have your husband?"

"Of course." Sylvia is right, her sister has figured them out in a minute.

"Is he still funny?"

"I guess you could say he's funny."

"She doesn't think he's funny," Bibi says, nodding. "Maybe they stop being funny when you're married to them. I wouldn't know. But I always thought he was very funny. He was part clown, a good clown."

Sylvia looks from Bibi to Inez—Bibi may not have her sister's beauty, but she does have a twinkle in the eye.

"One time," Bibi says, her face brightening with a memory, "Jake walked across the kitchen floor with a raw egg balanced on the bridge of his nose."

"And then he dropped it," Inez says.

"But he made it nearly across the room."

"Really?" Sylvia says, catching Bibi's excitement.

"Yes!" Bibi exclaims.

Inez wonders if she should have been satisfied that Jake nearly made it across the kitchen floor before the egg fell to the linoleum and shattered.

"I always wanted to try that," says Bibi.

"What?" Inez says, losing herself in the absurdity of the conversation.

"Walking across the room with an egg balanced on the bridge of my nose. I think I have the nose for it." Bibi giggles for a moment, then smiles demurely.

"You better practice with a hard-boiled egg," says Inez.

"Where's the fun in that?" Sylvia asks.

Bibi smiles at Sylvia. "That's just what Jake told me not to do when I said I wanted to try it. He said, 'Live a little, Bibi. Get yourself a dozen eggs you're willing to sacrifice and, for God's sake, practice without a net.' "

It's been years since they've seen each other, but here they are, standing together in the halls of Napa State Hospital, talking about Jake and his famous raw egg trick. She begins to hum the Schubert lied to herself—*everything in this life is precious*—but forces herself to look into Bibi's open face.

Mrs. Carlentini steps toward them. "If you'd like to go into the music room, that might be a nice place to visit."

"Do you think we could have some tea, Rose?" Bibi asks.

"Yes, that can certainly be arranged."

benediction

A FTER Bibi introduces her guests to Rose Carlentini, they all go down the hallway to a room with an upright piano, a scarred black beast of an instrument. A stack of folding chairs leans against one of the walls, which are checkered with old travel posters from great music cities in Europe.

"So let's have some music!" Mrs. Carlentini says.

"I'd be happy to play," Inez says.

"She's very good," Bibi says, beaming.

"I'm sure she is, Bibi." Mrs. Carlentini turns toward Inez. "How would you feel about some of the others coming in to listen?"

Inez looks at Bibi.

"It's okay with me," Bibi says. "Some might get up and start walking around. Some may hum along with you."

"That's fine, as long as no one insists on playing my instrument."

Rose Carlentini nods. "Of course not; we'll make sure that doesn't happen."

"My friend Sylvia plays the piano," says Inez.

"Not on that instrument," Bibi says, beginning her manic nod again.

"Is it that bad?" Sylvia strolls up to the black monstrosity and, crouching in front of it, picks out the melody, complete with a few dead tones, to "Wouldn't It Be Loverly."

Inez thinks of the opening lyric: "All I want is a room somewhere."

MRS. CARLENTINI sets up some folding chairs as a little flock wanders into the music room. Inez counts sixteen people in the audience as she tunes up.

During the war, Inez occasionally played at the veterans' hospital in the Presidio. It was a far more troubling experience than this. She was in her early twenties then and wasn't prepared for so graphic a view of the atrocities of war. Men with craters in the middle of their faces, or with heads that seemed strangely shrunken, men who limped or stumbled on crutches or even strolled into the social room in government-issued terry cloth robes smoking cigarettes, as debonair as walking ghosts. Once in a while, a man would sing out with a wolf whistle while she took out her violin. They probably would have been happier if she'd stripped for them. As she played, a steady stream of cripples were wheeled in and out. A good half of them were only shells of themselves, on respirators, with tubes jutting out of everywhere. Inez did her best to play to a single man in the room—there was always at least one whose eyes would brighten to the music and let it take him to a better place.

It isn't difficult to find her ideal listener in the music room at Napa State—Bibi sits by herself in the middle of the first row. Witnessing Bibi with her eyes already closed and her lips pushed out, in anticipation of musical rapture, Inez remembers her sister's girl face, open, rosy with good cheer, always eager to listen to Inez's latest recital piece. She remembers, as early as ten, being contemptuous of her big sister. Giving a Mozart recital at a mansion in Pacific Heights, she noticed Bibi beside her father in the front row, her hands clutched in her lap, her head swaying side to side. Was her sister simpleminded? Had she inherited their father's capacity for holding one, and only one, idea or pleasure in her head at once? Was there truly nothing in the world that made her happier than listening to her little sister play the violin?

SYLVIA has found a seat angled off to the side. It's the perfect spot for a voyant—she not only has a good view of the performer but can see into the faces of most of the audience as well.

As Inez tunes her instrument, Bibi smiles up at her. Somebody in the room is humming along with Inez as she tunes. Sylvia decides it's the middle-aged son of the ancient people. He has his head down, and his bespectacled mother, the one with the kooky hat dangling wooden cherries, is bent over him, whispering. The man has a decent ear. Sylvia can hear him accurately run the fifths with Inez. The high E flutters in his throat long after Inez is finished with it. The lapsed plumber, without his deck of cards now, is sitting a couple of rows ahead of her. Again, he meets her eye. He has something to tell her, but it will have to wait.

Inez stands, with the violin at her side, smiling at her little audience. "Hello, my name is Inez Roseman. Some of you may know that I'm Bibi's sister, her baby sister." This brings some general laughter to the room. Sylvia notices the worried husband clutching the hand of his smock-clad wife.

"I was thinking of playing a little Fritz Kreisler for you today and then a little bit of Mendelssohn and Bach. Usually, you think of Kreisler as dessert music meant for the end of a program, but today I'm going to play the Kreisler first. Let's have our dessert before the meal and if we want more afterward, we can do that too."

Inez's small audience purrs with pleasure as she speaks to them.

"When I was studying violin, my teacher used to tell me stories about Fritz Kreisler. Kreisler was even more famous as a violinist than as a composer. He had theories about practice that my teacher liked to tell me. I had a problem with practicing: I practiced too much. Bibi can testify to that. I stood on a spot in my room and practiced six, seven, eight hours a day. I wore a hole in the rug practicing. I wanted to be perfect. I'm sorry to report, I didn't make it."

The humor of Inez's remark, it seems to Sylvia, is lost on her audience, but that doesn't seem to faze her.

"'Practice,' according to Fritz Kreisler, 'is a bad habit. Too much practice and you'll lose the bloom of your musical imagination.'"

Why, Sylvia wonders, has Inez grown loquacious? What is she afraid of?

Sylvia turns to see a trail of latecomers, residents who aren't sure whether they want to be in the room, let alone sit in an audience, lurk nosily by the door. As Inez drops her violin to her side to wait for a measure of calm, Mrs. Carlentini rises to sort them out.

Inez stands still on her spot. Sylvia tries to imagine Inez when she was young. Did the girl who wanted to be perfect wear her wheat-blond hair in a long braided ponytail? Did she ever sneak a stick of gum into her mouth when she practiced, or entertain ignoble thoughts while her fingers whizzed up and down the fingerboard? Was there ever a time when little Inez was just a girl, not a prodigy yet, but a girl, with a girl's sometimes lavish or stunted imagination? Was she ever foolish or sad or penurious? Did she ever sit on her father's lap and play with the things inside his shirt pocket? Did she have a baby doll or a dollhouse or a pouch of lucky jacks or a secret collection of books? Did she ever steal things from her sister? Did she ever pick her nose or leave a snotty handkerchief in her sister's underwear drawer? Did she think of going to China as a missionary? Did she enjoy dangling her legs on the toilet? Did she ever get so angry that she walked out into the garden on damp mornings in search of snails to crush under her Mary Janes? Did she ever fart in a room and secretly enjoy the smell?

As Inez glances toward her now, Sylvia feels her lips pucker into a single word: *courage*, from the Old French *corage*, which reminds her of another word that you'd think was a cousin of the first: *corsage*, a bright posy, an orchid, the bloom of her imagination. She would love to pin a corsage to the front of Inez's dress. Instead, she mouths the first word three times.

INEZ has yet to play a note of music, but the little audience is already restless. Can you blame them? Rose Carlentini, with the help of a Negro aide, has seated a few stragglers and is wrestling a combative patient named Esther out of the room. "Esther, it's going be fine, Esther," purrs Rose Carlentini gently, leading her out. A wiry-haired man in the third row has begun to whimper.

Under her straw hat, Sylvia is blowing kisses. Either that or she's saying something that Inez doesn't understand. Dear Sylvia, offering comfort. Always offering comfort. The last time she and Sylvia were alone wasn't long after the old man had peeped at her. Inez hadn't dared tell Jake, but she told Sylvia in detail about the horror of meeting Isaac Roseman's eyes as she climaxed. "I was thinking about your tongue, Sylvia. It was so awful to see the old man when I opened my eyes."

Sylvia had prepared a fabulous lunch for that day. First she'd served a pungent round of white cheese, with slices of pippin apple dipped in lime juice.

"What is this?" Inez had asked, savoring the cheese. "It's the most glorious thing I've ever tasted."

"It's Bucheron, a French goat cheese. I stole it from Simon Brothers."

"You stole it?"

"Yes, force of habit."

"So you're a thief as well as a charlatan?"

"Only a few small things on occasion."

"What else have you stolen?"

"Besides your heart?" Sylvia said, nudging a slice of pippin with a smear of Bucheron into Inez's mouth.

After she swallowed, Inez said, "You didn't steal my heart; I gave it to you freely."

Sylvia had covered a large wooden crate with a pretty but washed-out cotton fabric and had set pillows for them to sit on at each side of the crate. She set the makeshift table with two mismatched china plates, silverware, a tall green bottle of Wente Grey Riesling that Inez had brought—her father's wine—and two embossed jelly glasses. After the Bucheron, Sylvia brought plates of roasted quail with wild rice. Sliced in crisp brown halves on her plate, the bird's tiny drumsticks seemed the size of a girl's thumbs. "Did you steal these as well?"

"No, these I purchased. I make it a point never to steal fowl."

"How do you eat them?"

"You pick them up with your hands. They're like us—not quite as fragile as we'd like to imagine."

"I'm more fragile than I like to imagine, Sylvia." She actually said that. She felt immediately shy, afraid that Sylvia thought poorly of her.

Sylvia pulled the cork from the bottle of Riesling and filled the jelly jars. Inez sipped at the wine but still hadn't touched the little bird. She watched Sylvia break off a drumstick. It didn't exactly snap, but lifted away like a peach from its stem. Sylvia put it on her tongue and sucked on it. "Next," she said, "I taste you."

Right now, in the mad music room, the tip of Sylvia's tongue, that beautiful sprite, is peeking at her. And, finally, Rose Carlentini returns to her seat and nods to Inez. It is quiet in the room, save for the occasional whimper from the third row. Bibi is sitting forward in her chair, her eyes open wide.

Inside her head, Inez hears two voices, the one reminding her of the

Schubert lied: *everything in this life is precious . . .* the other the voice of her teacher: *Play, already.* All right, she will play. She lifts her violin and dives into Kreisler's "Liebesleid." Love's sorrow. An impossibly sad song that has now found its way into the movies and is even being piped into the produce aisle of the supermarket. Isaac was always after her to play Kreisler's romantic pieces. *Sure,* he'd say, *they're schmaltzy, but you could use a little schmaltz in your tone, from time to time, just like you could use a little schmaltz on your body.* He'd wink at her, a pubescent girl scandalized by any reference to her body. How many years has it been since she's thought of this? *You know what schmaltz is?* he said, finding the shock on her face hilarious. *Schmaltz, it literally means chicken fat. You need some in your tone just like you need some on your body.*

As she plays, she hears Isaac's voice calling to her from decades ago. *Vibrate, Inez, vibrate. You cannot play this music without vibrato. You want to sound like a Swede? Why would you want to play this music with ice in your tone? That's right, relax. Vibrate.*

Inez remembers what she's managed so well to forget: Mr. Roseman, standing behind her as she played. His long fingers grabbing her breasts. Her mouth opened wide with the shock of it, but not a word came. Her job, as he reminded her over and over, was to keep playing.

Her greatest horror: she did what he told her. *That's right, keep the bow moving. Vibrate. Feel it inside, feel the pleasure, but keep the bow moving, continue to vibrate. You need to learn to keep your composure.*

Mr. Roseman became bolder, as the weeks went by, and she still did whatever he asked. *Today, let us consider your posture. Your legs, they are too close together. You cut off your power that way, you play stiff. Spread your legs apart. That's right.*

He came up behind her and put his hands on her waist. *Just like a dance instructor,* she told herself. But a week later he had a hand under her skirt, and soon after that he began fondling her between her legs. *That's right, keep the bow moving. Let yourself feel the pleasure, you must learn to keep your composure. That's the point of this exercise.*

This went on for more than a year. But one day—she must have been nearly fourteen—something in her snapped as she saw the bastard coming toward her. *Don't,* she said, trembling more than she had when he'd first touched her. *Never.* Mr. Roseman backed away. Inez brought the violin down to her side. Neither of them spoke for a moment. It was as if a live power line dangled between them in the room. *You mention this,* he said, *you ruin your career forever.* Just like that, they made their pact: he stayed away from her and she never spoke a word about it. What she hadn't accounted for was how skillfully she could push the trauma out of her head. By the time she and Jake began seeing each other, Jake's father was again her beloved teacher.

Once Inez finishes with "Liebesleid," a very short piece of music, she is drenched in sweat and wary of lifting her head toward the small audience. A few people applaud. For some reason, she curtsies like a girl would. She can hear Bibi crying in the front row. Inez turns away from her sister to take in the rest of the audience. The whimperer in the third row is now sucking his thumb. A woman with a pencil stuck in her nest of tightly coiled red hair noisily gets up from her chair, muttering, *It's just too sad. Too sad. It's too sad for me. I don't know why it has to be so sad.* Inez makes a point of not looking out front, but listens to the voice trail away—*It's just so sad*—as the woman leaves the room.

Inez notices Sylvia at the back of the room. She's taken off her dark glasses and is rubbing her eyes. So much for the Kreisler. If she plays any more Kreisler, she'll have everybody in tears.

It takes all she has to dig her way into Mendelssohn's bittersweet concerto. She'd meant to start with the second movement, but for some reason launches directly into the Allegro molto appassionato at the beginning of the concerto. Apparently, she can't let the death march alone. As a child practicing this concerto, or listening to her recording of Nathan Milstein playing it with the Philadelphia Orchestra—an album of five 78s whose weight she can still remember in her lap—she always associated its dominant motif with the death march. Something about E minor. All she had to do was hear an E-minor chord in her head and she could make herself cry on the spot.

Even as a child, she knew that the Mendelssohn was an exquisite piece of music. Once she'd learned the violin part satisfactorily, Mr. Roseman brought her the complete score, and she soon became so familiar with it that she could have conducted it. Whenever she practiced the concerto alone in her room, she heard the swell of the entire orchestra.

This is what her teacher wanted to have happen. If she believed him, she'd play it someday with the major orchestras of the world. The Mendelssohn wove its way into her brain and muscle memory.

The concerto is a demanding piece and Inez's bow arm begins to ache. Soon she is struggling with the the tight-bowing spiccato section at the end of the cadenza. The tips of her fingers start to throb.

BIBI, who's sitting directly in front of her, begins to keen in the low, steady voice of a small engine. This, Inez decides, is her sister punishing her.

Inez becomes undone as soon as she draws the black musical thread through Mendlessohn's glorious Andante.

> This charming solo should be played in as flowing a style as possible, and without the least broadening pathos. But at the same time the interpretation must not in any way be an insignificant or expressionless one; it must be performed with warm feeling and with well-calculated tonal graduations for the climaxes, especially in the 15th and 29th bars.

Or so said the commentary Inez memorized thirty years ago. As she plays the Andante, mindful of climaxes and careful not to broaden Mendelssohn's pathos or her own, she imagines that the composer is making love to her. As a teenager, during hours of practicing, she occasionally had such fantasies. Between movements, her left hand might sneak off the fingerboard and land in her crotch. How better to become one with the music?

Inez looks out at her audience at Napa State—lunatics and their caretakers. Everyone has his or her eyes closed, breathing with a certain rapture. Or so she imagines. Has she become crazed, too? Does she actually believe that she can send her audience into a fever with a bow and violin?

Before Felix Mendelssohn climbs on top of her, he strips off his forest-green velvet trousers. He chews on each of her fingers, his teeth as sharp as a wolf's. *Felix, dear Felix; if I had another child I'd name him Felix.* He rides her hard, but she wants more of him than he has to give. She wishes that she had fingernails so that she could tear into his flesh. It doesn't matter that her fingers ache.

At the crescendo, she closes her eyes and settles into a medium tempo, before forcing the accelerando. Everything falls away but the bare theme, which rises from her body, through the violin. It is an aria of plain majesty, a woman dashing through a fall garden, a woman who's never cared much for asters and marigolds and chrysanthemums, but who is now persuaded, despite the speed at which she's moving, to see the beauty of these flowers and their quiet testimony to living and dying.

THE Mendelssohn concerto has taken hold of the small audience. The music is no longer safe for her in this place, Sylvia knows that. She's thankful for her straw hat and sunglasses. She knows how to keep the music from affecting her, knows how to shut it off. Even as an inveterate observer, mindful of her mother's safety, she knew that she didn't need to see and hear everything. That would be impractical. The goal was to be strategic, which entailed having a shutoff valve. One of her mother's boyfriends suggested trying wax earplugs for those nights when her mother had a manic episode and sat at the kitchen table chanting three- and four-syllable words instead of sleeping. But Sylvia had tried to master a deeper form of not-hearing.

She could hear her mother chanting *melanoma, melisma, mellifluous, melopoeia,* just as she now hears Inez playing the Mendelssohn. The sound is distant, like something packed away in a bottle with a tight cap. Sylvia pictures a gallon of distilled water that glugs in its container as you carry it, but that's ready to hiss dangerously as soon as you pour it into a heated steam iron.

Once, after her mother returned from the hospital, she talked about her life on the psychiatric ward. Sylvia listened with grim attention to the characters her mother described, the way she spoke about a typical day, the rituals of meals and medication, the leisure hours spent at card tables and around the flickering television. The staff provided her mother with writing implements and ample supplies of paper as long as she stayed in the common room, but they wouldn't allow her to return to her bedroom with a pencil or a pen. *Did they think that I was going to gouge myself to death with a ballpoint pen?* Angela spent most of her days alone at a table in the common room working on lists of words. She made a list of fifty-six phobias and was cheered to realize that she truly suffered from fewer than a half dozen of them.

The most surprising thing on the ward, Angela Bran told her daughter, *are the patients who've lost their sense of modesty and masturbate in public spaces.* To Sylvia, who had just begun to appreciate the pleasure of touching herself, this was a terrifying image.

Now, as Inez plays with enough fury to save somebody's life, or end it, the music room at Napa State Hospital has grown swampy with sex. People are actually touching themselves, in the light of day. Sylvia allows herself to listen to the Mendelssohn. She can do it without losing her balance. Her mind is strong, as is her heart. She will not end up in a place like this. She adjusts her sunglasses and dips the brim of her straw hat low over her eyes, a mild form of insurance.

INEZ can hear her small audience engaged in rhythmic breathing. She catches a glimpse of their strange ecstatic faces. She draws back into the music. Felix Mendelssohn has her circling the theme again—it might as well be her own sad life. Inez is becoming weary of these recapitulations, but here she goes again. She sees her father, his white head bent over his workbench. She sees his arthritic fingers, his crooked digits moving ceaselessly as he crafts his wooden frames. What would she frame? What wonders of this world? She thinks of sweet Joey, passionate Anna, even Jake. She thinks of dear Bibi, wilting in the front row, and of Sylvia, cloistered at the back of the room, Sylvia, whom she can't see behind those dark glasses and the wide brim of that hat, Sylvia, petty thief and impostor, who clearly has stolen Inez's heart, because there was no way that she would give it freely.

As the movement draws to a close, Inez wishes for her shell to crawl into. She conjures up a phrase of funeral splendor: her "loved ones." How to explain to them that her instinct is true, that she is drawn more decidedly to death than to life?

The final movement with its glistening, brilliant passages of elf-like speed, is possessed of an unusually animated capricious character; at one moment graceful and cheerful in its flight, at the next with fiery, decided accent. Consequently its interpretation must neither be stiff and dry, nor one-sidedly brilliant.

The music is weaving its way through her sister's heart. Bibi, who took care of her, who worshipped her. Bibi, her fingers sewn together with thick, black thread. Sweet Bibi, whom she abandoned. Inez strives to be *graceful* and *fiery* with the Mendelssohn as she thinks again of her children. Anna, smart Anna, do not follow me. Joey, my cello boy, find happiness apart from the music. How can she leave them? Is her heart sewn shut?

Inez does not look up, but she can hear the audience whimpering now. They have traveled with her from sorrow to sex to sorrow. By the time Inez plays the final, descending scale, she is weeping, but she is not alone. The whole room is in a virtual downpour. She forces herself to look out into the audience. Sylvia, at the back of the room, has dropped her face into her hands. Some of the patients are tossed into convulsive wails. A middle-aged patient chews the air, emitting a wild Indian chant. E-WAH, OH-WEE, AH-OH. An old woman in a strange hat is trying to shush him. The wiry-haired man in the third row is sucking both of his thumbs at once. All Inez needs now is for a baby to begin wailing. A thin, balding man suddenly stands up, flinging his arms around wildly. Inez wipes her tears with the back of her bow hand and watches as the wild man turns to face Sylvia, who, hatless now and without her dark glasses, is mopping her face with a scarf.

"It must be the Cuban missiles!" shouts the balding man. "They thought they stopped the missiles, but look what they're doing to us!"

Inez feels inebriated. She holds the violin at her side, the fingers of her left hand pressed as hard as they can be against the strings and fingerboard. She doesn't want the ache in her fingers to go away. Her bow arm does not understand the rest of her body. It's poised to begin bowing the Allegro molto appassionato again, to start the concerto over like the girl on the frayed carpet of her bedroom. Finally, she forces her right arm to the side, and it flops like a fish on a pallet. If she had any sense, she'd bow her head and pack up her instrument. But she remains frozen. What is she waiting for? Applause? A call for an encore?

Rose Carlentini, who has ushered the balding missile man out of the music room, walks now toward Inez, teary-eyed, and with the nostrils of her broad nose flared. Inez expects an urgent message, perhaps a reprimand. *Enough is enough. Look what you've done. Don't you have any decency?* But Rose Carlentini wraps her arms around Inez and holds on to her for a long moment. Once again, she and Bibi have the same mother. This one is living. Inez wishes she could drop the violin and give herself fully to the embrace, but too many years of holding on to the instrument prevent that. Inez glances at her sister, who sits quietly in prayer, her hands folded but, thankfully, not sewn together over her face.

ROSE Carlentini leads the three of them into a small room and brings tea. Along with the tea service, she leaves a plate of anise cookies, a favorite of Bibi's when they were children. Bibi baked them all the time back then, but these are clearly store-bought.

Suddenly Inez is famished. Any appetite she has she owes to Sylvia. She counts: there are six cookies on the plate. She glances at Sylvia and at Bibi. Neither of them seems as cheered as she is to see the plate of cookies, which could be good since she feels like even two anise cookies are not going to hold her. It strikes her as odd to have an appetite at the same time as her longing for her shell, the private cure of withdrawal, so dreadful and appealing. She feels she has one foot in each world. What can she ask of a world that she's determined to protect herself from? A few anise cookies?

"I packed a little picnic, Bibi," she says, facing her sister, and then Sylvia.

Bibi laughs a big guffaw. "You're going on a picnic now?"

Apparently, the mental patient finds the two of them amusing. "We thought we'd take you outside, if we can," Inez says, "and have a little picnic. Or we could eat right in here. Maybe Sylvia wouldn't mind going out to the car."

"Not at all," Sylvia says, standing quickly.

"I'm not hungry," Bibi says, without a trace of petulance, "but you two go."

As Inez rifles through her purse to find her car keys for Sylvia, she has a chilling fantasy of Sylvia driving off in the Studebaker and leaving Inez behind at the hospital with Bibi—the two mad sisters together at last.

"Sylvia," Bibi says, with surprising force, "would you mind staying here a little longer? I'm beginning to get tired. I'll go back to my room soon and you two can have your picnic."

"No, I wouldn't mind at all."

"By the way, I love your string tie, Sylvia," says Bibi.

"Thank you." Sylvia loosens the string tie's treble-clef medallion. She thinks to offer the tie to Bibi—she'll probably never see the poor woman again—but a fleeting image of Hy Myerson on the showroom floor changes her mind, and she slides the tie's medallion closer to her throat.

Inez looks from Bibi to Sylvia, then plucks an anise cookie from the plate.

SYLVIA sits down again. She glances at Bibi, who seems to be thinking hard as she sips at her tea. Bibi has a little animal face. The face of a fox. Her small but sharp incisors, visible when she smiles, give her a feral look. For the first time, Sylvia can imagine her doing the thing Inez described, sewing the fingers of her hand together in a web. Sylvia notices Bibi's left hand, how clearly it is scarred with the needled stigmata of her madness.

Inez speaks to her sister. "I'm sorry I didn't play any Bach for you, Bibi."

"I can still hear it in my head, Nez."

"What's your favorite Bach, Bibi?" Sylvia asks.

"Hmmm," Bibi says. She cocks her head to the side as if she's considering her answer. "I think it must be 'The Art of the Fugue.'"

"Funny, Inez and I were talking about 'The Art of the Fugue' not so long ago."

"Yes, you would be thinking about that," Bibi says.

Sylvia stops herself from asking why.

"You realize," Bibi says, "that Bach didn't call it 'The Art of the Fugue.' Someone else named it that."

"That's right," Inez chimes in. "Bach called the pieces 'Contrapunctus,' but he died before they were published and the engraving was done."

It appears the two sisters are beginning a little fugue. Sylvia would just as soon keep her voice out of it and let the sisters wander.

The problem is, Bibi wants her attention. Bibi leans forward and fixes her large brown eyes on Sylvia. "There are a lot of people in this hospital who have tried to hurt themselves. Some people still try. I hurt myself once. Maybe Inez told you." Bibi briefly holds up her scarred hand. "But my intention was not to hurt myself. Nobody believes that." Bibi's head begins a rhythmic nod. "In the years I've been here I've never tried to hurt myself, but there are others . . ."

Sylvia watches Inez turn her body slightly to the side. This curious recital must be difficult for her lover to witness. Sylvia can't decide which is stranger: the way Bibi's eyes recede into her head as she speaks, or the fact that Bibi seems to know what Sylvia is thinking.

"There are others here who try to hurt themselves. It used to upset me. Well, it still upsets me. I've spoken to a doctor about it. He said that there really isn't much . . . much you can do about it . . . if . . . well . . . if a person wants to harm herself."

That said, Bibi's rhythmic nodding ceases. Of the three of them in the small room, Sylvia wonders whose harm is most at issue. She glances across at Inez, who's been slowly eating all the anise cookies.

Bibi fixes an eye on Sylvia, then on Inez. "So when did you two become such good friends?"

"Oh, I don't know," Inez says, warily.

"You can't remember, or you don't want to tell me? Does it get in the way of your marriage?"

"You're very curious about this, aren't you, Bibi?"

Bibi looks down at her hands. "Do you love each other?"

Inez picks the final anise cookie from the plate and nibbles on it. "I can't speak for Sylvia, but I certainly love her."

Bibi looks up and smiles at this odd declaration. Sylvia is elated. She opens her mouth and sighs. Inez appears too sheepish to show her face to Sylvia.

"Sylvia, do you love, Inez?"

Sylvia holds her head high. "I do."

"This is why you came to visit me," Bibi says and inhales a long breath through her nose. "May I offer you both my blessing?"

"Please," Inez says, and finally allows herself to smile fully at Sylvia. Sylvia watches Bibi stand, her small body rising into a formal posture, her arms forming an arch in front of her.

"Would you stand, please, both of you."

Sylvia takes the command to heart and can see that Inez has done the same.

"Take each other's hands, please."

They both rise to the spread wings of Bibi's benediction.

"May you be kind to each other in the world," Bibi says, rocking forward. "May you have happiness forever."

bigamy

B Y the time they walk out of Building Two, it is three in the after-noon. Although the air has turned chilly, it feels good. A stiff breeze blows a swirl of leaves and debris around the parking lot. The sun's still high in the sky, but it has begun its slow descent toward the west. Sylvia is tempted to take her jacket off, to experience the chill more intensely. She wants to feel something of the moment on her skin.

"So this is what it feels like to be married."

"I thought you'd been married, Sylvia."

"My final lie to you."

"Hmmm."

"I'm no longer going to keep anything from you, Inez. Nothing."

"That might not be a good idea." Inez unlocks the Studebaker and they climb in. She sits with the car keys in her lap, suddenly exhausted. "I'm not ready to go yet. I need to sit here a minute."

"Fine."

Sylvia flips down the windshield visor and studies herself in its mirror.

"Do you look different to yourself?" says Inez, leaning back and closing her eyes.

"Oh, I don't know. Perhaps a certain maturity has settled into my face."

"Just like that, huh?"

Sylvia senses Inez's retreat. She's not going to let it affect her. She doesn't want to be hurt by Inez now. Sylvia rolls down the window and sticks her head out into the cool air for a moment. She wishes it were colder still. She pulls her head in and touches Inez's arm lightly. "I was glad to meet Bibi," Sylvia says, as Inez's eyes open.

"Were you?"

"Yes. I think I won our bet," says Sylvia, turning sideways in her seat to face Inez. "Your sister doesn't miss a lot."

"It's hard to see her," says Inez, her hands encircling the steering wheel.

"I would think it'd be harder not to."

"You don't have to bother with the guilt, Sylvia."

"Oh, I probably would have done the same as you did."

"Left her in there? No, you wouldn't. Not if it were *your* sister."

"You're wrong about that. I'm just as selfish as you are, Inez. We're a good match."

Sylvia turns back to the mirror, takes a comb out of her purse, and runs it through her hair and then daintily through her eyebrows. She can see her mother's face in her own. Not as much in the features as the mannerisms, even its posture. Doesn't a face have a posture, a way of holding itself, an attitude? Despite leaving more and more of her mother behind each day—she really doesn't share her mother's distaste for life—Sylvia carries a bit of Angela Bran's defiance.

"Do you always comb your eyebrows?" Inez asks.

"Every day. That's something else you should know, now that we're married."

"I suppose this makes me a bigamist."

"I'm not big on technicalities."

"Your eyebrows are quite seductive."

"They're thick. A proper person would pluck them, but I do everything I can to avoid pain."

"Is that right?" Inez turns on the engine and gasses it a couple of times in neutral. "I'm hungry," Inez says. "I want to eat. Don't you think that's a good sign? A hearty appetite?"

"It's a wonderful sign."

"Hand me a sandwich, willya? I'll eat like a truck driver, while I'm driving."

Sylvia turns and kneels to reach into the backseat for the picnic basket while Inez smiles at her fetching behind.

"Stop that," says Sylvia.

"Stop what?"

"I know what you're thinking." Sylvia pulls the basket into the front seat, then flips open a lid at one end and pulls out a sandwich, lifting apart the wax paper. "What is this?"

"Chopped olive and capers on Roman Meal. Help yourself."

"Not exactly trucker fare," says Sylvia, handing the sandwich to Inez.

"There's shoestring potatoes in there," Inez says, taking a big bite, "and a container of strawberries. Mmmm. Nothing like chopped olive on Roman Meal."

THEY drive in silence along Highway 29, through the Napa Valley. Sylvia is content to look out the window as they drive through miles of vineyards. She doesn't need to know where they're going. She rolls her window down all the way. Most of the grapes are harvested by now, but the sweet dark smell of the crushings is everywhere. Some of the leaves along the rows of vines have turned an autumn red. Chilled, and with her hair blowing back, Sylvia feels happy, despite a sense of foreboding.

Sylvia reads the signs as they drive north: Yountville, Oakville, Rutherford—some looking less like towns, at least from the highway, than winemaking hubs with clusters of large outbuildings. Numerous signs, with arrows pointing down side roads, advertise wine tastings. Occasionally, Gothic wineries of prodigious scale loom by the roadside.

"I think I need a taste of wine," says Sylvia, smacking her lips together.

"Good idea," Inez says, looking back and forth across the road.

The highway spills through the town of St. Helena, and, just north of it, Inez spots a winery sign and a road to turn off on. They follow the twisting blacktop north along a hillside of grapes and come to a small storefront. The winery is called Venezia. An OPEN sign hangs over the door. A little bell tinkles when they open the door, and a man who appears to have been napping sits up on his stool behind the oak burl bar. He is a stout fellow in a green Pendleton shirt. Sylvia notices his large fists opening on the varnished bar.

"Afternoon, ladies."

"Good afternoon."

"Care for a taste of Prosecco?"

Inez and Sylvia nod and step up to the bar as the man pulls down a couple of champage flutes.

"This is all we're pouring today. It's all we ever pour. It's all we make."

The man reaches into an icebox below him, pulls out a bottle, and stands it on the bar for a moment.

Sylvia looks at the label—an elegant black affair with an embossed "V" logo. The gold script lettering reads:

Venezia

P R O S E C C O

1961

St. Helena

Napa Valley

"Are you familiar with Prosecco?"

"No," says Inez.

Sylvia shakes her head and watches the man deftly uncork the bottle. She looks at the man's fat fingers. He wears a gold wedding band. Why is there a comfort in that? Would she care to wear a wedding ring?

"The Prosecco grape grows in the hills north of Venice. It can be made into a light Spumante or Frizzante. Our style is closer to a Spumante Cartizze," he says, squinting for emphasis. "It's geared for the more sophisticated palate."

The wine man slowly fills each flute to the top with bubbly.

Inez and Sylvia turn to each other, forgetting their host, and clink glasses. Sylvia cups her lips and brings them close to Inez's ear, whispering, "To beautiful Inez, a long and happy life."

The Prosecco is sweet, perhaps too sweet, Sylvia thinks, as she drinks it down. Inez has gotten a bit up her nose and turns away giggling.

"May we buy a bottle?" Inez asks.

"By all means," the man says, standing for the first time since they came in.

As they step out into the cool sunlight, Inez asks if they should drive on to Calistoga.

"Why not?" says Sylvia, light-headed. "We're having an actual adventure."

EVERYTHING appears a little run-down along the main street of Calistoga. It is not yet five, but a number of the stores are closed, some, it appears, for good. An old couple, walking a tired-looking spaniel, straggle up the sidewalk.

"At one time this was quite the spa town," Inez says. "Nothing really fancy. Hot springs. Mud baths. Stout European women here for the cure. I used to wonder what exactly was being cured. You'd see them walking up the streets, in the late afternoon, with big strands of Baltic amber drooping from their necks."

"Seems like a ghost town now."

"Not quite. I'm sure there are quite a few spas that still operate."

"Can we take a walk here?" Sylvia asks.

"We can do anything you like."

"I like the sound of that."

ONCE on the sidewalk, Sylvia slips an arm through Inez's—to test the limit of her permissiveness—and they stroll, arm in arm, up the main street, like a pair of European women, sans the Baltic amber, until they reach a bakery that serves coffee.

They sit at a table by the window, sipping burnt coffee out of plastic cups and eating doughnuts.

"I always wanted to eat jelly doughnuts on my honeymoon. That is, after I had a glass of Napa Valley Prosecco," Sylvia says.

"Did you always expect to get married?"

Sylvia makes a grand sweeping gesture with her arm and tosses her head back like a diva. "Yes, I did," she says. "But not as suddenly as this."

"No, but seriously."

"I *am* serious. I don't think you want to know how serious I am, Inez. I expected to get married and I expected to have babies. The baby part may be a problem, but here I am, eating jelly doughnuts on my honeymoon. The only difficulty I'm having is trying to figure out if I'm the bride or the bridegroom."

"Which do you want to be?"

"I want to be both."

"You can't be both," says Inez, shaking her head with playful disapproval.

"Can't we switch off? I really like the idea of being a bride," Sylvia says, offering Inez a rapturous smile. "But I look dashing in a man's suit. You'll want to divorce your other husband as soon as you see me."

Inez shakes her head. "You're a true wonder, Sylvia."

Nibbling her doughnut, Sylvia looks out the window. Across the street is a small resort called Anderson's Healing Cabins. Sylvia tries to imagine herself and Inez, taking the cure.

"How about we get healed on our honeymoon?" Sylvia points to Anderson's neon sign across the street. "Let's spend the night there. I could call in sick at The Little Sweden."

Inez lifts her chin and, balancing it in her hands, appears to be considering the query.

Sylvia keeps her eye on the red bruise under her lover's chin, the living scar the violin has left.

"I suppose I could make a phone call home," Inez says.

"Are you kidding?" Sylvia asks.

"No, I'm not kidding. I don't think you want to know how serious *I* am, Sylvia."

the sharper, the kinder

THEIR room at Anderson's Healing Cabins has twin beds. They are fated, it seems, to sleep together in small beds. After they make love, they lie for a long while in each other's arms. Inez wishes it were dark. She wishes all the light in the sky still peeking through the curtains would disappear. They take naps and Inez dreams that Sylvia has become a rabbit cleaved to her side. It is not an unpleasant sensation. It grows dark. Sylvia is still sleeping. *Little one,* Inez thinks. *Little one.*

How cruel can she be, setting up Sylvia like this? *The sharper the knife, the kinder the killing.* A phrase Isaac Roseman employed whenever her violin playing grew tentative. Mr. Roseman could sense when she was worried about a particular passage. *You are thinking. Who told you to do that? Where's your authority? Sharper, kinder!* he'd shout, reducing the phrase to its essence. *You know where that expression comes from, Inez? The kosher butchers in the old country. It is written that the butcher with the dull knife causes the animal the most pain. The rabbis will not bless his killing; this butcher's meat will not be kosher. So when you play the Mendelssohn, especially the Mendelssohn, you bring your sharpest knife, Inez, and you remember that music, just like the cows and the lambs and the chickens, just like human beings, is made of blood. Sharper, kinder. Sharper, kinder. Sharper, kinder.*

Inez moves quietly to the other bed and calls home. She whispers into the phone, telling Jake she needs to spend an evening by herself.

"Why are you whispering?" he asks.

"I don't wish to speak loud."

"Who are you with?" Jake is whispering now.

"Not a soul."

"You're acting strange, Inez."

"Am I?"

She watches Sylvia sit up in bed and rub sleep from her eyes, watches her push her lips forward in a pout. Her little imp. Jake's insistent whisper produces a hiss of words that she can't make out. "What was that?"

"You're not acting like much of a mother."

"I'm doing my best."

"You're just a little out of sorts, Inez. We can find some help for you."

"Please, tell the kids good night," Inez says and hangs up the phone.

DESPITE her efforts, Sylvia cannot persuade Inez to take a mud bath. Just out of the shower, and wrapped in a towel that says *Anderson Healing*, Sylvia tries once more. "I thought you were looking for a little adventure."

Inez is sitting in her underwear, applying lotion to her feet. "I'm not interested in that kind of adventure."

Something has changed in Inez's mood. Rather than questioning her directly, Sylvia becomes the voyant again. Quiet, but fiercely observant. *Will you quit looking at me like that*, her mother used to say when Sylvia watched her closely. *Will you quit looking at me?*

Inez *is* willing to try a dip in the hot mineral pool. They've come, of course, without swimsuits, but a small selection of inexpensive suits and bathing caps are available in the front office. Sylvia comes out of the dressing room first. She tiptoes into the tiled pool area feeling pleasantly vulnerable in a mint-colored two-piece with a padded halter.

Inez surprises her, a couple of moments later, hopping out of the dressing room in a tan bathing suit—a garish print with tropical animals and jungle vines. "I feel like a mama kangaroo," Inez says, the tops of her breasts shiny in the mineral air beside the pool.

Sylvia takes a long look at her lover. Now, with her hair tucked into the white bathing cap, Inez's features have become stark and iconic. Her face is as mutable as her mood.

"I thought you'd be in by now," Inez says.

"I was waiting for you."

"You're sweet."

Sylvia watches Inez step directly into the pool.

Inez peels off her bathing cap and tosses it toward a lounge chair. "I don't need this."

Sylvia watches the heaps of scalloped blond hair tumble down and frame Inez's cheeks. In a moment, Inez has slipped fully into the pool and the beautiful face is shrouded in swirling steam.

"Aren't you coming in?"

Sylvia drops a foot into the pool. "It's hot."

"Hey, you're the great adventurer."

She'd like to remain the watcher but, wincing, eases herself in.

Inez smiles at her. "Isn't it nice? I wonder if death is anything like this."

"What do you mean?"

"Don't you love the way your body goes numb and your head feels like . . . I don't know . . . nothing more than an incidental orb?"

"You think death feels like this?" Sylvia asks, watching Inez as closely as she can through the steam.

"No, I don't think death feels like anything. That's the value of death; it's beyond feeling."

"I happen to like feeling."

"You're a sensualist, Sylvia."

"And you're not?"

"Not like you. Anyway, there's something about being in here, maybe it's the heat of the water, maybe the minerals, that makes me feel as comfortable as if I were dead."

What a strange thing to say, Sylvia thinks.

"It must be the minerals," says Inez, contentedly.

"Yes," Sylvia says and considers the word. *Mineral.* From the Old French and the Middle English. Her mother's favorite compound of languages. *Mineral,* something precious from the *mine.* Her mother tried to bring her down into the mine with her. Was she supposed to be the canary? Was she supposed to sing at the first breath of danger? She didn't sing, she only watched.

"If you let it," Inez says, "the water can take away your worries."

There is nobody else in the pool area. Sylvia would like to put her arms around Inez, but she doesn't. She must be the vigilant observer. She sidles next to Inez so that their steaming wet skin touches, but barely. She tries to imagine them as a seamless whole, inseparable as a pair of girls who don't believe there's anything wrong with loving each other. She closes her eyes and pictures a pair of teens after a swim meet, panting, invincible, in love with themselves and their bodies. But she and Inez are not schoolgirls.

Sylvia boosts herself out of the pool. The bones of her body have lost their edge; they've been rounded by the heat and have grown weightless.

"You've already had enough?"

"Yes, I've had enough."

"It takes a little longer for the mineral's healing powers to kick in."

"I guess I'll have to miss out for now." Sylvia sits on the edge of the steaming pool, drops a towel around her neck, and dangles her legs in the water.

SYLVIA offers Inez a towel once she boosts herself out of the pool, but Inez isn't interested in drying off. She never wants to dry off. How long can her skin glisten in the cool air? In the pool she'd begun humming the Schubert lied and making her plans. As much as she'd have liked to have gotten home before the final planning began, she couldn't stop herself anymore than she could stop the steam from swirling around her. Now, out of the pool, the lied has grown faint, but she can still hear it. How long can she suspend this moment? Sylvia, who is not foolish, has read the mood. Inez closes her eyes. The end of the world would have been easier if it had begun with a Cuban missile. She opens her eyes. Sylvia, reclining now in a chaise lounge, has a wistful expression on her face.

"What you thinking about?" Inez asks.

"My mother."

"Do you think about her often?"

"Lately I have."

"You've never told me how she died."

"Pills, lots of them."

"I'm sorry."

"Thank you. It could have been much messier, but my mother was fanatical about keeping the house tidy. The strange part is that she put on makeup just before, a kind of mask. Mother hated makeup, but there she was in heavy foundation, raccoon-eyed with mascara."

Inez walks over and stands beside Sylvia in the chaise. "You found her?"

"I did. A dazzling sight, my mother, Cleopatra in Sacramento."

"I'm so sorry."

"You don't have to be sorry for me, Inez."

The comment hurts her. What's surprising is how tender she feels. Just when she believes that any emotion has departed, it finds a way of streaming into the dark room like a final burst of evening sun. She faces Sylvia again, back to business.

"Can you let her go? Your mother?"

"I'm letting her go."

"Can you forgive her?"

"I'm working on it."

Inez places her hand gently over Sylvia's shoulder strap. "I want to tell you something important. An irreversible decision I've come to."

"No decision is irreversible."

"This one is. Please. I need to talk to you . . . I need to tell you . . . you may have a hard time accepting what I tell you, especially after what you've been through. I'm not asking for your blessing, but if you could just try . . ."

"I know what your plans are, Inez."

"What are you talking about?"

"I know."

"You may think you know."

Sylvia stands and walks toward the mineral pool.

Inez notices that her breath has become constricted. "Where are you going? Are you going back in?"

Sylvia sits down by the pool. "No, I'm only going to dangle."

Inez wonders what Sylvia knows, whether she's bluffing. It's certainly a specialty of hers. Inez walks over and sits beside Sylvia. She dips her feet slowly into the hot pool.

Sylvia scoots a distance away and smiles. "You are so beautiful, Inez."

"Thank you."

"So the decision is irreversible." Sylvia says it as a statement that hangs for a moment in the steamy air.

Inez is tempted to contradict it, out of reflex. She's tempted to mimic Sylvia's initial response. *No decision is irreversible.* "Yes," she says, "it's irreversible."

"Have you decided," Sylvia asks in a flat tone, "whether you'll paint your face like my mother did or destroy the body in the process?"

"How long have you known?" Inez asks.

Sylvia doesn't answer. She thinks of what Bibi said: *There really isn't much you can do about it, if a person wants to harm herself.* She slowly slips into the mineral pool and goes under, holding her breath for so long that she imagines that Inez is about to come in after her. When she finally shoots to the surface, Inez hollers at her: "What are you doing?"

Sylvia takes quick, shallow breaths, her hair matted to her face like seaweed, the skin under her eyes stinging. She looks up at Inez. "I've always known. I've watched you for a long time. I thought, for a while, that I could save you. I couldn't save my mother, but maybe I could save you. But Bibi knew better. She helped me understand."

THAT night they watch *The Red Skelton Show* on the motel TV. Neither of them laughs at any of the jokes or skits, but they watch the show with a curious fidelity. After Sylvia turns the television off, they lie awake for a long time in their twin beds like a pair of mute sisters. Then Inez repeats Red Skelton's sign-off line, the line of a red-faced clown, cloying in its sincerity: *May God Bless.*

THE next morning in the Studebaker, Sylvia turns her body toward the side window, which, despite the chill, she has rolled all the way down. She rolls up her sleeves, loosens her string tie, opens the top three buttons of her blouse.

"You seem determined to freeze me out," Inez says.

Sylvia doesn't bother to answer.

"More power to you." Inez turns up the collar of her wool coat and keeps her eye on the centerline.

Once they hit 101, Inez pushes the Studebaker to seventy, relishing the open lane ahead of her. All that's left to do is to put her *affairs in order.* A strange irony in that. Is it courtesy or vanity, she wonders, that fuels the desire to have her affairs sorted neatly at the end of her life?

Back in the city, Inez loses heart, as the time to drop Sylvia off nears. Is she not as cold-blooded as she believes? Will she ever see Sylvia again? She drives in circles for a while through the streets of the Marina.

"Where are you going?" Sylvia asks, peeved.

"To your place to drop you off."

"Don't you know your way?"

"I thought I did."

"You're driving like a fool."

"I probably am a fool."

"Why don't you just take Lombard from here?"

"All right."

Pretty soon she's advancing with other traffic through the timed lights on Lombard, past the rows of tourist motels. They all seem to have vacancies today. Each of the motels has a big sign that promises one thing or another. COLOR TV. FREE BREAKFAST. HEATED POOL. Most of the motels have a tiny swimming pool out front that nobody ever swims in. A middle-aged woman could rent a room at the Beauty Bay Inn, go for a chill afternoon swim, dry off with a whole day's worth of scratchy white motel towels, lie naked in her bed, ingest a bottle of barbiturates, and watch a nice hour of color TV.

Inez glances over at Sylvia, as if the faux reporter were privy to her mental motel scenario, but Sylvia still won't meet her eyes.

As Inez pulls up in front of Sylvia's apartment, a northbound cable car is trundling by, a syncopated hallelujah of bells rung by the thick mustached gripman, as tourists on the running board holler, everybody so glad to be alive.

Sylvia gathers her few things from the backseat. Inez turns to watch her and notices the bottle of Prosecco beside the picnic basket— they didn't even remember to bring it with them into the motel.

Sylvia, dark glasses in place, hat in hand, and jacket over her arm, is ready to duck out of the car. "Good-bye," Inez whispers, as Sylvia slips out of the front seat. No apologies to make at this point. No prolonged good-byes.

Sylvia, on the sidewalk now, turns back. She dips her head through the opened window and flips her sunglasses up onto her head. Inez wants to take Sylvia's small, intense face into her hands, just for a moment, and kiss her good-bye. She keeps her hands gripped on the steering wheel instead and listens to the engine idle.

"I'd like to try and stop you," Sylvia says, her eyes rimmed in red, "but I'm not sure there's any way . . . any way to do it. Is this really something you can talk a person out of? Certain people, perhaps. You? I don't know. You have a look in your eyes, Inez."

"What kind of look?"

"I don't know. Like somebody who's found God. . . ."

"Well, that's a surprise to me. I'm not particularly big on God."

"Smug is what I really mean. Somebody who no longer needs anything or anybody."

"If it's any comfort to you, I don't feel very smug."

"My mother was taken to the hospital five times. It didn't stop her. She always came back with that look in her eyes."

Inez draws in her cheeks, closes her eyes.

"Tell me what I'm supposed to do, Inez. Should I call Jake? Telephone your kids and tell them that their mother is very sick? Call the police? Get them after you with a paddy wagon, as if you were violent, or crazy, or drunk? Or should I just tell you in the simplest possible way that you're breaking my heart?"

"I'm so sorry, Sylvia." Inez turns the car engine off, opens her door, and steps out. Now they are both standing in the cool sunshine, the car very much between them.

"My mother turned herself into somebody who didn't need to feel anything, and I studied her for so long that it rubbed off on me," says Sylvia. "If you want to learn how to become numb, live with somebody who's always at the point of destroying herself. I could have gone on forever without feeling much. I could have been happy enough. I had no need to destroy myself. I learned how to enjoy the smaller pleasures. I didn't need anything as grandiose as you or my mother. I was happy enough to be a watcher."

Inez reaches her arm toward Sylvia, across the roof of the Studebaker.

"Don't. You can't have your cake and eat it. That was one of my mother's favorite phrases." Sylvia shivers visibly and folds her arms in front of her.

"You're cold," says Inez.

"I'm all right. My mother could talk a good game. She was steeped in arrogance. She didn't suffer fools and, when it came down to it, we were all fools in her eyes. If not, we would have been sensitive enough to understand her perfectly. Sounds like you, Inez."

"Don't play psychology with me, Sylvia."

"I'm not playing." Sylvia drapes her jacket over her shoulder.

"It isn't going to work on me."

"I know that. I know all about you, Inez. You're exactly like my mother. She loved the word *emotion.* From the French *émouvoir,* to move toward feeling."

"I'm not your mother, Sylvia."

"I used to wonder if she ever achieved anything beyond synthetic feeling. If you counted the frequency of usage, if a concordance of her most frequently used words existed, *grieve, grief, grief-stricken* might lead the way. The only genuine grief in our house is what she left behind with me. She used words that way. Language as decoy. Language as bluff. Language as a means of disassociation. She made a wall of language around herself. You're the same."

"Are you trying to torture me?"

"Listen to the pot calling the kettle. That was another of my mother's favorites."

Inez looks up the street toward a southbound cable car trundling their way. She glances back at Sylvia. "You talk a pretty good game yourself, with all your phony identities."

"I'm an amateur compared with you, Inez, because I take it all to heart. Nothing means anything to you. What happened to your soul, Inez Roseman? All this nonsense about me being the charlatan. We both know who the real fake is here."

"I think I've heard enough."

"I'm sure you have."

The cable car is bearing down on the double-parked Studebaker, the bells a bit terrifying in their urgency. Sylvia walks quickly toward the front door of her building. Inez is at the point of calling her back, but simply watches as Sylvia turns one more time to face her. The silver medallion of Sylvia's string tie, a shimmering orb in the sunlight.

old home

INEZ parks at a meter on Chestnut Street, feeding it all the pennies from her coin purse. This is Jake's childhood neighborhood, the place she came three times a week for violin lessons. Inez has no idea why she's parked here, except that she's so numb after dropping Sylvia off that she has to stop somewhere. She locks her violin in the trunk and walks into a fruit market, where she buys a single Santa Rosa plum, which she slips into her coat pocket.

Walking west on Chestnut, she finds a phone booth that she closes herself away in. She spills out seven dimes. Who does she think she's going to call? Her father and mother are dead, her sister is unavailable, her children are in school, she never wants to speak again with her father-in-law, her friend Mafalda is angry at her for disappearing, for becoming so poor a friend, and Sylvia will hang up as soon as she hears Inez's voice.

Still, she makes phone calls—to Jake at his office; to the symphony manager, Arn Burlingame; to Jan Smetna, her violin dealer—and ends up speaking with a secretary, an assistant, and Smetna's Czech apprentice. When one wants to conduct business without emotion, there's something to be said for the efficiency of good assistants. Inez is assured by her husband's gum-snapping secretary that he has nothing in the works that should keep him from being home by seven; she sets up an appointment with Arn Burlingame to discuss a leave from the symphony; and she gets penciled into Smetna's calendar to get her violin appraised.

Inez decides to walk through the old neighborhood. Soon enough she finds herself in front of Jake's old house on Francisco Avenue and she leans for a few minutes against a shiny blue Ford Fairlane that is parked exactly where her father used to park his Hudson. In the summers, after she and Jake had started seeing each other, he'd sometimes go out and sit with her father while she was inside having a lesson. She used to wonder why this bright modern boy, home for a couple of months from his classes at Berkeley, would care to spend time with her old-world father. Once, after a lesson, she found them sitting forward in the lumpy gray seats of the Hudson with pocketknives in their hands. Jake was whistling one of his Tin Pan Alley songs and carving a greenish block of alder. Her father, the funny old Swede, had his lips puckered as if he might whistle "Dear Old Stockholm" as a counterpoint while he worked away on a lop-eared bunny. A couple of weeks later, Jake gave her a gift—his only known carving, a misshaped miniature violin, a freak of love and nature, that she kept for years in an underwear drawer with sachets of lavender and potpourri.

Jake brought her father pictures from *Metronome* of his favorite jazz musicians, and her dad returned the next week with framed photos of Jelly Roll Morton, Fats Waller, and Earl Fatha Hines. Her father seemed happiest when he was making gifts and wrapping them up in colored pages from the *Saturday Evening Post.* Once, at the kitchen table, she watched her father wrap a just-framed photograph of Duke Ellington in a Pierce Arrow ad. "One thing I'll say for Jacob Roseman," her father said. "He certainly holds a strong appreciation for colored musicians."

Heavy drapes are pulled across the picture window of Jake's old house, but Inez can still see the living room as it was on the day that Jake first spoke to her. The matching chairs and sofa, covered in a creamy brocade, the warm light from the pair of olive wood floor lamps, the plump copper vase stuffed with huge white hydrangeas, the blossoms the size of a stout woman's face. Inez can also see Jake, twenty-five years ago, staring out the picture window at her as she climbed into the black Hudson.

Pretty soon a man walks out of the house, a handsome fellow in a tweed coat. Inez watches this polished character walk down the front steps of the Rosemans' old house. It is as if she is remembering somebody from her youth, but this natty man has no more connection to her past than he does to her present.

"Can I help you?" he says, surprising her. She'd almost felt invisible, but there she is, leaning against a car.

"No . . . no, I used to live here. Many years ago."

The man smiles at her, disbelieving.

"Well, actually my husband lived here as a kid."

That the man can accept. "Care for a look around?"

"No, thank you. I like it best in memory."

"I won't take away your memory. Promise." The man grins at her. He'd be happy to lead her through the house. Perhaps he is a gentleman and his intentions are pure. Or maybe he would ravage her. Maybe she could live like this. Meeting up with strange men in the middle of the day. Treating people as if they were interchangeable. Was this what Sylvia meant by a fugue state?

"Thank you very much," says Inez, smiling at the man in the tweed coat. "I have something I must tend to, otherwise . . ." She holds her hands open in apology, then turns and walks up the street.

She continues to walk, leaving the fate of her car to the meter maids. At the corner of Bay and Fillmore, she can't decide between Marina Green, the vast grassy expanse, with its dogs and kite fliers, jutting along the bay and marina, and the gentle beach at Aquatic Park with its long stone pier. Choosing the latter, she heads east. Across Van Ness, she smells the dark ferment from the Ghirardelli chocolate factory and realizes that she's famished again. In the last week her appetite has turned into a feast-or-famine affair. She buys a Hershey bar in a small grocery and thinks of standing, as she did in childhood, nibbling chocolate beside the boccie ball courts.

Aquatic Park was one of her father's favorite spots on Sundays. Sometimes they'd have an afternoon meal in North Beach and then walk down Columbus. Her father would say, "How about we walk it off?" When she was seven or eight, she always wished they could take the trolley or cable car, but wanting to be a good sport like Bibi, she kept her eyes on the sidewalk and tried not to complain. It seemed like miles and miles they had to walk. When they finally got to the bandstand at Aquatic Park, her father would say, "How about we take a little rest? Unless you want to keep walking, Inez." That made them all laugh. Her father winked at her and nodded. She felt proud to have walked so far without complaining.

They often heard the municipal band at Aquatic Park. "Inez," her father would say, "I hope this music doesn't ruin your ears." He was ashamed by how much he enjoyed "common music." Inez happened to like the sound of the big horns. She remembers sitting on the concrete steps, how her vision would wander from the wide bay, to the mustached members of the band, to the steady stream of sailors in their immaculate uniforms, strolling by in twos or threes, or with their dates, willowy young women who, like Inez, had to be at least as smitten with the uniforms as with the men inside them. As she listened to the municipal band, she'd wonder whether the ruin to a person's ears was ever visible. Did a form of rust set in like you saw on the fenders of old cars?

Although her father pointed out the sailboats and fishing vessels with particular pleasure, she preferred the large ships, steaming out to sea or being tugged back in. "Someday you'll sail the seas, Inez," he'd say, and she believed him. She used to wonder why he said this to her, but not to Bibi.

Their father often pulled a pair of plums from his coat pockets and wiped them off with a clean handkerchief before handing one to each daughter. Then he'd take the handkerchief and spread it across the lap of Inez's dress or her coat so that the drippings from the plum had somewhere safe to spill. Inez could never understand how Bibi managed to eat her plum so much more carefully than she did. When she handed the handkerchief back to her father, it was always stained in purple blood.

The boccie-ball courts were her father's favorite. He never told them that, but they knew. A chicken-wire fence enclosed the courts. She and Bibi looked through the chicken wire at the old Italian men and their funny wooden balls, and their father looked over the fence.

Her father handed them bars of chocolate, which they slowly unwrapped and nibbled as they stood watching the boccie-ball players. She used to wonder why her father enjoyed these funny men so much, the crazy gestures they made with their hands, their language one he didn't understand any better than his daughters did.

Once, she asked her sister why the Italians had so much to say about a silly game of wooden balls.

"They're not talking about boccie ball, Nez, they're talking about politics and business. They're talking about smart things to do with your money. Maybe they're talking about somebody's wife who got really fat.

Or somebody else who used to do magic tricks and just dropped dead on the streetcar."

This was a shocking thought; she didn't believe Bibi at first. How did Bibi know what they thought? She didn't understand Italian. Anyway, it seemed to her that all those men knew were wooden balls, how close the big one was to the little. They held their hands apart, scratched lines in the sand with the toes of their shoes, invented new methods of measurement as they went along.

The chicken wire is gone now, replaced by a short wooden fence, but the boccie-ball courts are still here. Inez leans against the fence as she nibbles on her Hershey bar. When she closes her eyes, the chatter of Italian, the rise and fall in pitch, sounds like chamber music. The agitated voices evoke a string section worrying itself into a dissonant corner before easing toward a resolution. She opens her eyes and watches the men play. Had her father wished he were one of them rather than an old Swede who had nobody to talk with about his life?

After she finishes her chocolate, she instinctively reaches into her pocket for something more to eat. And there's the plum. She wipes it off on her coat. She hadn't thought any of the men had noticed her, but just as she takes a bite out of her fat Santa Rosa plum, and feels the juice of it spilling down her chin, a short man from the other side of the fence holds out a clean white handkerchief.

"*Prego,*" he says.

"No, no."

"*Prego.*"

She looks into his small, animated face, an oval of light under his gray felt hat.

He wants to hand the handkerchief to Inez, but because she's so surprised by the gesture, he bends toward her with the white cloth and dabs at the juice spilling from her chin. "*Grazie,*" she says, and turns away.

human

INEZ hadn't expected it to go this way. The closer she gets to ending her life, the more human she feels. For better or for worse, the relationship with Sylvia has humanized her. Just a couple of hours after dropping Sylvia off, even after Sylvia's punishing diatribe, Inez aches for her.

On the way home, Inez stops at the Larabaru Bakery on Sixth Avenue for French bread and at Shenson's, on Geary, for a pound of lox—something special for the kids when they get home from school.

Her father-in-law is alone in the house when she gets there. The very sight of him calls her humanity into question. She thinks how nice it would be to slap his face and, perhaps, add a twist to his gimpy bow arm. She lets the impulse pass. "Hello, Isaac," she says. "How are you?" She doesn't hear a word he says in reply. Inez finds a cucumber in the fridge, peels it, and cuts it into thin coins. After slicing a half loaf of French bread and spreading the slices with cream cheese, she adds the cucumbers and fillets of smoked salmon. Once she's assembled a plateful of open-faced sandwiches, Inez opens the front door—her usual sign to the kids that she's home.

She hears Joey tromp in the front door first. "Hi, Mom," he shouts. Inez knows that Anna's not far behind—Joey, anxious for home, always runs ahead the last couple of blocks.

Inez meets Joey in the front hall, gives him a hug, runs a hand through his cowlick. She'll give him a bath tonight, shampoo his hair. As her eyes grow moist, Inez turns to the side.

"How was your trip, Mom?" asks Joey, dropping a math workbook and his *Weekly Reader* on the hall table.

"It was fine."

That seems to satisfy Joey's curiosity. "Is there a snack?" he asks, heading for the kitchen.

"Go and see."

Anna pushes her way through the open front door, blancing her binder and a stack of schoolbooks, covered in white butcher paper. "Hi, Mom," Anna says in a flat voice, without looking at her mother.

"God, Mom," Joey shouts from the kitchen. "Did we strike it rich?!" This in response to the lox, a delicacy that Jake refers to as "gold" whenever Inez brings home a pound of it.

"There's something in there you might like," Inez says to her daughter.

"No thanks, I'm not hungry," says Anna, climbing the stairs to her room.

Finally a little fallout. Inez watches Anna disappear up the stairs, resisting the instinct to follow her.

AS soon as he gets home, Jake goes off to mix drinks. He seems happy to see her. Relieved, may be more like it. Perhaps she put a scare in him. Given Jake's public life as a political agitator, an "agent of change," as one newspaper columnist described him, Inez has always been surprised by how much he favors the status quo in his home life. There's no way to prepare the poor man for what's coming next.

Jake returns with a whiskey sour for himself and a gimlet for her. He seems intent on pleasing her. He hands her a drink and a cocktail napkin, then drapes his arm around her shoulder. Inez suddenly becomes conscious of the whereabouts of everybody in the house. Anna, as far as she knows, is in her room doing homework, Joey is hacking away at the Dvořák. And the old man . . . she's not even going to worry about the old man. At the moment, she and Jake are alone in the living room, Jake in a black polo shirt and a pair of Bermuda shorts, the pale green hue of a breath mint. Inez glances at his tan legs and smiles.

"You seem happy, Inez. You must have found what you were looking for."

"I wasn't exactly on a pilgrimage."

"Did you see Bibi?" asks Jake, taking so hearty a gulp of his drink that a little spills over his lower lip.

"Yes, I saw her." Inez sips at her drink. "You make a fine gimlet, Jake."

"Thank you." Jake pats at his mouth with his napkin.

"Anyway, I found the whole thing a bit exhausting, which is why I spent the night in Napa."

"Did she look bad?"

"No, she looked okay. About as good as a forty-five-year-old woman in a nuthouse can look. She wanted to be remembered to you. She wonders if you're still performing your egg-balancing trick."

"Ha. She remembers."

Inez studies her husband as he leans back cross-legged on the sofa. She used to envy the ease with which Jake resided in his body. Now she thinks that he may have gone a little slack. Has a little too much self-satisfaction set in? At least that's not a problem that plagues Inez. "There's something else," she says, "that might shock you, Jake."

He sighs like a spent athlete, then pulls himself up straight on the sofa. "What?"

Inez takes a long sip of her drink. "I'm going to bring Bibi home next week."

"What do you mean?" Jake shakes a cigarette out of his pack but can't find a light for it.

"They're willing to let her out." Inez tosses Jake a book of matches from the coffee table.

"For a day?" he says, lighting his cigarette.

"No, for good. She's harmless, Jake. I know the house will be a little tight, but I think Bibi will get along very well with your father. Maybe she can teach him how to sew."

Jake's face freezes. He sits with three fingers pinned across his lips. It appears that she has a talent for petty sadism. If she'd discovered this fact a little earlier, her life might have taken another shape.

"You're not serious," he says, his brow still furrowed, smoke pouring out of his great nostrils.

She sips her drink and smiles at Jake. "Of course not."

Jake lets out a gasp of relief.

"Bibi's perfectly happy where she is. She's more content than the rest of us. When I was visiting, it occurred to me that people really do become who they're supposed to. It's like growing into your face. And Bibi is perfectly at home with being crazy. You could say it becomes her."

"And what becomes you, Inez?"

"To be unhappy, I suppose."

"You're not so unhappy."

"I'm sure it's all relative."

"You seem relatively happy."

"If you say so."

"It's not what I say."

Inez looks at her husband with a degree of pity, the way you might consider a child who you discover, while he stands beside you at the piano, is tone-deaf. "How about you, Jake? What do you think your natural state is, happy-go-lucky?" She can't quite disguise her contempt as she says the phrase.

"Well, I wouldn't say happy-go-lucky. I do have some depth, after all."

"It is all relative, isn't it," says Inez, again, cruelly. She sighs. "I think Bibi's where she belongs. What's the phrase? Let sleeping babies lie."

"I think it's dogs that you let lie, Inez, not babies." Jake stands and stretches out his arms extravagantly. "I remember when we brought Joey home. He never seemed to sleep, did he?"

"No," she says.

"Drove you crazy."

It's clear that Jake is aiming for a little tit for tat.

"I had to take him down to the basement to sleep. How long did that go on? Weeks? Months?"

Jake is standing in front of her now, shifted into attorney mode. "That wasn't a very good time for you."

"No, it wasn't."

"Did you ever figure out what it was?"

Inez glares at Jake. "Why are we talking about this now?"

"Was the doctor any help at all? What did the doctor say?"

"He mentioned hormones," Inez says, closing her eyes on Jake, on the conversation.

"Hormones. They blame everything on hormones, nowadays. Your pimples, your breath, your personality, the way you behave in public. You'd think that hormones were a disease. Polio, for Chrissakes. Might as well get Dr. Salk working on a vaccine for hormones. Next thing you know, hormones will be a leading legal defense."

Inez tells herself that it won't be long and begins to hum her Schubert lied. *Everything in this life is precious.* . . .

"Speak of the devil," Jake says.

When she opens her eyes, Joey's standing beside his father. "Are we going to have dinner tonight, or something?"

"Are you hungry?" Jake asks.

"Yeah, I'm really hungry," Joey says.

"How about we call Chicken Delight?"

Inez hears their advertising ditty in her head—*Don't cook tonight, call Chicken Delight*—and imagines the truck pulling up in front of their house, the teenager with a flattop and a Chicken Delight jacket walking up their front stairs with a large white Chicken Delight sack. The neighbors peering out from behind their venetian blinds. *Can't she even cook a chicken dinner?*

"How about we go to the Feed Bag?" says Inez.

"Sounds great," Jake says.

"That'd be neat," Joey says, bounding out of the room. "Cheeseburger in a basket!"

"Do you think we can go with the kids," Inez asks, "and leave the old man here?"

Jake grins at her. He likes the idea and seems pleased that Inez has adopted his moniker for his father. "I think we can manage that. We can heat up the leftover spaghetti for him."

THREE bites into his cheeseburger, Joey drops his bombshell: "I want a dog."

"Jews don't have dogs," Jake says, winking, between bites of his cheeseburger.

"I'm only a half Jew," Joey says.

"And the wrong half, at that," Inez says.

"Why the wrong half, Mom?" Joey asks.

"Yes, please explain," Anna says, a hard grin breaking over her face.

"We're getting a little off the subject," Inez says.

"Hey, Dad," Anna says, sticking out her tongue, "Jews don't eat cheeseburgers."

Jake holds his cheeseburger at arm's length as if it's contaminated. They all have a hearty laugh. For a moment, you'd think they were the happiest family in America, and Inez, the most normal of moms. Maybe that's how it is . . . for a moment.

Inez looks across the booth at Joey. "Since when have you wanted a dog?"

"Since always."

"I've never heard you mention it."

"I wasn't ready."

"What do you mean?"

"I thought I better wait until I got responsible."

"You think you're responsible now?"

"Enough for a dog," he says, dragging a french fry through a puddle of ketchup.

"What kind of dog do you want, Joey?"

"Let's not get started," Jake says.

Joey keeps his eyes focused on her. "I don't know, any kind."

"We can't get a dog," Jake says.

"Why?" Joey and Anna ask in unison.

"We've already got your grandfather to look after."

"Maybe Isaac will like having a dog around," Inez says.

"Don't kid yourself."

"It can keep him company while the kids are at school."

"I'd be worried about the poor dog having to be alone with the old man."

"Quit making excuses," Inez says, turning to face Jake, who's disappointed that his last comment produced no laughter. "You should get the boy a dog."

Jake looks at her, surprised. "*Me?* Why me? Why should *I* do it?" His eyes hold the same old question: *Why are you doing this to me?* Although it's become less frequent in recent years, she enjoys watching the look of the persecuted seep into Jake's eyes. Jake wants her to say something to undo the trouble she's started. Inez smiles back at Joey. "The truth is," she says, "I think this family could use a dog."

Joey sings an arpeggiated trumpet charge, and his sister obliges him by calling out: *Charge!*

"But let's let Dad get used to the idea."

"It's going to take a lot of getting used to," Jake says, frowning in mock anger.

Inez pats his hand. "I think you can manage."

Soon, everybody goes back to their meal. Jake eats with his head down. The kids, sensing a shift at the center of the family, can hardly contain themselves. With their mouths open wide, they spoon in hunks of ice cream from their root beer floats. Inez sucks hard on her straw, but there is nothing left of her strawberry malt.

"Don't slurp, Mom," Anna says, repeating the ancient family injunction.

"Yeah, Mom," Joey chirps in.

Inez looks across the table at her kids. Can she actually leave them? Of course, she can. It's clear that they love her and that she loves them. This is indisputable. It is also clear to Inez that, in the end, they will be better off without her.

little bird

JAKE often has difficulty getting much work done on days he's due to visit Christine. Awaiting an afternoon of unbridled sex can turn him into a horny old goat who has to be careful to keep his unbidden erections in check when a female client visits or his secretary, Grania, waltzes into his office. But since he's been unable to raise an erection, for all his ardor, during his last two visits to Christine, he's filled with trepidation this morning. The misadventures of his last visits have haunted him. He's tried to reason with himself, to regard the events, or nonevents, as nothing more than a couple of isolated incidents that happen to every man sooner or later. The first time, in Christine's sewing room, he could explain away as an aberration. But when the problem returned, two weeks later, after she led him, as a special treat, into her own bedroom, his frustration swelled into a knot in his chest. What if this became the norm rather than the exception? Was this the beginning of his demise? Who's to say that a man cannot become a eunuch at the age of forty-two?

As if this fear about his potency weren't enough, a certain madness is sweeping through his house. He has lingering, if unfocused, questions about his wife's behavior. Inez is up to something, he knows it, but he doesn't know what. The woman has a fierce resolve about her. One thing that's clear is that whatever she's planning, or in the middle of, doesn't include him. Inez seems perfectly content to go on without him.

After a morning of paper shuffling and innocuous phone calls, Jake strolls down to Market Street to buy lunch. A return to the aphrodisiac basics seems in order. Jake picks up a dozen oysters on the half shell, a pair of walkaway shrimp cocktails, and a large loaf of dark sourdough.

As soon as he steps out of the cab and approaches Christine's back door, he begins whistling the theme of "Yardbird Suite," a gracious and relaxed Charlie Parker song. That's Jake, gracious and relaxed. Christine meets him at the door.

"You sound chipper."

"I'm trying."

"Don't try too hard," Christine says, leading him into the kitchen. "I think my neighbors must know about you—here comes Christine's backdoor jazzman."

"How can you call them neighbors when you live in a mansion and the closest houses are so far away that you can't even see them?"

"What kind of question is that, Jake? Are you in one of your socialist moods?"

"I don't know, I'm in some sort of mood."

Irritated, Christine shakes her head.

Is he trying to make her angry? He stares at her for a moment as if he were. Maybe he is. It is a weird, fucking enterprise he's involved in here: getting his sex from a Pacific Heights matron, who he realizes is dressed today like a whore. He's been so distracted that it isn't until now that he notices Christine's getup: a short, clingy skirt matched with a close-fitting cashmere sweater, in which her nipples are visible. She's actually made up like a hooker, with a thick layer of foundation, heavy black eye shadow, and a swath of cherry red lipstick. Christine places her left hand on her hip as she's being appraised, and she dangles a small clutch purse, the color of her lipstick, from her right hand.

"What's the occasion?" Jake asks.

"Thought you might be up for a change of pace."

"Do I pay you now or later?"

"Your pleasure."

Jake's never gone in for prostitutes or found the look the least bit appealing. One evening when his daughter, Anna, was a young girl, six or seven, and riding in a car with him through downtown, she spotted a streetwalker and quite innocently pointed her out: "Look at that woman, Daddy. I like her dress. I want a dress like that someday." Jake hadn't bothered to explain who the woman was or why she was dressed like that. Jake sees plenty of prostitutes down at the courthouse. Once in a while they appear haughty, strolling the halls with their lawyer, but more often they seem like plain, working women, attending to another unsavory part of their job—getting booked and briefly jailed. No more glory in that than in treating their venereal diseases or drug addictions. Nobody, not even à whore, likes to be humiliated in the light of day. Christine gives him a hard stare. One more part of the act?

"You look like you're going to attack me with your little purse."

"Is that what you'd like me to do?"

"Not especially."

"You can never tell with a customer."

"I'm not a customer, Christine."

"Of course you are. What's interesting is that you fancy me as the aggressor. Maybe that's part of your problem."

"My problem?"

"Forgive me, Jake."

It would be smart, he thinks, to walk out of the kitchen right now. Leave his oysters and shrimp cocktails on the butcher block and say *sayonara*. But, instead, he tells himself to be a good sport, to go along with the game.

When the plates are set, Jake steps around behind Christine and slips an oyster into her mouth. She swallows.

"Thank you; does this mean you've forgiven me?"

"No."

"Oh, a man who holds grudges. Could I have another oyster, this time with hot sauce?" Christine tilts her head back and opens her mouth.

"How many shots?"

"I don't know. I suppose five will do."

Jake shakes hot sauce over the largest oyster, much more than she's asked for, and watches the hue of the gelatinous oyster meat gradually tint toward pink pepper.

Christine winces as she watches Jake's assault of the oyster. "Isn't that going to burn, Jake?"

"I think you'll taste it." Jake feeds Christine the oyster and watches her swallow it, blinking her eyes shut.

Christine inhales slowly through her nostrils, her eyes turning bleary. "Do you want to hurt me, Jake?"

"Do you want me to?" says Jake, his hands on his hips.

"We're not talking about my desire, Jake. Anyway, you should know, I have a high threshold for pain."

"I've never been a violent person."

"You've lived a very safe life, Jake."

Jake lifts Christine off her stool—she can't weigh much more than a hundred pounds—and lays her on the floor. "Have you ever been fucked on the kitchen floor?"

"Not this one."

"But others?"

"Plenty of others."

"You *are* a whore."

"Good, Jake, very good."

Jake pushes her skirt up to her waist and strips off her underwear. He pins her arms back with his right hand and starts to fondle her.

"So, tell me, have you ever hurt a woman, Jake?"

"Not in the way you mean."

"No, you prefer the more subtle approach, like driving your wife batty from neglect."

"Do you think that's what I'm doing?"

"I couldn't say for sure."

Jake twists Christine's left arm behind her back until she winces. He slaps wildly, and with little effect, at her face.

"Good, Jake; I mean your aim is lousy, but at least you're playing. Haven't you ever hit a woman?"

"No."

"Well, better late than never."

"Why are you doing this, Christine?"

"I want to see what you're made of. Hey, how about we get back to Inez?"

"Stop."

"Don't you think it's most fun when we're talking about her? You know, somebody might say she's my rival, but I never think of it that way. We're not in competition. We each get a piece of you and I happen to get the piece I want. At least most of time I get it."

"Bitch." Jake applies more pressure to Christine's arm. His face turns hot.

"Are you going to break my arm, Jake?"

"No," Jake says, letting her arm loose, then standing. He picks up an oyster from the platter, dashes it with hot sauce, and slips it down his throat.

Christine sits up, lifts her arm, and shakes it loose a few times. "You realize that I have no illusions about Inez, Jake. I know how it looks from the outside. She has the great career, the beautiful children, the outstanding husband, but things may not be as they appear."

Jake glares at Christine. "What the hell are you talking about?"

"Things may not be as they appear," Christine repeats. "Take me, exhibit A. People look at me from the outside, my *nonexistent* neighbors, for instance. What do they see? A happily married woman with wealth, a place in society, and, some might even say, a measure of beauty. Could they possibly guess that the chic little woman in the mansion thinks of suicide five days out of seven?"

"You do not," Jake says.

"You're right. But I could."

"Bullshit," Jake says, a knot of fury rising right up his throat.

"And how about Inez? Who knows what she's thinking about? She's liable to be thinking about anything."

"Shut up." Jake crouches carefully in front of Christine. "Will you shut up about Inez!" This time, he takes aim at the beauty mark, just above the cherry wedge of lipstick, and slaps Christine soundly across her mouth. Her head snaps back. The smack is loud. Jake's hand smarts from the contact. They are both stunned. Jake's breath is caught in his chest and burns for a moment. Finally, his breath heaves clear and he forces himself to look at Christine, a fallen whore on the floor. Her mouth is already swollen, her makeup smeared.

"I'm sorry," he says.

"I taunted you."

Jake stands. "You should put some ice on that."

"I don't need it."

Jake goes to the giant refrigerator and empties cubes from an ice tray into a large dish towel. In a moment, he kneels in front of Christine, holding the ice to her lip.

"Lie down beside me, Jake."

She takes the ice from him as he reclines beside her and lights a cigarette. They have nothing to say to each other. They may never have anything to say again. When he finishes his cigarette, he rises up on an elbow and starts to stand up.

"Stay," she says.

"I don't think it's a good idea."

"Come here."

Jake bends down beside her and she kisses his forehead.

"What you said about yourself . . . ?"

"Nonsense. All of it nonsense. Sometimes I think I'm nothing more than a frustrated actress. I don't even make a good whore, do I?"

"You have some potential."

"Don't be cruel, Jake. We don't need to hurt each other anymore." She reaches toward him and unbuckles his belt.

"It's not a good idea."

"What did you come for, Jake?"

It happens in a flurry. His zipper down. His pants yanked off. His prick in her hands.

"It's like a little bird, Jake."

"What did you expect?"

"It doesn't want any part of me."

"No," he says, "I'm afraid it doesn't."

play me a song

LOOK . . . look who's here," Hy says, when Toby ushers Sylvia into the living room. The poor man has a double-pronged tube coming out of his nostrils. Sylvia follows the tube to an oxygen canister, a massive orange tank that wreaks havoc on the Danish modern aesthetic of the living room. The furnishings surprise her. She imagined Hyman's house would be extroverted like him. She pictured massive overstuffed chairs and sofas, maybe a baroque daybed on which Hy's ample bride could pose for him as a mature odalisque. But clearly Toby holds the reins to the house. A blond baby grand, as homely an instrument as Sylvia's ever seen, broods like a giant Scandinavian across the room. It must be a form of revenge for Toby, given Hy's likely infidelities, to have him propped up on a thin-cushioned church pew of a teak sofa that offers better prospects for obedience than slouching.

Although Hy may be half-dead, his eyes brighten at the sight of Sylvia.

"Hy, I'm sorry I'm late." She kisses Hy's cheek. His skin is drawn and sallow like an old grandfather's, and, though the room is more than toasty, he is wrapped in a heavy wool blanket. Sylvia takes a quick look around and spots Miller Beem and a couple of younger people she doesn't know. Everybody seems to be holding down a separate corner of the large room. Sylvia feels the heat being pumped into the room through the floor vent. Too much heat. "Has everybody already done theirs?" she asks.

"Just about . . . everybody," says Hy.

SYLVIA coached herself on the bus ride over. She'd been weeping most of the afternoon and early evening. About Inez, about Hy. Wishing that the one who no longer wanted her life could pass it to the one desperate for his.

On the bus ride, she tried to get ahold of herself. She needed a strategy. She decided that she would respond to Hy—and his silly notion of a eulogy party—by being nurselike, warm but clinical. But he is dying before her eyes, and clinical warmth is a more difficult task than she imagined.

"I didn't think . . . you'd come," Hy says.

Sylvia, aware that the others are watching, squints her eyes at Hyman, clownlike. "You think I had a choice," she says, in her best Jewish-gangster voice. She hears some nervous laughter behind her. Now she tugs the cords of the string tie that Hyman gave her. Her only hope is to go through with the performance. She spreads her feet apart like a gunfighter. "I had no choice! I'm standing on the running board of the California Street cable car, you understand, going east toward the ferry building. I'm trying my damnedest to get out of town. Suddenly, I feel myself being strangled. It's not a pretty picture. There's an invisible rope drawn around my throat. The damn thing's practically yanking me off the running board into traffic. The other passengers—they think I'm crazy. I'm struggling to hold on, my hair's flying back, I begin to say my prayers, when it hits me like a shot—*it's old Hy, he's got his mind lasso working.*"

Hy breaks into a choked laugh, and the others are convulsed with laughter.

"Look . . . look at her," Hyman says for the benefit of the whole room. "She's even wearing the string tie."

"Nobody else would be caught dead in it, Hy," she says and turns, wishing she could withdraw the last comment. She recalls one of her mother's favorite phrases: *Aren't you just mortified?* Fortunately, neither Hy nor his guests seem to notice what she's said.

Miller Beem gives Sylvia a quick wave. A young man in a Hawaiian shirt, his hair shiny with gel, comes up to greet Sylvia.

"I'm Rudy," he says.

"You're Hy's son?"

"The one and only. Hey, that was very good, your routine, very funny. The whole world, you know, has heard about the mind lasso. He tried to teach me, back when I was in school. The secret to better grades."

"How'd it work?"

"It went the opposite way for me. My grades went down—couldn't go much lower—and I ended up spending more time in the principal's office. I don't think I was cut out for the mind lasso. How about you?"

"I'm just starting to catch on."

"You may be the first one."

Sylvia feels something tugging on the back of her blouse and turns to see Miller Beem, the left sleeve of his sport coat pushed up to reveal a shiny gold Longines watch that looks new.

"Miller, have you met Rudy?"

Miller nods his head confidently. "I've had the pleasure."

"Miller's a practitioner of the mind lasso," says Sylvia, noting the rose carnation in Miller's lapel.

"Have you had any success?" Rudy asks.

"Well, I haven't hurt anybody yet," Miller says with a chuckle.

"Hey, that's a start."

"Actually," Miller says, a full grin breaking over his face, "I think it's beginning to work for me. I sold two pianos the other day."

"You did?" Sylvia says.

"Just a spinet and an upright, but I'm working on a baby grand."

"That's wonderful."

"It's only a start," Miller says. He points to the ugly blond baby grand across the room. "That's what I aspire to." Miller pulls a handkerchief from his coat pocket and dabs at his brow. "A bit tropical in here, wouldn't you say?"

Sylvia can't get over the change in Miller Beem. A little success goes a long way.

Rudy Myerson, the perfect gentleman, nods to Sylvia and Miller. "My father's lucky to have such loyal employees."

Now Toby, dressed in a floor-length red kimono, the largest mass of silk Sylvia's ever seen in one place, approaches with a small silver tray of hors d'oeuvres. "By the way," Toby says, "I apologize for the heat— Hyman likes it warm."

Sylvia plucks a stuffed mushroom from the silver tray and remembers the night she sat with Hy and Toby at Inez's solo concert. How Inez came onstage in her sleeveless purple dress and Sylvia fixed her opera glasses on the bruise under the violinist's chin, wondering if she'd ever be able to kiss that bruise. She didn't imagine that she'd soon know that bruise well, that she'd discover even deeper scars. Despite the fact that Hy kept sneaking his hand onto her thigh, Sylvia remembers sitting in the Myerson box and feeling a certain comfort, like sitting beside a pair of adopted parents for the night. Sylvia recalls the moment she fell in love with Inez's bow arm, with the violinist herself. Sylvia wants to keep any thought of the violinist out of this house. She smiles at Toby, who has completed a circle of the room with her tray. "Your house is lovely."

Toby nods. "Tell Hyman. Personally, I don't go in for this Scandinavian look. It's too austere for my taste. But you know Hy, he likes everything to be modern. Have you met my daughter? Nina, come over here."

Nina, a small, dark-haired woman about Sylvia's age, comes over to greet Sylvia. The poor woman, who'd been sitting quietly in a teak chair, looks like she's been crying for seven days straight.

Sylvia takes her hand. "I'm so pleased to meet you."

Nina watches her mother move away with the tray of hors d'oeuvres. "Dad has told me a lot about you."

"He told me that you were the brightest person under the sun, Nina."

"So he'd like to believe."

"Hey, hey," Hy calls in a frail voice, "there's . . . a little problem here, you've all . . . forgotten about me."

"What do you mean?" Toby says. "You're the reason everybody's here!"

"Don't we . . . don't we have a couple more eulogies?"

"The man's a glutton for punishment," Sylvia says.

"That's all you have . . . to say for yourself?"

"You want more from me, Mr. Myerson?"

"You have more?"

Sylvia walks over to the blond piano, which turns out to be a special edition Steinway, then glances at Toby. "May I?"

"By all means."

Sylvia chords a jaunty intro to "I've Grown Accustomed to Her Face." Although the piano might be ugly, its responsiveness is extraordinary. She tries to play the song with a light, even comic touch, fearful that if she plays it soulfully, she'll make it sound mournful. Everybody, save Hy, who's tethered to his oxygen, gathers around the piano.

"Wait . . . wait," Hyman calls. "You all left me again. Listen, I'll be gone . . . soon enough."

Sylvia rises from the piano bench and leads the little group back to Hy on his teak sofa.

"You're certainly impatient tonight, Hy."

"I'm . . . running out of air."

"I don't believe you."

"She doesn't believe me," Hy says, clearly getting a kick out of Sylvia.

"What do you want me to do, say something nice about you? Is that the idea here? Butter you up, so you give me a raise?"

"Exactly. All the nice things . . . you can think of."

Sylvia puts a finger on her chin, thinking. "Somebody else is going to have to step in, I'm drawing a blank. How about you, Miller?"

"What?" Hy says, with a laugh. "You expect Miller . . . Miller Beem to make a speech?"

"I can talk," Miller says. He stands and takes off his suit coat, folding it over his arm. "Gosh, it's warm in here. Hello, Mr. Myerson," Miller says, standing across the coffee table from his boss.

"Miller, you can call me . . . call me Hyman."

"Hyman. Hyman, I was talking to my mother the other day. I called to tell her that I sold two pianos. 'This is a miracle,' she said."

"It is a miracle," Hyman says.

"I'm just getting the hang of it, Mr. Myerson. I told my mother, 'These pianos I sold were small ones, Ma.'

" 'How big do they have to be?' she said.

" 'That's not the right question,' I told her. 'The right question is *How big can they be?* Mr. Myerson taught me to think like that. He told me it would take time. He believed in me. He told me that I was much bigger than I thought. He said, *Miller, Miller, Miller, do you think the Pacific Ocean knows how big it is?* Then he taught me about the mind lasso.' "

Miller Beam steps into the center of the room, a man playing his audience expertly. He unfolds his sport coat and pushes his thumb through one of the buttonholes. "For me, the mind part was easier to understand than the lasso. Then, a couple of weeks ago, I went to a rodeo at the Cow Palace. Let me tell you, those guys are good with the lariat. We could all learn something from them. I practiced the lasso in my apartment. Locked my fat thumb in the buttonhole of my suit coat and swung it around like a lasso. Once I mastered the physical part, I began to integrate my prowess with the mind. Any of you care to come down to the showroom, I'm sure I could help you find just the instrument you're looking for. I'd consider it a real pleasure."

A cheer goes up in the room, and Miller Beem lifts his suit coat in a series of rising swirls until it is above his head and he is hooting like a cowboy.

Once everybody has settled down and congratulated Miller Beem, Sylvia lets it be known that she has no intention of following Miller's performance with one of her own.

"Only on the piano," she says.

"Fine," Hy says. "Somebody help me over . . . there with my juice." He flicks the oxygen canister with a fingernail. In a moment, Rudy is helping his father make his way slowly across the room with his oxygen. It's only then that Sylvia allows herself to feel her deep sadness again.

Hy, settled in a teak chair with armrests, says, "Play me . . . play me a song . . . Sylvia. Not one for the customers . . . one for me."

the right of first refusal

IT's been more than a week since their dinner at the Feed Bag, far longer than Inez expected to be around. As yet, there's been no action taken on the dog. Inez, however, has done a good job looking after her worldly business. Her Landolfi is appraised at $27,000, and her bows add a few thousand more. Given that she'd bought the instrument, not that many years ago, for $4,500, the news of its present value makes her blush with pride.

Her violin dealer, Jan Smetna, a Czechoslovakian flirt, is very fond of the instrument and offers to provide free maintenance for the right of first refusal should she ever choose to sell the violin.

"But I'm not looking to sell the fiddle, Jan."

"Someday you might be. Nobody's interested in trading until they see an instrument they like better. It's the same thing with marriage. My wife, she was perfectly happy with me until she saw a man six inches taller with a smaller nose and a Jaguar."

"Poor Jan," she says, even though she's heard about the wife and the phantom gentleman a dozen times. She doesn't believe any of it. Smetna is a Czech joker. He's made a small fortune trading violins. She's seen him pull up near the Opera House in a very nice Mercedes, accompanied by a big European girl who adores him.

"How about you and your Jake? He must be getting a little tired by now. You just let me know, anytime. I have the perfect instrument for you, Inez," he says, winking.

"I'm too old for you, Jan."

"Old? In this business, age is an advantage. Age is not an impediment, but a virtue."

"I'll bear that in mind."

"Please."

"So you're willing to maintain the Landolfi indefinitely, Jan?"

"For life."

"What if I live longer than you, Jan?" Inez says, looking directly into the eyes of the pudgy Czech. The man is a good five years her junior.

"I'll take my chances," he says.

Wise fellow, she thinks.

Inez signs a paper for Smetna granting him the right of first refusal, and he types up a formal appraisal of the Landolfi, which he signs with a flourish.

ARNOLD BURLINGAME, a buttoned-down fellow who likes to pretend he's above the nasty business of managing a symphony orchestra, is all sympathy when Inez expresses her need for a leave, yet, given half a chance, he'd do whatever he could to screw her out of any money or benefits coming to her.

Bent over his little desk, Arn Burlingame peers up at her. "Inez, I've been meaning to let you know how much I admired your solo performance. We all did."

"Thank you."

"What can I say? We are all very proud of you."

"Thanks, Arn."

"Are you okay, Inez?"

"Tired."

"Yes, this work can make you tired."

"I've hardly missed a concert or rehearsal in twenty years, Arn."

"Remarkable. Now, you've thought this over, and you want the rest of the season, starting immediately?"

"Yes."

"You understand that this sort of thing is frowned upon in the middle of a season, especially without giving the proper notice? You understand, and this is in your contract, that without giving proper notice, you forfeit a year of pension, and if the governing board chooses, for whatever reason, not to reinstate, you have no rights of grievance?"

Inez nods her head soberly. The man wants to shame her, but she is invulnerable. It is a lovely feeling.

"Look here," Arn Burlingame says, raising his finger in the air.

"Yes," she says, admiring the absurdity of the situation: her thought-fulness in requesting a formal leave before taking her life.

"If you have a change of heart, my door is always open." Arn inhales deeply through his nose. Inez watches his chest swell and his pale, lined face brighten slightly. Inez thinks of the ashy light of a lantern.

hang up already

INEZ is so pleased to have her business affairs behind her that she walks into a bar called Emperor Norton's, on Van Ness, and orders a martini. The middle of a Friday afternoon and she sits alone at the bar, an attractive, well-dressed woman, toasting herself in the filmy mirror.

The martini is not a good idea; it turns her weepy, and she begins to ache for Sylvia. She'd chosen to believe that she's over Sylvia, that she's over everything. Halfway through a second martini, as the bar starts to fill with girl Fridays and automobile salesmen just off for the weekend, Inez goes to the ladies' room, taking her half-finished martini with her. On the way back, she drops a dime in the pay phone, balances the martini on top of the black phone box, and dials Sylvia.

"Hello," she says.

"Inez?"

"Yes."

"Why are you calling me?"

"I'm not sure. I wanted to say I was sorry."

"Sorry for what?"

"Well . . . I heard about Hyman Myerson."

"You saw the obituary?"

Inez lifts her martini and sips at it. "Yes. I'm sorry. I know you were close to him."

"I was."

"Did you go to the funeral?"

"Yes."

"It must have been a large affair."

"Why did you call?"

Inez holds the phone for a minute and feels its weight. She hates how filthy the phone is, just like the hallway she's standing in. "I called to say good-bye."

There is a pause. She can hear Sylvia's breathing, her anger.

"I really shouldn't have called. It was just an idea I had without thinking. To say something to you, but I really don't have anything to say."

"Where are you?"

"Doesn't matter."

Sylvia is growing anxious on the other end of the line. It's as palpable as a static frequency, a note heard in the inner ear.

"Do you want company, Inez?"

"This is all I want . . . to talk with you a minute. I s'pose I have no right. To call."

"But that's what you've done."

"I wanted to tell you . . . that everything is going to be all right. You have such a bright future, Sylvia."

"Don't patronize me. You have a lot of nerve."

Inez pours down the rest of the martini as if it were medicine. She considers eating the olive. Her hands have grown sweaty holding the phone.

"What is it you want, Inez?"

"Just . . . to wish you well."

"You've already done that. Don't leave your children without a mother, Inez."

"Supposing that was in my plans, and I'm not saying that it is, don't you think they'd be better off in the long run?"

"Who told you that?"

"Oh, I know they would."

"Ask me if I'm better off."

"Sylvia, I only called to wish you well. And to tell you that I love you. Maybe you should hang up on me, Sylvia."

"You're the one who's going to have to hang up."

Inez looks at the filthy black phone. Who knows whose hands have been on it. "I wish you would."

"No chance."

"Good-bye," Inez says, finally. "Good-bye, Sylvia." She gently replaces the phone in its cradle.

intervention

A GAINST her better judgment, Sylvia calls Jake Roseman the next morning at his office, but his rude secretary, snapping gum into the receiver, claims that the attorney has no time available for the next month.

"It's an emergency," Sylvia insists.

"Check the yellow pages," the secretary says. "They're full of lawyers. Any kind you want. Divorce. Bankruptcy. Wrongful injury."

"It's about his wife," Sylvia says, playing her trump card. "I'm afraid she's in danger."

"What kind of danger? Are you making a threat, ma'am?"

"No, I'm not making a threat! I'd like to talk with Mr. Roseman about this."

After a short pause and a snap of gum, the secretary says, "He's with a client now; he should have a few minutes at eleven o'clock. I'll have him call you then. Name and number, please."

"I can be at his office by eleven."

"Name and number?"

"Natalie . . . Natalie Bucheron," she says.

"Number?"

"Graystone 4-2641."

SYLVIA dresses in a new pair of nylons and a navy blue thrift-shop suit, just back from the cleaners. She tops herself with a small, pointed hat in gray felt. The hat lends a sense of purpose, or so she thinks, when she sees her reflection in the window of the cab at Hyde and Washington.

At a quarter to eleven, she introduces herself to the horror at the front desk, a heavyset blonde with a well-shellacked bouffant. "I'm Natalie Bucheron."

"I told you I'd have Mr. Roseman call you. He's still in his conference."

"I'll wait."

In a few moments, Jake Roseman appears in the lobby with a tall woman in a sable coat, whom he pats on the arm and dismisses with a few kind words.

Once his client departs, his secretary says, "This is Miss Buscher."

"Bucheron," Sylvia corrects, standing. "Natalie Bucheron; I'm sorry to impose."

"I told her that you didn't have any time, Mr. Roseman."

"It's rather urgent."

Jake Roseman, who's dressed sportily in a pair of blue seersucker pants and a knit shirt, gives Sylvia a quick, friendly glance. "If you're looking for an attorney, miss, I'm sorry to say that I'm not taking on any . . ."

"I told her that on the phone, Mr. Roseman, but she insisted . . ."

"It's about your wife."

"My wife? Is she all right?"

"Can we speak in your office?"

"Of course."

The man holds the door and ushers Sylvia into his office. His face has changed hurriedly from easygoing charm to wrinkled-brow intensity. It's clear that the man loves his wife or is, at least, deeply concerned about her. Sylvia sits in the worn leather chair across from Jake Roseman's desk and is amused to see the disarray of books and file folders in his small office. The door of a small closet is open, and Sylvia notices more files, stacked haphazardly on a shelf beside an antique adding machine, a sack full of tennis balls, and a huge jar of pickles, worthy of a delicatessen. The pickles, she guesses, are the gift of a grateful client. A beautifully garish pair of purple shorts hang like an emblem from a hook on the closet door.

Jake Roseman swivels back and forth a couple of times in his chair. "How do you know my wife?"

"I've gotten to know her through the symphony."

"Are you a musician, Miss . . . ?"

"Bucheron. Yes . . . yes, I am." It's a good name she's given herself, but Sylvia is beginning to get weary of all the invention. Enough is enough. The absurdity of it—changing herself into a woman named after a goat cheese—has begun to make her nauseous. Her mind is racing. She might as well run off and join the circus, turn herself into a contortionist. At what point does she start being herself? Could she possibly screw herself into so many fresh identities that she'd wear through the threading of her own soul? Natalie Bucheron. She'd rehearsed her story on the cab ride over, but Jake Roseman doesn't seem a bit concerned with verifying who she is or isn't. To what purpose, this masquerade? Does she actually believe that she can prevent a suicide by telling secrets to the philandering husband? Jake Roseman shakes a cigarette out of a pack on his desk and quickly lights it. Then, embarrassed by his manners, he offers a cigarette to Sylvia.

"No, thank you."

"So what did you want to tell me about Inez?"

The question is how much to reveal. She could tell the man his wife's life story in such a manner that he'd not recognize her. "On second thought," she says, "I will have a cigarette." She hardly ever smokes, but she wants to stall a moment now and watch Jake Roseman go through the ritual of lighting her cigarette.

He holds out a Pall Mall toward Sylvia but, before lighting it, says, "I'm worried about Inez."

The familiarity with which the attorney says his wife's name is disconcerting. How odd to be sitting with a man who may love Inez as deeply as she does, and yet have no way to share the bond. What would she tell Jake Roseman about his wife, if she could share anything? That Inez actually likes to be kissed along the scars on her belly. That she can be persuaded to stand under the shower until all the hot water in the building runs out. That, despite her protests, food is important to her. That she likes to eat with her fingers and to have the nubs of her calloused digits sucked one by one. That sex makes her hungry. That if you are patient, you can help her have an orgasm. That she likes a good striptease. That she can be girlish and lewd. That she can walk around the bedroom naked under a man's shirt, doing miserable impressions of James Cagney and Bette Davis. That she loves French music, the simpler the better. That she likes to curl up in a shell when she's frightened, and she's often frightened. That, believe it or not, she dearly loves him and their children. That the best way for him to win her back, to keep her alive, might be to rent a little apartment along the cable-car line and take her there in the afternoons. What a mass of rot! How desperate is she, to concoct this bit of Hollywood rubbish, to give herself one more role? As what? The grandiose savior? Is there anything at all she can tell Jake Roseman about his wife? That a woman like Inez needs to be attended, not waited on, but attended? That she could be lost so easily. That, just like that, she could be gone.

Jake Roseman faces Sylvia expectantly.

Does he sense, like Bibi, that something's up between his wife and the woman in his office, whose name he can't pronounce? It doesn't seem likely. Perhaps if Sylvia and Inez were sitting in front of him. She looks directly at the man. "I'm afraid Inez hasn't been herself lately at the symphony."

"What do you mean?"

It strikes her that Jake Roseman knows exactly what she means, even if she's shaded her meaning. "Since her splendid performance of the Goldmark, Inez has not been playing with her usual, how shall I put it, her usual brio. She seems out of sorts, distracted. Since she is one of the leaders of the first violin section, and since she is such a beloved member of the symphony family, there is some concern. The management has spoken to her about the possibility of taking a leave, but she hasn't been particularly responsive. So they asked if I would come and speak to you, in confidence. It isn't a pleasant task, as you can imagine, and I'm embarrassed to have barged in on you, without even having the presence of mind to set an appointment. Forgive me, Mr. Roseman."

"Don't be silly. I'm grateful to you, Miss . . ."

"Bucheron."

Jake Roseman draws on his cigarette and puts a hand over his face. "I know she's been acting a little strange lately. What would you suggest?"

It's tempting to answer him, to lay it all out. Sylvia crosses her legs. "I'm not really in a position to say, but if it were my spouse I'd . . . I'd have them see someone. Soon."

"You don't suspect she's thinking of harming herself?"

Sylvia shrugs. "I couldn't say. Although, without meaning to alarm you, I would be concerned."

"She doesn't have any reason to harm herself."

"Of course not." Sylvia finds *harm*, the attorney's euphemism for suicide, rather touching. He can't bear to say the word out loud, or even to think it. He, like everybody else, equates the act with reason. Do people actually believe that a reasonable argument can persuade a suicide not to follow through? Or that suicides see their lives from the inside the same way we view them from without? Sylvia has never viewed the act as irrational. Her mother and Inez Roseman are the two most rational people that she's known in her life.

Jake Roseman has already traded reason for emotion. "She's so talented . . . it's always seemed to me that she has everything a person could want, a good family, a fine career."

The poor man doesn't have a clue.

"She's so important . . . to me . . . the kids."

Sylvia doesn't know how to offer the man comfort, but his concern is strangely comforting to her. Once the long ash of her unsmoked cigarette begins to curve, she tamps it out in the ashtray.

"You understand, Mr. Roseman, that this is only a supposition that the management has considered, perhaps nothing more than a misguided theory."

"Yes, of course."

"I've come to register my personal concern, as well as the management's. I ask, on behalf of the management, that we keep this visit in confidence. On a personal note, if I may, I'd suggest that you find her some help. I'd let her know how much she means to you. It's certainly clear to see. She's mentioned your family. I'd let her know, as you say, how important she is to you all. She's a wonderful woman, Mr. Roseman. I know that you will do what you can to help her."

Sylvia stands and casts her eyes downward.

Jake Roseman comes around his desk toward her and takes her hand. "Thank you, Miss Bucheron. Thank you so much."

olympian poise

THE time is getting close. There are signs everywhere. Yesterday, both Inez and Anna started their periods. She found her daughter's bloodied underwear in the dirty clothes hamper and a used pad in the bathroom wastebasket. A couple of years ago, when Anna began menstruating, Inez realized that mother and daughter had quickly become synchronized in natural time. She'd noticed the same thing, living in a house with Bibi, as an adolescent. It strikes Inez that she and her daughter will lose this wild synchronicity before Anna even notices it, a poignant thought, which she immediately banishes.

Practically everything Inez has wanted to accomplish in these last days has been done. But tonight, when Jake comes home and tells her, with a sullen bluster, about a visit he had with a woman who came into his office, she senses that her well-laid plans are, at least temporarily, in trouble.

"The conversation was about you, Inez."

"Me?" she says, genuinely surprised. It takes her a beat to realize who Jake's visitor must have been.

"Do you want to tell me about it?" Jake says.

Inez has no choice but to play dumb. "Tell you about what?"

"Do I need to spell it out?"

"I really don't know what you're talking about, Jake." Inez hands him a whiskey sour. She has a gimlet for herself. Nothing now but gimlets till the end. "So who was this woman?"

"She said she was a musician."

"A musician? Did she have a name?"

"Yes, I wrote it down so I'd remember it." He pulls out his pocket datebook and shuffles through until he finds the right page. "Here. It's French. Buch . . . Bucheron. Natalie Bucheron."

"Never heard of her."

Jake lights a cigarette and forces a charge of smoke out of his nostrils.

An image of Sylvia with a wheel of stolen goat cheese seeps into Inez's consciousness. She closes her eyes, remembering the last, blissful afternoon with Sylvia in her apartment. They ate Bucheron and quail, listened to Satie and Ravel, made love. The idea of Sylvia marching into Jake's office in a bid to save Inez from herself is almost more than she can stand. Inez is close to crying, close to giving it all up. But the thought of inviting anyone else into her sorrow, of turning her situation into a circus of suspicion and denial, keeps her from breaking. Her Olympian poise, acquired during a lifetime dedicated to disassociation, kicks in. She opens her eyes and looks at Jake. "So what did this woman, whom neither you nor I have ever heard of, say about me?"

"She said she was sent by the symphony and that I wasn't supposed to let you know about her visit."

"A promise you weren't about to keep."

"She said that everybody was worried about you. That since the Goldmark you weren't playing with any enthusiasm, or in her words, you weren't playing with your usual *brio*."

"My usual *brio*, that's choice."

"She said they can't figure out what's going on with you, and they're worried."

"Who is this woman, Jake?"

"I told you what I know. I had Grania call down to the symphony and the musicians' union, but nobody's ever heard of a Natalie Bucheron."

"See."

"I don't know what's going on, Inez, but I didn't hallucinate the conversation. She was very compelling. What she said was highly disturbing."

"What *did* she say?"

"She said they were worried you might harm yourself."

"Harm myself. This is preposterous. This woman, whoever she is, must be delusional."

"It sounded credible to me."

Inez makes a point of losing her temper. "Does it sound credible to you now, Jake? For God's sake, the woman is an impostor. Anyway, it's not true; I'm in a good place, Jake." Inez tells herself to stay calm now.

Her quick flash of histrionics will serve its purpose, jump-starting Jake's eagerness to deny the unpleasant.

"I'm concerned about you," Jake says, shaking out a cigarette, too agitated to look at Inez.

"Please. There's nothing to worry about, Jake. I'm fine, even chipper. I had a little slump after the Goldmark, that's true. That was such a high, you know, it's only natural that going back to regular symphony life was a bit disappointing at first." If she can maintain her smiling posture and offer a reasonable inventory, she'll be home free. It's heartbreaking to see Jake, nearly broken before the fact. But she has no choice. He, too, will be better off.

"You know," she says, "you and I had that lovely time in Carmel. And, when all is said and done, I really feel pretty good about the Goldmark. I can be hard on myself, but I feel like I did an honorable job with the concerto. And the kids and I . . . we seem close. Sometimes it's hard with Anna, but I think that will pass. The only real problem I see is with the old man."

"I know."

"But we'll figure something out. Really, I haven't felt this good in a long time." Inez smiles at Jake, observes the relief in his eyes, and then makes her final play, a true test of her resolve, which she hopes will put the issue to rest. "You know, Jake, I think I know who this woman is."

"You do?"

"Short, isn't she? Dirty-blond hair she wears in bangs. A pointy nose. A bit homely."

"I wouldn't say homely."

"No?"

"No, but that sounds like her."

"She's young, but well-spoken."

"Right. So who is she?"

Inez is amazed at herself. How easily she can call up an image of beloved Sylvia and dispassionately destroy it. She realizes now that she is capable of anything. "I'll tell you this, Jake, Bucheron is not her name. That's a made-up name. That's the name for a certain kind of French goat cheese."

"Come on."

"No, I used to pick up little hunks of it down at Simon Brothers. Bucheron. Her real name is, I don't know, Mindy . . . Cindy. She's not a musician, either; she's some sort of executive assistant at the symphony association. Too ambitious for her own good. Jealous little urchin."

"But why did she come down to see me?" Jake asks, still not quite satisfied.

"I don't know. Maybe she overheard a couple of people at the symphony association talking about me. I'll admit, I was sullen for a couple of weeks after the Goldmark. So the woman decided to do a little free-lancing. You're not going to like this, Jake, but I think this might have more to do with you than it does with me. Maybe she saw you on the news. Maybe she was just making a play for you, Jake."

Jake lights another cigarette and scowls at her, but the screw's been turned; he's on the defensive now.

"Come on, Jake, you can't deny that all sorts of women take a special interest in you. Who would have thought that I'd end up married to a Casanova?"

"I'm not a Casanova."

"Though I've gotta tell you, Jake, this woman, if we're truly thinking about the same one, she doesn't strike me as your type."

"Stop. Will you?"

Finally, she has him on the ropes.

bubbles

THE next afternoon, as soon as Anna's home from school, Inez asks if she'd like to take a walk to Sutro Super. Although Inez's appetite has gone spotty again, she has a sudden desire to prepare a nice meal with Anna. The two of them, Inez reasons, could use a bit of red meat. Anna isn't sure if she wants to come.

"Why don't you ask Joey?" she says. "He's just watching TV. You promise him a pack or two of baseball cards, and he'll go anywhere with you."

"I don't want to walk with Joey," Inez says. "I want to walk with you."

"Let me think about it."

This is one of Anna's teenage ploys—she is unwilling to say a quick yes to anything, but give her a little time and if she agrees, on her timetable, she appears to save face.

"Sure," Inez says. "Let me know."

Meanwhile, Inez takes a look through the half-dozen cookbooks she rarely uses, but settles again on "the dummy cookbook." Inez flips past "Easy Meals" to "Meats" and spends an inordinate amount of time staring at the two color pages of "Beef Cuts and How to Cook Them."

Inez studies each cut: boneless chuck, arm pot roast, blade pot roast, corned beef brisket, short ribs, shank cross cuts, standing rib roast, rolled rib roast, rib-eye roast, top loin, New York strip, tenderloin steak, rib-eye steak (or Delmonico, "as it is sometimes known"), T-bone steak, club steak, porterhouse steak, flank steak, sirloin steak, sirloin tip roast, bottom round, rump roast. Then she turns to the lamb. It's amazing how long you can look at red meat and not think of mortality.

Anna consents to walk with her to Sutro Super if Inez will buy her a magazine at the pharmacy next door.

"That's extortion."

"It's only thirty-five cents, Mom."

"But it's the idea," Inez says, but wanting to confound her, adds, "but I so much want your company, I'll buy you five magazines."

"You don't need to buy me five."

"Well, you pick out what you want."

IT is breezy walking along Geary toward the ocean. Inez wants to hold her daughter's hand but knows that Anna won't stand for that. Claiming her independence has become a primal event. Inez doesn't take it personally.

A loud 2 Clement roars west on Geary. "Your father and I used to take the streetcar out to the ocean when we were young."

"I know."

"He was always fond of Sutro Baths. I don't think we ever went swimming there, but we sat and watched the swimmers. Your father was particularly fond of the divers. We'd sit there munching crisp green apples. One time he said, 'Someday, I'm going to be a great diver.'"

"He said that?"

"Yes, and I don't think he'd ever dived in his life. He was big on doing things that his parents had never done. I don't think they'd ever even been in swimming."

"Yeah, can you imagine Grandpa swimming?"

"The funny thing is that, years later, your father did teach himself how to dive."

"But he's not very good."

"That doesn't matter," Inez says. "I love that he taught himself."

They walk in silence for a while. Inez thinks about Jake as a young man, how, during the late forties and early fifties, he would accompany her to Los Angeles for the short opera season. This was before the kids were born. They stayed at an old hotel called the Figueroa that had a beautiful pool, guarded by rows of palm trees. Jake was either sprawled out on a chaise lounge reading a fat novel or practicing his diving. How beautiful he looked, standing perfectly still at the end of the diving board. All the women adored Jake. Inez would get jealous seeing the general commotion he could cause. Still, she had sweet times at the Figueroa with her husband.

Anna takes a fat package of gum from her purse and offers her mother a piece.

"I didn't know you liked bubble gum, Anna."

"Yeah, some kid at school showed me how to blow bubbles. I'm getting pretty good at it. Just don't tell Joey. He always wants my gum. Sometimes he even goes into my purse."

Inez doesn't care for gum and can't remember the last time she chewed any, but she takes the rectangle of gum, unwraps it, and sticks it in her mouth. She resists her initial impulse to spit the gum back into its wrapper after the first burst of sugar syrup and walks beside her daughter, making a point of chewing loud.

Anna blows a small bubble and sucks it back into her mouth. "How long did it take before you first knew you loved Dad?"

"About ten minutes."

"I don't believe you."

"You don't believe in love at first sight, Anna?"

Anna blows a formidable bubble now and turns her head toward Inez so that she can appreciate it. Inez nods and watches the pink skin of the thing shine in the air a moment before it goes slack.

"Love at first sight is just something that happens in the movies," Anna says, chewing.

"You're a born cynic."

"How long until you realized that it wasn't going to be as good as you thought?"

"Huh?"

"You and Dad. I mean, how long before you figured out that that kind of love is transient?"

Inez is so surprised by the question that she needs to stall. The word Anna chose is a surprise in itself. *Transient.* What would Sylvia make of it? Love as somebody you'd find loitering in a bus station. She thinks to deflect the question, to ask Anna if she has a crush on someone, but that doesn't seem fair. Where did Anna come up with an idea like that? Inez has always wondered if all the time Anna spends in her room reading is reason for concern. Inez spreads the leathery hunk of gum across her tongue and blows, accomplishing less a bubble than a weak flutter of pink.

Anna repeats the question: "How long before you knew, Mom?"

"I knew early."

"You did? Weren't you sad?"

Inez nods. "I was terribly sad. I was devastated. But that wild love that you say you don't believe in, it can turn into something else, something calm and lasting."

Anna blows a fresh bubble that swells to the tip of her nose. She quickly retracts it and looks as if she's going to cry.

AS they get closer to Sutro Super, Anna asks if they can walk on to the ocean and shop on the way back.

"Only if you show me how to blow a decent bubble."

"Are you serious?"

"Serious as a heart attack, ma'am," Inez says, repeating a line she'd heard a month ago, when she and Sylvia hopped on a cable car outside of Sylvia's apartment. They had just made love, and Inez told Sylvia that the only thing she was left craving in the world was a crab cocktail. Sylvia jumped up from the bed and started yanking on Inez's arm. *Let's get a cable car down to the wharf.* In a few minutes they were dressed. They hadn't even washed. When they heard the clang of the car, they raced down the stairs to the street and leapt onto the running board, a couple of randy girls in love.

Heading toward the wharf, a tourist queried the driver, *Brakes ever go out on these things?* The gripman, a corpulent Irishman who assumed a mythic heroism as he worked the grips, didn't miss a beat, *Happens all the time.* The tourist looked a little pale. *You're not serious.* The driver gave the tourist a sideways look, *Serious as a heart attack, ma'am.* Inez and Sylvia burst out laughing and, later, as they walked along the wharf with their crab cocktails, Sylvia pitched the question to Inez. *How about you and me? Do you think it's serious?* Inez winked, *Serious as a heart attack, ma'am.*

Now Inez stares at the sharp edge of blue on the horizon and thinks of Sylvia, how much she loved holding Sylvia's small, winning face in her hands.

Anna is shaking her head. "You sure you want to learn how to blow bubbles?"

"Positive."

"Look, I'll try, Mom, but I'm not responsible if you're too spastic to figure it out."

"I might surprise you, you know. It all depends on how good a teacher you are."

Anna shakes her head, works her gum a minute, and then blows a majestic bubble.

"Not bad. Now show me how to do that."

"Don't get your hopes up." Anna reaches into her purse and pulls out another hunk of gum. "You need reinforcements."

After Inez has softened up the gum, Anna goes into her patter. "You got to make it thick, right at the center where your tongue is. Think of digging a pocket with your tongue and make sure it's good and sturdy right where your tongue is. Then blow, really gentle."

Inez does her best to follow her daughter's instructions. The first few times she gets something going it snaps right away. But, finally, she gets the feel, and a small bubble opens in front of her face.

"Hold it, Mom, hold it."

Pretty soon, Anna has one of her own. They stand at the corner of Forty-sixth and Geary, mother and daughter, swaying back and forth, proud of their pink bubbles.

lantern

THE next night Inez makes mashed potatoes and a nice gravy to go with the leftover roast. Although Inez referred to the dummy cookbook to make gravy, she resisted the hurry-up recipe and tried her hand at "Perfect Pan Gravy." At this point, she figured she might as well go for broke. Serving it all with broccoli and a green salad, she feels as if she's fulfilled her duty as a mother and wife, at least once.

Joey is the best eater. Inez enjoys watching him feast on the meat and the mashed potatoes. Anybody with an appetite like that, it strikes her, will always want to stay alive.

"If you have to eat leftovers, Mom," Joey says, "this is the way to go."

Only her father-in-law seems to take issue with the meal. He is angry at her because she's done her best to avoid him since he's been in the house. Tonight Isaac slouches at the dinner table in a tweed sport coat, frayed at the elbows, and a stained yellow necktie that she thought she'd already thrown out. But, as it happens, all of his neckties are stained and live somewhere in the spectrum of yellow.

"Why don't you try some mashed potatoes, Pop?" Jake says.

Isaac shakes his head. "We never had such food."

Jake smiles. "When, in the old country, Pop?"

"I thought you moved here when you were two years old, Grandpa," Anna says, innocently enough. "How can you remember whether you had mashed potatoes?"

Jake begins to laugh. It starts as a giggle, but pretty soon he has let loose an infectious peal of laughter. Inez thinks of an adolescent boy— the Jake she first knew—getting a kick out of what a buffoon his father is. Pretty soon Joey joins in with his high-pitched cackle, and even Anna begins to purr with amusement.

"I never said anything about the old country!" Isaac shouts.

Jake and Joey smile at each other, a conspiracy of sorts, but Anna is clearly disturbed by her grandfather's shouting. Inez tries to catch her eye, to let her know that she loves her, but Anna keeps her head down near her plate.

"Mashed potatoes and gravy are goyish food," Isaac says, quieter now.

"What exactly does that mean?" Inez asks.

"Jews don't eat this kind of food, with the fat and all the starch."

"Jews don't eat potatoes?" Inez asks.

"Of course, they eat potatoes, just not mashed potatoes with all this butter."

Inez looks Isaac directly in the eye and keeps staring at him, wishing she could work a curse into his addled brain, a kind of telepathic lobotomy, that would ensure that he'd be forever harmless to her children. Isaac, feeling the heat of her stare, the incision being made in his frontal lobe, is forced to turn away.

"The thing is," Inez says, "with a gentile cook you have to expect this kind of food sooner or later."

Inez has managed to shut the old man up, but rather than feeling any joy from the act, she's steeped in a sudden melancholy. There's no joy in watching Isaac Roseman dip his fork into the mashed potatoes. She remembers how much she learned from the man and how beautifully he once played. Does his betrayal take all of that away?

When she was nine years old, already studying with Isaac, he left a pair of symphony tickets for Inez and her father at the Civic Auditorium box office. She can't remember what was on the program that night. It was a warm evening, and her father sweated in his flannel suit. He had a tin of fancy candies that he kept offering and she kept pushing away. Suddenly, in the midst of a big orchestral work, there was a power outage in the auditorium and the lights went off. The music came to an abrupt stop. Unable to see their music, the musicians, unnerved by the ensuing hubbub, began to climb out of their seats and worry about the safety of their instruments. There was quite a panic in the audience, as if, rather than a power failure, an act of willful anarchy had taken place. Inez grabbed a handful of her father's candies. Then she heard her teacher, Isaac Roseman, the concertmaster, speak into the dark auditorium.

"So, we seem to have lost our electrical lights and there's no telling when they will come back on. Some of you, you'll probably be more comfortable going outside. Maybe nobody wants to sit in a dark auditorium. But for anybody who does, for anybody who'd like to hear a little more music, I'd be happy to play the Chaconne from Bach's Partita in D Minor. I don't need any electric lights to play that."

There were murmurs in the vast, dark hall. Some people decided to scurry from their seats for the exits. Mr. Roseman waited a moment for the commotion to subside. When he finally drew the bow across the D and the A strings, the open majesty of the sound caused a huge, collective gasp through the hall.

Inez had just begun to study the Chaconne. "A little bit at a time," Mr. Roseman said. "Technically, it's difficult, but someday you'll master it. Will you understand it? I can't tell you that. Maybe in a lifetime. I'm hoping someday to understand it. I'll tell you this, if somebody were to ask me what piece of music contains all of the universe, I wouldn't think for a moment before I said the Chaconne."

Inez remembers sitting beside her father in the dark, listening to her teacher in awe. Midway through Mr. Roseman's playing, an usher walked onstage with a lantern and set it on the floor of the stage a few feet from the violinist. The only glow in the hall illuminated Isaac Roseman. His left side was a bit outside the circle of light, but Inez could see his powerful bow arm and the determination carved into his face as he soared through his thirteen minutes of seized glory.

Now, Inez watches her father-in-law, his bow arm twisted like a dead branch, lifting a forkful of mashed potatoes to his mouth.

"So what do you think?" Inez asks.

"What do I think?"

"About the mashed potatoes."

"You want me to tell you I like this?—butter and mashed potato?—I'll tell you I like it."

"No, tell me what you think, Isaac."

"I'll tell you what I think. I could live without it."

"Not me," Joey says, her little man, standing up for his mother. "I want more. Pass me the mashed potatoes, Mom."

the splintered white

AFTER they finish clearing the dishes, Inez lures Jake out for a walk. From the start, she finds it difficult to establish the right tone. How do you tell your husband that you care deeply for him, even though your departure is imminent?

"How long a walk?" Jake asks, as soon as they step outside.

"A walk of indeterminate length."

"Why the cryptic answer? Is there something you want to tell me?" Jake asks, suspicious. "Has something happened? Have you met with that Bucheron lady? Was she onto something?"

"No, it's nothing like that. I just want your company." She places her open hand on Jake's bare neck—Sylvia's gesture—and leaves it there until he begins to fidget.

Jake doesn't know what to make of the sudden affection. "It's cold out here," he says, zipping himself into his parka.

"Good for you to walk, especially after eating all that goy food."

"You really put the old man in his place."

"That wasn't my intention."

"Still."

At the corner of Forty-first and Geary, Jake stops, shakes a cigarette from his pack, and lights a match, expertly cupping his hands around the flame so that it won't die in the breeze. Inez watches him take a hungry gulp of his cigarette once it's lit.

"How far do you want to go?"

"To the ocean."

"That far?"

"It's not so far."

Jake exhales a long stream of smoke. "But you realize that once you walk there, you have to walk back."

"Yes, your basic round-trip."

They walk a couple blocks in silence, past Forty-sixth Avenue, the spot where, just yesterday, she and Anna had blown bubbles and stared at the horizon. But tonight, given the low overcast, there is no horizon. Inez wonders if the word *horizon* can indicate the line of separation between any two things. Not just the sea and sky, but a woman from a man. Can the mind imagine a vertical horizon existing between a wife and her husband as they walk toward the ocean? Can people draw an impermeable horizon between their present and their past? What form of horizon separates the sane from the insane? And how does one picture the horizon line between the living and the dead?

As they walk past the Seal Rock Inn, Inez watches a couple get out of their car with a pair of young children. Their license plate says Ohio. They've come from so far to see the ocean that they're determined to stay as close to it as they can, even if their motel is a little on the damp and spartan side. As the parents gather their suitcases, Inez sees that they're happy to be here, the woman draping an arm around her husband's waist.

"Care for a drink?" Jake asks, as they come to The Cliff House.

"How about on our way back? I want to walk on the beach."

"You sure seem to know what you want."

"Yes."

"Don't you think it will be a little cold down there?"

"I think we can handle it."

The wind is quite a bit stiffer once they get down the hill to the beach. Jake leans over the beach wall. "We're the only fools down here."

"Do you feel like a fool, Jake?"

He turns his back to the ocean to light another cigarette.

The tide is out, but Inez loves the way the splintered white of the waves leaps out of the darkness.

"I'm going to go down there," Inez says, as she kneels to take off her shoes.

"You're going to walk on the beach?"

"Yeah, you coming?"

"What's the idea? You've become a natural woman all of a sudden?"

"In fact, I have. Every now and then I try to remind myself," she says, feeding him his old silly line, "that I too am a part of nature."

"Touché."

Inez walks down the concrete steps to the beach, and Jake, still with his shoes on, follows.

"Aren't you going to take off your shoes?"

"I don't want to get my feet all mucked up. What's the idea anyway?"

"A walk on the beach? It's not exactly a revolutionary thing, Jake."

"In the middle of the night?"

"It's not even nine o'clock. Anyway, you're supposed to be my nature guide. And I've heard you're an unconventional man. I read it in the paper. 'If Jake Roseman is anything, he's unconventional.' I saw that in Saul Rose's column. 'Jake Roseman, our bohemian attorney from the Caribbean, was sighted the other day in a fresh pair of Bermuda shorts.'"

"Stop."

"I like to tease you."

"Why?"

"I don't know. Maybe because I'm surprised that a savvy old fellow like you can still be teased."

"Surprise, surprise."

Inez leads Jake across the soft sand, sliding her bare feet in and out of smooth pockets of sand. There is still a slight warmth in the sand even though the sun is down. Inez closes her eyes to listen to the gather and heave of the waves. Even with the tide out, the roaring breath of the waves surprises her.

"You shouldn't walk out here barefoot, Inez. There's broken glass all over the place."

"It's better than getting sand in your shoes."

"If we stayed up on the top, we wouldn't have either problem."

"My, you're resistant, Jake. Pretend you're out on an adventure with a new girl."

"Don't, Inez."

"Well, pretend anything. How often do I ask for your company?"

Jake nods his head, a beaten man, falling into step.

In a moment they are walking along the packed wet sand. Her feet are cold, but she's happy to be in contact with the ocean. Inez wonders if a woman could put rocks in the front pockets of her slacks and walk straight into the ocean. She'd heard about a famous writer doing that. A brilliant white-haired Englishwoman, whoever she was, with rocks in her pockets. Inez reaches into the pockets of her slacks. They are nearly empty. Nothing but a cake of rosin. What's she doing with a cake of rosin? She must have picked it off the counter at Smetna's—a half-dollar of German rosin, glued to a green felt backing. It doesn't have enough weight to sink a kitten.

Inez takes ahold of Jake's hand and thinks of the woman in the parking lot at the Seal Rock Inn. The woman from Ohio. The way she roped her arm around her husband's waist. Inez tries, for a moment, to think of Jake as her lover.

"You know what the problem is, Jake?"

"No, I don't know what the problem is."

"The problem is . . . you've never pleased me."

"What are you talking about?"

"I'm not trying to hurt you. I'm not even talking about sex, though I could talk about that as well. The trouble with sex for somebody like me is that I didn't know that I was supposed to expect anything. Most people have an expectation of how it's supposed to be, but not me. Which begs the question: would I have been better off not to have found out? I suppose I *am* talking about sex."

"I'm having trouble understanding you."

"You wouldn't have trouble if you listened. If you listened really hard, I bet you wouldn't have trouble. At some point, I realized it's supposed to be about pleasure. It came to me very late, I'm ashamed to say. *Pleasure.* It's supposed to be the instinct that drives us. The pleasure principle. But I didn't know to have it. So there, you see how flawed my thinking is? Did I imagine pleasure as an elective? It's not for you, Jake. You've always had the instinct. So here's the question: if pleasure isn't what's been driving me, what is? Was I born without it? Did I have it bred out of me? Sometimes I think it was all that practicing on my violin. I can't remember, Jake, did you ever see the carpet in my bedroom, the hole I wore in it from standing on a single spot? Your father . . . your father used to say that training a young violinist was like binding the feet of a Chinese girl. If you were successful, you created a cripple. I heard him say that a hundred times, but I never knew what he meant. Should I blame it on your father? Blame it on the old man?"

Jake shrugs. "Sure, blame it on the old man."

They both laugh a moment. Inez thinks about Sylvia. How she learned more from Sylvia about pleasure in a weekday afternoon than she did during all the years with Jake.

Jake bends toward her now and kisses her forehead.

Inez closes her eyes. Lets herself feel Jake's lips. His sweetness. "You think I'm going mad, don't you, with all this crazy talk. Don't worry, I'm not going to sew my fingers together, or do myself any harm. It's just that thinking has become one of my curses. You're lucky to be free of it, Jake," she says with a laugh.

"Hey, I've been known to have had a thought or two."

"Of course you have."

They come to a good-sized log, and Inez asks Jake if he'd consent to sit a moment. He doesn't answer. She sits down on the log and looks up at Jake, standing there. More than six feet tall and still pleasing to the eye, even as a dark silhouette standing at the ocean. No matter what has come between them, she knows that she still loves the man. He is simpler than she is. Part of him has never needed to grow up. That's one of the privileges for a nice-looking man with a measure of intelligence and charm.

"Won't you sit?"

"There's tar on that log."

"And you don't want to get your pants dirty."

"Not especially."

"I've thrown all caution to the wind. How's that for a cliché?"

"Are you okay, Inez?"

"I'm fine. Just having one of my introspective moments. I get an idea sometimes, like this notion of pleasure, and it doesn't let me alone. I only wish that you'd tried to please me more."

"How come you've never mentioned it?"

"How come it never occurred to you?"

As Jake sucks on his cigarette, Inez watches the pulse of ashy red light brighten a small corner of his face.

countdown

THE time comes when your business is all but done. That's when the
real countdown begins.

After doing a final shop at Sutro Super, Inez picks up Jake's laundry
at the cleaners—a box of shirts and three pairs of pressed Bermudas on
hangers. The shorts make her laugh. It is getting very late in the year,
but Jake is determined to keep wearing them.

"Bet you don't get a lot of shorts this time of the year," she says to
the Chinese laundryman.

"No time of year," he says.

"My husband's."

"Yes." The man nods and makes an amused sound in his throat.

He knows Jake, Inez realizes, and is putting the pair of them
together in his mind. Or does he even bother with such nonsense? Every
time she's come into this cleaners—and she's been coming for years—
she's seen this man, maybe sixty now, buttoned up in his beige cardigan,
no matter how warm the day or how much steam is rising from the back
room. Today is the first time she's spoken any extra words to him. As he
bends over the cash register, she notices that he wears a gold wedding
band, that his fingers look arthritic, that he's getting thin on top. She
knew him when he had a lot more hair on his head.

"Thank you," Inez says as he hands her change.

"Say hello to Jake," the laundryman says, surprising her. But why
should she be surprised? Jake speaks with everyone and he has an effect
on people. He can even get taciturn men to speak.

At home, Inez fills the fridge with groceries and waits for Isaac to go
do his business. She's learned how to time him. His habits are as pre-
dictable as a rat's. Around four in the afternoon, he makes a trip to the
bathroom that lasts a good half hour. Glory to a man and the passing of

his bowels. With Isaac indisposed, Inez goes down to the music room in the basement for a little practicing. It's hard for her father-in-law to get downstairs, virtually impossible, but Inez is still phobic about the old man walking in on her while she practices.

Today, she only wants to noodle around with a little Bach. She's not been able to get the Chaconne out of her head since thinking of Isaac playing it in the dark. It's something she's played most of her life. She knows nothing that possesses a more severe and blistering beauty. Even for nonbelievers, the Chaconne has a holy architecture. Inez takes the violin out and, as she tunes it, wonders if she has ever been a believer, wonders if she is, in fact, a believer now. It might seem a foolish question for a woman in her situation to ask, and yet she answers affirmatively to both the past and the present. Belief can be as simple as realizing that your children will thrive beyond your life. Can't a person who does not see herself as necessary believe in the world?

Inez draws a cake of rosin across her bow and decides to play the entire Partita in D Minor. All she needs is to bow the initial open Ds of the Allemande and she is inside Bach's simple cathedral.

She closes her eyes—she always closes her eyes when she plays Bach. It was good of Bach to keep the Allemande so free of double-stops—they will arrive with a vengeance in the Chaconne. To begin this way, a player gets to dive into the beauty of the single line, relatively unencumbered. Inez, a woman in full control of her instrument and, surprisingly, of her life, plays straight through the Allemande, the Courante, the plaintive Sarabande, and the Gigue.

She takes a minute and a couple of deep breaths before launching into the Chaconne itself. It used to help her when working on its technical aspects to think of the Chaconne as a mechanical man. You put your penny in and the sequence of meticulously calibrated gears shift one into another. But with the Bach, unlike, say, the Paganini, the mechanical man comes alive almost immediately. He is flesh and blood. His large heart beats against his ribs. The more difficult the bowing, the more arduous the double-stop fingerings, the more emotional it becomes. Not emotion like we experience in the movies, which is to say histrionics, but rather a controlled emotion, rising indomitably along the parallel arcs and ridges.

Even though Inez is fully clothed as she plays the Chaconne, she feels herself stripped down to her essential skin. She'd like to believe that it's the Bach that's banished her protective shell, that a massive dose of Johann Sebastian has balanced her evil hormones and eliminated the heavy armor that's accompanied her for years. But she knows better. The peace she's made with herself is responsible.

Four strings and a dozen voicings. How can one woman hold so much within her? How can she stop? The engine keeps pulsing, the fingers, curled into knots, tighten and loosen, the bow, a circular fury of pistons. When the engine hums with such harmonic majesty, an entire civilization grows, treelike, in her ear. Everything she's imagined, in tune, all she's desired, in time, each person she's loved, baring themselves, gently insisting, right through the final held D, that she do what she must.

AT five, she gets a call from Jake that he won't be home for dinner. A late meeting or a new girlfriend? She doesn't bother to ask. Either way, she's indifferent. She'd planned to make a nice meat loaf, but now with Jake gone and Joey having discovered the prodigious supply of TV dinners she's stuffed into the freezer, she opts for the lazy mother's choice. It seems such a strange final meal, at first, but both Joey and Anna are delighted that she's willing to join them. Frozen dinners are usually reserved for the kids, for the nights when she and Jake are both out.

Only Isaac grumbles at the idea of a TV dinner. Alone with her in the kitchen, he gives her a sad-eyed look—like an old animal betrayed. "I don't want a ready-made frozen dinner."

"Why's that, Isaac?"

"Who ever heard of a man eating ice for his dinner?"

"It's warm when you eat it."

"It's one thing for the astronauts, but not for me."

"If you don't want one, I won't put one in for you."

"I don't want one. I don't want to go to space, I don't want to eat their dinner. What's it going to do for my digestion anyway?"

"That's hard for me to say."

He picks up a TV dinner package with his good hand and waves it in the air. "Frozen white turkey, frozen mashed potatoes, frozen peas, frozen goyish gravy. A meal like this could kill me."

"Isaac, aren't we being a little dramatic?"

"I might as well drink white paint," he hollers, raising his twisted bow arm like a twirling arc in the air. "Make me some soup!" he commands.

"You don't give me orders anymore. I am no longer your student."

"Orders," he laughs, feigning a jovial attitude. "Who's giving orders?"

"Shhhh." She puts her finger over her lips and tries to freeze him with her eyes. Inez holds him there a moment and then walks to the kitchen chair in which he's sitting. Before she takes his tight, shriveled face in her hands, her father-in-law's eyes cast around the room for something that might save him. Inez holds his face in a vise and forces him to look at her. The audacity of the act surprises even her.

"When I was a child, you did things to me that were wrong. You should have been punished. Do you understand?"

Isaac closes his eyes.

"Do you understand?"

Finally, he nods.

She lets go of Isaac's face and watches him shrivel into his seat.

"Would you like me to fix you some soup?"

Isaac nods.

In a moment, she opens a can of tomato-rice soup for the old man. "How about some liverwurst crackers?" she asks, knowing how fond Isaac is of the smelly liver paste.

Again, he nods.

This will be the last time, she thinks as she stands spreading liverwurst on saltines.

Inez leaves the old man sitting alone with his meal in the kitchen.

She and the kids do something they haven't done for ages: they set up TV trays in front of the television and watch a quiz show, drinking pop while eating their astronaut dinners. The three of them are happy. Nothing can take that away.

matchmaker

THIS afternoon, out of the blue, he got a call from Christine. Given how painful their last visit was, he doubted if he'd see her again.

She offered no greeting, and, at first, he thought it might be a crank call. He'd been getting them lately, people unhappy with the labor work he'd been doing on behalf of Negroes. He liked listening for the fear in the anonymous voices, the idle threats, the words *Nigger lover.*

Her voice was softer than usual. "Can you talk, Jake?"

"Sure, I can talk," he said, before he was sure who it was, and then he had it. "What's up, Christine?" He half expected her to say something ugly, racist.

"Your secretary isn't listening in?"

"Grania, are you there?" he said into the phone, holding it silently for a few beats. "No, we'd have heard her chewing her Aspergum by now. I think the poor woman's in perpetual pain. Nothing specific, you realize, but the human condition in general."

Christine offered a warm chuckle. "Aspergum helps with that?"

"Best thing on the market."

"You're funny, Jake. I've missed you. You know, I felt terrible after you left. I hate ending things on a bad note." She paused then, perhaps expecting him to agree with her.

He said nothing. He enjoyed having her a bit off balance.

"Anyway, when the fog started rolling in this afternoon, I thought of you, Jake."

"You equate me with the fog?"

"Well, I know you live out by the ocean. I pictured you going home after work and the fog getting thicker and thicker around your house."

"It does that."

"And I thought that perhaps I could get you to take me out for a drink, before you went home to the deep fog."

"Out for a drink?" Jake said, amused. It struck him as a strange request. During the course of their affair, he'd often asked Christine to do something, anything, outside of the confines of her mansion, but she always demurred, reminding Jake that maintaining their happy arrangement required them to honor their vow of discretion.

"Derek's out of town, in case you want to know, and I thought that if we went out to a place like The Cliff House, we'd probably have it to ourselves. Don't you think we could safely get lost in the fog out there, at least for the duration of a cocktail? That's assuming that you're willing to meet me. There's something I need to say to you."

"I'll pick you up," Jake said, fancying the idea of this unexpected diversion. "I actually drove to work today. It's a rarity."

"I'd prefer to meet you there, but I'm curious—what do you drive?"

"My car? You'd find it fetching, Christine. A white Plymouth Valiant with push-button transmission."

"Can I have a rain check on the ride? And tonight, say six o'clock," said Christine and signed off.

IT'S so socked in by the time he hits the Avenues that the cars only inch along Geary Boulevard. His headlights seem to be illuminating nothing more than the transient vapor. But he can see the car in front of him. That's all that matters. He thinks to turn the radio on but finds himself enjoying the white silence.

Despite his cautious driving, Jake still manages to arrive before the appointed time. He stands outside The Cliff House for a moment, listening to the foghorns. The damn things sound human. They manage to sound patient and insistent at the same time, a mother whose only purpose in life is to issue warnings. Like all warnings, there's something about them that makes you want to disobey, that creates a sense of longing.

The smell of the sea wrack makes an even more intimate claim on Jake's senses. The memory of taking the streetcar out here with Inez twenty-five years ago is clearer than his sense of their walk the other night. He used to love sitting across from Inez on the streetcar and admiring her beauty. He thought then that for the rest of his life he would never love anyone as he has Inez. And he was right. Of course, Inez is far different now from the woman he married. That woman expected him to guide her through every portal of her life. This woman doesn't even regard him as a factor, but she has a curious resolve about her. The other night, when they strolled out to the ocean, he was reluctant to go with her. She can see right through him these days, and, in her company, he feels like a hale fellow lacking substance, a hollow man. Not only does she find him lacking, she's made her peace with the fact.

As they walked along the beach, he wondered if he could do anything to regain her love. If not, he feared that he'd be irrelevant to her for the rest of their lives together.

CHRISTINE is quite striking standing in the entryway in dark wool trousers and a quilted turquoise jacket. It's odd to see Christine outside of her house and realize that, though she's small, she occupies a clear and forceful presence in the world.

Christine gives Jake an amused look. "A couple of adventurers, aren't we?"

"Indeed."

"I wondered if they'd close the place due to excessive fog."

"Happens too often."

"Not like this."

"You'd be surprised." Jake takes her arm and leads her into the large, open room. There is no hostess. The Cliff House has fallen on hard times. Seat yourself. Christine sneers at a loud group of tourists who sit at a table in the center of the room. "Let's sit as far away from them as we can."

Jake chooses a small table by the massive picture window. "Normally, you can see the seals from here." Now all that's visible are swirling layers of fog. Jake lights a cigarette. He feels curiously awkward with Christine. It strikes him that they have very little in common. The years of good sex and amusement have accrued no real history. The present tense that he gloried in has left little in its wake.

"So you're wondering why I asked you to meet me," Christine says, signaling to the waitress.

"I haven't been holding my breath."

"I'm glad to hear that," says Christine, twisting her lips into an exaggerated smile.

Jake is grateful to see the waitress, a tall Irish girl, approach the table and orders a tequila on the rocks after Christine asks for a glass of Harvey's Bristol Cream.

ONCE they have their drinks, Christine narrows her eyes at Jake. "I know what happened to you toward the end, even if you don't."

"You do, huh?" Jake looks away. He isn't sure he wants to hear it. He takes a gulp of the tequila and decides to hold it in his mouth for as long as he can before swallowing. "You realize what you did, Jake; you fell in love with your wife again."

Jake swallows his mouthful of tequila. "What makes you think . . . ?"

"I watched it happen. I've seen it happen before. A man returns to his wife and he's no good to me anymore. I just wasn't sure you realized what you'd done."

It seems as plausible a theory as any, and yet Jake has an overwhelming desire to tell Christine to go fuck herself. He thinks of Inez. The other night, after their walk, he saw her in the bath. How beautiful she was. Christine is watching him, waiting for a response.

"You don't have to worry about me, Jake." Christine sips her sherry and smiles at him. "We had an absolutely perfect affair, Jake; the best of my life. I'm not wrong, am I, about Inez?"

"I don't know." Jake smiles at his former lover. Nothing like being patronized by a Pacific Heights matron. She's probably a fucking Republican, Jake decides, despite making claims to the contrary.

"It happens sometimes to men your age—your heart, or shall we say your capacity for actual love, grows larger than your prick. Don't worry, your glory days aren't over."

"I'm glad you understand me so well, Christine."

"Oh, I don't know about that. A man can fall in love with his wife again. I think that's what's happened to you."

Jake shrugs.

"You have to woo her all over again."

Jake slugs down the last of his tequila. "I don't know that I have it in me."

Christine fingers the beauty mark on her upper lip. "You have it in you. Just let it unfold naturally. It will be the most important seduction of your life."

Jake shakes his head. "Listen to you, Christine, you sound like a goddamn matchmaker. You should set up a little shop in the Mission District with a big heart outside. And how about you, Christine?"

"Me? You needn't worry about me. I met a young man. He's really too young for me." Christine runs a finger along a furrow in her forehead.

A young Republican, no doubt. "You're shameless, Christine."

"I am."

Jake's ready for this little escapade to be over. Christine's become like an unpleasant client whose business he's done with.

Jake laughs lustily. "Does the poor boy know what he's in for?"

"I don't think he has a clue."

AFTER Christine declines a ride home, Jake waits with her for a cab. They stand together at the curb, each in their own pocket of fog. He can't wait to get in his car and drive home. To see Inez. The damn thing is, Christine is right. But how does a middle-aged man woo his wife? As the cab appears from out of nowhere, he opens the door for Christine and kisses her good-bye. He stands at the curb, watching her cab disappear into oblivion.

chef's choice

AROUND nine, sipping a gimlet, Inez hears Jake's car pull up out front. Isaac has gone to bed and the kids are in their rooms. Inez pulls the curtains back to look out on the street. The fog has come in so thick that she can't even see Jake's car at the curb. Inez hears the slam of the car door and also hears the foghorns wailing in their insistent fifths. Then she hears the sweetest sound of all: Jake whistling. He's whistling a beautiful tune, not his usual agitated jazz, but a minor ballad that she's heard somewhere before.

Jake comes in the door whistling. The song has a hold on him, not unlike the way the Bach had taken her in the afternoon.

"What's the name of that tune?"

"Hi there," he says and looks up surprised.

She watches him drop his briefcase. Now he walks over and kisses her. Strange. When was the last time he came into the house and kissed her? "What's that thing called?"

"What I was whistling?"

"Yeah."

"'Round Midnight.'"

"It's a pretty tune."

"Thelonious Monk."

"Monk," she echoes. "Tired?"

"I am."

"Hope you picked up something to eat along the way; the kids and I just had TV dinners. Your father waged a boycott. Too goyish for him."

"Are there any left?"

"Yeah, I stocked the freezer with them. Give the kids a little break from my illustrious cooking. Turkey or fried chicken?"

"Turkey."

"Get you a drink?"

"Be nice."

"Whiskey sour?"

"Sounds good."

Inez turns the oven back on, and without waiting for it to warm, puts in his tin tray of turkey. As she fixes Jake a drink, she tops off her own. The song Jake was whistling is still in her head.

They sit across from each other in the living room. After the conversation at the beach the other night, she worries they may have nothing left to say to each other. He's looking at her strangely. As if he wants something from her, as if he wants to make a confession. She'd rather not hear it. She hereby forgives him everything: his infidelities, his princely indifference, his years of taking her for granted. Still, he smiles at her. He lights a cigarette and smiles at her some more. Must she suffer a fool, before she gets on with it?

"You seem very happy tonight, Jake."

"I love you."

It's the last thing in the world she'd have expected the man to say.

"Jake, would you teach me the song you were whistling?"

"''Round Midnight'?"

"Yes."

Jake blows out a steady stream of smoke. "Do you want me to whistle it?"

"Sure."

Jake whistles the first five notes of the minor dirge. The man may not play an instrument, but he is a hell of a whistler. Perhaps she has an inflated sense of his talent, since, as a whistler, she's barely able to produce a sound. Jake can make bright, clear notes that flow easily, one to another. Plus, he's got a decent ear. He whistles the plaintive song beautifully.

"Let me get my violin."

Strange. Jake just stands still and smiles at her.

Once she has her violin out, she bows easily through "'Round Midnight."

"No, no," he says, "it's too stiff. You've got to goose it a little bit here and there. Nothing's staccato, it's not meant to be staccato." He winks at her. "This is jazz, baby."

"How's that?" Inez says, playing it legato.

"Now, get rid of the vibrato. Can it. You sound like some creature out of the thirties."

That makes her laugh. "You're just as dictatorial as your father."

"That's right. You want to play jazz, you listen to me, girl."

Inez plays through the theme several times until Jake finally nods his approval. He walks over to her and puts his arm around her waist. Please don't let the man get amorous. The last thing she needs now is a scene. Miraculously, Jake answers her wishes and backs away.

"My jazz baby," he says and sits down.

In another world she would have played jazz and lived with a person like Sylvia. Inez sniffs at the air and can smell Jake's precooked turkey dinner beginning to warm.

She puts down her violin. "Let me get your dinner and freshen your drink. Then I'm going out for a little drive."

Jake stands up out of his chair. "You can't go out now. The fog . . ."

Inez peeks out the dining room window. "It looks like it's beginning to lift."

"I'm not going to let you go out there," says Jake, giving his wife a hard stare.

"Jake, come on. Don't be silly."

"You can't go out there."

"I'm not going far, Jake. And the fog's lifting."

Jake looks out the street window. "You can hardly see out there."

"I just want a little air. I've been all cooped up. First with your father . . ."

"If you really want to go out, Inez, I'll go with you."

"No, no, you sit down and eat your dinner. I'll be back before you finish." She walks into the dining room with a place mat and a table setting. "I'll drive slow. Promise." A moment later she returns with the frozen turkey dinner and a glass of ice tea. The last supper she'll serve her husband. The tin dish looks odd floating on a china plate. It's more natural on a TV tray.

"I need to run upstairs for a jacket," says Inez. On her way past Joey's bedroom, she peeks in at her sleeping boy, his thumb nestled in his mouth. Let him give himself what pleasure he can.

Downstairs, Jake has sat down to his humble dinner. He turns to face Inez as she starts toward the door. "Be careful."

Inez feels a momentary pang at the door. She puts on her jacket. She wants to say one more thing to Jake, anything, a small kindness to leave him with.

"Jake," she calls. "The Chinese man at the cleaners sent his best to you. 'Say hello to Jake.' It's the first time he's ever spoken to me."

"How often have you spoken to him?" Jake calls.

"Well, maybe I'll become a social being in my old age."

"Fat chance," he says, his mouth full of Swanson's turkey. "How about you become a cook instead?"

"And what would you have me prepare?"

"I don't know. Chef's choice. Be careful, darling; be careful out there."

force of habit

ONCE she's backed the Studebaker out of the garage, she notices the car is nearly out of gas. That's no way to begin a journey. She drives to the Mobil station on Thirty-eighth and Geary, thinking she'll fill it up with ethyl. But there's no need to buy that much gas, no need to waste. She runs over the bell in the station, a minute before closing. She and Jake have brought the cars here for years. Inez can see a light in the office, a yellow pulse in the fog. She pictures the two middle-aged men standing in the cluttered office, grease on every surface. Jim, the older of the two men, surprises her at the driver's-side window, an apparition standing in the swirl of fog. Bald, and missing teeth, he hunches down so that his face is framed in the window. At another time she might have been frightened. But tonight she's calm. The engine is still humming. Inez rolls her window down.

"Evening, Mrs. Roseman. Heck of a night to be out. Fill 'er up with regular?"

"No, two dollars, of ethyl, Jim."

"Two dollars?"

"That's all I have with me, Jim."

"Put it on the charge?"

"No, two dollars is fine."

He jerks his head back, as if to say, *suit yourself.* "Better turn off your engine."

Inez doesn't want to turn it off, but she does.

"Wouldn't want to be driving very far tonight in this fog."

"Nope, not far."

As Jim cleans the windshield, taking great deliberate swipes with his squeegee, she wonders if this is the last conversation she'll have.

"No real point in cleaning this," he says, shrugging. "Be all dewy in a minute."

"Thanks for doing it though."

"Force of habit."

The same phrase Sylvia used when she described her theft of a little wheel of goat cheese. She can't imagine two people with less in common than Sylvia and Jim the garageman. There you go—life will surprise you right down to the end.

Inez hands Jim two dollars, the whole transaction having the feel of a child's game.

Jim nods as he takes her money. "Nice picture of Mr. Roseman in the paper the other day."

"Yes, it was," she says, trying to remember Jake's latest newspaper splash. She's ready to drive away, but Jim has more to say.

"He's getting so famous, I wonder if he'll be buying his gas here anymore. Might have to head down to Van Ness Avenue to fill up. Place they'll make a little more fuss over him."

"I think he'll keep coming here, Jim."

"Well, you say hello to him, ma'am."

She might as likely be heading out of *Our Town* in a shiny-fendered Model T as easing into the San Francisco fog in her five-year-old Studebaker Scotsman.

Instinctively, Inez drives down the hills to the park, entering at Forty-third Avenue. She can see a few yards ahead of her, but no farther. Alone in the park, she drives east. She rolls down the window and smells eucalyptus. If the fog were a noxious gas, she'd be dead in a hurry. Even though her right foot is aching to floor the gas pedal, she drives slowly. *Force of habit.*

At Tenth Avenue, she turns left. Once out of the park, she doubles back to Park Presidio and heads toward the bridge approach. Inexplicably, the fog has cleared enough at the tollbooth for her to read the big clock—11:27. A man in a stiff cap takes her quarter. This one a mute transaction. There is hardly any traffic on the bridge. Inez drives across, swerving a couple of times over the bumpy yellow reflectors that divide the lanes. She has no desire to pull over. The bridge has always struck her as a bit of a cliché. A more grandiose statement than she'd care to make. She favors an ambiguous approach. She'd heard of an entertainer in the fifties—he might have been a musician for all she knows—who told friends that he intended to either jump from the Golden Gate or move to Mexico, disappearing forever. When his body wasn't found, his friends decided he'd made the Mexican choice. You had to salute the man and the cloud of ambiguity he left behind. Let every survivor come to their own conclusion, let each decide whether surviving is worth the price.

The fog is not as dense when Inez comes through the Marin tunnel. She takes the first Sausalito exit and weaves along the hilly road toward the quaint hamlet of boats and tourist galleries and discovers more fog. She'd really only wanted to turn around. On a night like this, a woman could drive off the road into the white abyss without meaning to. She wants to mean to but doesn't care for this setting. She takes the first intersection and manages to turn back toward the bridge. She's not sure where she wants to go.

Another quarter, another stoic toll taker. The big clock reads nine minutes before twelve, and the song comes into her head. Jake's song. One regret—can she allow herself any?—that she didn't have a chance to play this song for Sylvia. "'Round Midnight." The idea of Jake teaching her jazz makes her laugh out loud. They should have tried that years ago. Somehow jazz is a better fit for her now than Mendelssohn. A better fit than Bach, although Inez could swear that all the music she has ever loved is playing now at once. One voice layered atop another. Inez is a musician in her glory, and this is the art of the fugue.

Across the bridge and through town, she connects to the Bayshore, heading south, and finally pushes the gas pedal to the floor. There's a pinch of tension in her Achilles tendon. It's the feeling she's been after. Invulnerability. Two dollars of gas is more than half a tank. She can keep driving through the fog, the blinding ambiguity of it. The miracle is that there's nobody else out here. Finally, she's by herself.

living fish

SYLVIA reads the news about Inez, like everybody else, in the newspaper. "Noted Symphony Violinist in Fatal Crash." She pours herself a glass of plum wine, then stacks the recording of Satie's Gnossiennes atop the Ravel string quartet on the hi-fi and sits by the window. She's grateful for her familiar perch. From time to time Sylvia gets up to turn the records over—that's when she tends to feel Inez's presence in the room.

A week after her mother died, Sylvia walked into the country, east of Sacramento, and spent half the day sitting in an almond tree. She didn't think to bring any food but carried a canteen of water and a small *Webster's* pocket dictionary in her pack. Words and water and the right tree to climb—what else did a woman in mourning need?

Her mother had just been buried. Sylvia thought she'd be perched in the tree for an eternity, she had so much to figure out. How to measure the loss? Which to mourn most, the dozen years of dying, or the final death? Could she, Sylvia, have done anything differently? Would she be able to forgive her mother? How does one forgive the dead? Did she have a chance of living a life that wasn't wrapped in the gauze of her mother's dying?

By midafternoon, Sylvia began to wonder how long a woman with a quart of water and a dictionary could survive in a tree. At what point would the birds begin roosting in her hair?

Late in the day she opened the dictionary. It was like having a container of her mother's ashes with her, even though her mother was buried in the ground. Perhaps, because it was a cheap dictionary, hardly a holy thing, she thought to tear out certain words and drop them, as ashes, through the leaves of the almond tree. She flipped through the dictionary and chose words at random. *Actuary, bridle, contrarian, dictate, enticement, finite, gullible, horror.* Of course, nothing is truly arbitrary. As her eyes traveled the page, they chose the words that wanted to come. She ripped whole pages from the dictionary and carefully tore her words from the pages. But once she had each word in hand, each a tiny living fish pulled from the water, they became precious. Each word had its pedigree, its part of speech, its key to pronunciation, its tide of meanings. She wished that she had brought some form of an adhesive so that she could attach words to the branches. Failing that, she stuffed each word into the pockets of her jeans.

On her return walk to Sacramento, Sylvia kicked a stone along the side of the dusty highway and wondered if what she'd done in the tree was just a bunch of mood making. Could anybody out there tell her what a natural response to an unnatural death might be?

At her window, Sylvia is pleased to see that people leap on and off the cable car's running board with the same grace as ever.

the torah

THE day after the funeral, Mafalda takes the kids for the afternoon and Jake brings his father's friend Silvio Manatelli back to the house to play chess with the old man. After he's set them up at the dining room table, Jake goes down to the basement with a large red radio from the forties and plugs it in beside the twin bed.

When Joey was a baby, they'd sectioned off this part of the basement and tried to make a little room of it. For months, Jake slept with the baby down there. Jake would wake sometimes with a crick in his neck— he slept at an odd angle because he was afraid of crushing Joey. It pleased Jake to think that he was being a good father and that an irrevocable bond had formed between him and Joey. Some nights when Joey woke up crying, Jake paced with him along the narrow track of basement carpet. Once, while trying to walk him back to sleep, he dozed off himself and dreamt that instead of a baby hoisted on his shoulder, he was carrying the Torah.

Jake tunes the red radio to KKHI, the classical music station. He and Inez used to joke about the station's imperious announcers, but no one is talking now. Instead, it's what he feared and hoped for—a violin concerto. He thinks the Brahms but isn't sure. He doesn't really hear the music so much as know that it's playing. This is his first waking hour alone. He lay on the small bed—just a bare mattress now—as he did with baby Joey. Watch him end up with a crick in his neck.

The worst part was Inez's face in the morning. Jake would creep into the bedroom hoping not to wake her as he laid the sleeping baby in his crib. Half the time, Inez was already awake in the bed, staring stone-eyed, like a person who'd committed a crime for which there was no forgiveness. Jake tried to comfort her when he could. *This is something that's easier for me*, he'd say, *than it is for you. That's all.* Usually she closed her eyes in response, sometimes she nodded. At least once, Inez offered a verbal response that Jake found chilling. *You're good, Jake,* she'd said, her eyes closing. *But this isn't about you, it's about me. It's about me and the baby.*

Jake had always wanted to tell Inez about the night Joey became the Torah in his arms. He wasn't sure what it meant but he thought it was a good thing. That, no matter what, the boy had a soul and was connected to a long history, and that, by extension, their little family was linked to a past and a future. But every time Jake thought to tell her, he worried she'd misunderstand, think that he was boasting about the special bond between the baby and him. Nonetheless, he wishes he'd told her.

There's a racket overhead. His father sounds as if he's both shouting and stomping around the dining room. Jake climbs the basement stairs, wishing he'd had a little more time to himself. The old man is standing beside the dining room buffet holding a china gravy boat in his good hand. He looks like he wants to throw the gravy boat at his friend, who's sitting with a fat smile on his face, the chessboard in front of him.

"You took your hand off the bishop, Manatelli," his father shouts, cocking his frail left arm. "Once you take your hand off the bishop you can't move another piece."

"It's checkmate, my friend," Mr. Manatelli says.

Jake sees no reason to break up the argument. He looks toward the little shrine for Inez that's on the buffet beside his father. Three photographs in standing frames. Inez with her violin. Inez with the kids in front of the blue hydrangeas in the backyard. Inez with Jake beside a hotel swimming pool in Los Angeles, the two of them clearly happy.

His father turns to look at the photographs and begins to cry.

"You're a cheater, Manatelli," the old man shouts, his voice cracking.

Jake wonders two things: will his father throw the gravy boat? And how long until Jake lets himself cry?

the chignon

THE first Tuesday after Inez's funeral, Sylvia dresses in trousers and her herringbone sport coat. She spends some time deciding between Hy's string tie and the red silk dickey that she stole from Toole-James. Which accoutrement will be the more natural? She chooses the red dickey, because she's yet to wear it in public. The Blindfold seems a perfect spot to break it in, and to read the twelve-line poem she wrote after Inez's funeral. It may not be a particularly inspired poem, or even especially natural, but since Sylvia wrote it she's wanted to read it to somebody.

Sylvia arrives early and signs her name on the poets' sheet. When her turn comes, she climbs to the stage with her handwritten poem and looks out at the crowd of noisy faces, covered in all assortment of fabrics. She stands a moment to behold herself and her place in the room. "I have a new poem," she says, then reads the poem.

THE CHIGNON

Courage, I say to her,
pronouncing it as the French would.
You have no business, she says,
telling me how to live my life.
Au contraire, it is my business.
We have these conversations,
fluted glasses of Prosecco in our hands.
I say, haven't you heard of the pleasure principle?
And she, don't you have your nerve?
Not at all, beauty. I want to see you
as an old woman, your white hair
coiled in a chignon.

When she's finished reading the poem, a man whose eyes are covered in a paisley cloth calls out to her: "What did you say the title of that poem is?"

"It's called 'The Chignon.'"

"Would you please read it again?"

Sylvia looks out at the small crowd. A few people, along with the man in the paisley cloth blindfold, nod their heads, so she reads the poem again. Sylvia had never seen Inez wear her hair in a chignon, but she is sure that Inez would have looked beautiful with her hair that way.

After Sylvia finishes reading a second time, the man in the paisley blindfold calls out again: "Read another poem."

"I don't have any others," she says.

"Then write some," he hollers back.

"There's an idea."

Once she climbs down and finds a stool near the back of the coffee-house, Sylvia slips off her red silk dickey and eases it over her head the opposite way, so that the ribbed neck part now covers her eyes. She wears it as a blindfold for the rest of the evening, feeling no compulsion to peek.

hidden

A T Inez's funeral, there was no need to climb a tree in order to gain
distance. Sylvia sat toward the back of the chapel but got a good
look at the family when they streamed out after the service. Jake
Roseman appeared reasonably destroyed, the children, distant, perhaps having anesthetized themselves in that way children have when
situations become unbearably grave; the old man, with his twisted arm
and body, appeared an emblem of ruin. Sylvia looked closely to see if
Bibi was present, but apparently they had left her in "dear old Napa
State."

A F T E R Jake Roseman left the chapel, nobody among the more than hundred people remaining could have had any idea who Sylvia was or that
she'd played a role of any significance in Inez's life. How could a relationship that had affected them both so profoundly—and Sylvia had no
doubt that this was true—be so immaculately erased? What remained of
the two of them was as hidden as a tiny word torn from a page and folded
into a pocket.

When Sylvia started to leave, an old woman tapped her on the shoulder. It took a minute for Sylvia to remember her. It was the elderly usher
from the symphony, her white hair, again, coming loose from her
chignon. She was the woman who'd told Sylvia about Inez, who'd spelled
out her own name.

"You're the reporter, aren't you?"

"Yes . . . yes, I am. And you're . . . Elizabeth Mier. Spelled M I E R."

A brightness came into the old woman's face. It's a good thing to be
recognized once in a while.

"Isn't it terrible what happened to beautiful Inez?" Elizabeth Mier said, her expression retreating back into grief.

"Yes, it is." Sylvia looked into the old woman's face, which was just about the saddest thing she'd seen in her life. There was nothing to do but grab her hand and hold on to it for a long time.

ACKNOWLEDGMENTS

This was a very difficult novel to write; it went through more drafts than I'd like to admit. Many thanks to Anne Czarniecki, Brigitte Frase, Patrice Koelsch, George Rabasa, and Kasi Williamson, early readers who offered encouragement or solace, some of them sacrificing themselves to more than one draft.

I am grateful to my agent, Marly Rusoff, for believing in the novel and for finding a fine publisher and editor in Shaye Areheart. It seemed clear that *Beautiful Inez* called for a female editor, and I feel doubly fortunate to have gotten two: Shaye and her brilliant colleague Deborah Artman. The way they worked in concert was sheer wizardry. Thanks also to my longtime friend Philip Patrick for his help and encouragement.

My most satisfying research for this novel involved long phone conversations with my father, who was a violinist in the San Francisco Symphony for fifty years. I particularly enjoyed having him walk me through the trouble spots in the Mendelssohn Violin Concerto as I sat with an open score. But more than that, it was the countless stories of musicians, the years of music in the house, the challenges my father set for himself. I remember, as an alienated adolescent, waking in my basement bedroom every day to the sound of my father practicing the very difficult Roger Sessions Violin Concerto. He carried on for more than a year, piecing together the impossible architecture of the thing. I am still not sure what inspired more awe in me: the daily doggedness with which my father pursued a concerto considered too difficult to play, or the splendor of hearing it for the first time with a full orchestra, when he gave the concerto its West Coast premiere with the San Francisco Symphony. Most of all, I thank him for sharing his sense that even in a frighteningly cynical world, one must push forward and find joy.

Finally, I am very grateful to the friends who sustain me and to my family; my wife, poet Patricia Kirkpatrick, who inspires me with the high standard of her work and her vision of the world; and our children, Simone and Anton, who keep me both off balance and whole.

Beautiful Inez

Rich with the bohemian romance, music, and ethnic melding of 1962 San Francisco, *Beautiful Inez* beguiles even as it explores such explosive issues as sexuality, obsession, and authenticity. The title character, Inez Roseman, is a leading violinist with the San Francisco Symphony, a noted beauty, and a dedicated wife and mother. As charmed as her life may appear, however, Inez is preoccupied with thoughts of suicide. Enter Sylvia Bran, a waitress and showroom pianist ten years Inez's junior, who sees the violinist perform and develops a fierce attraction to her. Her seduction is shockingly simple. But based as it is on a series of harmless—though unsettling—lies, their love affair forces each woman to face her demons, with lasting, deeply moving repercussions.

The questions that follow are designed to enhance your reading of *Beautiful Inez.*

1. On page 5, we're told that "Sylvia Bran's career as a voyant is about to begin." What did you imagine that meant when you read it? What do you think it means now? Who turns out to be the more successful voyant, Sylvia or Inez?

2. What part does language and etymology play in the story? How does Sylvia use language as a barrier? Or a weapon?

3. Throughout the novel, questions of role and identity are raised: Sylvia pretends to be a reporter to meet Inez; Jake wears Bermuda shorts to court as a sort of costume; Christine dresses like a hooker for her final rendezvous with Jake. What role does Inez assume? Is she convincing?

4. On page 141, Inez admits to herself that "she doesn't care who Sylvia is. Let her be whoever she wants." Why is Inez willing to continue the affair after such a grave deception? How does their relationship change as a result?

5. How does the Cuban Missile Crisis impact the various characters? Do you think they might have behaved differently if it weren't for the specter of imminent death?

6. Do you believe in Hy's concept of a "mind lasso"? Which characters wield it best? Do they know they're doing it?

7. Music is woven throughout the novel: Inez plays Paganini for Sylvia on their first meeting, then plays with the symphony; Jake whistles jazz everywhere he goes; Sylvia plays piano in the showroom, and for Bibi in the mental hospital. What does each character's relationship to music tell us about him or her?

8. On page 221, Inez thinks, "A woman like her isn't brave enough to walk away from her family, her children, and go on living. She cannot make so sharp a left turn in her life, nor can she sit idle." Why do you think Inez feels this way and continues to contemplate suicide, even while she seems so happy?

9. Food has a different significance for each character, seen, for example, in Inez's fluctuating appetite or Jake's gourmet assignations with Christine. How does Sylvia's simple, sensual attitude compare? What does Isaac's disdain for "goyish" mashed potatoes reveal?

10. Was it wrong for Jake to bring Isaac home to live with them? Did he have any other options?

11. How does Bibi's benediction alter the relationship between Inez and Sylvia?

12. How does the fact that Sylvia's mother committed suicide influence her response to Inez's initial confession? How does it influence her response when Inez announces her "irreversible decision"?

13. What role does religious belief play in the story? Is it a help, or a liability?

14. Consider the theme of betrayal in the novel. Christine has a speech on page 223 in which she says: "Who's betraying whom. Isn't that the question we're always at the point of asking our spouse? Or have we already decided? It's them." Who is betraying whom?

15. What do the chapter titles signify? Why do you think the author chose to use chapter titles?

16. Did the ending surprise you? How might it have been different if the story took place in our era, or in a different era?